HIGHEST PRAISE FOR
DIAMOND HOMESPUN ROMANCES:

We at Diamond Books are thrilled by the enthusiastic critical acclaim that the Homespun
Romances are receiving. We would like to thank
you, the readers and fans of this wonderful
series, for making it the success that it is. It is
our pleasure to bring you the highest quality of
romance writing in these breathtaking tales of
love and family in the Heartland of America.

And now, sit back and enjoy this delightful new
Homespun Romance . . .

ANNA'S TREASURE
by Dorothy Howell

ANNA'S TREASURE

DOROTHY HOWELL

DIAMOND BOOKS, NEW YORK

This book is a Diamond original edition,
and has never been previously published.

ANNA'S TREASURE

A Diamond Book / published by arrangement with
the author

PRINTING HISTORY
Diamond edition / January 1995

ISBN: 0-7865-0069-7

Diamond Books are published by The Berkley Publishing Group,
200 Madison Avenue, New York, New York 10016.
DIAMOND and the "D" design
are trademarks belonging to Charter Communications, Inc.

PRINTED IN THE UNITED STATES OF AMERICA

10 9 8 7 6 5 4 3 2 1

To David, Judy and Stacy—
for your unfailing patience and support.

CHAPTER 1

NORTH CAROLINA—1884

It was a man and he was—naked.

Ann Fletcher gasped and turned her head away. Heat rose in her cheeks more intense than the afternoon sun overhead. She crouched lower behind the stand of pines and fanned herself with her open hand. A man undressing by the pond was not what she'd expected to find when she'd spotted the wisps of smoke from the ridge and came down to investigate.

She heard a splash and parted the branches once more to peer at the valley floor. The man was in the pond now, his arms churning the cool, still water as he swam. A short distance away a chestnut stallion was tied to the limb of a sycamore and a stone-ringed campfire smoldered in gray ashes. A single bedroll and rifle lay against the trunk of a tree.

He was alone. Probably just a drifter camped for the night, she decided. No reason to worry over why he'd come to the farm.

Anna sighed with relief. Her secret was still safe.

Nor was there a reason to hesitate confronting him when she held so decided an advantage, Anna reasoned. Her hand tightened on the shotgun beside her.

Cautiously she made her way down the steep, rugged hillside keeping to the cover of the trees and bushes. Briars pulled at her dark skirt, and stones pressed against the thin soles of her slippers.

At the bottom of the hill Anna pushed away a stray lock of her brown hair and raised the shotgun to her shoulder. The gun was slippery in her sweaty palms. Her stomach twisted into a knot as she advanced on the pond.

1

The man's dark head bobbed on the surface of the water, then disappeared as he dove under. His long body moved fluidly in the clear pond as he swam toward the grassy bank where she stood.

Anna waited, adjusting her grip on the gun, until he surfaced, sending up a spray of water around him. He gulped in a mouthful of air and ran his fingers through his wet hair, slicking it back off his face.

She pointed the shotgun at his chest. "I want you off this farm by sundown." Beneath her long skirt, her knees shook.

His eyes blinked open and widened in disbelief. He froze. Quickly his gaze swept the area then returned to Anna and the gun barrel bearing down on him.

He held up his palms. "Now be careful with that thing, ma'am. Somebody's liable to get hurt."

"I know how to use this." Anna swallowed hard but her voice held steady. "And you're going to get your head blown off if you don't get off this farm."

The man's left eyebrow crept upward and the corner of his lip curled into a slow smile. "Is that a fact?"

"It's a fact," Anna replied. His apparent amusement shook what little confidence she clung to.

"In that case, I guess I'd better get going." He waded forward, the water cascading from his broad shoulders. Droplets clung to the dark hair that covered his wide chest.

"What—what are you doing?" Anna lowered the gun.

"Just doing like you said. I've gotten right attached to this head of mine in these past thirty-two years, and I don't want it blown off." The waterline fell lower to the hair that grew in a line down the center of his taut belly.

Anna backed up a step. "But you can't—I mean—I didn't want you to—"

His navel appeared amid a swirl of thick fur. "If somebody points a gun at me, I take them seriously, especially if it's a woman."

She felt as defenseless as she had intended to make the stranger feel. "St—stop."

He kept walking.

"Stop! Or—or I'll—"

His lean hips rose out of the water. "Or you'll what? Ogle me to death?"

Anna's cheeks flamed. She turned to run but the man vaulted up the grassy bank and tore the shotgun from her grasp. His fingers closed firmly over her arm, holding her in place.

She whirled around to face him, her cheeks red with anger now. He towered over her. His blue eyes taunted her. His whole body gave off an overwhelming heat, despite the cool water that clung to his skin.

Her breath came in short puffs. "Ogle you? I wouldn't ogle you if you were the last man in the country!"

"I almost am."

Fear cut through her anger as she realized how vulnerable she'd made herself. There was no one around for miles, no one who knew where she'd gone, no one who expected her to return.

"Let go of me." She wanted to push him away but didn't dare touch him.

His gaze held hers for a tense moment. "It has been a long time, but I'm not desperate enough—"

Anna kicked him squarely in the shin. He howled with pain and loosened his grip slightly. Anna pulled her arm free. She dashed to the horse tethered by the tree, grabbed the reins, and scrambled into the saddle. Panic seized her and she dug her heels into the stallion's sides. The horse lunged forward with unexpected power. Anna grabbed the saddle horn with both hands.

The stranger was a blur as she swept past, hurling obscenities at the top of his voice, hopping on one foot, holding his shin. Anna held tight and kicked the horse again.

The stallion picked its own way up the rugged hillside through thick trees and underbrush, across rain-washed gullies, and around outcroppings of rock. Anna was too frightened to do more than hold on.

When they reached the top of the ridge, she pulled back the reins. The horse danced in a tight circle before responding to the pressure of the bit in its mouth.

She turned and the leather saddle creaked beneath her. Far below, she could see the stranger watching her. He was dressed in his long johns, opened to the waist, and black trousers. The dark hair on his chest glistened in the sunlight. His expression was unreadable from so great a distance, but she could feel his piercing blue eyes boring into her. She could well imagine his thoughts. Defiantly, she stuck out her tongue.

Anna urged the stallion down the other side of the hill just out of the stranger's view. He would follow her to get his horse back. She'd make sure he could find it easily; she'd be long gone by the time he dressed and made his way up the steep hill on foot.

Heat surged through Anna at the sudden memory of the stranger's strong, muscled body rising out of the water; then embarrassed by her thoughts, she pushed them away. It wasn't proper to think such things, though at age twenty-four she was old enough to be married and have a half-dozen children by now. Anna slid to the ground and tied the reins securely to a tree branch.

Bob, the workhorse she'd ridden this morning, was waiting patiently by the tree stump where Anna had left him. She climbed onto his bare back and urged him through the woods. The stranger was best forgotten, she told herself. Her visit to the farm would be brief, and she had no time for such distracting thoughts.

Hours later as the sun was dipping toward the horizon, Anna turned the plodding workhorse north. They descended the rolling, wooded hills and crossed the small creek that ran diagonally across the valley floor past the two-story farm house that had once been her family home. She was unaccustomed to riding, tired and frustrated by how poorly the afternoon had turned out, and felt worse seeing the farm as she approached it from the rear.

The house sorely needed a fresh coat of paint, and the broken window needed replacing. The couple who had rented it after she and her mother left ten years ago had taken good care of the farm. But they'd moved out last fall, and the whole place had fallen into disrepair. Part of the barn roof had blown off, the fields were barren, the front lawn was thick with weeds, the fencing was down. It was a sad tribute to the memory of her parents.

She put Bob in the corral with Bill, the other workhorse

she'd purchased along with the wagon and supplies for the trip to the farm. There was enough grass for them to eat, and though many of the rails were missing from the corral, the horses were content to graze near the barn.

Anna hurried into the house and set to work right away so as not to notice the silence that hung heavily in every room. Since her arrival at the farm the day before, she spent much of her time making it livable. It helped that most of the furniture had been left behind.

She'd chosen for herself the bedroom that had belonged to her parents because of the fireplace her father had insisted on when he'd done the extravagant addition to the house years ago. Next to it was the room that had belonged to her as a child. The upper floor had been blocked off for as long as Anna could remember.

Evening shadows stretched across the bedroom as Anna stood back and appraised her work. She'd dragged the mattress outside and beaten it until her arms were numb. Now covered with fresh linens and the crazy quilt she'd spent last winter stitching, it looked inviting. She'd scrubbed the floor, washed and rehung the priscillas, polished the windows, and knocked all the cobwebs from the corners. A small supply of firewood had been left in the woodshed, and she'd stacked several logs by the hearth. The room wasn't as fashionable or grandly furnished as the bedroom that had been hers in her uncle's home in Salem, where she and her mother had lived these past ten years, but it was clean. Uncle Lloyd was a prominent physician, and he'd been generous in providing for them.

Juggling the mop, broom, cleaning rags, and pail of dirty water, Anna made her way down the hall. She refused to look in the parlor, which was covered with dirt and grime. She had no intention of cleaning it. If all went as planned, her task here would be complete and she would be gone from the farm in a few days.

She passed through the kitchen, the room she'd spent most of yesterday cleaning, deposited the supplies on the back porch, and tossed out the dirty water. She hesitated for a moment, her eyes drawn to the ridge and the orange and

golden sunset. The stranger came into her thoughts and she
wondered if he'd gotten his horse back all right.

Anna shivered in the cool evening breeze. What did she
care, anyway? He was gone, and all that mattered was that
she was alone to finish what had started here ten years ago.
She left the pail by the door and hurried back inside.

It was dark by the time Anna reheated last night's stew and
sat down at the kitchen table to eat. She was almost
accustomed to the silence, enough so that the noise she heard
set her nerves on edge. She sat up straighter, her ears
straining. It could have been the wind or one of the horses or
maybe an animal searching for food, she told herself.

Cautiously she crept to the window beside the cookstove
and looked out at the sagging clothesline, the oaks she'd
played beneath as a child, the plot of weeds that had once
been a fertile garden. All was still.

Conscious of how isolated the farm was, Anna made her
way to the front of the house and rubbed a circle in the dirty
window by the door. Shadows lay across the yard; she could
barely see the horse standing just inside the chipped and
peeling picket fence. Its rider had fallen forward onto the
animal's thick neck.

She pressed her face against the dirty glass and scanned the
yard and the road in both directions as far as she could see.
No one else was around. She opened the door. The creaking
hinges sounded like thunder in the stillness. She slipped out
onto the porch, her eyes searching the darkness. Still she saw
no one; the horse and rider were alone.

"Hello," she called. "Are you all right?"

The man moaned and tried to push himself upright in the
saddle.

She went down the stairs, careful to avoid the second step
that sagged precariously. "Do you need some help?"

When he didn't answer, Anna ventured closer. She stopped
beside the horse. "If you need—"

The man toppled sideways and fell from the horse,
flattening Anna beneath him.

"Get off me!" Anna struggled against him but his weight
pinned her to the bed of overgrown weeds. She pushed at his

arms and chest until she realized that he had not moved. Not once. Not an inch. She squirmed beneath him to free her arm and rolled his head onto her shoulder.

Scratches marked his cheek and forehead, and he lay still, so still that it frightened her. Pressing her ear against his mouth, she heard the faint sighing of his breath. She realized then that the wet stickiness in his dark hair was blood.

Her limited training in the medical field look over. She managed to roll him off her, then crouched on her knees at his side.

Gently she shook him. "I need your help. I've got to get you into the house. I can't possibly carry you. Wake up."

Finally he roused. Disoriented and groggy he struggled to his feet. Anna wedged herself under his arm and circled his waist.

"Come on, walk." She pulled his arm over her shoulder and lurched forward. He was more than a head taller than she and his weight was crushing, but she pulled and tugged, begged and encouraged until she got him up the steps and into the house. He staggered drunkenly across the foyer and slammed into the wall, dragging Anna with him. He groaned and his knees buckled.

Quickly she wrapped both arms around his waist and pressed his back against the wall. If he fell now, she'd never get him up. "We're almost there. Keep going."

Exhausted and nearly out of breath, she gathered the last of her strength and jerked him toward the bedroom door. He leaned heavily on her as they crossed the darkened room and fell across the bed together.

He mumbled incoherently as Anna untangled herself from him and rolled him onto his back. Breathing heavily, she scrambled off the bed and lit the lantern at the bedside.

The flame danced to life illuminating the room. Gently she turned his head to examine the wound. Her fingers froze. Her heart skipped a beat.

It was the stranger. The man at the pond. And by the look of the deep graze cut above his right temple, someone had tried to make good on the threat she'd issued.

Someone had tried to blow his head off.

CHAPTER 2

Anna sat back and wiped her hands on the hem of her apron. She'd done her best. She'd done everything she knew to do. Still, she wished her uncle Lloyd was here.

Flickering lamplight bound her to the stranger as she bent over the bed once more. The bullet had grazed his right temple. At the base of his skull she'd found a large knot; she guessed he'd struck his head when he'd fallen. She'd applied a healing salve and bandaged the wound. There was little else she could do but let him rest and keep him comfortable.

She dipped the corner of the cloth into the pan of water she'd brought from the kitchen and carefully wiped the dirt and dried blood from his face. The man looked different than at their encounter at the pond this afternoon. Vaguely she wondered if that was because he had his clothes on now.

He was a big man, well over six feet tall. He'd towered over her at the pond today. Now his feet nearly hung over the end of her bed. The boots he had on were covered with dust, expensive at one time, she guessed, but now old and worn; probably the only pair he owned. As he lay on the bed, one leg rested at a lazy angle stretching the fabric of his trousers. They fit like his boots, soft and worn, conforming to every curve and bulge. Anna's cheeks colored at the memory of him climbing out of the pond; the trousers did little to conceal what she'd seen firsthand this afternoon.

He worked hard for a living, she decided, judging from the look of his broad chest and heavily muscled arms. His were the hands of a working man, tanned and calloused.

She remembered that his eyes were blue. Deep blue, alive

with mischief. They were closed now against the pain his body was enduring. His brows were black and thick, like his hair. There was a slight crook in his nose, suggesting it had been broken. Was it during a fight? A fight over a woman? Anna wondered. His lips were full, opened slightly now as he slept, displaying a line of even, white teeth. He had a strong chin with a cleft in the center so tiny it wouldn't likely be noticed. Except by someone blatantly ogling him as she was doing now, Anna thought. He'd accused her of the same this afternoon at the pond.

Anna rose and gently placed her palm on his forehead. He tossed his head fitfully for a moment then settled down again. His skin was cool to the touch; it was a good sign.

Anna went to the foot of the bed and eased off his boots. He groaned and mumbled but didn't wake up. She folded the quilt over him and left.

With lantern in hand she took his stallion to the barn and bedded him down in a stall near Bill and Bob. She gave them all an extra measure of grain and a fresh pail of water.

Her own shotgun was among the stranger's possessions and she brought it back into the house along with his rifle and saddlebags.

In a dark corner of her bedroom, Anna changed into her night rail as she listened to the stranger's deep, even breathing. She slipped into her wrapper and lit the fire in the hearth to drive away the night chill.

Nothing was going as she had planned, Anna fretted as she stood looking down at the sleeping man. Everything had seemed much easier two weeks ago when she'd decided to leave her uncle's home in Salem and return to the farm. But the wagon, horses, and provisions had cost more than she'd anticipated, and the journey was harder than she'd imagined. She hadn't thought that being in this house again would evoke such painful memories or that making the place livable would be so time-consuming—time that would have been better spent pursuing her real purpose for being here.

And now this.

The man shifted and groaned. Anna moved to the foot of the bed and gazed down at the sleeping figure. What was she

going to do about him? His presence here would only delay
things further.

Anna sighed heavily. She'd come back to the farm to put
an end to the nightmare that had driven her and her mother
from this house ten years ago, and to dispel the cloud that had
hung over her head since that fateful night so long ago. And
nothing—not stray bullets, bad memories, or naked men in
her pond—was going to stop her.

Finding some comfort in her resolve, Anna curled up in the
upholstered chair beside the bed and covered herself with her
woolen cloak. Her last thought before drifting off to sleep was
that she wanted to be near the stranger in case he needed her
during the night.

A soft moan jolted Anna awake. She sat up and pushed her
dark hair off her face. In the bed beside her, the stranger
mumbled and groaned.

"What is it?" She sat down beside him on the edge of the
bed. His face was drawn, his brow creased. She leaned closer.

"Have to . . ." His head tossed restlessly on the pillow.
"Have to . . . hide. . . ."

Anna's breath caught in her throat.

"Hide . . ." He licked his dry lips but didn't open his eyes.
"Can't let . . . find me. . . ."

A chill ran up Anna's spine. The silence of the night and
the isolation of the farm bore down on her. She bit her bottom
lip. "You just hit your head—that's all. You're not thinking
clearly. No one is going to hurt you. You're safe." And so was
she. Wasn't she?

He mumbled again, but she couldn't understand the words.
She only saw how frightened he was, how vulnerable.

Anna took his hands in hers and placed them on his chest.
His fingers were powerful; she took strength from them.
Gently she stroked the backs of his hands with her thumbs.
Finally, he relaxed, and after a while the stranger drifted off
to sleep again.

For a long moment Anna studied him. What had she done?
Who had she taken into her house?

Anna rose and paced the floor. Was he adrift in some

nightmare, imaging he was being pursued? Or was he really hiding from someone? The law perhaps?

The hardwood floor was cold beneath her bare feet as she stopped at the end of the bed and stared down at the man. What if he hadn't been hit by a hunter's stray bullet as she had first thought? What if he was a wanted man? Maybe she should go to the sheriff.

A cold, hard knot formed in the pit of Anna's stomach. Alerting the sheriff would mean going into town, and that was the one place she wanted to avoid at all costs. There were too many memories there; unpleasant ones that she didn't want to confront.

Anna began to pace again. What if the stranger was an outlaw? She could be branded his accomplice for taking him in. Or worse—.

She wrapped her arms around her middle, suddenly chilled to the bone. What if the stranger told the sheriff what she'd said to him at the pond? She herself had threatened to shoot him. What if she couldn't convince the sheriff she'd had nothing to do with the man's injuries. What would they do to her?

Jail. Anna shivered with revulsion. She never wanted to see the inside of a jail again as long as she lived.

Anna drew in a deep breath. She had to learn who this man was.

Silently she crossed to the armoire and pulled out the saddlebags she'd taken from the man's horse. She settled into the chair and pulled the lantern closer.

Anna emptied the contents of one of the bags. It was clothing. Trousers, shirts, a vest, socks that needed mending, all neatly folded. Wrapped in a pair of long johns was a flask of whiskey. She ran her fingers inside all the pockets of the garments searching for any clue to his identity. She found nothing.

The man moaned and shifted in the bed. Anna glanced up and saw him trying to rouse himself from sleep. His effort failed and he fell asleep once more.

Slowly she opened the other bag and poured its contents onto her night rail over her lap. The collection of items was slim, but it told her what she had suspected at the pond: the man was a drifter; everything of value was with him.

Wrapped in a piece of tattered, black velvet, Anna found a silver-framed miniature. She turned it toward the light. Pictured there was a man and wife with a small boy. She had never considered that the stranger might actually be married and, certainly, had not guessed he would have a child.

But the man in the picture looked different, she realized. At first glance she was sure it was the stranger. But no, she decided, he was the boy.

The dark-haired child with the playful grin was the man who now rested in her bed. Anna smiled. She'd had seen that same look on his face yesterday afternoon at the pond. It meant trouble. She wondered if his parents pictured with him had known where that look could lead.

Anna's smile faded. It touched her heart that he would carry with him a miniature of his family. Anna felt a sudden pang of regret that she had no such treasure of her own.

Pushing aside the photograph and her own feelings, Anna opened the leather wallet. It contained a surprisingly large sum of money, and it took all her will power not to count it. Tucked behind the bills were several neatly folded pieces of paper. She skimmed them quickly, not wanting to delve any deeper than necessary into the man's personal business.

This was it, she realized as her eyes squinted in the dim light. She'd found what she was searching for. With a sigh of satisfaction, Anna turned the document toward the lamplight and read the birth certificate declaring this man to be one Samuel James Rowan, born to James Henry and Margaret Rogers Rowan on November 22, 1849, in the town of Lynchburg, Virginia.

Anna returned all the items to the saddlebag and curled up in the chair. He was no one. Just some poor soul who had the misfortune of being in the wrong place when a hunter's bullet strayed; luckily he hadn't paid for his misfortune with his life.

Anna pulled the woolen cloak over her. If in fact the man was hiding from someone, he presented no threat to her. If he'd wanted to hurt her, he could have done so at the pond. He'd be well in a day or two and go on his way.

She yawned and closed her eyes. This Samuel James Rowan meant nothing to her. Or her future. She was sure of it.

He was hot. Hotter than he'd ever been in his life. Sam flung off the quilt and opened his eyes. Light from the midday sun pouring in through the window sent sharp pains shooting through his head. He cursed and pushed himself up on his elbows.

A wave of nausea swept over him forcing him back onto the pillow. His head pounded.

He lay there, silent, eyes shut, his mind clouded with the unbearable pain that wracked his entire body. Where was he? He struggled to think, but the effort was too great.

Sleep overtook him, then he woke, unsure how long he'd slept, or if, indeed, he'd even slept at all. Sam cursed again and pushed himself up.

He struggled to his feet, lost his balance and crashed into the table at his bedside. The lantern fell. Glass shattered across the hardwood floor. He braced his arm against the wall to keep from falling. Sam touched his head. He cursed and pulled off the bandage and flung it aside.

His stomach pitched. He clamped his hand over his mouth to keep himself from vomiting.

The pain in his head worsened as he shuffled to the window and pulled it open. Cool air wafted in. The effort sent another wave of aches through his body.

It was hot. Stifling hot. Clumsily, he opened the buttons on his shirt and shrugged out of it. He dropped his trousers onto the floor around his ankles. He wavered as he stepped out of them and headed back toward the bed, working the buttons of his long johns. He had to rest before—.

The angel spoke.

Sam stopped quickly, his ears straining. The angel who had hovered at his bedside, caressing his injured body with her gentle touch, soothing his fears with her melodic voice was speaking again. It drew him across the room. He pulled open the door.

Across the foyer was a woman, and beside her stood a man

dressed in a suit. Sam squinted his eyes against the sunlight streaming in through the open door and the room swayed violently.

He felt the woman against him, holding him. She was soft. She smelled of wild flowers in the spring.

"Easy there, man."

Sam felt rougher hands holding him now. He looked down at the man who'd wedged himself under his arm.

"Say now, ma'am, he's a big one," the man said to the woman beneath his other arm.

Who were these people? Where was he? Sam opened his mouth, but no words formed. He tried to pull away.

"Slow down," the man called out. "Have a little mercy on this wife of yours."

The woman's dark head came up quickly. Big brown eyes—doe eyes—looked up at him. Dark lashes blinked against her porcelain skin. She drew in a sharp breath. "What?"

Sam shook his head. It was the angel's voice. He looked down at her. "Wife?"

The man tightened his grip on Sam's waist. "Let's get you back into bed."

Sam didn't budge. He looked down at the woman. She was supposed to be an angel. "Wife. . . ."

The man peered across Sam's chest. "You are his wife, aren't you?"

She hesitated a moment then smiled sweetly. "Of course I'm his wife." She looked up at Sam. "Come along, dear, let's get you back into bed."

Sam still didn't move. His brows drew together and his head wobbled. "Wife. . . ."

"Honey, come on now." She urged him back toward the bed. "Honey . . . sugar . . . now, don't be difficult."

"But. . . ."

"You'll have to excuse my hu—husband," she said to the man peering across Sam's wide chest. "He took a nasty blow to the head yesterday."

He nodded. "So I can see."

The woman pulled Sam forward into the bedroom. "You must get into bed."

Sam's head pounded anew. Wife? She was his wife? He allowed her to guide him across the room and fell into bed. How could she be anyone's wife? She was the angel. Sleep overtook him.

Anna slumped against the door as the drummer's wagon pulled away from the house. She wished she'd never opened the door for him, especially after the stranger had suddenly appeared in the bedroom doorway dressed only in his long johns unbuttoned to his navel. But she was glad for the drummer's help. She couldn't have gotten the man back into bed on her own.

She turned toward the bedroom again and bit down on her bottom lip. The man had undressed. Was he too hot? Was a fever coming on? Anna returned to his room.

His clothing and the broken lantern littered the floor, but the man was sleeping soundly. She placed her palm on his forehead. It was cool. Satisfied he wasn't feverish, Anna turned to leave.

The man grabbed her wrist and urged her back with unexpected strength. Anna gasped as he pulled her down and anchored his other hand behind her head.

"Wife. . . ." He sighed the word.

His mouth covered hers hungrily as he worked his lips against hers and thrust his tongue deep inside. Slowly, he acquainted himself with her thoroughly, seeking out and caressing the sweet recesses of her mouth.

For a stunned second, Anna didn't react. Feelings of excitement and fear coursed through her, coiling deep inside her. She pressed her palms against his chest and pushed herself up. The strength of his muscles seared her hands even through the thickness of his long johns. He was reluctant to release her, but finally she broke free of his hold. His hands fell lifelessly beside him and he drifted off to sleep again.

Standing over him, her lips tingled. Anna felt her cheeks flaming. Her mouth felt hot. Her stomach glowed. No one had ever kissed her like that before. Ever.

Anna hurried from the bedroom, unsure if what she was feeling was fear or something entirely different.

She spent the afternoon at his bedside checking his forehead, watching for signs of fever. She was cautious of him now, and had considered tying his hands. But she looked at those heavily muscled arms of his and doubted she could tie a knot tight enough to hold him.

She fed him an herbal broth her mother had always used to ward off a fever. The day's escapade had cost the man most of his strength, but he resisted the broth. Anna knew it tasted bad, but he needed it, so she was as persistent as he was evasive. By nightfall, her lower back was aching, and she was nauseous from the broth's vile smell; her own head was beginning to hurt.

But it was worth it, Anna told herself. Without her help the man might have died. He needed her. She'd be there for him.

Sam came awake with a start. Quickly his gaze swept the darkened room. Beside the bed the lantern burned low, and sleeping in the chair near him was the woman.

She was huddled beneath a woolen cloak. Thick dark hair curled around her head and fell softly over her face. Long lashes lay against her porcelain skin. The lamplight caressed her, cast her in pale-pink light.

A feeling of calm overtook Sam as he watched her. He'd thought she was an angel, but gazing at her now, though she indeed looked angelic, he knew she was only a woman. She was the soft, delicate creature who had comforted him. She was the woman who had cared for him. She was—.

His stomach clenched. Raw fear coursed through him unchecked. He knew who this woman was; and, by God, she was no angel.

He wanted to run but his limbs were lifeless. She'd given him something, some drug. Some evil brew. He remembered her feeding it to him. Panic set in.

Darkness closed over him once more, dragging him into a great downward spiral. His last conscious thought was one of sheer terror.

He was alone and helpless.
And in the hands of Anna Fletcher.

Anna felt his gaze upon her, caressing her as if it were a living thing. She turned and clutched the sash of her wrapper close around her. Her gaze met and held with the steady, blue eyes that impaled her from the bed across the room.

"Good morning." Her voice was a soft whisper. She approached the bed. "How do you feel?"

He dug the heels of his hands into his eyes and drew in a deep breath. "Like I've been pushed through a keyhole."

She smiled. "You managed to acquire a large assortment of bumps, bruises, and scrapes."

Cautiously he touched his fingers to his head, then looked up at her. "And a wife as well, it seems."

Anna blushed. She'd only gone along with the drummer's assumption that she was his wife so that the man wouldn't spread word through the whole country that not only was the old Fletcher house occupied again, but that she was harboring a half-naked man with a gun shot wound to the head.

"Oh yes . . . that. I can explain. . . ."

He pushed himself up on his elbows.

"No, you mustn't try to get up." Anna hurried to the side of the bed. "You're not strong enough."

He disregarded her warning with a wave of his hand and tossed back the quilt. He looked down at himself then threw her an accusing glare. "Where the hell are my pants?"

Anna pushed against his shoulders. "Lie down, Mr. Rowan. You can't walk yet."

He shrugged to avoid her grasp. "I'll decide when I can walk—Mrs. Rowan."

Anna's back stiffened. "You—you'll fall."

He pushed her hands away and swung his legs over the side of the bed. "I ought to know whether I can stand or not."

Anna planted her hands on her hips. "You could at least have a little consideration for me. If you fall, I don't know if I can pick you up again."

His jaw tightened. "I've been taking care of myself since long before I got here. I can keep on doing it."

Anna's temper flared. She'd worked day and night nursing this man back to health, and she wasn't about to let him injure himself further simply because his male pride had been offended.

She crossed her arms under her breasts and stood directly in front of him. "You are not getting out of this bed."

His glassy gaze met hers, answering the challenge. He heaved himself to his feet.

Anna fell back a step as he rose in front of her, overwhelmed by his height, the broadness of his chest, the surge of strength he exuded. For an instant she thought she'd been wrong, that he was well enough to be on his feet. Then he moaned and his eyes rolled back in his head. He swayed toward her, his arms flailing.

"Oh. . . ." Anna threw herself against him and he plopped down, bouncing on the mattress. "Lie back."

Sam pushed her hands away and fell against the pillow. He grimaced and blew out a heavy breath.

"Would you please stay put from now on, Mr. Rowan?" Anna yanked the quilt over him. "Before you get another knot on your head."

He snorted and turned away from her.

"You're a very difficult man, Mr. Rowan."

"For better or worse," he told her. "I believe that's what the marriage vows state."

Further irritated with him now because she still had to explain why she was passing herself off as his wife, Anna changed the subject.

"Do you remember the accident?"

He cast her a sour glance. "I remember." He wasn't about to tell her that he'd fallen off his horse. He considered himself an expert rider. He didn't know how he'd fallen. But his pride was already smarting, and he wasn't about to explain it to her.

Good, Anna thought. He remembered being shot and obviously didn't blame her, as she had feared he might. And he didn't seem concerned that she might have alerted the sheriff. Proof conclusive, she decided, that it was a stray bullet from a hunter somewhere in the woods. Nothing for her to concern herself with.

A tense silence yawned between them. Sam lay in bed, his chest puffed with wounded pride, refusing to look at her. Annoyed, Anna turned on her heels. She grabbed clothing from the armoire and left.

She dressed in the kitchen by the warmth of the cookstove, sipping coffee and stirring the pot of bubbling oatmeal. The man in her bed was most annoying. Much too bullheaded for his own good—a decidedly irritating man. Anna sighed heavily as she loaded the breakfast tray. Maybe it was just as well she didn't intend to marry. She didn't have the patience to put up with the Sam Rowans of the world.

He was resting quietly when she entered the bedroom and placed the tray on the bedside table. "Mr. Rowan, your breakfast is here."

He opened his eyes. "I'm not hungry."

Anna gritted her teeth. "You have to eat. You need your strength. Sit up."

He didn't budge.

She squared her shoulders. There were a thousand things she should be doing right now. He could at least cooperate.

"Really, Mr. Rowan, if you don't sit up I'll have to spoon-feed you myself. Would you prefer that?"

A string of mumbled curses tumbled from his lips as he struggled to a sitting position. Anna stuffed pillows behind his back and placed the tray on his lap. He looked pale and drawn. Frail.

A pang of sympathy touched Anna's heart. "I'll help you eat if you'd like," she offered softly.

He shot her a scathing glare and snatched up the spoon.

"Fine." Anna turned on her heels and left the room.

Sam heard her return a short while later, but he kept his eyes closed and pretended to be sleeping. She lingered for a moment. He sensed her beside him, her delicate scent tantalizing his nose. He felt her palm on his forehead. She had the softest touch he'd ever known. The dishes rattled on the tray he'd left at the bedside and she was gone.

Maybe, just maybe, she didn't know who he was, Sam thought. He kept his eyes closed, concentrating as best he could with his head throbbing. No, he finally decided, she couldn't know. If she knew, she surely wouldn't be caring for him with such tenderness and compassion.

His belly was full and he wanted to sleep again. He drifted off, confident that his identity was safe. After all, he was the last person she would expect to show up at her farm. She probably hadn't given it a thought. Surely, Miss Anna Fletcher had had more pressing matters to contend with since she'd walked out of the prison at Raleigh two weeks ago.

An early dusk had settled over the farm as Anna took her shawl from the peg by the back door and went outside. The breeze had picked up, heavy with moisture, suggesting a rain shower was on its way. Light from the kitchen window and her own memory guided her to the woodshed behind the house. There was barely enough wood left for the night, and she dreaded the idea of chopping more in the morning. Irritably she blamed the thankless Samuel James Rowan and his unexpected appearance here for causing the shortage in all her supplies, not to mention wreaking havoc with her plans.

She took the logs back into the kitchen and dumped them into the wood box by the stove. The last of the stew that waited for her didn't seem the least appealing, so she poured herself a cup of coffee and sat down at the table. The brew tasted bitter but she didn't want to waste her precious sugar ration on it. She lit the lantern in the center of the table and sat down listening to the still, quiet house. In the distance, thunder rumbled.

Presently, her thoughts turned to Sam. There had been no sound from his room since she'd last checked on him. He was still sleeping, she guessed. He'd been asleep all day. Head injuries caused that, or so her uncle had always said.

She slipped into the pantry and dressed in the night rail she'd left there this morning. Anna almost wished Sam would wake up so she would have someone to talk to. Traveling all the way from Salem and living out here so far from town had left her feeling lonelier than she'd expected. But her life had been empty for a while, she admitted to herself, and not just because her mother had died last fall. Lloyd Caldwell, her uncle, was a doctor, and Anna and her mother had gone to live with him ten years ago. Elsa had assisted her brother with the medical practice he ran out of his home in Salem. Later, Anna had joined them, learning her uncle's medical skills and her mother's home remedies. Anna seemed destined to turn to nursing and everyone was glad she would have a profession to fall back on since she'd shunned every prospective husband who had come along. But Anna couldn't stomach the ordeal of surgical procedures, thereby ruling out any possibility of a real career in the field. And so as everyone had predicted, Anna was a spinster at the age of twenty-four, with no skills and no husband. It was a small consolation that her mother was no longer alive to see how her life had turned out.

Her uncle was always busy rushing from a patient to the hospital, then to another house call, when he wasn't away studying new medical procedures. Most of her friends were married now, so she rarely saw them, feeling out of place around them without so much as a steady beau of her own. It had been her charity work that had filled her idle hours. And that was the only thing which would take her back to Salem once her purpose here had been achieved.

Feeling melancholy and lonely and slightly sorry for herself, Anna took from the pantry shelf the special box she'd brought with her from her uncle's house in Salem, and placed it on the kitchen table. It was a gaily decorated hatbox; she fondly remembered the day her father had presented it to her mother. The hat inside had been extravagant beyond their means, but that was just the way her father was. If he had a little extra cash in his pocket, Cyrus Fletcher would spend it on his wife, Elsa—his angel, he called her—because he loved her so much. She would always fuss at him and gently remind him that it was far too expensive, but she always wore his presents proudly, telling herself that for all his other shortcomings, Cyrus was a generous and loving husband. He never worried about money, no matter how empty their pantry became. He truly believed that one day his big chance would come and he would have all the money he needed. It was only a matter of time.

The hat had long since gone out of style and been cast out,

but the box had remained as a place to store what became the most important documents in Elsa Fletcher's life. And finally, when the papers had failed her, the life had gone out of Elsa too, Anna thought as she eased off the lid.

Anna sank into a chair and dumped the box's contents onto the table. Odd, she thought, that after ten long years seeing it all now could still make her feel so angry, so hurt, so abandoned.

She sifted through the documents to find the series of newspaper articles that recounted her father's arrest, his trial, his sentence. How different it would have turned out, Anna thought—his life, her life, her mother's life—if Cyrus Fletcher had not gone to his job as railroad guard that fateful night. The night the infamous Jimmy Rowe Gang executed the most daring, ambitious robbery in the history of North Carolina.

The night they stole a hundred thousand dollars from the Charlotte mint.

CHAPTER 3

Anna settled herself at the kitchen table and read the newspaper articles again. Now yellow with age, they told of Jimmy Rowe, a man who had come out of obscurity to capture the hearts and imagination of the public. He was considered a genius at planning and executing the most bold, daring, well-orchestrated hold-ups ever heard of. His four accomplices were trained to perfection. There wasn't a bank or train anywhere in the South considered safe from Jimmy Rowe.

His exploits made front-page news. Gradually, he became almost a folk hero as word of his exploits spread. He never fired a shot, seldom even drew his gun, and never allowed his gang to mindlessly shoot up a town or train during a holdup. The sight alone of the five riders in identical white dusters, wearing black hats, riding jet-black horses was enough to intimidate most anyone.

And Jimmy was generous with his wealth. There were numerous accounts of people whom he had simply given money to—widows, elderly folk, struggling young families. The recipients were reluctant to come forward, of course, but word got out, and it happened with such frequency that not even the biggest skeptic doubted Jimmy Rowe was responsible.

Jimmy and his gang would vanish, sometimes for months, leading to much speculation as to where the men went and what they did. Were they ordinary folks living among the general public, in plain sight, right under the noses of the many federal marshals who sought them? Or did they have some secret hideout that even the most ambitious posse could not uncover? Then, without warning, they would reappear in a different county, a different state, and pull off another amazing robbery, leaving both citizens and lawmen mystified.

But to Anna, Jimmy Rowe was no hero, no larger than life legend, no charitable Robin Hood. He was a thief, plain and simple. He'd robbed her of her father, her home, her family's respectability, and finally, her mother.

It was painful, but Anna read the other newspaper clippings contained in the hatbox. The story they told was one-sided and surely had helped turn the tide of public opinion against her father. Cyrus Fletcher had never fit in with the community. He had only been tolerated because he had married Elsa Caldwell, the daughter of a respected, long-time resident. It hadn't taken long for the townspeople's attitude to change once the accusations had begun to fly and gossip had run rampant.

Anna read over the many newspaper articles that detailed that fateful night. It seemed every newspaper had carried the story, then printed updates in an attempt to get the most out of the story; certainly that had added to the distortion of the facts at the time.

But Anna knew the entire story by heart, as her father had told it, as her mother had retold it, as she had heard the attorneys discuss it. Cyrus Fletcher had been on the train that night when it pulled out of Charlotte carrying two strongboxes containing fifty thousand dollars each from the mint. He was a guard for the railroad, one of two stationed in the baggage car responsible for watching over the shipment. A few miles west of Charlotte, Jimmy Rowe and his gang stopped the train and relieved it of its valuable cargo with well-laid and perfectly executed plans. But Jimmy had no way of knowing the railroad had anticipated the holdup, and that four U.S. marshals lay in wait in the next car. A gun battle broke out. When the smoke cleared Jimmy had been shot, as had three of the four marshals, and Cyrus Fletcher had been taken hostage to aid in the gang's escape. A posse was formed in no time, and despite the closing darkness, followed the thieves into the hills between Charlotte and Kemper. There the four remaining gang members split up, each pair taking one of the strongboxes. It was after midnight when they tracked down Buck Kyle. He'd been shot in the leg. At his side, cradled in his arms, was the lifeless body of his younger brother, Arlow. Neither Cyrus Fletcher nor the strongbox were anywhere to be found.

Anna laid aside the faded newspapers and looked over the correspondence her mother had devoted years to. She had written to other attorneys asking them to take over the case. She'd sent letters to congressmen, senators, the governor, even the President himself, pleading her husband's innocence, asking for a pardon, a reopening of the case, another appeal—anything. One by one they all turned her down, and Cyrus Fletcher stayed in his Raleigh prison cell; the reason for living had gone out of Elsa Fletcher's life.

Things were never the same after that, Anna thought as she rose from the table and poured herself another cup of coffee. Elsa, of course, always believed in her husband's innocence, even after all attempts at appeal had been exhausted. The people of Kemper were divided on the issue; the subject had been rehashed on street corners, in the barber shop, the saloon, the church yard—anywhere people gathered. Everyone had their own opinion of what happened that night. But in the end, the only opinion that mattered was that of the jury—the jury who had decreed that Cyrus had been a party to the robbery all along, that he wasn't kidnapped at all, but went willingly, then he shot the Kyle brothers out of greed and hid the strongbox of money somewhere in the hills. Cyrus's contention that the brothers had shot each other in an argument and that the strongbox had been in the possession of the other pair of gang members all along had fallen on deaf ears.

After all, the prosecution had argued, Buck and Arlow were brothers, close brothers, and Buck had been in tears when the posse found them. It hardly seemed likely that greed would have driven them to shoot each other. And what of Cyrus's movements that night? He hadn't shown up in town again until after daylight the next morning. More than enough time to bury the strongbox. Cyrus's explanation that he had escaped on foot during the brothers' shoot out, only to become lost in the woods hadn't evoked any sympathy from the jury. The other gang members had been tracked halfway across Mississippi before the posse had lost their trail, so it was not possible to confirm or deny that they had both strongboxes.

Anna uttered a short, bitter laugh as she gazed out the kitchen window into the darkness and listened to the soft rain that had begun to fall. She believed Cyrus, as had her mother and a few of the townsfolk. If only they had known what she knew now, she thought. Her eyes searched the darkness. If only they had known that out there, at this moment and for the last ten years, fifty thousand dollars was buried on Cyrus Fletcher's own farm.

Waves of humiliation washed over Anna as she thought of it. She had been completely shocked two weeks ago when she stood in the prison infirmary at her dying father's bedside and he had confessed the truth to her. He'd actually had the gall to try and explain his motives. He'd seen his big chance to be wealthy and had jumped at it. He'd told her that the money was hers now, her inheritance. Cyrus had instinctively known he had but a short time left to live and was clinging to life until Anna could make the trip to the prison to see him. He died that same night. And with the knowledge of what her father had done, something inside Anna died, too.

Damn that Jimmy Rowe, she thought as she turned away from the window and set aside the coffee that had grown cold in its cup. If it weren't for him—that conniving, thieving outlaw—none of this would have happened. She hated him. Hated his name. Hated the sight of him, though she'd never actually seen him in person.

Angrily, she dug to the bottom of the pile of papers, letters, and documents spread out on the table and pulled out a "Wanted" poster of Jimmy Rowe. Her harsh gaze raked over his square jaw, his aquiline nose, his expressive eyes. She hadn't seen the poster in years, but now she was struck by the familiarity of his face. It was no longer a flat, one-dimensional drawing. The image of Jimmy Rowe seemed to come to life before her eyes. Suddenly, he no longer looked like a criminal. He looked handsome, yet ordinary. The type of man one would expect to find living in one's own town or on a neighboring farm—a man with a wife, a son, a. . . .

Anna shuttered violently and her stomach rolled. She glared at the poster as the initial shock gave way to cold reality. This man—this outlaw—was the same man pictured in the miniature she'd found in Sam Rowan's saddlebag; the man who looked so much like Sam she'd thought it was he.

A hot rush swept through her as she realized the full scope of her discovery. Jimmy Rowe was the man in the miniature, and that could only mean that the man who called himself Sam Rowan was actually. . . .

The "Wanted" poster slipped from her fingers as Anna charged out of the kitchen, her night rail blowing in the breeze she created. She ran down the hallway and into the bedroom. Anna froze in the doorway as her eyes impaled the man lying in her bed, lounging against her pillows. Rage consumed her.

"You bastard!"

He no more than raised his head and opened his eyes before Anna flew to the opposite side of the bed.

"Get up! Get your despicable, filthy, rotten self out of my bed!"

He stared at her. "What's gotten into—"

"Get up! Get out of my bed! Get out of my house!" Anna flailed her arms, fists clenched.

Sam shook his head to clear his thoughts. "What the hell. . . ."

"Out!" Anna leaped onto the bed and shoved his shoulder with both hands. When he didn't budge, she pounded him wildly with her fist. "You snake!"

Sam quickly grasped both her hands in one of his. "Just a damn minute. I—"

Enraged, Anna pulled against him, then swung her feet around and delivered a series of quick, hard kicks to his side and belly. She wanted to hurt him as she never wanted to hurt anyone before.

If his body hadn't been so sore, the blows would have meant nothing. Sam pushed her back onto the mattress then rolled out onto the floor and came up on his knees at the bedside facing her.

Anna struggled for a moment to untangle herself from the coverlet, her own dark mane hanging loose about her shoulders, her night rail ridden up to her knees. She scrambled to her hands and knees, her brown eyes riveting the object of her fury, their faces only inches apart.

"You bastard." Her voice was now low and measured, filled with hatred. "You thought I'd never find out, didn't you. You thought I'd never know."

His brows furrowed and his eyes grew stormy. "I don't know what the hell—"

"I know who you are!"

Sam's jaw tightened and his cheek twitched.

The change in his expression confirmed Anna's suspicion. "He was your father, wasn't he?"

His bare chest, visible through his unbuttoned long johns, rose and fell as Sam drew in a deep breath. "Yes."

Anna's rage bordered on uncontrollable. "I should have shot you myself! I should have killed you at the pond when I had the chance!"

Her face lit up as she realized that yes, the possibility was still within her power. Anna leaped from the bed and dashed out of the room.

Sam raced after her. She was quick. She made it to the kitchen before he caught up with her.

Blinded by her own anger, Anna jerked open the pantry door and grabbed the shotgun from the shelf. She had no thought save killing the son of Jimmy Rowe. It burned through her. She'd do it, without a second thought.

Standing inside the pantry, Anna wheeled the gun around. Sam stood only a barrel-length away. With lightening-quick speed he tore the gun from her hands.

After a stunned second, Anna shouted, "Give me that!"

He raised his long arm high in the air holding the gun out of her reach. His eyes bored into her. "Hell, no." He saw her small hands curl into fists. "And don't you dare hit me another time."

They faced each other in the pantry doorway for a long

moment, glaring their anger at one another. Finally Sam deposited the gun on the top shelf well out of Anna's reach.

Seeing her only weapon made useless, Anna fell back to her verbal assault. "You bastard. You stinking—"

He pointed a threatening finger at her. "Don't call me that name again."

"I'll call you anything I choose!" Anger flowed through her. "Just what kind of game are you playing? What do you want here! What are you doing here!"

Sam took a step closer. His eyes narrowed. "I'm here for the same reason as you, lady. So don't try to play innocent with me."

His words drove away her anger. Silently she cautioned herself to be careful. She shifted her shoulders casually. "I don't know what you mean."

"The hell you don't."

Anna's chin went up a bit. "I'm only here to fix up the farm so I can sell it."

Sam snorted his disbelief. "You're here for the money. You know it and I know it, so let's not waste time claiming otherwise."

Anna folded her arms under her breasts. "I don't know what you're talking about."

"You know. You know exactly. But to put an end to this useless discussion, I'll explain it to you. Two weeks ago you went to the prison in Raleigh to see your pa. Before he died he confessed the truth of what he'd done, that he'd actually taken part in that robbery, that he'd hidden the strongbox right here on his own farm."

Anna was stunned that he knew, and it showed in her expression.

Sam almost laughed aloud. The look on her face confirmed that the hunch he'd played in coming here had been correct.

"You're sadly misinformed, or hallucinating from that bump on your head. How could you possibly know that I was even at the prison?"

"You don't know anything about prison," he said flatly. "For the right amount of bribery money, a man can live as good on the inside as on the outside."

"That doesn't explain—"

"Buck Kyle was in that prison. You didn't know that, did you." Sam took her silence as the response he'd expected. "Buck was my pa's best friend from the time they were boys. He knew Fletcher was dying, knew you were there to see him. Buck figured that finally Fletcher would tell you where he'd hidden the money and you'd go after it. So he got a message out to me. I knew you'd lead me right to it."

"So that's why you were camped out on the back of my property," Anna realized. "It was me that you were hiding from." Her contempt for this man doubled. "You were watching me, waiting. How long had you been out there before I discovered you?"

He shrugged his wide shoulders. "A couple of days."

A wave of caution calmed Anna's tirade. "So, when I found this supposed money—which doesn't even exist—you planned to take it from me."

"Damn right."

She eyed him bitterly. "Like father, like son."

Sam's face hardened. "Don't look so self-righteous, lady. It was your pa that shot the Kyle brothers and took that money in the first place."

"He did not!" Anna's eyes flashed. "The Kyles shot each other. Papa told me. He wasn't a thief. Not like your father was!"

"You don't know a damn thing about my pa!" He jabbed his finger at her as he spoke.

"I know he was an outlaw and a thief." Anna flung the words at him with all the venom her heart held. "He didn't have guts enough to get a real job and work like other men. He had to steal what he wanted. He was nothing but a spineless, no account, worthless varmint! He deserved to die in that robbery!"

Sam's temper blew. "He didn't deserve to lie in the dirt and bleed to death while the marshals stepped over him! He deserved every cent he took—that and more! The government owed him!"

"Owed him! What kind of twisted logic is that? He was a criminal—"

"He was a man! A man who—" Sam's chest heaved with rage, but he stopped himself.

They glared at each other for a long moment. Then Anna shrugged indifferently. "Well, you've wasted your time in coming here, Mr. Rowan, or Rowe, or whatever your name really is."

"It's Rowan," he told her. "My pa shortened his name, hoping there'd be no link to me."

She shrugged indifferently. "I want you off of my property tonight."

He laughed aloud. "I'm not going anywhere."

"Then I'll get the sheriff."

"And tell him what? That you don't want to be disturbed while you recover the fifty thousand your pa stole from the United States government?"

Anna sucked in a quick breath realizing her dilemma. She tried another tack. "You're a fool to stay here, chasing after something that doesn't even exist."

A confident smile parted his lips. "It's here, and I intend to stay no more than two inches off your sweet little fanny, Mrs. Rowan, until you lead me to it."

Anger flickered inside her. "We'll see about that."

"We sure as hell will."

The battle lines drawn, they eyed each other, sealing their vows.

Anna was the first to look away, realizing suddenly how loud the rain sounded in the quiet house, how cool the air had become, and that she was wearing only her night rail, arguing with a man clad only in his long johns.

Suddenly feeling self-conscious and vulnerable, Anna wrapped her arms around her middle. "Well, uh, I'm going to bed—sleep now."

She took a step forward. He reluctantly moved aside and let her pass. Anna hurried down the hall, anxious to escape his bold gaze, and went into her bedroom only to find Sam on her heels.

"What do you think you're doing in my bedroom?" She eyed him coldly, stopping him in the doorway.

"I'm tired too."

Her eyes widened and she tightened her grip on the doorknob. "Well, you're certainly not going to sleep in here. This is my farm, my house, my room, and my bed. And I'm sleeping in it."

"And where the hell am I supposed to sleep?"

"Why don't you ride into town? I'm sure you will have your choice of hotel rooms there." She offered the suggestion with a sickly sweet smile.

He shook his head. "And have you grab the money and leave before first light? Oh no. I told you, I'm not letting you out of my sight."

Anna gave an exaggerated yawn and stretched. "Suit yourself. I'm going to get into that warm, soft bed now and get some sleep. Goodnight."

She stepped back and closed the door in his face.

. . . drip . . . drip drip . . . drip . . . drip drip . . . drip . . .

Sam groaned, cursed, then tried to roll over on the narrow bed. He banged his elbow on the wall bringing an even more lurid curse to his lips. This was without a doubt the most uncomfortable contraption he'd ever had the misfortune of trying to sleep in, he thought. The tiny bed he'd found in the bedroom next to the kitchen was so short his feet hung over the end, and the straw mattress was thin enough that the support ropes cut into him like daggers. The room itself was a near-nightmare. Several panes were missing from the window, which allowed a cold breeze in, and the rain dripping through the leaking roof was enough to drive a man crazy.

But still, it was somewhat more acceptable than the other places in the house he'd attempted to sleep in tonight. Sam had abandoned the short, narrow settee in the parlor, because no matter which way he lay, a spring jabbed him in the backside. He even tried to sleep sitting in the kitchen chair with his head resting on the table, but that had given him a backache, a crick in his neck, and no rest at all. And there was no way on earth he would even consider sleeping on the floor.

Sam rolled onto his back, bringing a threatening creak

from the little bed, and tried to spread the cloak he'd found by the back door over him again. No matter how he turned, half of him was left uncovered.

All he could think of was how cold he was, how much his body ached, and the big comfortable bed down the hall. He rolled over again and struck his already bruised shin on the bedframe. Cursing, Sam leaped to his feet, wadded up the cloak and flung it to the floor, and limped down the hallway.

He threw open the door to Anna's bedroom. It banged against the wall sounding like another clap of thunder in the rainstorm. A low fire burned in the hearth and he could see Anna stir from the depths of the warm, cozy coverlet. Sam went to the opposite side of the bed and yanked down the covers.

"Move over."

Anna came fully awake in a heartbeat. She sat straight up in bed, clutching the quilt to her breast. "What—what do you think you're doing? Get—get out of here!"

"I'm tired," he barked. "I'm sleeping in here."

"You most certainly are not." Her heart pounded wildly as she took in the sight of him in the soft firelight. "Go sleep somewhere else."

"There is no other place! In case you hadn't noticed, this is the only decent bed in the house." He sat down on the edge of the bed.

"In case I hadn't noticed!" Hot indignation filled her. "I suppose you don't remember, but I slept in that chair for the last two nights taking care of you while you were ill."

He glanced at the small chair by the fireplace then looked across the bed at her. "You did?"

"I most certainly did." She flung her hand toward the door. "Go away."

He scowled again. "I told you, there's not one other decent bed or chair to sleep in."

"Then sleep in the barn."

He laughed bitterly. "It's probably got a better roof on it than this place does."

Her brows drew together. "The roof leaks? Oh, dear, what's next?"

"I'll tell you what's next—I'm sleeping in here."

"Sleep on the floor," she told him.

He shook his head. "Hell, no. This place is full of mice, and I'm—"

"Mice!" Anna sprang to her knees in the center of the bed, clutching the covers closer, her eyes searching the darkness as if she expected the little rodents to present themselves upon command.

"Yes, mice. And I'm not about to sleep on this floor and have my fingers and toes—or anything else more vital—nibbled on. Now, move over."

Sam climbed in the bed beside her and when Anna opened her mouth to protest he silenced her with a pointing finger. "Don't you know that denying your husband admittance to your bed is grounds for divorce, Mrs. Rowan?"

Anna's temper flared. How irritating of him to keep throwing that in her face. "You're not my husband and you have no rights!"

"Yeah, yeah, I know." He took one of the pillows she'd been using. "Look, lady, you don't mean anything to me. Your virtue is perfectly safe. Tonight, I just haven't got it in me."

Sam rolled onto his side presenting his back, effectively ending their conversation.

She was left stewing. How dare he barge into her room and crawl into bed with her! Then tell her she meant nothing to him! After all she'd done to care for him and nurse him back to health!

Realizing the ingrate was taking no notice of her outrage, Anna settled back in bed suddenly acutely conscious of the warmth of his body, the sight of his big muscular back through his long johns, and the rhythmic sound of his breathing. Annoyed with herself, Anna turned her head away and clamped her eyelids shut.

God, this was the most comfortable place he'd rested in his entire life. Sam snuggled deeper into the soft mattress, soaking the warmth of the quilt into his chilled body. The pillow beneath his aching head smelled sweet, like wild flowers blooming in the spring. The scents and sensations all blended together to promise the restful night's sleep he desperately needed.

So if everything was so damn perfect, Sam thought irritably, why was he lying here wide awake? And why was his body strung tighter than a banjo string?

It was her. It was that woman. And the realization caused Sam's eyes to fly open and stare blankly into the darkness. It was her fault, all right. It was Anna Fletcher.

Vague impressions began to surface in his mind and Sam recalled bits and pieces of the last few days. Anna's soft, reassuring voice, her gentle touch, the comfort of her presence.

When Sam had come into this room tonight and forced himself into her bed, he had no interest in Anna Fletcher at all. A warm comfortable place to sleep was the extent of his desire. But suddenly, everything had changed. She was no longer just a means to an end, the key to the fortune he sought.

Sam cursed aloud in the heavy silence, threw off the covers and stalked from the room slamming the door behind him—Goddamnit, Anna Fletcher was also a woman.

CHAPTER 4

The sound of footsteps caused Anna to look up from her pencil and paper. Sam walked into the kitchen. It struck her as odd to see him fully clothed. He was wearing the same dark trousers and shirt he had on when she found him in her front yard. Whisker stubble shadowed his jaws and chin, and his eyes were hooded from fatigue. She wondered where he'd slept last night after he'd stormed out of her room—and she still didn't understand what that had been about. She wondered now if he had slept at all. He looked tired—and handsome.

Anna forced down that startling revelation with the last gulp of her coffee and turned back to her writing pad. She'd already decided how to handle Sam Rowan's unwanted presence in her house. She wouldn't be swayed from it.

"What's for breakfast?" Sam ambled into the kitchen and raked his hands through his hair at the temples. He winced as his fingers brushed the scab that had formed on his forehead.

Anna almost offered him some of her headache powders but stopped herself. She glanced at the empty bowl on the table in front of her. "Oatmeal."

His lips curl downward. "Is that all you've got?"

Anna's temper heated up a notch. "In case you didn't notice when I practically carried you into my house the other night, nearly wrenching my back in the process, there was no sign over my door declaring this place 'Anna's Restaurant.'"

He ignored her sarcasm and went to the cookstove. His eyes riveted her as he held up the empty pot. "It's all gone."

"And it was quite tasty, too." She smacked her lips and turned back to her writing.

Sam slammed the pot down on the stove, then searched the cupboards until he found a blue-speckled cup. He poured from the coffeepot. Three drops of thick, dark liquid and a teaspoon of grounds splattered into the cup. He growled low in his throat and slammed the pot down onto the stove with a bang. He lifted the lid from the kettle on the back of the stove and took a whiff.

"Good God! What the hell is this stuff?" He wrinkled his nose and quickly covered the foul-smelling concoction.

Anna looked up at him. "That happens to be your medicine."

His eyes widened. "Is that the stuff you fed me! Jesus Christ, it tastes like pond scum."

Anna's back stiffened. "That is an old family recipe, and for your information, it is largely responsible for your recovery." That and the time she spent caring for him, she wanted to add.

He snorted in disbelief. "I'd sooner eat tree bark."

"Tree bark!" Of all the nerve! She'd nursed him back to health, and he had the gall to compare her healing remedy to tree bark! Anna's anger smoldered.

Sam shuddered. "That stuff could rob a man of his capabilities."

"Well, it certainly didn't rob you of any," Anna said angrily as the memory of his lusty kiss and demanding embrace came back to her.

His eyes came up sharply, their blueness filled with concern. "I didn't hurt you, did I? I mean, while I was unconscious, I didn't . . . force you . . . or—"

"No." Anna's reply was quick. She couldn't bear to see the worry on his face over what he might have done. Color rose in her cheeks and she turned back to her writing pad once more.

Sam looked around the kitchen, uncomfortable, and ran his hand across his chest. "I, uh, I need a bath and a shave."

Startled, Anna looked up at him, and the image of his long, muscular frame sitting in her wooden washtub sent her senses reeling. Afraid that she would blush again, Anna hardened her feelings.

With exaggerated precision she folded the paper she'd been writing on. "Why don't you ride into town? There's a public bathhouse there that should suit your needs perfectly."

His eyes narrowed and he shook his head. "Nice try. But I'm not going anywhere without you."

Anna rose from her chair. "Suit yourself."

"I always do."

She ignored him as she deposited her dishes in the sink and headed out the back door.

"Hey, hold on!"

She turned and sighed impatiently. "What do you want? I have things to do."

The morning sun was behind her, outlining her trim figure. He licked his dry lips. "What am I supposed to do about breakfast?"

"Why don't you eat some of that tree bark you mentioned a while ago that you thought would be so tasty?" She gave him a sweet smile, then closed the door behind her.

The harness jangled as Anna slapped the reins and the horses pulled the wagon out of the barnyard. Preparing the team was a task that had not come easily to Anna, and though she had done it many times in the past two weeks, her hands were no better practiced.

The morning sun was warm and bright and everything seemed to glisten after last night's rain. It almost looked pretty here, she thought as she guided the horses toward the house—almost.

Anna wished she could block out the view of the overgrown yard, the broken fence, and the general state of disrepair that existed everywhere she looked. She wished she could see it as it had looked so many years ago; it was so ugly to her now.

Her nostalgic reverie was abruptly halted by the sight of Sam Rowan standing on her front porch. Evidently he had found the washtub and his saddlebag containing his shaving razor and his clothing she'd hung in the armoire. He looked fresh and clean, dressed in dark trousers and vest and a pale-blue shirt that made his eyes sparkle beneath the brim of his black hat.

He came down the steps, avoiding the broken one, and strode purposefully across the yard. "Where do you think you're going?"

Anna pulled back on the reins, pretending not to notice the edge of his voice and the suspicious tilt of his head. "To town."

His strong fingers closed around the bridle. He planted his other fist on his lean hip. "You're not going anywhere."

Anna looped the reins around the brake lever and stood. She felt a certain satisfaction in looking down on him. "When I planned for this trip I hadn't expected I'd have to feed a bottomless pit from the dredges of humanity. I need more supplies."

Considering the subject closed, Anna turned and cautiously climbed down from the wagon. She felt his big hands close around her waist and lift her to the ground easily. Anna whirled around. "Don't ever touch me again."

His left eyebrow crept upward. "It's nothing personal, but I've got manners and I use them."

The warmth of his hands radiated up her body. "Well— well, just use them on somebody else."

Sam chuckled. "Yes, ma'am. I'll do that."

Irritated at both him and herself, Anna pushed past him and headed toward the house. "I'll be back by midday. Just don't—"

"I'm going with you."

She stopped and turned to him. "There's no need. I'm quite capable of—"

"I'm sure you're capable of a lot of things," he told her. "That's why I'm not letting you out of my sight."

She sighed heavily. "Oh, all right. I don't care what you do. I'll be out as soon as I change," she called as she walked toward the house once more.

"Wear that frilly pink thing, will you?"

Anna froze in her tracks and turned slowly toward him. The coolness in her features belied the pounding of her heart and her sudden shortness of breath. His gaze was steady but unreadable. Finally, she turned and went into the house.

Just for spite she ignored the "frilly pink thing" Sam had requested and dressed in a pale-blue dress. It had rows of ruffles down the tight-fitted bodice and around the high collar and sleeves; the bustle accentuated her small waist and swayed with her hips when she walked. She coiled her hair atop her head and pinned a matching hat among the curls.

It gave her an odd sensation knowing that Sam had gone through her clothing in the armoire and had selected a favorite. She wasn't sure it was at all proper. But nothing about Sam Rowan had been proper.

Anna checked her appearance in the mirror one final time, then made certain her grocery list and coin purse were in her reticule. She'd have to shop carefully since her resources were limited.

When she left the house, she saw Sam leaning against the wagon, one ankle crossed over the other and gazing at the Blue Ridge Mountains in the distance, patiently waiting. He turned his attention to her and watched intently as she crossed the yard. She was glad she hadn't worn the dress he'd requested.

Anna pointedly ignored him and began to climb into the wagon. Sam grasped her elbow. She pulled away and shot him a defiant glare. Unperturbed, he grasped her waist and lifted her up onto the seat.

Anna fumed silently as Sam walked around the wagon and climbed into the seat beside her. She reached for the reins but he picked them up first.

"I'll handle the horses," he told her.

Anna pursed her lips and looked away. It was about time he did something around here, she decided. Anna straightened her skirt and moved as far away from him on the seat as possible.

"You look real pretty." His voice was mellow. She felt his breath on her cheek. Anna turned and found him lazily perusing her from head to toe. A devilish gleam appeared in his eyes, and the corner of his lip curled into a smug smile. "Blue is my favorite color."

Anna's shoulders sagged slightly and she turned away.

Sam called to the team and slapped the reins. The wagon lurched forward.

"I'm only going to Kemper," Anna said when they reached the road. She pointed to the west.

The town of Kemper, only three miles away, was the closest, and adequate for the supplies she needed to purchase today. Charlotte, several more miles away and to the east, was reserved for the every-two-month trip to the city when more than staples were needed.

Sam turned the team westward onto the road. "Who bought these horses? Some blind widow woman?"

Anna's mouth fell open then snapped shut. "There is nothing wrong with these horses."

He shrugged his big shoulders. "They're both well past their prime. I'm surprised they got you down here."

"And I suppose you're an expert on horses?"

"As a matter of fact, I am. I've worked on horse farms since I was a boy." Sam looked out at the road again. "Other peoples' horse farms."

They were silent for a long while before Sam spoke again. "What do we need from town?"

"Just some staples I'm running low on. Because I have another mouth to feed." She waited for his comeback, or at least a thank you for the meals she'd fed him, but he said nothing. "You can wait in the wagon. I won't be long."

He looked at her from the corner of his eye. "Won't people think ill of a husband who lets his wife do all the work?"

"Don't start that again," she told him. "You're not my husband."

"You're the one who started it," he pointed out.

"Well, that was an emergency, of sorts." It was a feeble excuse for what she'd done, but it was the only one she had. Anna tugged at her skirt, smoothing it down. "I wish you wouldn't bring it up again."

"Don't you think your friends in town might ask who I am?"

She looked away, out across the fields that lined the road. "I don't have any friends there."

His brows rose. "Didn't you grow up here?"

"Yes. But I never kept in touch with anyone, me or Mama either. No one is going to remember me here. I left ten years ago. I was only fourteen then."

Sam shrugged. "I don't know. It's a small town. People have got long memories in a small town."

Anna nodded confidently. "We're not going to be in town long enough to raise an eyebrow. No one knows I'm at the farm, no one will be looking for me. You just stay in the wagon. I'll pick up what we need and we'll be on our way. Believe me, no one, not one soul, is going to recognize me. No one."

"Anna? Anna Fletcher? Is that you?"

"Anna? My goodness, it is her."

"Why, it's little Anna Fletcher! I can hardly believe my eyes!"

Anna cringed as Sam pulled the wagon to a stop in front of Palmer's General Store. Mildred Palmer stood with a broom in one hand and a welcoming smile on her face, gazing up at her. Clara Abbott and Irene Sanders beside her gaped at Anna with unmasked curiosity.

"It's her," Clara declared.

Irene's eyes widened behind the lenses of her spectacles. "I'd know her anywhere. The very image of her mother."

The three ladies gathered beside the wagon gazing expectantly until Anna was forced to say something. She drew in a deep breath, mustering what cheer she could. "It's so good to see you again."

"My little Anna's been having a fit to come into town and see all of her old friends again."

At Sam's words Anna's head snapped around. He was grinning smugly. A feeling of foreboding rose up inside her. She'd seen that look before.

The ladies turned their attention to Sam and he gave them a charming smile. "And I've been anxious to see all of her friends. It's a pleasure to meet you ladies. I'm Sam Rowan, Anna's husband."

Anna gasped and her eyes widened in horror. He shot her
smirk and jumped down to the boardwalk.

"We had no idea Anna was married," Mildred said.

"Why, we didn't even know she was back in town," Irene
added.

Sam grinned and looked sheepish. "It's my fault. I've been
keeping her all to myself."

The ladies tittered.

He smiled proudly. "But I just had to bring her into town
today and show her off." He looked up at Anna. "Come on
down here, honey."

If looks could kill, her glower would have incinerated him
to ashes. She barely contained her anger, her temper threatening to explode.

The ladies turned their bright, happy faces up to Anna.
Words were on the tip of her tongue, words that would surely
shock the three fine ladies into a silence they might not
recover from.

But Sam spoke first. "We've been out at the farm together
for days now. Just the two of us. Just Anna and me. Alone. All

___ ___, _dies smiled and nodded their understanding.

_ _ds," Mildred concluded.

_e bobbed their heads in unison.

_y gaze bored into Sam. Her lips pressed
_ent outrage. There was no way she could deny
_s her husband. Not now. Not after he'd just told
_e women—the town's biggest gossips—that she'd
_one with him at the farm for days. She was caught in
_e she'd created, however innocently. Though she hadn't
_gined it possible, her contempt for Sam Rowan grew.

"Come on down, honey." Sam lifted her from the wagon
and planted her stiff body at his side.

"Anna, we still have prayer group at my house on
Thursday morning," Irene told her. "You'll have to come."

"And the Founders' Day Festival will be coming up soon,"
Clara added. "We can certainly use another pair of hands."

Sam spoke quickly. "That's mighty kind of you ladies, and
I know she'd love to join in, but the truth is I don't believe I

can do without this little wife of mine." He squeezed Ann
shoulder affectionately.

Anna kept her mouth clamped shut, knowing that if s
uttered one sound, it would unleash a verbal assault th
might never end. Sam couldn't have cared less about her, th
prayer group, or Founders' Day; he only wanted her under hi
thumb to keep watch on the hidden money.

"Well, that's all right, Anna," Mildred said. "We understand how newlyweds are."

Mildred returned to her sweeping; Irene and Clara went on
their way.

"I don't think I've ever seen a man set such a store by his
wife," Irene declared.

"I just hope she realizes how lucky she is," Clara replied as
they disappeared into the crowd of Saturday shoppers.

Anna cringed at the overheard comments. She felt Sam's
smile beaming down at her.

"Come on into the store, Mrs. Rowan." Sam applied gentle
pressure to the small of her back.

She dug in her heels. "Stop calling me that."

Sam glanced around. "Better keep your voice dow Mrs
Rowan, unless you want to give these good people som
else to gossip about after we're gone."

He had her. Anna was galled to admit it. He'd fixed it s
could stay as long as he wanted, and if she spoke up and t
the truth she'd only make herself the object of the m
unsavory gossip. And the last thing she wanted was to onc
again be the grist for the town's rumor mill.

She gave Sam a scathing look, put her nose in the air and
glided inside Palmer's General Store.

Hugh Palmer recognized her on sight and called a greeting
that made everyone in the store turn and stare. He was a little
balder than she remembered and thicker around the middle,
but he was as kind and friendly as when she'd been in his
store as a child. It was always a gathering place for the
townspeople. Men would sit in the cane-bottom chairs on the
porch or crowd around the potbellied stove in the winter and
talk about the weather, the crops. The shop was also a favorite
among women, as Mildred Palmer saw to it that they carried

the most fashionable yard goods and the latest in housewares. Children loved the array of colorful candies displayed in glass jars on the counter.

Anna walked around the store. She studied the list she'd prepared, but her thoughts were anchored in the past. The wooden floor creaked in the same spot, and the room smelled of coffee, exactly as it had when she'd accompanied her parents here years ago. The store was crowded with Saturday shoppers. So little had changed in Kemper, Anna thought. Ten years had made no difference at all. Except in herself, she realized. She had changed immeasurably. Now she was a grown woman who wanted no part of this town. She had her own life. She had her own dreams and goals. She had a—husband.

Anna's spine stiffened as she spotted Sam across the store shaking hands with the men crowded around the pickle barrel. Without a doubt, he'd introduced himself as her husband to every person in the store. Her anger stirred, and Anna decided it was time to conclude her shopping and get out of town.

She hurried to the counter and waited until Hugh had dispensed with his other customer and turned his attention to her.

"What will you be needing today, Anna?"

She consulted her list. Her funds were limited, and she knew she'd have to shop carefully to get everything she needed.

"Give me a half-pound of coffee, a pound of flour, two pounds of—"

"Whoa here. Let me see that list, sugar."

Sam was suddenly at her side. Casually, he rested one hand on her waist and leaned over her shoulder.

"That's won't be nearly enough food, darling. Hugh, give us ten pounds of sugar, a couple sacks of flour and meal, a slab of bacon. Have you got any fresh eggs?"

The shopkeeper nodded. "Sure thing, Sam." He called to his son across the store who hurried off to fetch the order.

Furious, Anna wheeled to face Sam. "I am not paying to feed you," she whispered through clenched teeth.

He looked unconcerned as he helped himself to a licorice stick from the jar on the counter. "I believe it's a husband's duty to provide food for his wife."

Her hands curled into fists. "You're not my—"

"Hugh," he called over Anna's head. "Can you tell me where I can get a new mattress? The one I've got is worn out."

Hugh and the men gathered at the pickle barrel all exchanged a knowing look that turned Anna's cheeks crimson.

"I stock them," Hugh replied. "Here in the back room. What size do you need?"

"Something long," Sam said as he crossed the store. "But no sense in having it too wide."

Mortified, Anna bolted for the door.

The man was insufferable. Totally and completely. Anna silently berated Sam with every foul name she knew as she made her way down the boardwalk. And the most frustrating part of it all was that there was nothing she could do about it.

When she thought of all she'd done for him—taken him in, nursed him around the clock, gave him the food out of her own mouth—it made her all the more angry. He'd never even said thank you. Instead, he made her life a living nightmare.

Anna was halfway through town when her anger cooled enough to slow her steps. She couldn't lose her head anymore, she realized. Sam was a cunning man. She'd need all her wits about her if she were going to get rid of him. And that's exactly what she would have to do. She was going to recover that stolen money herself. She had a very specific plan for it, and it did not include Sam Rowan.

Calmer now, Anna saw that she was outside Reynolds Dry Good Store. She looked at the clothing displayed in the window and debated a moment before hurrying inside.

The work she did on the farm was hard, and her skirts were always getting in the way. She'd toyed with the notion of buying herself a pair of men's trousers but hadn't had the nerve to do it—until now. Maybe, she thought, she could drive Sam Rowan away simply by looking terrible.

It was out of the question to try them on, so Anna took a

pair of the denim trousers from the shelf and held them up; the best she could do was guess at the size. She did the same with a tan workshirt and paid for them with the money she'd intended to spend on supplies.

As she stepped out onto the crowded boardwalk again, a man blocked her path. She stepped to the left, and so did he. She moved to the right. He followed. Annoyed, she looked up to find a mischievous grin bearing down on her.

"If it's not Miss Anna Fletcher. I was determined I'd find you today if it meant turning this whole town upside down."

It took a moment for Anna to mentally match the face of the man before her to that of the boy she'd known so long ago. She smiled in earnest.

"Brett Morgan. What a surprise."

He swept the tan Stetson from his blond head. "It's good to see you, Anna."

"How did you know I was here?"

Brett gestured toward the street. "It's all over town."

Well, that didn't take long, Anna thought ruefully. Still, she was pleased to see Brett.

"How have you been?" she asked. Then she saw the star pinned to his brown vest. She giggled. "A deputy? You're the deputy? The last I remember of you, Brett Morgan, you were stealing apples from Parkers Orchard."

"I still do," he told her with a sly grin. They both laughed.

"So, are you and your pa both keeping the peace in Kemper now?" Anna asked.

Brett shook his head. "No, Pa hung up his badge last fall. He and Ma moved down to Charleston near her sister. The winters are easier on her there."

"And you're carrying on the family tradition."

He grinned and shrugged. "I didn't have much choice. It's in the blood."

They laughed again, then Brett grew serious. "I'm glad to see you again, Anna, truly I am. I wanted to write to you after you left town, but I didn't think your ma would take too kindly to it, seeing as it was my uncle who handed down your pa's sentence."

She hadn't expected to hear that from Brett. She'd known

him since she was a child, and because he was four years older than she, they'd seen a lot of each other in school and in church. That was normal in a small town. But back then, he was more likely to tease her unmercifully, pull on her pigtails, and chase after her with a jar full of spiders than to stand before her twisting his hat in his hands and looking at her with puppy-dog eyes as he was now.

"I didn't keep in touch with anyone here, Brett. It was easier for Mamma that way."

Brett pulled on his Stetson and took the package from Anna's hand. They walked slowly down the boardwalk. "What have you been doing all these years?"

"Helping my uncle with his medical practice, mostly," she explained. "He's a fine doctor. He's been studying new surgical procedures in Boston for the last two months. It's been a bit lonely without him around. Mamma died last fall."

Brett nodded solemnly. "I heard about that. I'm real sorry, Anna. I should have written you with my condolences, but I'd just moved back to town then and taken on my deputy duties. It's no excuse, though."

Apparently her family was still talked about in Kemper. She wondered how word of her mother's death had reached town, but didn't ask.

"I was sorry to hear about your pa passing on, too."

Anna's steps slowed. "You know about Pa?"

"My Uncle Chester is a guard up there at the prison." The corner of Brett's mouth curled upward. "My whole family is involved in the law. Don't you remember the time we stole rock candy from Palmer's and hid under the church steps when my pa came after us and threatened to toss us in jail?"

Anna giggled. "I'd forgotten that. But you're the one who stole the candy, not me."

"Yeah, but you helped eat it."

They laughed together, then Brett gazed off into the street. Wagons and buckboards made their way through the rutted roads, still damp after the night's rain. Children hurried behind their fathers, and women with shopping baskets on their arms roamed the stores.

"Yeah, I left Kemper for a few years," Brett said. "Spent

some time in New Orleans, then over in Galveston. But I came back home, finally. I'm glad you did too, Anna."

"I'm not staying in Kemper." Somehow it was difficult telling him that.

"You're not? But I thought—"

"I just came back to sell the farm." It was the lie she'd planned to tell everyone. It rolled off her tongue easier than her conscience liked.

Brett's brows drew together. "Is that what you want?"

"Yes, Brett, it's for the best."

He tucked her package under his arm and hung his thumbs in his gun belt. "I don't know. I might have to arrest you for stealing rock candy again and put you in my jail to keep you here for a while."

A giggle tumbled from Anna's lips and she swatted his arm playfully. "Don't you go trying to get me in trouble again, Brett Morgan."

He closed his hand around her wrist. "Maybe I should take you over to the jailhouse right now and let you get a look at your new home."

She laughed harder and tried to pull away. "I'm surprised these townspeople ever made you deputy. You've been up to no good ever since I can remember."

Brett laughed with her. "That's another good reason to put you in jail. I can't have you telling these folks what I'm really like. Come on, now."

Anna hadn't laughed in ages. She'd forgotten that Brett always had that effect on her. Suddenly she felt young and carefree with no worries or problems weighing her down.

Until she saw Sam walk out of Palmer's General Store a few feet ahead and level a cold stare at her and Brett.

She froze. Instinctively Brett released her wrist. Sam walked toward them with slow, measured steps. Beside her, Brett's frame went rigid. Anna heart skipped a beat.

She sensed the deep tension between the two men when Sam stopped beside her. Anxious to fill the awkward silence, she introduced them.

"Brett, this is Sam Rowan. Sam, this is Brett Morgan, an old friend of mine."

The two men eyed each other sharply. Neither offered his hand.

"I'm Anna's husband," Sam said in a low, even voice. It wasn't a statement of fact. It was a warning.

As though he'd been struck a physical blow, Brett fell back a step. He looked hard at Sam as if he couldn't trust his own eyes.

Anna glanced nervously between the two men. Sam was taller by several inches but Brett nearly matched him in weight and build. They were opposites in every other way. Sam, with his black hair and ruggedly handsome face tanned by the sun, countered by Brett's boyish looks and fair skin crowned by a head of golden hair.

Finally, Brett spoke. "It was good seeing you again, Anna." He handed her the package he'd carried for her but Sam reached out and took it. Brett tipped his hat and left.

Sam turned on his heels and walked back to the wagon.

Anna was struck with the need to explain as she hurried after him. "It was all perfectly innocent. I've known Brett since I was a child."

His gaze was cold as he tossed the package into the wagon.

"He's just an old friend."

Without a word, Sam turned and walked away from her.

Anna was overwhelmed with guilt. She felt dirty, as if she'd done something wrong—as if she'd cheated on her husband.

CHAPTER 5

He'd gone only a short distance before he stopped and came back for her. Sam grasped her elbow, and they walked to Nettie's Cafe together. Neither spoke as they sat at a table by the front window. Anna fiddled with the silverware and gazed out at the street, doing anything but looking at Sam. When their meal arrived he ate hungrily, reminding Anna that he'd had no breakfast this morning. He appeared tired now, and weary. He was still weak from his injuries and he should have stayed home and rested today; she was sure his head was hurting.

"Maybe you should see Dr. Sawyer while we're in town," she suggested softly.

He paused over his steak. "I don't know what he could do that you haven't already done."

It was the closest thing to a compliment she'd gotten from him. Still, it brought her little comfort.

Anna could hardly eat. Sam was quiet and withdrawn. Then she became angry with herself for caring what he thought of her conduct with Brett earlier.

She snatched up her fork. "If my behavior doesn't suit you, you're free to leave."

He looked up from his plate. "If you want to shame your husband in public, go ahead. It's your reputation."

Anna clenched her knife. "You're not my husband."

"I know that." He inclined his head toward the street. "But they don't."

She hated it when he was right. Anna calmed herself and

began to eat, reminding herself of her earlier resolve to keep her head and her wits about her.

"You're being foolish to stay here, anyway. There is no money buried on my land."

"It's there."

"If that's so," she proposed, "why would I have waited until now to get it?"

He pushed his empty plate aside. "Your pa planned to recover the money himself when he got out of prison. It wasn't until he realized he was dying that he told you about it."

Anna shrugged off his logic. "That's speculation on your part."

"A conclusion drawn from facts," Sam told her. He signaled the serving girl and ordered a slice of apple pie.

"You're wasting your time," Anna told him.

"And you're wasting your breath."

Yes, it seemed she was. It would take something more than words to convince Sam Rowan there was no money hidden on the farm. Anna knew she needed a solid plan to drive him out of her life for good.

"I heard the rumor. Seems it's true."

The sultry voice came from the redhead who appeared beside the table. Anna looked up at her, certain this was someone she should remember. The woman, however, seemed more interested in devouring Sam than renewing old friendships.

"Maggie Nesbit?" Anna ventured.

"That's right. Only it's Fry now." She arched her brow at Sam. "And you must be the new husband."

He introduced himself. "Pleasure to meet you, ma'am."

"The pleasure is mine. All mine." She spoke the words in a breathy sigh, then turned to Anna again. "I got married a few months ago. You probably remember Jonas Fry."

Anna gasped. "You married Jonas Fry? Deacon Fry?"

"His wife took sick and died just after Christmas. I run this cafe for him now, and take care of those kids too."

"That must keep you hopping," Sam said.

Maggie swept her tongue across her bottom lip. "More than you'd know."

Anna didn't know how Maggie could make a simple statement sound so lurid—hardly the kind of thing one would expect to hear from a deacon's wife. But Anna couldn't imagine them together anyway. Jonas had been an old man ten years ago when Anna had last seen him and Maggie was only a few years older than herself. She was round and soft everywhere, with shapely hips that sashayed when she walked and bosoms that threatened to pop out of every dress she wore.

Annoyed, Anna picked up her reticule and rose. "We've got to be going."

Maggie stood there another few seconds blocking Sam's path so he couldn't rise from his chair. She ran her finger down his arm, from his shoulder to his wrist resting beside his plate. "You come on back, Sam. I've got a house special I think you'll like."

Sam stood and pulled on his hat. "Good day, Mrs. Fry."

Anna led the way out of the cafe ahead of Sam, but she could feel Maggie's gaze upon them. Vaguely, she wondered if this was what Sam had felt like when he'd seen her with Brett. No, she decided. That was different entirely.

Outside Palmer's General Store they found the wagon had been loaded with supplies, including a crate of live, cackling chickens. Lashed to the top of it all was the mattress. Anna cringed. Was he going to parade that thing all over town!

Anxious to leave, Anna simply allowed Sam to help her into the seat and kept her mouth shut.

Sam climbed up beside her and picked up the reins. "Is there anything you want before we leave town?"

"What I want can't be purchased in a store," she said pointedly as she tugged down her skirt.

Sam shrugged and eased the team out into the street.

They made one final stop before leaving town. Anna waited in the wagon in front of the blacksmith shop while Sam talked to the smithy inside. He came out a short while later carrying a large white cat.

"Oh, Sam, he's adorable," Anna cried as he passed the fluffy animal up to her.

"Adorable or not, he's the best mouser the blacksmith owned." Sam climbed onto the wagon and turned the team toward the farm.

The cat settled onto Anna's lap. She stroked his soft fur. "What's his name?"

Sam lifted his shoulder. "I don't know."

"You didn't ask?"

"Doesn't matter much one way or the other, as long as he rids the place of those mice."

"We have to call him something." The cat purred contentedly in Anna's lap. "What sounds good to you?"

"Right now a bed and a soft, feather pillow are the only things that sound good to me."

Anna considered his words. "All right. We'll call him Feathers."

Sam looked down at the cat curled comfortably in the folds of Anna's skirt. It was the first time he'd ever felt envious of an animal. The cat looked so comfortable and Sam had never felt more miserable in his life. His head was pounding. His body ached, every inch of it. And he was bone tired.

The trip back to the farm seemed endless, and by the time he'd unloaded all the supplies, he was going on sheer force of will only. Anna had suggested he rest a bit before unloading everything, but Sam wanted the chore over with.

"Why don't you sit a while and catch your breath before you see to the horses," Anna suggested as he dropped the last sack of flour in the pantry. She'd been busy in the kitchen while he made trip after trip to the wagon out front. She pointed to the table. "I brought a fresh jug of water up from the spring house this morning. It's still cold."

Sam eased his bruised body into the chair and kept his mouth shut tight so as not to moan. He drained the glass Anna had set out for him. She was humming as she moved about the kitchen. And what a pretty woman she was, he decided, though that mouth of hers was something to be reckoned with. She was still dressed in the blue dress he liked so much, and her bustle was bobbing all over the room. Lord, it was a sight to watch.

And then he saw two of them. Sam blinked and shook his head. The room tilted to the left. He grabbed the table to steady himself. Sam rubbed his eyes and saw Anna standing over him.

"Let's get you to bed." Her voice was like a melody as she took his arm.

A heavy haze clouded his mind, and he struggled to form a clear thought. The drink. She'd put something in his drink.

"You . . . you gave me . . . something."

"Come along, Sam." She pulled him to his feet. "The bed will be so comfortable, and your head will stop hurting. You want that, don't you?"

"Yes . . . no. . . ." Something warned him not to give in, but Anna's voice was the angel's voice, and her words conjured up the most pleasurable images he'd ever experienced. He followed as she guided him to the bedroom and stood where she told him to stand as she helped him remove his vest and shirt and pulled off his boots. The last thing Sam remembered was Anna's sweet fragrance hovering around him and the feel of the soft pillow as his head sank into it.

He dreamed of Anna. She was laughing and her deep brown eyes shone with merriment as she looked into the face of the deputy sheriff who held her wrist. Her voice was like a song adrift on the summer breeze, drawing Sam closer, tapping a well of emotion deep in his soul.

Then she wasn't laughing anymore and her face was gaunt with horror. She transformed into Mary, screaming as the men held her arms and dragged her across the porch. Sam ran toward her, but he was small, so small that a blue sheathed arm scooped him up and carried him away. The sky darkened with smoke, and orange flames crackled and popped. Hooves pounded the earth, chickens squawked, dogs barked viciously. And above the chaos rose Mary's voice, screaming . . . screaming . . . screaming. . . .

Sam bolted upright in the bed, his chest heaving. A drop of perspiration trickled down his brow. Anna was beside him speaking softly. She was all right. Thank God. Her hands tenderly pressed him back onto the bed. His eyes closed. The screaming stopped.

It reminded her of a grizzly bear awakened too early from winter's hibernation, filling the kitchen doorway when Anna looked up from her seat at the table and saw Sam standing there. He towered ominously above her; his wide, muscular shoulders, rigid; the dark fur of his chest curled out of the opening in his long johns; the lines of his face set in a deep scowl.

"What did you give me?" He ground out the words in a low, menacing voice.

Anna closed the Bible she'd been reading. "You ought to stop frowning so much. You're going to make your headache come back."

His eyes narrowed. "What was it?"

She could see he was feeling much better, and it annoyed her that he had no appreciation of the precious medical supplies she'd used on him. "It was laudanum."

He stepped into the kitchen and hitched up his trousers. "Don't ever do that to me again."

"Fine," she snapped. "The next time I see you in pain and too stubborn to lie down, I'll just whack you over the head with the frying pan."

His jaw twitched. "I mean it. Don't do it again."

The man was a total ingrate, she reminded herself. "It's all gone, anyway. I used the last of it on you. So if I should become ill, I'll just have to suffer."

Sam snorted and went to the sink. He pulled up his sleeves. The tight muscles of his forearms rippled as he pumped water into the basin. He splashed his face. "What have you been doing?"

The suspicious tone in his voice spiked anger through her. "Well, after I put away the ton of supplies you bought, I unhitched the team, brushed and fed the horses, and put the chickens in the coop—" Sarcasm dripped from her words. "I recovered fifty thousand dollars in stolen money, went into town, and spent every cent of it."

Sam stared blankly at her, water from his hands and face

dripping onto the floor. "Nobody asked you to do all those things yourself."

"Oh!" Furious, Anna rose from the table. "You're the most ungrateful creature I've ever known. And stop dripping on my floor!" She grabbed the linen towel from the sideboard and flung it at him.

It hit him square in the face and dropped into his hands unnoticed as his eyes widened. "What in the hell have you got on, woman?"

Suddenly self-conscious, Anna looked down at the trousers she'd purchased in town this morning. They had served their purpose well for doing the chores while Sam slept, infinitely more comfortable and practical than her skirts. But she had selected the size poorly. They were a little more snug than she had intended. She'd decided, though, that it was of no consequence how bad she looked. In fact, it might even work in her favor. Because if Sam liked her frilly pink dress, and the blue one was his favorite, he would surely hate her in these plain, ill-fitting men's trousers.

Anna ran her hands down her thighs. "I got them in town this morning."

Sam felt as though he'd been kicked in the gut. The trousers clung to the gentle curve of her hips and outlined each of her legs with clarity. The fly in front drew his eye, and his insides knotted at the thought of what lay just beyond. Every fiber of his body sprang to life. Those damn trousers were positively indecent!

"You can't wear those things," he blurted out.

Her chin went up a notch. "I can and I will. Now, I have to go take care of some chores."

"But—"

As she headed out the back door, Sam's gaze locked onto her backside; two big pockets cupped her bottom, and a double-stitched seam ran up the center—of everything. His knees went weak. He'd been sick for days, but now as the familiar craving took hold, his body made him aware in no uncertain terms that he was well again.

Sam followed Anna down the back steps. "Get back in here."

She walked determinedly onward. "We need wood."

The back pockets tantalized him with each step she took. Good Lord, the woman was making him crazy. She stopped at the three-sided wood shed and looked around until she spied the axe on the ground. Sam froze. His insides flamed. She was going to bend over!

"No! Wait! Don't—"

Too late. Sam's mouth went dry. Heated blood surged through his veins. His trousers suddenly felt as confining as hers looked.

He had to get her out of his sight. He'd spent weeks on the trail getting here and had stopped only once to avail himself of a whore whose face he never looked at, and so, seeing Anna in her trousers was more than he could bear.

Sam charged across the yard and jerked the axe from her hands. "Give me that thing. I'll chop the wood around here. You go back in the house."

The line of her lip tightened, and Sam knew he'd made a serious mistake. He'd never met a woman as stubborn as Anna Fletcher!

"Don't tell me what to do."

She'd stay outside with him now, just for spite. Annoyed with himself and his mutinous body, Sam said, "Then keep out of my way."

Anna glared at him for a second then moved aside. Sam raised the axe over his head and thrust it into the wood, sending chips flying.

She couldn't imagine what had gotten into him. He attacked the chore as if the devil himself was nipping at his heels. Maybe it was only because he'd been ill for so long and now felt up to doing something, Anna speculated. She couldn't imagine any other reason.

With nothing else to do—she certainly couldn't go back into the house after she'd made such a fuss about staying outside—Anna sat down on a log. The afternoon was warm but a gentle breeze stirred the leaves of the oak tree overhead. She wrapped her arms around her knees and watched Sam.

He kept his back to her and continued chopping. She used to come outside with her papa and watch him perform this task, but she didn't remember the bulging and flexing muscles she saw in Sam's back and arms. She'd never noticed how narrow a man's hips were, either, or how muscular thighs could be. Not every man had so tight a waist, Anna was sure of that.

Heat rose in Anna's cheeks when she realized how blatantly she was staring at him. Thank goodness his back was to her.

Feeling useless while he worked so hard, Anna gathered the wood that had been cut.

Sam stopped chopping. Perspiration dotted his brow. "That's too heavy for you. I'll take it in."

"I can manage."

"You're going to hurt yourself."

She balanced another piece of wood on the load in her arms. "Who do you think did this while you were in bed?"

Sam slammed the axe into the chopping block. "How did you expect me to do anything around the place when you kept me out of my head with that witch's brew you fed me and the sleeping potion you slipped into my water?"

"I only did that because you were ill," she told him.

"Well, I'm not sick anymore. I'll take care of the chores."

Sam reached for the wood in her hands. All he meant to do was to take it from her. Nothing more. But the breeze stirred at that instant and he sniffed the sweet fragrance that clung to her. Her deep-brown eyes captured his gaze and her bottom lip crept out in a pout. And instead, he grasped her upper arms and pulled her against him. Her breasts brushed his chest and her thighs touched his. The desire he'd tried to work off by chopping the wood flamed inside him, consuming him. His mouth covered hers. She tasted so sweet that he moaned and his knees went weak.

The wood slipped from Anna's fingers and she was held captive by an unseen force that bound her to Sam. His lips moved over hers with such reverence, yet such command, that her heart rose in her throat. Tentacles of fire spread through her where her body touched his. No man had ever kissed her like Sam, and no man had ever touched her as he did. Yet she had no thought, no will to pull away.

But when he ended the kiss, a cool breeze struck her face, bringing reality with it. Anna turned and ran into the house.

Sam chopped enough wood to last a month, repaired the chicken coop so the feathered critters would stay inside, and saw to the horses in the barn. As she had said, Anna had put the team away and fed his stallion as well.

Sam stood at the stall door and stroked the horse's soft muzzle. The stallion needed exercise but the corral fence was down.

"Things aren't going like I'd planned, Fortune," he confided. The horse nudged his chest. "This is going to take more time than I thought. She's a mighty stubborn woman. Hell, she's a firecracker. But, if a man ever tapped into that hot streak of hers she'd be—"

Sam stopped himself. Lustful thoughts of Anna Fletcher were best avoided. He pulled on the tight muscles in his neck. Even if she was a decent woman who seemed to very much like his indecent kiss. . . .

He brought a load of firewood into the house with him when he entered a few minutes later and was glad that Anna wasn't there. He spent the rest of the afternoon cleaning the tiny room he was going to sleep in, reinforcing the bed, and making it up with the mattress and linens he'd bought in town. Sam replaced the broken windowpanes with those Hugh Palmer had in stock. It wasn't grand, he admitted as he assessed his work from the doorway, but it was a hell of a lot nicer than most of the places he'd slept in.

The kitchen was filled with evening shadows when he walked in and saw Anna sitting at the table slicing potatoes. He wondered if he should apologize for kissing her, though he wasn't the least bit sorry he'd done it, but decided it was best to leave it alone. He'd already sworn to himself it would never happen again. And she was dressed in a proper skirt and blouse now, so that made things easier for him.

He walked to the table. "That's not going to be near enough potatoes."

Her eyes widened as she turned her gaze up at him. She

was ready for most any comment, an apology at the very least. But all he cared about was the food.

"Certainly you don't think I'm going to cook for you."

His expression told her that yes, that's exactly what he expected. Anna uttered a tight laugh and walked to the woodbox. "I'm cooking my own supper. You'll have to fend for yourself."

Sam blocked her path. "No, ma'am. You're not cooking your supper with my firewood."

"This is my firewood." She planted her hands on her hips.

He shook his head. "It was your log. I chopped it. That makes the firewood mine."

She could find no argument to refute his logic, and that made her madder. "Fine, you can have your wood. I hope you'll enjoy it while you're sitting square in the middle of the road. Because you're not going to use it to cook on my land or on my stove or with my pots and pans!"

Anger roiled through him and he bent down until his chin was only inches from her stubborn one. "Fat lot of good they're going to do you, Mrs. Rowan, when you've got no food to prepare."

"I don't have any food left because I shared it all with you!"

Sam flung out both hands. "All right, we'll both just stand here and starve to death!"

They glowered at each other another moment. Finally logic set in.

"I'll let you use my stove and pots if you'll let me use your firewood and food," Anna reluctantly offered.

Sam nodded. "I'm agreeable to that."

"But I'm not doing all the cooking," she added quickly.

"We'll cook together." He'd agree to anything to get the meal underway.

"Or the cleaning."

"We'll divide the work—all of it—in half."

She sighed heavily. "Under those conditions, I agree."

"Praise the Lord."

Anna fetched more potatoes from the pantry as Sam pumped water into the basin. "What are you doing?"

"Washing up so we can cook. Do we have to divide up the water now too?"

"Outside." She gestured toward the back door. "Go outside and wash. I don't want you dripping all over my floor again."

Sam grumbled under his breath but headed for the door. Getting this meal on the table was liable to take an Act of Congress.

After he'd washed at the backyard pump, Sam came into the kitchen to find that Anna had put the potatoes on to boil and was kneading the biscuit dough at the sideboard. He ambled across the room and looked over her shoulder. "What else are we having?"

She stepped away, uncomfortable with his nearness. "Chicken."

Sam rubbed his hands together. "What else?"

Her brows rose. "What else? Nothing else."

"Whoa here, Mrs. Rowan, your husband doesn't intend to eat like some dowager at a tea party."

"You're not my husband!" Anna slammed her fist into the dough. Flour billowed up and settled on her face.

Sam chuckled and wiped the white mess from her nose. Anna pulled away.

"Go set the table," she told him and cleaned her face with the hem of her apron. "And shuck some corn."

After completing the chores she'd given him, he hovered around her and the stove, much to her dismay. Every time she turned, every way she turned, Sam was in front of her, blocking her path, asking questions, advising her on which spices to use, how much salt to put in. He was constantly underfoot as he went about preparing his portion of the meal. For Anna, it was maddening because he was so big, so tall and broad-shouldered. It was like having a tree planted square in the center of her kitchen.

Finally they got the meal prepared and sat down across from each other at the table. Sam reached for the plate of chicken.

"We have to say grace."

His hand froze in midair, and he looked as he must have looked as a child, Anna thought, caught red-handed and guilty. She asked the Lord's blessing over the meal and his deep, resonant amen sounded after hers.

They ate in silence, both hungry after the long afternoon of chores. Finally, Sam spoke.

"Why is the upstairs blocked off?" He dished out seconds for himself.

"It's always been that way," Anna replied. "Ever since I was a child."

"What's up there?"

"Bedrooms. Five of them."

Sam's eyebrows rose. "Sounds like somebody was expecting a big family."

"My grandfather." Anna picked at her potatoes. "He owned the land and built the house. He intended it to go to his oldest son, but he died of influenza. My uncle Lloyd—he's a doctor—didn't want to farm the land, so my mother inherited it all. She was the youngest, and all her sisters had already married and moved on."

Sam poured the last of the gravy over his biscuits. "How much land?"

"Two hundred acres."

It was dark outside now, and the lamp on the kitchen table cast a soft, golden glow. A look of profound envy crossed Sam's face.

"Your pa owned two hundred acres?"

Anna nodded. "Mama met him when she was in Syracuse visiting her sister. They married and moved back to the farm."

"Your pa owned two hundred acres? He had a farm of his own? Land that was his—given to him?" Sam leaned closer. "And he worked for the railroad?"

Anna shifted uncomfortably. She'd heard the men in town say those same words for as long as she could remember. Ultimately, it had helped lead to her father's downfall when public opinion had turned against him. He wasn't a farmer like the other men. He'd never really fit in. Some had even turned against her mother, wondering why a pretty girl like Elsa had shunned the beaus in Kemper and married a Yankee in the first place.

But Anna didn't take offense to Sam's questioning, as she

had to the men in town. His words weren't a condemnation of her father.

"He wasn't a farmer." It was all she could say.

Sam shook his head slowly. "Two hundred acres. It's not a big farm, but with that kind of start a man could—"

He stopped, embarrassed by his outburst. He focused on his plate once more.

"Do you have a farm, Sam, in wherever it is that you come from?" By the look in his eyes, she doubted it.

"Kentucky," he told her. "And no, I don't own a farm. But I've worked on plenty of them."

"I suppose it's hard for you to understand why my father didn't work the land."

Sam pushed his plate away. "No, I understand. I understand that a man's got to do what he's called to do."

Anna understood his point and recognized, too, that it was probably the way he justified having a father who was an outlaw.

The meal finished, Anna stacked the dishes and carried them to the sink. She rolled up her sleeves and gave Sam a pointed look.

"I'm not doing all this myself," she reminded him. "You'll have to do your half."

He grumbled, but pumped water into a pot and heated it on the stove. Anna put away the food while he prepared the dishwater and plunged the frying pan in. He swished it around then held it up, dripping.

"There. I washed my half of the pan. Now you do your half."

Anna's mouth dropped open and her hands went to her hips. "Of all the—"

A sly smile tugged at the corner of his lips and his eyes twinkled with mischief. "You said I only had to do half, and this is half."

Anna giggled despite herself. "Your half is washing. My half is drying."

Sam scowled. "Ah, dammit. I hate the way my fingers get when they're in the water for a long time."

Anna tried to swallow her smile. "I'll wash next time."

When they finished the dishes, there was really nothing else to do. A real married couple might sit in the parlor after supper and watch the fire. The husband might read aloud or play a tune on a fiddle or mouth harp while the wife did mending or stitchery. Or, with the fading light, they might walk together in the garden, talking about crops, the farm . . . the future.

But Sam and Anna had none of those things between them, so they stood facing each other in the kitchen for an awkward moment.

"I guess I'll turn in," Sam finally said.

Anna nodded. "Me too."

From her bed she could hear Sam locking the front door, then rummaging around in his room, beside hers. She imagined him undressing and fitting his tall frame into the small bed.

The house seemed suddenly still, and the breeze through her open window brought not a sound. She felt isolated on the farm, alone with Sam.

Anna pulled the quilt around her middle and turned up the flame of the lantern at her bedside. She opened her Bible to the book of Genesis and the story of Adam and Eve.

CHAPTER 6

Anna entered the kitchen the next morning tying the sash of her wrapper and pushing her thick, dark hair off her shoulders. It startled her to see Sam standing by the stove sipping coffee as if he belonged there. He was dressed in dark trousers and a white shirt and a string tie at his throat.

"What are you doing?"

He glanced over his shoulder, did a double take, and then straightened. She looked tousled and rumpled—and very appealing.

He finally found his voice. "It's Sunday."

Now conscious of her appearance, Anna folded her arms across her middle. The intimacy of sharing a house with a man was nerve-wracking.

"So?"

"Church," he said. "You do go to church, don't you."

"Yes, I go. But not in this town."

He tilted his head. "Do you think the Lord can't hear you from here?"

"No." Anna sighed heavily. "I don't like this town or these people."

Sam sipped his coffee. "So you only do your Christian duty when you're in a place that suits you. Is that it?"

"No, and I don't expect that you would understand." Her anger simmering, Anna pivoted on her toes to leave the room and end the discussion. "Just go, if that's what you want."

"I plan to." Sam poured another cup from the pot on the back of the stove. "And when people ask where Mrs. Rowan is, I'll tell them you didn't want to go to services."

"Don't tell them that!" Anna whirled around. The town would gossip about it for weeks. "Just tell them I'm sick, or something."

Sam eyes widened. "I don't go into the house of the Lord and tell a barefaced lie."

It was plain as day what he was trying to do. Anger seethed in her. "I'm sick and tired of you manipulating me."

His gaze held steady with hers. "I can be gone from here for good. All you have to do is tell me where that money is hidden."

Anna's jaw tightened. "There is no money. And even if there was I'd never tell you where to find it."

He shrugged indifferently. "In that case, Mrs. Rowan, you'd better get ready for church."

Within the hour they were seated in the wagon heading for the white clapboard Baptist church that sat on the edge of Kemper. Anna had refused to speak to Sam as they prepared breakfast, dividing the work into halves as they had done the night before. She'd picked the least favorite of her dresses to wear, a brown with cream ruffles, having sworn never to wear the pink one Sam liked so much. She hoped he hated this one.

The sky was overcast and there was a chill to the air when Sam stopped the team at the edge of the churchyard. Wagons, buggies, and horses were already tethered there, and the last of the congregation was climbing the steps, shaking hands with the Reverend Hiram Langford at the door.

Anna moved to leave the wagon, but Sam laid a hand on her arm. She looked up at him.

"I thought you ought to have this." He dug into the pocket of his shirt and pulled out a gold wedding band.

Confused, Anna's brows drew together. "But. . . ."

"It belonged to my mama." He turned the worn band over in his fingers, eyeing it, remembering.

"Why do you want me to have it?"

Sam shrugged. "I thought it might look better if you wore a wedding band."

"You mean, if I wore it, it might ease your conscience for lying to the whole town," Anna snapped.

His blue eyes rose slowly to meet hers. "Does that mean you don't want it?"

Anna jerked her chin. "I most certainly do not."

"Suit yourself." Sam closed the ring in his palm. "But I don't have to tell you how people talk. Lord knows what people will be speculating on when they notice you've got no wedding band."

"Oh!" He had her again. Anna pried open his hand and pulled the ring from his grasp, then jammed it on her finger.

"Fit all right?" Sam asked as he jumped to the ground.

Anna flexed her fingers, surprised the ring was a trifle small. "I expected it to fit like a bracelet. Any woman who could have given birth to a moose like you must have been as big as a cow."

Sam shook his head as he stopped beside her. "I wouldn't know. I never knew her."

Anna looked down at him, sorry for what she'd said, sorry to know anything personal about Sam Rowan. She allowed him to help her from the wagon.

"You look real pretty in that dress," Sam said as he set her to the ground. "The color sets off your eyes."

Anna turned away. She looked across the churchyard and felt as uncomfortable with Sam as she did with the people filing into the church. They used to be her friends, all of them, back when she'd called this place home. But no more. This wasn't her home. And they certainly weren't her friends.

Reverend Langford smiled and took both her hands as she and Sam reached the door to the church. "I'd heard you were with us again, Anna, and I'm so pleased. The Lord has truly blessed us. And this must be your husband."

The men shook hands and Sam introduced himself. He grasped Anna's elbow and walked inside with her; he could feel the tenseness in her.

Heads turned and whispers rippled through the congregation as Sam and Anna found an empty pew near the back of the church.

"You sure cause a stir," Sam whispered as he laid his hat beside him. "What did you do to these people?"

"I never did a thing to them," she hissed. She leaned closer to Sam. "Do you see that woman near the front? The one with the big hat?"

Sam gazed across the church and wrinkled his nose. "The one with the bird's nest on it?" he whispered.

"Yes. That's Edna Mae Huntberry, and she's got her nerve staring at me after the things she said about my pa. And that woman beside her—"

"With the nose like a busted wagon wheel?"

"That's the one. She's Lula Jones, and she had the gall—the gall—to suggest that my mother was somehow connected to that robbery. And over in the corner is—"

"Do you hate all these people, Anna? All of them?" Sam asked in a low voice.

Anna's back stiffened. It was true. She hated them all. At that moment with the memories assailing her, she could feel no other way.

"Yes. I hate every one of them."

"Try to find some charity in your heart," Sam said softly. "What's done is done."

Anna turned her head away. She didn't want any charity in her heart for the people who had hurt her mother so badly.

Reverend Langford opened the service with prayer, then announced the shut-ins who couldn't make it to church. He reminded everyone of Wednesday's prayer meeting and asked for volunteers to help with the church booths for the upcoming Founders' Day celebration. He called attention to the newcomers in the congregation, Charles Hampton who had just moved down from Richmond, and Sam and Anna, the newlyweds. Anna managed a thin smile when they rose and everyone turned to stare. Sam circled her waist with his arm and smiled broadly.

Reverend Langford's sermons hadn't toned down at all in the last ten years, Anna decided, as he announced the scripture for the morning: John, Chapter Eight. She wondered if the reverend had somehow known she would be in town when he'd prepared the morning's message. Was it divine intervention? And if so, was it intended for the congregation, or herself?

"The woman was brought unto Jesus, accused of, and

caught in the act—the very act—of adultery." Reverend Langford's gaze raked the congregation. "And Jesus, according to the law, knew she must be stoned to death—stoned, my friends—stoned until she was dead! But when called upon, Jesus did not condemn her. No, no he did not. He looked out upon the faces of her accusers and said to them, 'He among ye who is without sin, let him cast the first stone.'"

Reverend Langford clutched the pulpit with both hands, his eyes boring into the upturned faces of his flock. He pointed a finger. "I say to you, my friends, look first at yourselves before accusing others. Look at yourselves! God will stand in judgment of each of us, not we ourselves."

There was as much fire and brimstone in his message as Anna remembered from her childhood. When the sermon was concluded, Miss Marshall struck up the organ and led the choir, now grown to ten people. Deacon Fry and Deacon Dooley still passed the collection plates as they had when Anna attended this church with her parents.

Sam held the collection plate between him and Anna when Deacon Fry sent it down their pew. "Do you want to go halves on this too?" Anna asked.

"Only if they ask us to wash it."

Anna giggled aloud and they shared a grin that bound them together for a long moment before Sam dropped coins into the plate and passed it on.

When the service ended, Anna headed straight for the wagon. Sam caught her arm.

"They'll only talk more if you run out and don't face them."

"They don't want to be my friends," Anna told him as she glanced at the congregation filing out of the church. "They only want something to talk about. You don't understand."

He tensed. "You think I don't know what it's like to be talked about?"

He was the son of a notorious outlaw and, surely, the target for gossip for most of his life, Anna realized.

"You can't make them stop talking," Sam told her. "If you

shy away and keep to yourself, people are going to make up things to talk about because they don't know the truth."

Sam's words struck a nerve. He had just described her mother, shy and withdrawn during her father's trial. Could that have contributed to the gossip that had eventually driven her mother from Kemper?

"People ought to mind their own business," Anna said.

Sam blew out a heavy breath. "Yeah. There's a lot of things that people ought to do."

He gave her another minute, then slid his hand into hers. "Let's go give them something good to talk about."

His hand was warm, and though his fingers were gentle, Anna felt the strength of his grip. It radiated up her arm. He grinned and gave her a wink that made her stomach roll, and together they walked back across the churchyard.

The first friendly faces they encountered belonged to Hugh and Mildred Palmer.

"How are things going at the farm?" Hugh asked Sam as they shook hands. "Are you going to get your crops in the ground pretty soon."

"We're not staying," Anna interrupted.

Hugh and Mildred looked at each other with raised eyebrows.

"But everyone thought you were back for good," Mildred said.

"No," Anna told her. "We're only here to fix up the farm and sell it."

Hugh turned to Sam for confirmation of this startling news.

"I haven't made my mind up one way or the other," Sam told them.

"You're a welcome addition to the community, Sam," Hugh said with a look of relief. "Glad you're with us."

How quickly everyone believed Sam, Anna realized. Was it only because he was the man of the house, her supposed husband? He was but an intruder in her life. He had nothing to do with the decision.

After the Palmers left them, Anna turned her angry eyes on Sam. "Why did you say that?"

"No sense in arousing suspicion." He shrugged noncha-
lantly.

Anger coiled deep within her. It was only the money he
was after. He didn't care what the town thought of her. This
was only another of his ploys. Why had she let herself trust
him?

Charles Hampton approached, tipped his hat to Anna and
offered his hand to Sam. "I guess that since we're both
newcomers we should get to know each other."

He was a distinguished looking man in his fifties with a
weathered face and strands of silver showing at his temples.

Reluctantly, Sam shook his hand. "What brings you down
from Richmond?"

"I finally had enough of city life," Hampton explained. "I
retired and decided to settle here."

"What sort of work do you do, Mr. Hampton?" Anna
asked.

"I was a clerk for the Richmond Paper Company."

She felt Sam tense beside her. Maybe he had no liking for
men who worked indoors, she guessed.

"It was good meeting you." Hampton touched the brim of
his hat and moved on.

Anna was approached by many other people she remembered. Everyone was anxious to welcome her back and meet
Sam. He kept an arm around her, smiling down at her until
Anna felt like a prize heifer on display at the county fair. She
gritted her teeth and forced herself to be pleasant.

Emma Langford, the reverend's daughter, approached as
Sam was discussing crops with two other men, Ben Atkins,
who owned the farm adjoining hers, and Al Wright, the owner
of Kemper's feed store.

Emma was a few years older than Anna, but Anna
remembered well her freckled nose and fiery red hair, hidden
now under the most outrageous hat Anna had ever seen.

"I never thought I'd see the day you'd come back to
Kemper." She gave Anna a thin smile.

Anna remembered, too, Emma's tendency to grate on her
nerves. "I'm only back to sell the farm."

Emma squinted her eyes and nodded. "I suppose that's

understandable, what with your ma dying last fall." She leaned closer. "Do you remember Joanna Reynolds and those things everybody used to whisper about her? Well, they must have all been true, because I heard she owns a disreputable business in Abilene, if you get my meaning."

"Emma, I—"

"And Polly Whittaker? She ran off with an actor from a traveling theatrical company that passed through town about four years ago, and no one has heard from her since." She pressed her lips together tightly with self-righteous indignance.

Anna didn't want to hear this barrage of gossip. "Emma—"

As if Anna hadn't spoke, Emma went on to the next subject. Her brows bobbed. "Brett Morgan is back in town, too."

Anna cautioned herself to be careful. As the daughter of the preacher, raised without a mother and forced to live by her father's rigid rules, Emma got what joy she could from life through gossip and speculation. But this was fact, not idle talk, so Anna took a deep breath and tried to join the conversation.

"Yes, I saw Brett in town yesterday."

Emma's eyes narrowed as if that information held some special significance. Then she pursed her lips prudishly. "Personally, I don't think they should have let him be deputy. If his own pa hadn't been the sheriff, I don't think it would have ever happened, what with his checkered background and all."

Anna didn't respond, hoping another abrupt change in topics was coming, but Emma warmed to her subject.

She leaned closer to Anna and lowered her voice. "He was one of those gamblers on a riverboat, I heard, and someone told me he had killed a man over in Texas in a fight with—"

"Emma, I love your hat. You must tell me where you got it." Decorated with pine cones, thistle, and wooden apples, it was the worst looking hat Anna had ever seen. But she wouldn't be a party to gossip about Brett—or anyone—and

Emma had worked up a head of steam that gave every indication of continuing on for some time.

Emma blinked her lashes and touched the back of her hat. "I made it myself. Do you really like it? I work at the millinery shop, when I'm not helping Pa, of course. I'll make one for you, if you'd like."

"No, no," Anna said quickly. "I couldn't ask you to do that."

"Well, maybe it's not the best color for you. But you've got to promise to come by the shop. Now, promise."

"I promise," Anna said, but at the same moment made a mental note to avoid the millinery shop at all costs.

Emma's eyes narrowed and she leaned closer to Anna. "I suppose you know about that Maggie Nesbit. Or Maggie Fry, I guess I should say."

Anna glanced around to see Maggie standing with Deacon Fry at the foot of the church steps. "I heard she'd married."

"Humph!" Emma tossed her head. "The gold digger. Everybody in town knows she only wanted Jonas's money."

Jonas? Emma was on a first name basis with the Deacon? Anna began to wonder if there was something more than idle gossip here.

"I imagine the marriage came as a shock to some people."

Emma jerked her chin. "Jonas is a fine Christian man. He could have had a decent woman to care for those children of his, someone who understood his work in the church and helped with his businesses. I'll never understand why he took her over—"

"Over you?" Anna asked.

Her chin went up a notch. "It's no secret that Jonas was courting me. But instead he married that Saturday-night, good-time girl."

The injured pride was still evident in Emma's eyes, though Anna knew the marriage was months old now. "It must have been very hard for you."

"Humph! It's a disgrace, just a disgrace. That Maggie chases everything in trousers—the whole town knows it. Only no one will say anything in front of Jonas, out of respect." Emma tossed her head. "She'll get hers one day.

The Lord will see to it. You just watch out for your husband, Anna. Mark my words, that Maggie will stop at nothing."

Emma moved on to talk with Edna Mae Huntberry and Lula Jones, clustered together with Reverend Langford. Anna was ready to go home. She cast Sam a pleading look that he read easily. Sam cut short his conversation with Ben and Al.

"I've pretended to be nice to these people as long as I can for one day," Anna whispered. "If I don't get out of here this minute, they're going to have more to talk about than they ever imagined."

Sam grinned and cupped her elbow. "I guess I can't expect a miracle, even if we are in the Lord's house."

They started across the churchyard when Anna heard her name being called. She wanted to ignore it, pretend she hadn't heard, but Sam stopped and turned.

A warm smile spread across Anna's mouth, reaching to her eyes. Sarah Norris, her best friend from her school days, stood among the crowd in the churchyard. Anna held out her arms as the young woman approached.

"Oh, Sarah, it's so good to see you," Anna said, and realized it was true.

The women hugged and laughed together.

"Anna, I'm so happy you're here. I'd heard you were back in town, and I knew you'd be here today."

Anna caught a glimpse of Sam and he rolled his eyes. But even his I-told-you-so look wouldn't spoil her joy at seeing her old friend again.

"You look wonderful," Sarah said. "You haven't changed a bit."

Anna smiled broadly. "You certainly have."

They both looked down at Sarah's belly swollen with her unborn child. Aside from that, she was the same dark-haired, even-featured girl Anna remembered.

Sarah lay her hand on her belly. "I'm used to seeing it this way. This is my fifth."

Anna's mouth flew open. "Fifth!"

They laughed again, the special laugh that only good friends share. It was as if the years spent apart had never passed, and they were young girls again eyeing fabrics in the general store, skipping rope at recess, helping each other with lessons, and dreaming about the future.

"Yes, my fifth." Sarah looked across the churchyard at the man and children approaching. "You probably remember Jamie Calhoun. We've been married nearly eight years now."

She remembered Jamie well, a quiet, gentle boy with a head full of blond curls. It was hard to equate that recollection with the tall, slender man she saw now carrying a daughter in one arm, holding another's hand while two sons followed. So many years had passed. So much had changed.

"This must be the man I've heard so much about." Sarah looked up at Sam.

Anna glanced at him too. "Oh, yes, this is my hus . . . my hus. . . ."

"Sam Rowan." He introduced himself and tipped his hat. "Anna's husband."

Anna cringed when she heard him say the words. Words she never could bring herself to speak.

Jamie and the children joined them, and they talked until the baby started to fuss.

"We'd better get home and feed these young 'uns," Jamie said. "Sam, will you and Anna join us for Sunday supper?"

"I'd love it," Sam answered without consulting Anna.

Jamie gave him directions to their house on the edge of town and told Sam to come on over.

"You should have asked me if I wanted to go," Anna told him as they walked toward their wagon.

Sam pulled his hat low on his forehead. "I'm going whether you want to or not, because I can guarantee you, your friend Sarah is not going to make me cook half the meal or clean anything."

Anna jerked her chin. "That's because you waited to be invited into her home and didn't just barge in unwanted."

"I assure you, Mrs. Rowan, if it was your friend who had fifty thousand dollars buried in her backyard, I wouldn't have waited for an invitation from her either."

"That money," Anna swore in disgust. "It's all you ever think of. Maybe you should try to focus your thoughts on something more uplifting, since there is no money to find in the first place."

They stopped by the wagon. "Lying is a sin, Mrs. Rowan."

Her gaze held steady with his. The lines of his face were cold and determined. "Do you intend to cast the first stone?"

He circled her waist and set her on the wagon seat without replying.

From nowhere, it seemed, Maggie Fry appeared at Sam's side. Her Sunday dress fit no better than her work dress from Nettie's Cafe. The buttons strained to join the fabric over her round bosoms.

"Hello, Sam." She purred the words like a cat charming a bird.

He tipped his hat. "Morning to you, Mrs. Fry."

"You'd better call me Maggie or I'll just throw a fit." She touched his arm. "A fit like you've never seen before."

"We can't have that happen, can we." A slow smile spread over his face. "Maggie."

In the wagon seat above them, Anna's back went stiff. "Hello, Maggie," she called. "How is Deacon Fry? He looked a bit tired and drawn this morning."

The other woman cast her a frosty glance then turned to Sam once more. "He had a . . . busy . . . night. Now, Sam, you just let me know when you'll be back at the cafe. I've got something special in mind for you."

He nodded. "I'll be sure to do that."

Maggie crinkled her nose at him and moved on. Anna rolled her eyes and heaved a heavy sigh.

"Is something eating you?" Sam asked after he'd climbed into the wagon.

She refused to give him the satisfaction of thinking she cared one way or the other what he did or said, even with the likes of Maggie Fry. "Nothing," she said tightly.

Sam jiggled the reins. "Okay."

It annoyed her that he'd dropped the issue so quickly. "All right, then, I'll tell you."

The wagon lurched forward. "I figured you would," Sam mumbled.

"Maggie Fry is a married woman, and I think her attention

to you is uncalled for." Anna twisted her fingers together in her lap. She gazed off in the distance. "Of course, Deacon Fry is so old, I suppose it is understandable. He is awfully . . . awfully old. And she's only a few years older than me."

"So?"

"So, how often could they—" Anna felt heat flood her cheeks as she realized where her thoughts had been heading. And she'd almost spoken them aloud!

Sam leaned closer. "How often could they . . . what?"

He knew what she'd been thinking and now she was doubly embarrassed. She pressed her lips together primly. "Nothing. Never mind."

Gently he elbowed her. "Go on, what were you saying? How often could they. . . ."

Annoyed now, Anna straightened her shoulders. "I was wondering how often they could . . . go dancing."

"Oh, yeah, dancing." Sam nodded. "Well, I imagine Deacon Fry couldn't dance with her near as often as I could."

Miffed, Anna tightened her grip on the reticule in her lap. "You are free to go into town to . . . dance . . . any time you choose. Why, you could . . . dance . . . the entire night away."

Sam shook his head. "I can do without dancing for as long as it takes."

He called to the team and worked the reins. But having such a desirable dancing partner under the same roof with him sure was going to make it difficult, as his own body told him several times already.

Jamie and Sarah lived in a small frame house on the edge of town surrounded by trees and carefully tended flower gardens. Inside, it was cozy and warm, and neat as a pin. It smelled of the chicken that had been roasting in the oven all morning.

Anna helped Sarah with the meal preparations while the men walked through the backyard, looking over the garden, the barn and the fields. Elizabeth, the baby, was fussy, so Anna gathered her in her arms.

Sarah wiped her hands on her apron. "I'll put her down for her nap."

"No, let me hold her. Please?" Anna patted the child's back. "I love babies."

Sarah smiled and pointed to the rocker beside the cookstove. "The swaying will put her to sleep in no time."

Molly, the three-year-old, brought her doll over and laid her head on Anna's knees. "My baby, too."

"No, honey—" Sarah began.

"It's all right," Anna told her as she settled into the rocker. She held Elizabeth against her shoulder and urged Molly onto her lap as well. "Come on, Molly. We'll rock the babies together."

Molly rested against Anna's other shoulder. Anna rocked the three of them, feeling as content as the children.

Just as Elizabeth dozed off, the back door flew open, and in ran Nathan, age seven, and his five-year-old brother, Derek.

"That's not fair. You cheated!" Derek cried.

"Shut up, baby pants!" Nathan slugged his brother in the arm.

"No hitting." Jamie came through the door, followed by Sam. "I've told you that before, Nathan."

Derek grabbed his arm and moaned. Tears pooled in his eyes. "It hurts, Papa. Nathan hurt me."

Nathan sneered at him. "See? I told you you're a baby pants."

Derek began to sob.

"Come here." Jamie lifted the crying child into his arms and gave him a hug. He turned to Nathan and pointed a finger at him. "And you, young man, are about to spend supper time in bed. Is that what you want?"

Nathan wrapped his arms across his chest and his bottom lip popped out in an angry pout, but he didn't say anything.

"Is it?" Jamie repeated. "Do you want to go to bed?"

Sam stepped in. "If it's okay, I was hoping one of the boys could show me that tree house out back."

Jamie nodded, grateful for the interruption. "Nathan, do you want to show Sam your tree house?"

The boy's eyes lit up. He looked up at Sam and nodded quickly.

"Let's go." Sam held open the door and Nathan ran out ahead of him.

As he turned to leave, Sam caught sight of Anna in the rocker. Stunned, he did a double take. Elizabeth was sleeping peacefully on one shoulder. Molly was cuddled against the other, sucking her thumb. And Anna looked as comfortable and contented as the children, rocking slowly and humming.

Was this the same woman who had threatened to blow off his head? The one who hadn't cared if she starved him to death? The same woman who hated every single person in the entire town of Kemper? Sam shook his head and followed Nathan out the door.

Anna chose to ignore the look Sam had given her. Nothing—and certainly not Sam Rowan—was going to ruin these cherished moments with the children. She hugged them tighter against her.

Sarah stirred the pot of beans simmering on the stove. "I don't know what's gotten into Nathan lately. He's so mean to Derek."

"Maybe I ought to talk to Reverend Langford about it," Jamie said. He rubbed Derek's back while the child was whimpering. "Let me try and get this one to take a nap."

"I just don't understand it. It's so unlike Nathan to act that way." Sarah frowned and gazed through the window at the backyard.

Outside, Sam looked up at the half-finished structure nestled in the limbs of the oak. "So, this is your tree house?"

Beside him, Nathan nodded. "Yeah, only it's not done yet. Papa don't never have time to do it."

"Pa's are busy, usually." Sam stroked his chin. "How about if you and me climb up and take a look?"

Nathan's eyes widened. "Yeah? Really?"

"Sure. Come on."

Sam followed the boy up the steps nailed to the trunk of the oak and climbed through the hole in the floor and into the house. The framework was in place, and two of the walls were complete.

Sam stepped over the pile of boards and nails and gazed out over the field. Nathan stood on tip toes, straining to see whatever it was Sam was looking at.

"Looks good." Sam nodded his approval.

Nathan nodded too. "Looks good."

"You know, I'll bet we could get these walls up before your ma has supper on the table," Sam said.

"But today is Sunday. Pa says we can't do no work on Sunday."

Sam grinned. "This isn't work, son. To me, this is playing."

A big smile lit up Nathan's face.

Sam picked up a board. "Grab that hammer."

"Pa won't let me hammer nothing. He says I might hurt myself."

"Well, we can't go against what your pa says. But how about if I show you how to drive a nail proper. Then you won't hurt yourself, and when you get good at it you can show your pa."

"That'd be great!"

Inside the house, Sarah turned to Anna, smiling. "I declare, seeing those two working on that tree house together, I'm not sure which one is the child. Sam seems to be enjoying it as much as Nathan."

Anna didn't answer. So far, she hadn't seen Sam enjoy anything except finding new ways to make her life miserable.

Molly became bored and wiggled off her lap and, reluctantly, Anna put Elizabeth in her crib. She and Sarah talked while they got supper ready. Jamie came into the kitchen yawning.

"I was trying to get Derek to take a nap and I fell asleep myself." Jamie rubbed his eyes.

"I figured as much." Sarah gave him a kiss on the cheek. "Call Sam and Nathan in to eat, would you? It looks like they've gotten that tree house finished."

They all ate supper together around the kitchen table. Nathan asked to sit beside Sam, and Anna readily agreed it was a good idea. The meal was delicious, the children were quiet and mannerly, and Jamie and Sarah were obviously deeply in love.

Anna was happy for her friend, happy that she had a wonderful home and beautiful children and that she and Jamie were so well-suited for each other.

"Your life seems so perfect," Anna said as they were leaving. "I can't help but feel a little envious."

Sarah gave her a quick hug and looked out at Sam, standing with Jamie beside the wagon. "Your husband is a fine man, Anna. You'll be having babies of your own before you know it."

Anna hugged her friend and hurried away fighting back the tears that threatened. There would never be any babies for Anna, none she could call her own.

The warm relaxed feeling she'd experienced during the afternoon vanished as they drove home. The sky had been gray all day and now the wind picked up. It was a long, chilly drive home.

The house looked wretched, much worse now after having been in Sarah's home. Anna walked through the parlor while Sam put away the horses.

It was horrible. Just horrible. Shrouded furniture covered with dust, grimy window panes, cobwebs in the corners, ashes spilling out of the fireplace.

She would have been gone from here by now if it hadn't been for Sam Rowan. Resentment hardened in Anna's stomach as she walked through the room, her footsteps echoing in the silence. If it hadn't been for that man she would never have had to confront the people in town, would never have taken a second look at this house, would never have seen how happy her friend was. Sam Rowan had ruined everything. Just as his father had ruined it all before him.

"You ought to come into the kitchen before you get a chill. I started a fire."

Anna whirled around to see Sam standing in the parlor doorway. Shadows lay between them in the fading light.

"And you ought to get out of my house." Her voice shook as she struggled to control her anger.

He stepped into the room. "I told you, I can be gone any time. You just tell me where—"

"There is no money!" Anna fought to curb her anger.

"Don't you think that if there were any money here, I would have gotten it while you were ill? Or yesterday while you were sleeping for hours? I could have taken it and been long gone if there were anything to get. Doesn't that prove something to you?"

He nodded his head. "Yes. It proves what I've suspected since I saw you at the pond: that money is out there in the hills somewhere and not close enough to the house so you can get to it in a couple hours time."

"No!"

"And I don't care how long I have to stay here. Days, weeks—"

"No! No!" She wouldn't be trapped in this horrid place that long. She wouldn't!

"If it takes months, I'll—"

Anna clenched her fists. "I won't stay here! I won't."

He closed the distance between them with long strides. "Then tell me where it is."

"No!" She swung her fist at him.

He grabbed her wrist. "Tell me!"

She tried to pull free but he held her easily. It only enraged her further. A knot hardened in the pit of her stomach, and she looked up at him with hatred in her eyes. "I swear to God, I'll let that money rot in the ground before I allow you to see one dime of it."

Stunned, Sam released her arm. "You know where it is. You really know." Until this moment it had only been a hunch. Now he knew for certain.

Anna rubbed her wrist. The pain stoked her anger. "Yes! You were right. That's why my father called me to the prison just before he died. But I'll take that secret to my grave like he nearly did before I let a lying, conniving thief like you have it!"

Sam's temper exploded. "That money belongs to me! My pa died because of it!"

"He was an outlaw! A low down, common, thieving bastard!"

"Shut up!"

"He was! He involved my father in that train robbery and it turned the whole town against us."

"Cyrus Fletcher involved himself in that robbery when he shot Arlow and Buck and made off with the strongbox they were carrying, then kept it for himself. He had no right to that money."

"Don't try to justify what your pa did by trying to make mine look as guilty." Anna spat the words at him. "Jimmy Rowe got what he deserved for the life he led."

Sam's jaw tightened. "You don't know a damn thing about my pa."

"I know all I need to know." She tried to walk past him, but Sam blocked her path. "Get out of my way."

Anguish burned in his steel-blue eyes, as if years of pain had seared his soul. "He was a farmer," Sam said softly. "You didn't know that, did you? It was a small place, but it was his. He worked it alone because he couldn't afford slaves. He didn't want to go off and fight in the war, but he believed the government shouldn't dictate a man's life. So he joined up with the Confederate army."

Sam drew in a ragged breath. The anger was gone. His voice shook. "Then the Yankees came. They burned it all. Everything. To the ground. The house, the barns, the fields . . . everything. After that, my ma left me with some people who took me to Kentucky, because they needed another pair of hands. My pa came back from the war, finally, to find nothing, not even his family. It took him eight months to find me. Eight months of not knowing if I was alive or dead. He never did find his wife."

Anna's anger was gone now too. "She left you? Your mother disappeared without—"

"My mother died when I was born." Sam pressed his hands to his head, his palms covering his ears, as if that might block out the memory of the haunting screams. "Mary was my stepmother."

A long silence passed as Sam seemed to be lost in his recollection.

"You never knew what happened to her?" Anna asked softly.

He pulled at the tight muscles of his neck and squeezed his eyes shut. "She probably took her own life after what the soldiers—"

Anna blanched and her stomach heaved.

Their emotions spent, neither spoke for a long moment. Finally Sam blew out a heavy breath.

"The government robbed my pa of everything he had. They owed him every cent he ever took—tenfold."

"And that's why you believe the money from the train robbery should go to you," Anna concluded.

Sam nodded. He turned and walked away.

"I can't let that happen."

Sam froze in the doorway. His gaze impaled her when he turned.

"You see, that money broke up my family." Anna's emotions were drained, too, so she simply told him what she wanted him to know. "My mother had to leave the home she grew up in after her friends turned against her. My father died in a damp, rat-infested prison cell. Because of that money, my whole life changed. And now I intend to do something about it."

His body went rigid. "What are you going to do?" He spoke as if the answer frightened him.

"I'm going to do the right thing." Anna's chin went up a notch. "I'm going to turn the money in and clear my family's name."

CHAPTER 7

"Jesus Christ. . . ." Sam raked his hands through the hair at his temples. "You're going to do *what?*"

Anna folded her arms across her middle. "That money has caused nothing but heartaches. I'm going to turn it in and remove the blight from the Fletcher name."

"You're going to take fifty thousand dollars and just hand it over to the government?"

"Yes." The nobility of her intention caused her chin to lift a little higher. "There's still a reward offered for the money. I intend to use that five hundred dollars to open an orphanage in Salem."

Sam could only stare at her. Finally, he blew out a heavy breath. "That is the goddamn dumbest idea I have ever heard."

Her mouth flew open. "How dare you—"

"You are crazy, lady." He stalked back into the room. "Crazy!"

Anna planted both hands on her hips. "Well at least I'm going to do something decent with it! Not squander every nickel in one week's time on liquor and—and soiled women."

"Soiled women!" Sam flung out both hands. "That sounds mighty tempting, after being stuck in this godforsaken place with a woman like you, but—"

She gasped. "A woman like—me!"

"—but it's not what I had in mind."

"And what is wrong with a woman like me?" she demanded.

86

"I'm using it to buy me a farm."

She tapped her foot against the wood floor. "Is what's wrong with a woman like me perhaps the way I took you in and nursed you back to health instead of leaving you for dead?"

"I've spent my whole life sweating to make some other man's dream come true."

"Or, maybe, the way I gave you the food out of my own mouth?" Her whole body was rigid.

"Now, I'm going to have a place of my own."

"Was it the last of the medicine I used on you?" Her eyes blazed. "Well, which is it?"

He glared right back at her. "You want to know what's wrong with you. Okay, lady, I'll tell you. For one thing, you're so damn tight, you're liable to pop something you're going to need in later life. And you're so mired down in what happened ten years ago that you won't let yourself enjoy anything now. You're too goddamn worried about peoples' opinions—you won't let yourself have a good time."

Anna pulled herself up to her greatest height, her back ramrod straight. "Decent people are always concerned about what others say."

"There's a difference between being concerned about it and being crippled by it." Sam pointed his finger at her. "You're afraid to live your life for fear of what everybody will have to say about it. And now you're set on some damn-fool notion of clearing your family name. That will never get done, Anna. You can never stop people from saying what they want to say." He looked hard at her. "What I want is real. I'm getting married soon and I'm going to have a family and land, and that money is going to be my start."

"You're what?" The words slipped from her lips in a breathless sigh. "You're getting . . . married?"

"Damn right," he told her. "I'm going to have a home and a wife. I'm going to have kids who wake up in their own beds every morning and sit down to eat at a supper table where they belong. I need that money. And I'm not leaving here without it."

He gave her a curt nod and strode out of the room.

Anna stared at the empty spot Sam had occupied. He was getting married? Soon? It had never occurred to her that there was a woman somewhere waiting for him. She'd never considered the possibility.

Anna sank down onto the shrouded settee. It was logical, of course, that he would marry. He was certainly handsome, and though she hated to admit it, at times he had been considerate and caring. He did have a sense of humor, too. It was easy to see why a woman would find him attractive. And a man like Sam would need a wife.

The memory of his kiss sent a hot rush through her. Anna touched her fingers to her lips. She could still feel his mouth covering hers with an intimacy that had shocked her. No one had ever kissed her the way Sam Rowan did. Is that what it would be like to be married to him?

Anna sprang to her feet, perturbed by her thoughts. Her imagination suddenly ran wild conjuring up images of Sam and the faceless woman who was to be his wife. But instead of the shame she should have felt for such thoughts, she felt something strange, something deeper.

Irritated with herself, Anna shook away the thought. Marriage or no marriage, she wasn't about to finance Sam's future at the expense of her family's good name. Not when she was this close.

Driven with purpose, Anna hurried to the kitchen expecting to find Sam there. Instead she caught sight of him through the window riding his stallion toward the hills. She scooped up Feathers, curled beside the cookstove, and stroked his soft head. It was a relief to see Sam leaving, though she didn't believe for a moment he was gone for good.

She was tired and achy after the tension at church this morning and then the argument she'd had with Sam. She wanted to go straight to bed. But she didn't know when she might have the house to herself again and she couldn't let an opportunity like this pass her by.

He needed a hard run as much as the stallion did, so Sam touched his heels to Fortune's sides and gave him his head. The animal's long legs chewed up the ground, quickly leaving the farm behind. At the creek that meandered out back of the house, Fortune never broke stride as he sailed across. At Sam's subtle command they turned eastward to race along the base of the hills. The ground was damp, covered with a carpet of leaves and newly sprouted grass. Fortune picked his way through the trees and bushes and over an occasional fallen log. Sam kept low, feeling the rhythm of the horse's movements.

The forest thickened, forcing a slower pace. Sam turned in the saddle. The farmhouse was out of sight now.

If only Anna and her damned orphanage could be blocked out so easily, he thought, along with her notion of clearing her family's reputation. She was full of high and mighty ideals that didn't amount to a wad of spit. Not in the real world, the world that Sam lived his life in. He'd get that money from her, no matter what it took.

He forced himself to push aside the image of Anna surrounded by a dozen small orphaned children, their smudged hopeful faces beseeching her. He deserved the money. He'd get it.

Feeling even more confined now, Sam urged the stallion deeper into the hills.

It was dark when Sam returned to the farm. He hadn't meant to stay away this long, so he made quick work of bedding down his horse, then hurried toward the house. The place was pitch-black. Not a light shone in any window. It was early for Anna to be in bed, and it irritated him that she hadn't left a lantern burning for him. He bounced up the back steps and turned the doorknob. It was locked. He shook it, then grumbled to himself as he made his way to the front door. It was locked too.

"Anna!" He pounded with his fist and paced the porch. "Anna! Open the door!"

The house was so silent that if he hadn't known better he would have sworn no one was home.

Same froze in midstride. Could something have happened to her? What if she'd fallen and hurt herself? The farm was so isolated, what if some stranger had forced his way into the house?

Fear gripped Sam's heart as he ran from the porch. In his haste he forgot about the broken step, fell through it twisting his knee. He cursed and hobbled around the side of the house. His bedroom window was slightly open, so he wedged his hand beneath it, driving a splinter into his fingertip, and pushed it open. He climbed onto the sill but misjudged the distance, bumped his head, and toppled onto the floor inside. Sam let fly a mouthful of curses as he struggled to his feet, holding the shoulder he'd landed on.

It was completely dark in the house, leaving him to feel his way to Anna's bedroom, then back down the hallway. What was he thinking to go so far from the house and leave her all alone? What if something terrible had happened to her?

A faint light in the kitchen drew him to the pantry. His senses heightened, ready for the worst. Sam strode to the doorway, then froze. He sucked in a quick breath.

Anna was there and she was all right.

She was also naked.

Seated in the wooden washtub, her back to him, she squeezed water from the sponge with slow, languid strokes. It cascaded down her back, sheeting the curves of her hips. Her hair was pinned loosely on top of her head, and damp, stray locks curled at the nape of her neck. The pale glow of the lantern cast a golden hue against her dewy skin as she reached for the towel beside the tub. Slowly she rose, water trickling down her thighs. A mole the size of a nickel drew his eyes to her soft, round bottom.

Sam's heart slammed against his ribs. His lungs ached from the breath he'd been holding. His mind wallowed in a stupor as his gaze held steadfast to the delicate, virginal visage stepping from the tub. Only as an afterthought did his loins react.

His brain was the last to respond. Quickly he stepped back from the doorway.

Anna walked out of the pantry carrying the lantern, her wrapper cinched tightly around her waist. She gasped when she saw him. "What are you doing in here?"

"Nothing—I—I wasn't doing anything. I—" He felt like a school boy caught with his hand in the cookie jar. Sam swallowed hard and thrust out his fingers. "I got a splinter."

She took his hand and held the lantern close. Her touch sent hot waves pulsating through him. "Come over to the sideboard. I'll pluck it out."

Sam stumbled along behind her, his whole body seething from within.

She looked back at him. "Did you hurt your knee?"

He'd twisted it when he fell through the front step. "I, ah, I . . ." His mouth went dry. "No."

"How did you get in? I thought I locked the doors." Anna took the tweezers from the medical supplies in the cupboard. "I was coming to let you in. Couldn't you have waited a minute?"

Was she naked under her wrapper? He didn't remember seeing a night rail in the pantry. "I didn't think you heard me calling."

"Old Ben Atkins down the road could have heard all that racket you were making." She held his hand closer to the lantern.

Did she have other moles beside the one on the left side of her bottom? In more private places? Others that no man had seen before? Sam's chest tightened.

"Hold still, now, this might sting."

She was the sweetest-smelling woman he'd ever known. Sam breathed deeply savoring the fragrance. Standing at her side, he was close enough to touch her if he eased himself over an inch or two. And the temptation to do so was strong in him. She was fresh, untouched by another man, and that fueled the flame that was building in him—in his heart.

"That wasn't so bad, was it?" Anna let go of his hand and put away her tweezers.

"Huh?" Dumbly, Sam stared at his finger and realized she'd gotten the splinter out. He'd never felt a thing except for the slow burn that consumed every fiber of his body. He ached to touch her.

Anna closed the cupboard door. "Just as good a job as my Uncle Lloyd could have done, if I must say so myself."

He looked into her eyes. God, she was beautiful. "You did a fine job, Anna."

A little smile crossed her lips. "I do believe that's the closest thing to a—"

His mouth clamped over hers, and he drew her against him. He couldn't stop himself. His lips moved over hers with an urgency to claim her. Yet she didn't respond. She was stiff, unyielding. Unpracticed.

The revelation struck Sam like a bolt of lightning. She was no whore, who knew exactly what to do because she'd done it to so many other men. She was untouched. Except, now by him.

The thought shook him to the core. Sam pulled away. She looked at him with those big doe eyes, her lips wet with his kiss. He felt as confused as she looked. And as frightened.

"I—I have to go." He backed away from her. "I need a—a bath."

Her head spinning, Anna pointed toward the pantry. "The tub is—"

"No!" He couldn't sit in the same tub she'd just used. "I'm going to the creek."

"But the water is freezing this time of year."

"Good," he mumbled and bolted out the door.

Teeth chattering, Sam climbed into his narrow bed and pulled the blanket over him. The creek water had been freezing, and it had helped. He was thinking more clearly now, but his problem remained unsolved.

Sam rolled over and stared at the ceiling. He couldn't keep his mind on his real purpose for being here when thoughts of Anna Fletcher were always intruding. She'd looked so vulnerable at church, facing the people she feared. But she handled the situation well. He was proud of the way she stood up to them and showed them what she was made of, regardless of what her folks had done. And she looked even more vulnerable when he kissed her.

He rolled over again and buried his face in the pillow. The woman had touched something in him. He'd never told anyone the truth about his pa or his own life. The understanding and compassion he'd seen in her face left its mark on him. One that he'd never felt before.

But he was here for one reason, and one reason alone. He couldn't afford any entanglements, no matter how beautiful Anna Fletcher was or how good she smelled. Sam pounded his pillow with his fist. From now on, he was going to tend to business and ignore everything else.

He sighed heavily. He didn't know how he was going to manage that when he couldn't even get within arm's length of the woman without kissing her.

CHAPTER 8

After a night of tossing and turning and having dreams like he hadn't had since he was fourteen, Sam dragged himself into the kitchen as the gray light of dawn was lifting. To his dismay he found Anna at the cookstove pouring coffee—and wearing her trousers.

He dropped into a chair at the table and dug the heels of his hands into his eyes. "I told you I'd do the chores."

Anna glanced back at him. The single braid of her hair fell across her shoulder. "It's Monday. Wash day."

"Wash day. . . ." Sam ran his hand through his hair and pulled at his neck. He didn't stand a chance of getting her into a skirt now.

Sam pushed himself to his feet. It was going to be a long day.

Preparing breakfast was no easier than the other meals they had fixed together. Anna was more quiet than usual, though, giving him only occasional directions. She kept her distance as he hovered near the stove watching her fry the eggs, standing by the sideboard while she rolled dough for biscuits. Finally, when she turned to retrieve the salt and found him standing in front of her, she spoke up.

"Would you please get out of my way," she said in a level, controlled voice.

He looked down at her and shrugged. "You told me I had to help."

She sighed. "Every time I turn around or reach for something, you're in the way. It's like having a moose in the middle of the floor."

Sam looked around the kitchen. It was a small room, as kitchens go, and there were only so many places he could stand. "Do you want me to do my cooking out on the back porch? What am I going to use for a stove?"

He could use the heat he'd generated last night when he kissed her, she almost said. They could have baked biscuits in here. Instead, she turned away and busied herself by wiping down the sideboard. "If you'd make an effort to move out of the way when you see me coming, I'd appreciate it."

Sam nodded. "Fine, Mrs. Rowan, I'll try not to be such a moose."

They ate in silence, both on edge. Sam complained when she told him it was his turn to wash. He grumbled but got on with the chore anyway. He noticed that Anna was standing as far from him as possible as she dried the dishes. An arm's length away. Good, he thought. It's better that way. But despite his best intentions he found himself inching closer. Those trousers she was wearing were enough to drive a man crazy, and her hair braided down her back wasn't helping anything. A breeze drifted in the open window carrying her delicate scent. Good Lord, why'd he have to smell her this morning?

Anna decided her plan had been a failure, as she eased farther from the sink. Surely the men's trousers and the unflattering, plain coif would discourage Sam, but instead, he seemed drawn to her. At this rate, she'd be in the parlor trying to dry the dishes!

She'd hardly been able to sleep for thinking of it, remembering his touch, the intimacy of his hands and lips on her. Having the wide, gold wedding band stuck on her finger hadn't helped things either. Last night his kiss had frightened her. It wasn't until sometime around dawn that Anna had realized the reason she was frightened by his kiss. It was because she liked it.

And that brought on an avalanche of feelings, questions, and problems. None of which were likely to be answered, she'd decided, given the conflict which existed between her and Sam. So she dressed this morning with the intention of looking as unappealing as possible; a plan which, obviously, was making little difference to Sam.

Daylight was spreading across the sky as Anna set up the washtubs on a bench in the backyard, as her mother had done so many times before. Sam hauled buckets of water up from the well and filled them, then headed off toward the barn.

Anna pulled her white pantalettes and chemises from the bottom of the laundry basket she'd brought from her bedroom and washed them quickly. She wrung the water from them and dropped the garments in the other basket, then went to work scrubbing her skirts and blouses.

Sam returned from the barn and gestured at the tub with the hammer he was carrying. "I'll get you more water as soon as I fix the clothesline."

Anna looked up, breathing hard from scrubbing and wringing the heavy, water-soaked clothing. "You're fixing the clothesline?"

He looked surprised by her question. "Sure."

A little smile tugged at her lips. She'd thought she'd have to repair it herself, recalling how difficult it had always been for her mother to get her father to fix anything around the house. "Thanks."

He shrugged. "I'll get you the water in a minute."

Anna swept back a stray lock of hair with a dripping hand. "This is enough. I'm nearly finished anyway."

"Finished? What about my clothes?"

"What about them?"

His brows drew together. "Aren't you going to wash them?"

"Me?" She planted one hand on her hip.

"Yeah, you. We agreed to split things in half." He pointed the hammer at her. "I did my half."

"You think hauling a few buckets of water and hammering a couple of nails is half?" She held up her shriveled fingers. "Look at my hands. This is a lot harder than it looks. You can wash your own things and I'll haul water for you."

Sam shuddered. "You know I hate to be all wet like that." It was why he disliked washing dishes so much.

"Then why don't you take them to the laundry in town?" She forced a big smile. "You can make a day of it. Stay gone as long as you want."

"You know I'm not leaving this farm."

"Then I guess you'll have to wear dirty clothes." Anna turned back to her scrub board.

"Dammit." Sam threw the hammer across the yard. "We made a deal—halves on everything."

"The deal was for cooking."

"Was not."

"Was too." Anna folded her arms. "I'm not washing your clothes and that's final. So there." She stuck out her tongue.

Sam was taken completely aback. He walked slowly toward her. "I think a bit of that lye soap in your mouth will take some of the starch out of you."

Anna stuck out her tongue again. "You'll have to catch me first, you big moose."

He lunged at her. Anna squealed and darted away. She raced behind the woodshed and across the garden with Sam right behind, then gained some ground when she ran beneath the sagging clothesline he had to duck under. Anna made a beeline for the back door, intending to lock him out of the house, but his long strides closed the gap quickly, and he wrapped an arm around her waist and pulled her off her feet.

Anna let out a scream that dissolved into laughter as she tried to pry his fingers loose. "Let me go!" His fingers were strong, his grip like iron.

He carried her to the washtub and plunged his hand in. "I've been dying to wash your mouth out with soap for a long time now."

His powerful arm held her easily and her kicking and squeals were useless, so Anna reached into the tub, too, and splashed a handful of water across Sam's face. Stunned, he loosened his grip enough for her to drop to the ground. She tried to run away, but their feet tangled. Sam fell backwards and sat down hard in the washtub. He pulled Anna down with him. She landed sideways on his lap. Water sloshed over the rim and rose to soak them both. They fell into a laughing fit.

"There. That ought to teach you," Sam declared. "Are you going to do my wash now, woman?"

Anna giggled and captured the scrub brush that floated beside Sam. "Oh, yes." She swiped the brush across the front of his shirt leaving a soapy trail.

Laughter rumbled deep in his chest as he fought her for the brush. It seesawed between them, neither willing to give up. Finally it slipped from both their hands and sailed across the yard.

"I swear, Mrs. Rowan, you're about the feistiest thing I've—"

Sam glanced away. The laughter died on his lips. He pushed himself out of the tub, taking Anna with him and steadying her on her feet with his hand at her waist. He stepped in front of her.

She peered around him. "What's— Oh."

Charles Hampton was standing by the back steps. "Didn't mean to intrude," he called. "I knocked out front but I guess you didn't hear."

Color rose in Anna's cheeks. She and Sam were both soaked and undoubtedly Mr. Hampton had witnessed the entire incident. What must he think of them? They were carrying on like children.

But one look at Sam told her that he was feeling something far different. The lines of his face were hard, his stance rigid. He looked back at Anna.

"Get in the house," he told her in a low voice. She opened her mouth to protest but Sam silenced her with a hard look. "Go inside. You're not decent for another man to look at."

She glanced down. Her wet clothes were molded to every curve. Doubly embarrassed, Anna nodded at Mr. Hampton as she ran past him and into the house. He tipped his hat politely as she went by.

"I came over to talk a little business," she heard him say to Sam as she closed the back door behind her.

Anna peeped out the kitchen window, but the men were too far away for her to overhear their conversation. Sam didn't look pleased about what Mr. Hampton had to say so the man didn't stay long. Feeling guilty about trying to eavesdrop, even unsuccessfully, Anna hurried into her bedroom when she saw Mr. Hampton leave and Sam coming toward the house. She changed into a deep-green skirt and white blouse and pinned her hair up. Sam was already dressed in dry clothes and in the kitchen when she got there.

"What did Mr. Hampton want?"

"He claimed he wanted to buy the farm." Sam stroked his chin and braced his arm against the hutch. "Seems he heard a rumor in town that we were here to fix up the place and sell out."

The laughter they'd shared a few moments ago was gone now. Anna took down her apron from the peg by the door. "You sound like you don't believe him."

"It's not that I don't believe him. I just don't trust him."

"He appears to be a very nice man."

"He might be nice, but he doesn't look like any clerk I ever saw." Sam sank deeper into thought.

"Well, how much did he offer?"

He shrugged indifferently. "Nothing. I told him it wasn't for sale."

"What?" Anna tied the apron around her waist. "You had no right to say that. I need the money from this place to open my orphanage in Salem. The reward money won't be nearly enough."

"Don't start talking that nonsense again." Sam waved her words away.

"It's not nonsense."

He strode to the table and gathered the clothes he'd brought from his bedroom. "I've got wash to do. I'm not going to stand here and argue with you over something that's never going to happen anyway."

"You keep your nose out of my business, Sam Rowan," she warned. "I want this farm sold and I don't care if you like Mr. Hampton or not. I'm going to find him and tell him it's for sale."

Sam spared her no more than a backward glance. "He's not going to believe a word you say and neither will anyone else in this town, Mrs. Rowan, because in their eyes I'm the man of the house and what I say goes."

Fuming, Anna watched as he walked out the back door. She knew he was right and it angered her all the more.

She was about to follow Sam into the yard when she heard a knock at the front door. Hoping Charles Hampton had returned, she hurried through the house. Instead, Anna found Brett Morgan on her front porch.

He swept his hat from his head and flashed a wide smile.

"For you, Miss Anna, a flower for the prettiest flower of them all." He presented her with the rose from behind his back.

"Oh, Brett, it's lovely." She stepped out onto the porch with him and whiffed its delicate fragrance. "Wherever did you get it?"

A devilish grin curled his lips. "I stole it out of Ben Atkins front yard."

Anna laughed and shook her head. "Brett, you're terrible."

"I know. It's part of my charm."

That was certainly true, Anna admitted to herself.

"Well, thank you. And the next time I see Ben Atkins I'll thank him also."

He wagged his finger at her. "That's your problem, Anna, you never could get over your want for justice. You feel like you've got to do the right thing—all the time."

She held up her hand in surrender. "Guilty, deputy."

Brett laughed along with her. He could always break her foul mood and lift her spirits when they were children. That hadn't changed, she realized.

"What are you doing so far from town?" Anna asked.

They walked across the porch, past the swing that dangled by one chain and stood by the railing.

"I come out this way real often." He looked down at her and his expression became serious. "I've kept a close eye on the farm since I've been back. I felt like your family was done wrong, Anna, and the least I can do is keep squatters and drifters away."

Sincerity showed in his blue eyes and it touched Anna. She'd never seen this side of him before.

"That's sweet of you, Brett, truly it is."

He put a finger under her chin and lifted her face.

"You let me know if you have any troubles, Anna. I want to help you."

His touch was warm and gentle. "Thank you, Brett. I'll remember that."

"Any kind of trouble." He looked deep into her eyes. "You just come to me and I'll take care of it."

Anna held the rose and watched as Brett climbed onto his horse and disappeared down the road. Maybe, she thought, just maybe she could trust him.

She had no vase so Anna put the rose in a water glass and placed it on the kitchen windowsill. Outside she could see Sam scrubbing his clothes at the tub. She joined him in the yard.

"You seem to know how to wash clothes," she said. "I don't know why you made such a fuss about doing it."

Sam looked up from the scrub board. His sleeves were rolled up past his elbows, and the front of his shirt was wet. "I didn't say I couldn't do it, I said I didn't like to do it." He nodded across the yard. "I'll fix the clothesline as soon as I'm finished here."

Brett had touched her by bringing a rose. Now the gesture paled at Sam's offer to repair her clothesline.

Anna sidled up beside him at the washtub. "I'll finish this while you make the repairs."

He looked down at her, his brows drawn together as if questioning her motives.

"You've almost finished, anyway," she said. "And all in all we'll have split the work in half."

His silent debate ended with Sam handing her the scrub brush. He wiped his hands dry on his pants legs and set to work repairing the clothesline.

Anna watched him as she scrubbed. He was a very capable man, and that was a quality she admired. She wondered if the woman who was waiting for him back in Kentucky appreciated it as well.

Thinking of Sam's unknown wife-to-be, Anna scrubbed harder on his shirt.

It didn't take Sam long to have the clothesline looking good as new. He picked up the basket of clean laundry and carried it to the line.

"No! Wait!" Anna rushed over, flinging soap suds as she ran. She couldn't let him hang up her pantalettes. She'd die of embarrassment. "I'll do that."

"And have you complain because I'm not doing my half? No, thank you, ma'am." He bent to pick up a garment, and

Anna snatched the basket away. A frown creased his forehead. "What's the matter with you?"

She licked her lips nervously. "I have some . . . personal . . . things in here."

Understanding dawned on him. Sam sighed heavily. "This may come as a surprise to you, but I've seen women's pantalettes before."

Anna gazed at him with what she hoped was regal grace and willed herself not to blush. "Perhaps that's so. But you haven't seen mine before, and I'd like to keep it that way."

She was a respectable woman and as silly as it sounded to him, Sam couldn't fault her for her feelings. "My apologies, Mrs. Rowan. I'll go tend to the chores in the barn."

"Thank you." Anna watched as he walked away. She wondered if he'd seen that Kentucky woman's pantalettes.

It was pointless now to have made such a fuss about her underwear, Anna realized as she looked out the kitchen window at the laundry hanging on the clothesline. There they were for anyone to see, her pantalettes flapping in the breeze alongside Sam's long johns. She was glad her mother never knew what she'd gotten herself into.

Feathers curled up in her lap when she sat down at the table. Her Bible was open to Revelations, and she read as she peeled potatoes for their noon meal. Sam came in a short while later and pumped water into the basin.

"I asked you to wash outside." Quickly, she stashed the Bible under her skirt. "You drip all over everything."

Sam cursed under his breath and went back outside. The cat scampered out the door behind him. Anna dashed down the hall and hid the Bible under her pillow. When she got back to the kitchen, Sam was there again, his face and hands damp, but not dripping. He popped a slice of raw potato into his mouth.

"Are you planning on telling me where that money is hidden in the next few days?"

The question was asked in a casual way, so she answered in kind. "No. Not even in the next few decades."

"Then I'm going to buy a milk cow." He took the pot of potatoes she'd sliced and carried them to the sink.

"Shouldn't you be saving your money? After I claim the reward, you'll need all your cash to get back to Kentucky."

"I consider it an investment." Sam pumped water over the potatoes. "Is there a stockyard around here?"

Anna joined him by the sink and put a pinch of salt into the pot. "The closest is in Charlotte. Do you like corn bread?"

"I like anything you'll cook." He placed the pot on the stove. "That uncle of yours ought to be shot for letting you come down here alone, and with no better supplies than you had."

"I hadn't planned on being here for more than a few days." Anna broke an egg into the cornmeal she was mixing. She lowered her voice. "Besides, he doesn't know I'm here."

"He doesn't know?" Sam looked over at her. "Don't you think that by now he's figured out that you're not sitting across the supper table from him every night?"

Anna avoided his probing gaze by concentrating on the mixing bowl. "He's been in Boston for the last few months. But I wrote him a letter and explained what had happened."

"You told him about the money?"

Her eyes rounded. "Of course not. As far as anyone knows I'm only here to sell the farm." She threw him a sour look. "At least that was my plan until you came along and ruined it."

Sam ignored her barb. He needed to know if he'd have her uncle to contend with as well. "What will he do when he gets your letter?"

"Nothing," Anna said as she stirred. "Uncle Lloyd is a dedicated physician, who has traveled all the way to Boston to study new medical procedures. He's not going to drop everything and come to Kemper just to check on me."

Sam grunted. It didn't set right with him that the man had such a lack of concern for Anna's safety. But still, he didn't need any more obstacles in his way.

He pulled the butcher knife from the drawer and gestured toward the window. "Where did you find a rose bush?"

Anna pause as she poured the corn bread into the skillet.

Suddenly it didn't seem right that she'd taken it from Brett. But she could hardly lie about it when it was sitting in plain sight.

"Brett came by today. He gave it to me." She focused her attention on scraping the bowl clean, avoiding Sam.

His shoulders squared. "Morgan was here? Today? What the hell did he want?"

"He said he'd been keeping an eye on the farm." She kept her voice even, hoping it would calm Sam. It didn't.

"Did you tell him not to bother?"

"No, I didn't." Sam's ill feelings for Brett were obvious, but Anna didn't share them. She slid the skillet into the oven. "I think it's sweet of him to watch out for things here. Brett's been very kind to me since I've been back. And that's more than I can say for some folks in town."

Sam whacked a slice from the ham that was waiting on the sideboard. "What's he done that's so all-fired sweet beside try to compromise your reputation?"

She wasn't going to let him goad her into an argument. Not over Brett. "I just appreciate his concern, that's all."

Sam turned back to the ham. He didn't like it. Not one damned bit. He didn't like Morgan in the first place, and the man had no business coming around the farm. And he sure as hell didn't like him bringing flowers to Anna.

Sam attacked the ham. "Those were probably his tracks I saw up in the hills yesterday. Next time he shows his face around here, I intend to have a word or two with him."

"The tracks were more likely from someone hunting game. You, of all people should realize that." How could he not, she wondered, when his head had been nearly blown clean off by a hunter. Anna wiped her hands on her apron. "Besides, Brett was only watching out for squatters. He wouldn't be in the hills."

Sam snorted. "I've still got a few things to say to him."

Anna turned away and took plates from the pantry. She didn't want to talk about Brett anymore for fear that she would betray the feeling that had been growing inside her all morning. Brett had sounded sincere when he'd offered to help her.

Maybe he could do just that.

CHAPTER 9

Sam drove in the final nail and stepped back to inspect his work. Sweat dotted his forehead; he pulled his hat lower to shade his eyes from the midday sun.

It wasn't a perfect job, he conceded, but it was the best he could do with the tools he'd found in the barn. At least now with the corral repaired, the horses could escape the confines of their stalls and get some exercise.

Fortune snorted and pawed at the ground when Sam stepped into the barn's cool interior, as if the animal knew something was about to happen. Sam led him to the corral and turned him loose. The stallion galloped around the perimeter, tossing his head.

Bob and Bill, the workhorses, were considerably less enthusiastic when Sam let them into the corral. They plodded aimlessly sampling the grass and weeds.

They were a sorry pair, Sam thought as he closed the barn door. It irritated him that someone had sold two such useless animals to Anna simply because she hadn't known better.

Sam headed for the house. He could see Anna sitting in the shade on the back steps studying something in her lap. Since they'd finished their noon meal, he'd fed the chickens, chopped wood, fed the horses, and repaired the corral, all the while mulling over a problem that had nagged him since he and Anna had stood in the kitchen cooking together.

She was a stubborn woman, and things here were taking much longer than he had anticipated. And the longer he stayed, the greater the risk that he would be found out. Now other people were nosing around—Brett Morgan and Charles

Hampton. Morgan, he'd just like to punch in the face; Hampton made the hair on his neck stand up.

Sam had wrestled with the problem and had come to one conclusion: he needed to talk to Otis DuBerry.

Buck Kyle, the only member of Jimmy Rowe's outlaw gang to serve time, had saved Otis DuBerry's life in a knife fight on the third day of DuBerry's sentence for bank fraud. The small, bespectacled man had sworn an allegiance to Buck and had not gone back on his word even after he had been released. It was Otis who had gotten word from Buck to Sam that Anna had been to see her father just before he died. Now, with time growing short and things closing in, Sam needed information from Buck. And the only way to get it was through Otis.

Sam's pace slowed as he neared the back porch. He had to get a telegram to Otis. But how the hell was he going to get that stubborn woman off her farm and into town with him?

"What are you reading?"

Startled, Anna slammed the Bible closed. It disturbed Feathers beside her. The big cat stretched lazily and trotted away. Anna looked up at him with wide eyes. "Nothing."

Sam dropped his hat on the porch. Should he just hog-tie her and throw her into the back of the wagon? "I fixed the corral."

She gazed off toward the barn. "The horses seem much happier."

What if he told her he'd take her by her friend Sarah's house for a visit? Sam dipped his handkerchief into the rain barrel by the porch and wiped off his face. "The chickens are laying."

The breeze blew a stray lock of hair over her cheek. "We'll have fresh eggs for breakfast."

Sam sat down on the step above her. Maybe he could get her to go if he offered to buy her something. "I got in more wood."

"I saw that. Thank you." She gave him a faint smile.

He braced his elbows on the step behind him and studied the back of her. Wisps of hair curled against her neck. The fabric of her dress outlined the delicate frame of her shoulders and back and clung to her bottom where it met the hard, wooden step.

"Would you like to go into town and have supper with me?"

She looked back at him and her thick lashes batted once. "Yes. I'd like that."

Anna, hardly believing her luck, went into her bedroom to change, and Sam went into his. She'd been pondering all morning on how she could get into town. Then out of the blue, Sam asked if she wanted to go. He wouldn't be so anxious, she thought as she stepped into her dark-green dress, if he had any idea what she was up to.

He'd never let her off the farm again if he knew she wanted to go into town to talk to Brett Morgan.

Mildred Palmer was outside the store and called a greeting. Sam tipped his hat and Anna smiled as they drove by in the wagon.

"It's early," Sam said as he pulled the team to a stop outside the Kemper Feed Store. "I figure we can spend some time in town before we eat."

The idea fit her plan perfectly. "I'll meet you at the Kemper Hotel restaurant in about an hour."

That was more than enough time. "Sounds fine."

Anna watched as Sam disappeared down the street, then turned and headed for the sheriff's office. To her dismay, no one was there. But Brett's horse was tied out front, so she knew he was in town somewhere. She had to find him quickly. She only had an hour.

Sam ducked between the tobacco shop and the office of the Kemper Gazette and turned down the alley behind the businesses that faced Main Street. He wanted to get to the express office and didn't want to attract any attention. Since everybody in town knew Anna, it was hard for him to go anywhere unnoticed; he'd been on the receiving end of a lot of finger-pointing and whispering since the first time the two of them had gone into town together. Sam didn't understand how Anna could hate the people here, the people who had so easily welcomed her back among them.

"Why, hello, Sam."

Maggie Fry stepped from between the barrels and bushel baskets sitting outside Nettie's Cafe and blocked his path. He had to stop quickly to avoiding running into her on the narrow boardwalk.

Sam touched the brim of his hat. "Afternoon, Mrs. Fry."

Her deep-green eyes traveled the length of him and her brows arched. "What am I going to have to do to get you to call me Maggie?" She inched closer, her massive bosoms pointing straight at his chest.

Sam fell back a step. "Well, ah, I. . . ."

She moved nearer. "Shall I give you something to remember me by?"

Sam backed into a barrel of smoked pork, lost his balance and sat down on the lid. The straining buttons of Maggie's blouse were at eye level—and moving closer. Sam sprang to his feet.

She laughed a deep, throaty laugh.

Sam eased his way around her. "If you'll excuse me, I've got some business to tend to."

Her bottom lip crept out and she batted her eyelashes. "I was hoping you might lend me a hand with these supplies. I've got to get them inside before the supper crowd shows up."

Sam looked at the clutter on the boardwalk. He was anxious to leave, but he couldn't refuse to help. He picked up a bushel basket of apples. "Where do you want them?"

"Just come inside with me." Hips swaying, she sauntered in ahead of him.

She'd looked at almost every respectable place in town, but Anna hadn't found Brett anywhere. There wasn't much time left before Sam expected to meet her at the hotel—and she certainly didn't want him to come looking for her.

Standing on Main Street debating on what to do next, Anna heard a tapping noise behind her. She turned and saw Emma

Langford's freckled face in the window of Millie's Millinery Shop.

"Come in, come in." Emma mouthed the words and waved at her through the glass.

Anna's heart sank. This was the last thing she needed. But she plastered on a smile and went inside.

The reverend's daughter was holding a hat decorated with huge, yellow sunflowers, the largest of which was crowned with a felt bumblebee.

"Don't you love it? I just finished it and was about to put it in the display window. Come sit down. You can be the first to try it on."

Anna swallowed hard. "Oh, no, Emma. I couldn't. Really."

Emma lifted her shoulders. "Well, it is a bit fancy for you." She placed the hat in the window, turning it on just the right angle so that the bumblebee showed. "Come look around the shop, Anna."

Among the more stylish hats on display were the ones Emma had created herself, and it was those she pointed out. Anna smiled and complimented Emma on her creations.

"Now let me show you the workroom."

Emma led the way through the curtained doorway into a small room in the back of the store. It was dominated by a large worktable and rows of shelves that lined the walls. On the table were swatches of fabric, bows, and ribbons.

"I'm working on this one for the Christmas season." Emma held up a green-brocade hat with an evergreen tree wired in front and tiny gift packages sewed around the brim.

It was even worse than the other hats Emma had showed her, and Anna was trying desperately to think of something nice to say when she caught sight of Sam through the window. He was across the alley carrying a sack of flour into the back entrance of Nettie's Cafe. Maggie Fry was lounging against the wall devouring his every movement. He disappeared into the store. Maggie followed, closing the door behind them.

A fire sparked in the pit of Anna's stomach. Her whole body went rigid. "I have to leave."

Emma followed her to the door. "But—but what about the hat?"

"It's beautiful," Anna called over her shoulder. "I'll take it."

Anna wasn't the kind of woman to let things go by and say nothing. She believed in tackling situations when they arose and dealing with them on the spot.

And this one she intended to jump squarely into the middle of.

Anna charged around the building and across the alley to the back entrance of Nettie's. She strode inside without knocking. From the storeroom on the left she heard Sam's deep muffled voice, then Maggie's playful laughter. The spark in her belly flamed to consume her.

Anna walked to the doorway of the supply room. In the dim little room she saw Sam leaning casually against a stack of crates and Maggie in front of him, her hand resting on his arm. Sam saw Anna and straightened.

"It's time for supper, Sam." Her chilly words cast a blanket of frost over the room.

Annoyance showed on Maggie's face, but she gave Sam a sultry smile and winked. She squeezed his arm. "Thanks."

He tipped his hat and followed Anna out onto the boardwalk. "Is it time for supper already?"

"No. It is not time for supper," she hissed.

Anna set a blistering pace through the alley and Sam had to lengthen his strides to stay with her. He gestured back toward the cafe. "But you said—"

"Never mind what I said. I don't want to talk about it." Anna squeezed the words through clenched teeth.

Sam shrugged. "Whatever you say."

Anna clamped her mouth shut and walked on. But her silence lasted only a few more steps. She couldn't hold it in.

Anna turned on Sam. "How could you have done that?"

He fell back a step. "Done what?"

"How do you think that looked? You and Maggie— Maggie Fry, of all people—alone together?"

Sam held out his hands helplessly. "She just asked me to

carry her supplies. I don't know why you're getting your dander up."

Anna drew in a sharp breath. "Because everybody in town is gossiping about her marriage to Deacon Fry—it's the only thing being talked about as much as me! She was a loose woman before she married him, and everybody says she's after anything in a pair of trousers."

Sam's brows crept up. "Did your mother know you talked that way?"

Anna pursed her lips and lifted her chin. "I would think that if you don't have a care about what people will say about you or me, you might at least remain faithful to your fiancée." She turned smartly and walked away.

"Who?" Sam caught up with her and touched her shoulder.

She sighed impatiently and stopped in the shade of the bank. "Your fiancée," she repeated. "The woman you're engaged to in Kentucky. Your wife-to-be."

Sam stroked his chin. "I don't have one of those."

Anna rolled her eyes. "Yes, you do. You told me you were getting married soon and that's why you wanted the money."

"Oh, that." Understanding dawned on his face. He nodded his head. "I do plan to get married. But I haven't picked out a wife yet."

"You're not—. You haven't—"

"No." Sam shook his head. "But I've been looking around for one."

He made it sound as though he was selecting a heifer at the stockyard. Anna drew herself up to her greatest height. "Honestly, Sam Rowan, for a man who claims to have seen so many pantalettes, you know nothing about women." Anna flounced away in a huff.

Left at a loss, Sam blew out a heavy breath and watched her go. He thought he could handle women, until the day he'd awakened in Anna Fletcher's bed. She was unlike any he'd ever dealt with before.

But she was right, to a point, Sam admitted. His knowledge of women was gained mostly from Saturday nights in saloons all across Kentucky. He'd worked on horse farms since he was hardly more than a child, and there had been no girls for him to court properly. He'd thought on it a lot, though, and he'd pretty well figured out how a women ought to be treated.

Sam watched Anna's bustle bobbing down the alley ahead of him. He knew how to treat a woman. Especially this one.

Sam hurried to catch up with her. "So why do you care?"

She froze. Anna felt as if the ground beneath her feet had crumbled away. "I—I don't care." And she didn't. Did she?

He moved in front of her. "No? Well, you're sure acting persnickety."

Was she? "I am not," she insisted.

Sam folded his arms across his wide chest. "You're mighty upset about something."

No! She didn't have any feeling for this man. She wouldn't allow it. She wouldn't!

"Don't stand there looking so smug," she told him angrily. "You've been nothing but a nuisance since you barged into my house, thinking of only your own selfish needs. And if you want the likes of Maggie Fry, or if you're just plain stupid enough to be lured by those tricks of hers, then it's fine with me. You don't mean a thing to me, Sam Rowan, and the sooner you get out of my life the better I'll like it."

Sam's expression hardened. His eyes grew distant and harsh. "If you want to stand here and see who can say the meanest thing, then I'll concede right now. You win. And don't fret anymore, I'll be out of your life for good real soon. I'm not waiting for you anymore, Mrs. Rowan. I'm going to find that money myself. If I have to take that house apart board by board and dig up every square foot of land on that farm, I'm going to find it. And when I do, nothing will suit me better than never having to hear that sharp tongue of yours again." He turned on his heels and walked away.

Tears welled in Anna's eyes and a hailstorm of emotions pelted her. She felt confused about Sam. Was he just angry? Or had she heard pain in his voice as well? She wondered now if what she'd gotten was what she really wanted.

Then panic set in. He was going after the money. Alone. He wasn't waiting for her to lead him to it.

Anna pressed her fingers to her lips. What would she do if he got to it before she did?

*   *   *

He'd had it. He was finding that money, and he was getting out of town, come hell or high water. Determination hardened in Sam's belly as he cut through the alley headed for Main Street; he refused to think that what he was feeling was anything but anger. He would send his telegram, Sam decided, and would go back to the farm, and he didn't care if he had to work from sun to sun. Nothing was going to slow him down.

Sam rounded the corner and ran straight into Clara Abbott and Irene Saunders, whom he had met on his first visit to town. The ladies were standing in a tight little circle with another woman he didn't recognize. For a moment it seemed they would not remember him, but Clara called out to him, shattering all hope of completing his errand quickly.

"Sam, there is something we simply must talk with you about," Clara insisted as she waved him over.

Dutifully he joined their circle.

"The church is in desperate need." She clenched the handkerchief in her hand. "We must have your help."

"We must have your wife." Irene peered at him over the top of her spectacles.

"You want Anna?"

"We've fallen behind on the stitchery for the church's booth at the Founders' Day celebration and we need every pair of hands we can get to finish on time," Clara explained.

Irene took over the plea. "We're all meeting at Clara's tomorrow and working straight through until we're done. You're a fine Christian man. Please allow your wife to lend a hand."

Sam could hardly believe his luck. To be rid of Anna for a whole day, to not worry that she was recovering the money from one end of the farm while he was searching the other, was more than he could have hoped for. It was a miracle.

A grin parted his lips. "I'd be proud to have her join you. Count on her being there."

The three ladies sighed with relief and excitement.

"That's wonderful!" Clara exclaimed. "Wait until Anna hears the good news."

"There she is now!" Irene pointed down the street as Anna emerged from the alley.

Sam's grin blossomed into a smile. "Anna, honey, come on over here. I've got something to tell you."

This wasn't right. Anna knew the look that Sam wore and knew it meant trouble. He was up to something. Cautiously, she approached the group.

Sam circled her waist with his arm and drew her into the gathering. He beamed down at her. "I've got some good news, sugar. I've given my permission for you to work on the church's stitchery with these fine ladies. Tomorrow. All day."

The ladies tittered with excitement.

No! Anna wanted to scream aloud. No, she couldn't leave Sam alone at the farm.

She glanced at the smug grin on his face and realized that was exactly what he had intended. That cunning, conniving fox, she swore silently. He'd manipulated her again for his own purposes. But no more, she decided. Two could play at that game.

Anna smiled sweetly. "Oh, Sam, darling, how kind of you. This will be so wonderful. Me helping with the sewing, and you joining the men building the booths." She turned to Clara. "You still do it that way, don't you?"

"Oh, yes, of course," Clara replied.

"Fine, then it's all settled," Irene declared. "We'll see you both tomorrow morning at Clara's and we'll—"

"Hold on a minute." Sam waved his hands frantically. He wasn't about to let Anna ruin his plans. "I'm awful sorry, ladies, but I won't be able to go."

They all looked at him expectantly, their silence demanding a reason.

"I'm feeling a little under the weather today," Sam said. "I can't commit to going and then not show up."

"You're sick? This is the first I've heard of it—sweetie."

He looked down at Anna. "I didn't want to worry you—darling."

She wouldn't allow him to pull this off. And the way to stop him was standing right in front of her.

Anna gestured to the third lady in their circle. "Sam, have you met Mrs. Sawyer? Dr. Sawyer's wife?"

Behind her, the office door opened and a portly man with gray chin whiskers walked out.

Sam shifted uncomfortably. "Uh, no, I—"

"And here's Dr. Sawyer now. What luck." Anna took Sam's arm and pulled him across the boardwalk. "Dr. Sawyer, could you spare a few minutes to see my husband? He's feeling poorly today."

Dr. Sawyer peered over his spectacles perched on the end of his nose. He eyed Sam up and down. "Come on inside."

The ladies were all staring. He couldn't go back on what he'd just said or he'd end up building booths all day tomorrow, instead of searching for the money. Trapped in his own lie, Sam gritted his teeth and went inside the doctor's office.

"Dr. Sawyer?" Anna moved closer and whispered to the doctor. "Sam won't tell you this himself. You know how silly grown men can be about these things."

The doctor nodded wisely and leaned toward her.

"He needs a dose of castor oil," Anna confided. "But don't let on that I told you. Tell him it's mineral water, or something."

"I understand." He started inside his office.

"Dr. Sawyer." She touched his arm. "Make it a big dose."

Through the open door she could see Sam looking uncomfortable standing among the medical equipment. Anna waved and smiled sweetly as the door closed.

He might have gotten rid of her for tomorrow, but she'd made sure he'd be in no condition to hunt for the money.

Sam left the doctor's office, smacking his lips distastefully. Lordy, but the medicines in this town were awful. The stuff the doctor had just given him reminded him of something he'd had as a child, though he couldn't say exactly what it was, since he couldn't remember ever having taken mineral water before. And somehow it had tasted even worse than the witch's brew Anna had fed him.

To his surprise Anna was waiting on the boardwalk. The ladies were gone and Ben Atkins was talking with her.

"Sam, I have some good news." She smiled sweetly and batted her lashes at him. "You remember Ben? He owns the farm next to mi—ours."

Suspicious, Sam shook hands with him. Ben was a frail, weathered looking man; a lifetime of hard work showed in the creases of his face.

"Ben is going to take you to the stockyard with him on Thursday," she announced. "All the way over in Charlotte."

Her ploy was painfully obvious. And Sam wasn't going to let her get away with it. "I appreciate it, Ben, but I've got too much to do around the farm."

"But Sam, you promised we could get a milk cow." Her voice trembled.

Sympathy showed on Ben's face. "It won't take long," he said to Sam.

"I'll care for the cow myself, Sam. I'll milk and feed it. I won't bother you with it at all." Her big brown eyes pleaded with him.

Ben fumbled with his battered hat. "We can be back before supper if we get an early start."

Anna pulled a handkerchief from her reticule and twisted it in her hand. "You can use my egg money, if you need it."

Ben looked at him expectantly.

What an actress, Sam thought. She belonged on the stage. She was sure putting on a show for Ben Atkins—and he was believing every word of it.

"I could come by your place and help you get caught up on things," Ben offered.

Sam squirmed uncomfortably.

Anna sniffed. "I won't ask for another thing. I swear I won't.'"

Sam threw up his hands. "All right, all right." She had him looking like a fool. What else could he do?

Anna touched the handkerchief to the corner of her eye. "Thank you, Sam. I don't deserve you for a husband."

Looking relieved, Ben said, "Be over to my place at first

light on Thursday." He pulled on his hat and crossed the street.

"That was quite a show, Mrs. Rowan."

"Wait until you see the show I've planned for Thursday." She raised her brows in mock surprise. "Oh, but you won't be home on Thursday. Too bad."

Her haughty little grin didn't discourage Sam. He might be gone all day, but he'd find a way to keep her from the show she was planning. He'd get to that money first. Regardless.

"There's something I still need to do," Anna said as she edged away from him.

He was glad because he still needed to send his telegram. "I'll meet you at the restaurant in a little while."

Sam never gave Anna a backward glance as he headed for the express office.

Jonas Fry was at the counter when Sam walked in. Sam remembered him as Deacon Fry from church.

"Afternoon." The bell over the door jangled as Sam closed it. "I need to send a telegram."

He filled out the paper Jonas gave him and paid for it while the Deacon made small talk.

"See you on Sunday," Jonas said as Sam left.

On the street again, Sam sighed with relief. Otis DuBerry would have the telegram by tomorrow, and soon he'd put an end to Sam's nagging suspicions. Feeling more confident, Sam headed for the Hotel Kemper.

Anna quickened her pace. She had to find Brett. He'd said he could help her, and he'd seemed genuinely sincere. She felt she could trust him to keep her problem confidential. He'd proved that he wasn't one to gossip. Brett knew about her father dying in prison and he hadn't told a soul. She was sure of that because no one in town had offered her condolences over his death while nearly everyone had expressed sympathy over her mother passing on. Brett wasn't like the others in town. She knew it in her heart. He didn't talk about her family problems.

Anna went from shop to shop all along Main Street hoping to find Brett. She couldn't ask anyone if they'd seen him, as that would surely arouse suspicion. She needed to talk to him alone when she could explain this whole mess to him. With Sam searching for the money on his own, confiding in Brett might be her only hope of opening her orphanage and clearing the Fletcher name.

Anna took comfort in the thought of Brett's help. How good it felt that she could trust him.

From the shadow of the bakery shop, blue eyes watched as Sam entered the express office, then waited patiently until he appeared once more and went about his business. Lazily the man crossed the street and went inside.

"Afternoon, Jonas." He rested his elbows across the counter in front of the Deacon.

Jonas gave him a sidelong glance as he paused over his log book. "Afternoon, deputy."

"How's things down at the church?" Brett asked.

Jonas squeezed the stub of a pencil between his fingers. "They're fine . . . fine."

"How long have you been deacon down there?" Brett pulled a cheroot from his shirt pocket.

"Twen—" Jonas cleared his throat. "Twenty-three years."

"Has it been that long? My, my, that's a long time. People in this town must think pretty highly of you." He rolled the cheroot between his fingers, toying with it.

Perspiration broke out across Jonas's upper lip.

"And say, that's a mighty fine-looking wife you got for yourself. That Miss Maggie is a good Christian woman, too. Not a Sunday goes by that I don't hear somebody comment on what an upstanding family you head up." Brett hung the cheroot between his lips. "But you know what? I could have sworn it was your wife I saw sneaking out of the back door of Luther Tillman's place one night last week while his wife was over nursing the widow Craighead."

The lead point on Jonas's pencil snapped.

Brett straightened and pulled a match from his pocket. "But that couldn't have been your wife. Could it, Deacon?"

Jonas swallowed hard.

Brett dragged the match across the counter and it sparked

to life. He picked up the telegram that lay on Jonas's logbook waiting to be sent. "That wasn't your wife. Was it?"

Jonas looked at the telegram, then at Brett. "No." The word came out in a hoarse whisper. "No, it wasn't."

Brett smiled and touched the match to the corner of the telegram. "I didn't think so."

Fire consumed the paper, turning it black and sending tiny sparks into the air. Brett dropped it onto the counter and lit his cheroot.

"See you in church, Deacon." He tossed the match on the floor and left.

CHAPTER 10

It pained her to admit it, but she'd had a good time.

Anna sat on the wagon seat with Jamie and Sarah, who had offered her a ride home, feeling surprisingly happy about the day spent sewing in Clara's parlor. Many of the women there were Anna's age, most married now with children. But this different stage in their lives had affected them little today, and Anna had fit in as if she hadn't lived the last ten years in another town. She'd known nearly all of them from her childhood spent in Kemper, and they felt like friends now, as they had then.

The sun was setting behind the Blue Ridge Mountains as Jamie stopped the team in front of the farmhouse and the final chorus of "Turkey in the Straw," led by the children in the back of the wagon, ended on a ragged note. They all laughed, and the baby Anna held on her lap clapped her chubby hands.

"Sam! Good to see you," Jamie called.

Reality struck hard and fast. The weeds, the peeling paint, the broken step. And Sam, of course.

Anna saw him standing on the front porch, his arms folded across his chest, a stoic expression on his face. Guilt feelings assailed her as she watched him cross the yard. Even though he deserved it, she felt bad about the castor oil she'd tricked the doctor into giving him yesterday. He looked pale and wrung out.

"Could have used your help today," Jamie said. "Anna tells us you're quite a carpenter."

He stopped beside the wagon and slid his hands into his trouser pockets. "Did she now?"

"In fact, Anna bragged about you all day," Sarah told him. She smiled. "I'll bet your ears were burning."

"No. It wasn't my ears." His gaze shot daggers at Anna. She ducked her head and looked away.

"Hi, Sam." Nathan leaned over the side of the wagon.

Sam reached up and ruffled the boy's hair.

Derek's head popped up along side his brother. "Hello, Sam. When are you coming over to our house again?"

"Shut up, stupid." Nathan elbowed him in the chest. "Sit down."

"That's enough, boys," Jamie called. "Nathan, I told you to be nice to your brother."

An angry frown crossed Nathan's face as he plopped down in the back of the wagon, arms folded across his chest. Derek wagged his tongue at him then climbed up next to their father.

Sam gave Nathan's shoulder a squeeze, and when the boy looked up at him, Sam winked. A small smile spread over Nathan's face.

"There's a barn-raising at the Huntberrys' tomorrow," Jamie said to Sam. "Most of the men will be over there. Anna thought you'd want to come too. How about it?"

He glanced at Anna. A faint grin played on her lips before she turned to adjust the baby's bonnet. Sam rubbed his chin. "Would that be Edna Mae Huntberry?"

Jamie nodded. "Their barn was struck by lightning a couple of weeks back. Burned right to the ground."

"What about Lula Jones?" Sam asked. "Will she be there too?"

Jamie grinned. "Those two ladies are nearly inseparable."

Sam nodded slowly. He looked at Sarah. "Are you going?"

She lifted the baby from Anna's lap. "I wish I could. But after being gone all day today, none of us will be there. Edna Mae and Lula will have their hands full feeding all you men themselves. They'll have to manage best they can."

"In that case, count me in." His voice grew cooler. "Anna will go too and help with the cooking."

She'd anticipated this move. "No, Sam, I can't go. I have too many thing to catch up on after being gone all day."

"I did your chores."

"But—"

"All of them."

"But—"

Sarah smiled warmly. "Sam, what a dear you are. Oh, Anna, you're so lucky."

"But—"

Sam lifted her down from the wagon and waved as the Calhouns drove away.

Anna whirled around, trying to hold her temper. "You probably don't remember, but I pointed out Edna Mae and Lula to you in church, and I told you I despise them both."

He leveled a cold stare at her. "I remember."

Sam walked into the house and closed the door in her face.

What a dirty trick. Anna's temper simmered, then cooled. As dirty as the castor oil stunt she'd pulled? Yes, she decided. After all, it was Sam who had barged into her life, and Sam who wanted to keep the money for his own gain.

Anna stared at the closed front door. No, nothing she could do was too bad if it rid her life of Sam Rowan.

The next morning they were up and on their way to the Huntberrys' farm at dawn. They'd hardly spoken the night before or while preparing breakfast. Anna feared Sam was contemplating some other way to get her off the farm for a day; she was doing the same.

"Did you ladies get all your stitching done yesterday?"

Sam's voice jarred her out of her plotting. "I hope so. I must have sewn ten rag dolls myself."

He looked across the wagon seat at her. "Rag dolls?"

She always felt uncomfortable when she was this close to Sam. She could sense the power in his muscular arms. His scent disturbed her.

Anna tossed her head. "I'd rather sew them than doilies or samplers."

"Why? Did you pretend they were all me and stick pins in them all day?"

She giggled. "No. But I wish I'd thought of it."

Sam laughed with her. "What's this Founders' Day all about, anyway?"

"It's a celebration of the founding of Kemper," Anna explained. "There's booths, horse races, a box-lunch raffle, contests for the children, and a dance at the grange hall."

"Sounds like fun."

Anna nodded. She remembered it as lots of fun, going with her parents, meeting her friends there. It was at the Founders' Day celebration that Cyrus had bought her mother the extravagant hat, the one that belonged to the box that now held all the legal documents, correspondence, and newspaper clippings from her father's trial. Now, she could never think of the two separately.

"Thinking bad thoughts again?"

Sam's words interrupted her thoughts. Anna realized she was frowning at the recollection. She shook her head to clear her mind. "Yes, I was. I can't help it."

"You can help it." There was an edge on his voice. "You'd better, or you'll be living in the past forever."

"You don't know what it was like. You don't know what my family went through." It irritated her that he was so insensitive.

"Every family has its problems, Anna."

She folded her arms. "I don't know why you're involving yourself with any of this. You don't know anything about it. You never even had a family."

He turned away. "No. But it wasn't because I didn't want one."

Anna squirmed in her seat. She didn't know why she'd said such a hurtful thing. Sam seemed to bring out the worst in her at times.

The Huntberrys' farm came into view when they crested the next hill. Neighbors had begun to arrive, and there was a line of horses and wagons leading to the spot behind the house where the barn had once stood. Sam stopped the wagon under the oaks in front of the white farmhouse and lifted Anna from the seat. He carried their contribution to the day's food to the porch where Edna Mae Huntberry and Lula Jones stood and greeted both the ladies.

Dread filled Anna's stomach as she followed Sam onto the porch. She despised both these women and hated the thought

of spending the entire day with them. She hated Sam, too, for
his part in this, even though it was her own stunt to get rid of
him for the day that had backfired and landed her here.

"It's real neighborly of you to come over and help," Edna
Mae said to Sam.

"We hardly expected that Anna would be here too," Lula
added, eyeing her as she lingered by the steps.

Sam smiled. "She wouldn't have missed it for anything."

He crossed the porch and felt Anna's harsh gaze on him.
Quickly he circled her waist with one arm and crushed her
hard against him. His lips smothered hers with a long, hot
kiss. Then, just as abruptly, he set her away.

"Be nice," he whispered. Sam climbed onto the wagon and
drove off.

Stunned, knees wobbling, Anna stared after him. Her flesh
burned where he had touched her, and her mouth tingled from
the taste of him. The pit of her stomach glowed.

Anna turned to find Edna Mae and Lula gaping at her. A
silly smile spread over her face. "I guess we'd better get busy.
These men are going to be hungry."

The spell Sam had cast over her didn't last long once she
got into the kitchen and meal preparations began. Edna Mae's
two daughters were there as were Lula's three daughters-in-
law, and they all fell into a well-practiced routine. Being the
only outsider, Anna didn't fit in. Conversation was awkward
and strained, because the others talked about people and
things Anna knew nothing about.

By mid-morning the kitchen was like an oven. Anna was
given the most undesirable tasks. Grease popped on her from
the frying chicken. Her arms ached as she rolled out and cut
dozens and dozens of biscuits. She stirred the pots of boiling
vegetables while the other women laid out the table settings,
sliced the bread, the cold beef and ham, and fetched water and
cider from the spring house. The grandchildren ran screaming
through the kitchen in an uproarious game of tag, using Anna
as home base.

Anna wiped perspiration from her brow as she stood in the
serving line doling out vegetables to the men as they passed
through the kitchen. She tried to smile and have a pleasant

word, but her nerves were frayed and her patience was nearly
at its end.

And then Sam passed in front of her. He was deeply
involved in conversation with the two men on either side of
him in the line as if they had been friends for a lifetime. He
looked cool and refreshed, just having washed up; being
outdoors obviously agreed with him. It seemed he couldn't be
enjoying the day more.

Sam held out his plate to her. He smiled, then winked.

Anna's temper flared. Her feet ached, her head hurt, no one
had spoken a civil word to her all morning. And Sam had the
gall to wink at her!

She flung a spoonful of mashed potatoes at him. It landed
on his plate and splattered over his hand and up the front of
his shirt.

The serving line stopped. Every eye turned to Sam, then to
her and back again to Sam. Slowly he looked down at the
mess she'd caused, then lifted his gaze to meet hers. She
thought, for an instant, he was going to throw the potatoes
back at her. She wished he would. But instead he simply
licked the potatoes from his fingers, winked again, and
moved on.

Completely flustered, Anna focused her thoughts on serving, trying to ignore the stares she felt burning into her. No
one said a word about the incident, but no one asked for
potatoes either.

After the men had all eaten, they headed back to the barn.
Anna watched from the doorway as Sam walked with several
other men. Everyone liked Sam and treated him as though
he'd lived here his entire life. It bothered her. He fit in here
better than she, Anna realized.

The women sat down to eat, now that the men were fed and
back to work, and Anna took a seat at the opposite end of the
table from Edna Mae and Lula. She hardly had an appetite for
the food she'd worked so hard cooking, and here with these
ladies was the last place she wanted to be. She picked at her
plate while the Huntberry and Jones women talked among
themselves. Anna gazed off toward the barn and found herself
wishing she was up there with Sam.

Daylight had faded to dusk when the men stopped their work. The barn's main structure was up, the sides completed, the roof intact. They stood around talking and drinking cold cider while Anna was in the kitchen with the other women washing the last of the supper dishes. She was nearly exhausted after helping clean up and cook two full meals. But she was angry also. She'd worked hard, without a single complaint, and still Edna Mae had said nothing more to her than to give orders on what to do next. Anna had seen her whispering to Lula several times during the day, and she was sure they were talking about her.

Anna rinsed the last plate and stacked it on the sideboard. The more she thought about it, the angrier she became. Edna Mae and Lula were the ones who had gossiped so shamelessly about her mother and father and had said some truly unforgivable things. Yet here Anna was, working like a dog, helping them.

Frustrated, angry, and tired, Anna pulled off her apron and tossed it on the sideboard. She'd done as Sam said—she'd been nice—but no more. She wasn't staying in this house another moment.

Without a word, Anna headed out the back door. She was going to find Sam and make him take her home this instant.

"Anna! Anna, dear!"

She was tempted to keep going when she heard Edna Mae calling, but didn't. Anna waited as the older woman hurried down the back steps and across the darkened yard.

"I wanted to thank you for helping today. I appreciate your hard work."

With only the glow from the kitchen windows, Anna couldn't see Edna Mae's face clearly and was left with just her tone of voice to judge her sincerity. It wasn't enough to draw a conclusion.

"You're welcome." Anna turned once more to leave.

"You're a very good cook," Edna Mae called. Her voice shook a bit.

Anna was obliged to stop again. "Thank you."

Edna Mae laughed nervously. "Though I wish I had your

courage in serving potatoes. You've no idea how many times I've wanted to do that very thing."

The tension between them eased. Edna Mae twisted her apron in her hands and stepped closer.

"I said some things about your mother that I wish I hadn't said. I never got the chance to apologize to Elsa, so I'd like to tell you, Anna. I'm sorry."

She was too stunned to reply. Then it occurred to her that this was her chance, the chance she'd wanted since she was fourteen years old, to lash out at the town and make everyone suffer for what they'd put her mother through. Anna's stomach coiled into a knot.

"Lula wants to apologize too, but she's afraid of what you might say." Edna Mae wrung her apron. "Your mother was a good woman. She stood by her husband. I wish I could take it all back. I'm very sorry."

The knot rose to form a lump in her throat and Anna couldn't speak. With only silence between them, Edna Mae turned back toward the house.

Hurting someone else, like the town had hurt her mother, didn't feel right after all. Tears welled in Anna's eyes and she swallowed hard. "Thank you."

Light from the kitchen shone on Edna Mae's face when she turned, and Anna saw relief reflected in her small smile. She released her apron and hurried into the house.

Anna's bottom lip began to quiver. Tears filled her eyes. Emotions, so long bottled inside her, wanted to pour out. And she was all alone—in the dark—standing in a strange backyard. She wanted someone to hold her. She wanted to tell someone what had happened. She wanted—

Anna hurried up the road to the barn, her dress hiked up to her ankles, mindless of the rocks and ruts and darkness.

"Sam! Sam!"

Some of the men were hitching up their teams by the lantern light, others were still gathered by the new barn talking. A few were heading toward the house now.

Anna stopped. Her heart pounded. She didn't know where he was. She didn't know where to look. And she wanted him—now.

Through the light in the corral, she saw him running toward her. A tear trickled down her cheek. She couldn't move a step.

"What happened?" Sam grabbed her upper arms. He searched her face in the dim light and saw the tears. "Jesus . . . what happened?"

"I—they—" Words wouldn't come. Only tears. Anna curled her fists into the front of his shirt.

He tightened his grip on her arms. "What happened? Did someone hurt you? Anna, talk to me."

Frantically she shook her head. "Ed—Edna Mae said. . . ." Anna sniffed. "She said that she . . . that she was so—sorry."

"Sorry?" He relaxed his hold on her. "Sorry? For what?"

Anna tried to rein in her feelings. She could see he was desperately trying to understand what was happening. She was making too much of it, Anna decided. Sam would think she was silly. She choked back her tears, but her voice was ragged with emotion.

"Ed—Edna Mae said she was sorry for—" She hiccuped. "—for all the things she s—said."

His brows drew together. "What things?"

Anna drew in a deep breath. "About my mo—my moth. . . ."

"Your mamma?"

Anna nodded. A torrent of tears threatened; she pressed her lips tight to hold them in. She expected him to laugh or say she was being stupid. But he didn't. Sam smiled and pulled her into his arms and held her. Fresh tears poured down her face as she sobbed into the front of his shirt.

When the tears finally stopped, she turned her face up to him. He wiped her eyes with his handkerchief, holding her close with a strong arm around her shoulders.

"You must think I'm some simpering half-wit."

Sam tilted her face upward. "You're a lot of things, Anna, but a half-wit isn't one of them. Besides, a little crying every now and again can be a good thing."

His lips met hers softly, gently kneading them together.

The kiss deepened, and Anna snuggled against him, taking strength from the warmth and tenderness of his touch.

Jangling harnesses and boots scuffling against the hard ground broke the spell that held them together. Sam ended their kiss but still held her in his embrace as two men walked past leading their horses.

"I told you they were newly married," one said to the other and elbowed him in the ribs.

Both men laughed. Then the other called, "As long as she don't throw nothing worse than potatoes at you, you got nothing to worry about."

Anna stepped away from Sam and wiped her eyes.

"Are you all right now?" he asked her softly.

She'd always be all right if Sam was near.

That thought stunned her, frightened her. Anna pushed it from her mind. "I'd like to go home now."

He studied her for a moment before replying, "I'm hitching up the team right now."

A few minutes later Sam drove the wagon down from the barn and stopped for her. Jamie pulled his team up beside them.

"We're mighty glad you could join us today, Sam."

He jumped to the ground. "Glad I could help out."

"And that was some good food you ladies fixed," Jamie said to Anna.

She smiled. "Thanks. But I missed seeing Sarah today."

Sam placed his hands around her waist to lift her into the wagon.

"Sarah and I both appreciate you taking care of the young 'uns for us," Jamie told her.

She slapped her hands over Sam's, stilling them. Suspicion crept up her spine. "Taking care . . . the children?"

Jamie braced his foot against the brake handle. "Sam said you'd keep the girls on Friday while Sarah and I go into town."

Anna dug her nails into Sam's hands. He winced and released her. "Sam said that, did he?"

"It's all right, isn't it?"

Anger welled inside her. What a fool she'd been a few

moments ago to want Sam's comfort. There was nothing
between them. Nothing but fifty thousand dollars.

She curbed her anger, determined that Sam wouldn't
outsmart her again. She'd never let him have a day alone on
the farm.

Anna smiled. "Sure, Jamie. But you must bring all the
children over. Why, Sam was just saying this morning how
he'd love to take your boys fishing."

"Huh?"

"That's mighty kind of you, Sam."

"But—"

"Have them bring their fishing poles," Anna said. "I'll pack
them a basket and they can make a day of it."

"But—"

"I'll tell the boys tonight." Jamie picked up the reins.
"Thanks a lot. Nathan and Derek will be tickled pink to hear
this."

Sam and Anna glared at each other as Jamie drove away.
Then, abruptly, he lifted her into the wagon and dropped her
onto the seat. Anna straightened her dress and scooted to the
edge of the seat.

So far, she'd thwarted his every attempt to get rid of her
and managed to arrange an entire day alone at the farm for
herself. Tomorrow, Sam would be with Ben Atkins at the
stockyard in Charlotte, and she would have the whole day and
the whole farm to herself.

The wagon lurched forward and Anna drew in a deep
breath. She had him this time; there was nothing he could do
to keep her from the money now. Nothing.

An unnatural darkness hung over her bedroom as Anna
fought to clear away the heavy veil of sleep. Her thoughts
were fuzzy, but she felt something was wrong. Instinctively,
she knew it was morning, yet her room was still dark. And the
pounding noise that had awakened her was out of place.

Anna pushed back the quilt and sat up. Light from the
window was completely blocked except for a crack along the
sill. She threw her dark hair over her shoulder and realized
the pounding noise was coming from outside. It sounded like

nails, she decided, nails being driven into wood. But why
would anyone be nailing a board over her window? There
was no one else around except for—

"Sam!" Anna bolted from the bed. He was sealing her shut
in her room!

She dropped to her knees and through a four-inch crack,
peered out at him driving nails into a sheet of plywood
covering her window. "Stop that! Stop it this minute!"

His dark hat was pulled down but she could see the hard,
determined lines of his face.

"You let me out of here!" Anna pushed the window all the
way up and pounded the rough plywood with her fist. Sam
drove in another nail.

"You rotten, stinking skunk! Let me out of here!"

He didn't answer, didn't even look at her.

"Oh!" Anna dashed to the door. The knob turned but it
wouldn't open. She braced her foot against the casement and
pulled with all her strength, but it didn't budge.

She ran back to the window and dropped to her knees,
peering out at him. "You can't just leave me in this room all
day!"

Sam stepped back from the window and surveyed his
work. "It's a hell of a lot nicer than the outhouse, where I
spent my day, thanks to your little talk with the doctor."

Anna gasped. "But—but that was different."

He gave her a curt nod and walked away.

She lunged at him, her arms flailing wildly through the
crack. "Come back here, you filthy rat!"

Sam climbed onto the wagon and called to the team.

"I wish I'd never laid eyes on you, Sam Rowan! I wish I
had shot you! I wish I'd left you for dead and let the buzzards
pick your miserable bones!"

He drove the wagon away from the farm without a
backward glance.

"I hate you!"

Anna stood and pounded her fist against the plywood. It
was solid as a rock. She whirled around and scanned the
room. The fireplace tools were missing from the hearth. Even

the logs were gone. He'd taken everything from the room that could be used to pry the window open.

She tried the door again. It was closed tight, and she guessed he must have strung a rope from the knob to the one on the front door.

Frustrated and angry, Anna paced the room. He'd left a tray of cold meat and cheese and biscuits by the fireplace so she wouldn't go hungry, and the chamber pot was under the bed. But these courtesies brought no favorable thoughts of Sam Rowan.

Anna gripped the bedpost. She'd get even, she swore. Somehow, someway she'd get even with him. She would make Sam Rowan sorry for the day he dared to come into her life.

Early the next morning, Jamie and Sarah were at the farm with the children. Derek jumped from the wagon, pushed Nathan for no apparent reason, and ran off screaming while Nathan chased after him. Shadow, the family dog they'd brought along, followed, barking furiously. Baby Elizabeth burst into tears when Sarah passed her down to Anna, and Molly sprayed a shower of spittle in Sam's face when he lifted her from the wagon.

"I hope this isn't going to be too much trouble," Sarah ventured, watching her children.

"Oh, no. No trouble," Anna assured her above the baby's wails.

Molly wiggled from Sam's arms. He wiped his face with the back of his hand. "You two just go on. Don't worry about anything."

"Keep an eye on Nathan, will you Sam?" Jamie asked. "He's gotten so rough with Derek, I'm afraid he might hurt him. I've read him the Bible on what the Lord says about fighting, but the boy just won't listen."

"I'll see to it."

Anna patted the baby while Molly wrapped herself in Anna's skirt. "You two have fun. We'll be fine."

Sarah and Jamie called to the boys, who were wrestling on

the porch, and drove away. Elizabeth screamed louder. Molly pulled on Anna's sleeve. "I hungry!"

Overwhelmed, Anna looked at Sam.

"You want to run an orphanage, Mrs. Rowan? Here's your chance to try it out. I'll see you tonight."

Anna's mouth fell open at the sight of his disappearing back. No! She wasn't going to be left alone with these children all day while he was out treasure-hunting.

"Nathan! Derek! Come quickly. Sam is going to take you fishing now."

The boys let out a whoop and clamored off the porch. Shadow loped along behind. They surrounded Sam.

"I gotted my own pole. Want to see?" Derek looked up eagerly at him.

Nathan elbowed his way to Sam's side. "I got worms. See?" He pulled a handful of the slimy creatures from his pocket. "I got enough for you too, Sam, so you don't have to dig for none."

Sam glared at Anna standing in the yard. He drummed his fingers against his thigh.

"I'm gonna get the biggest fish in the whole, whole world." Derek spread his hands wide apart.

"Shut up," Nathan told him. "You're too stupid to catch nothing."

"Am not!"

"Are too!"

Sam's icy gaze held steady on Anna.

"Am not!"

"Stupid!"

"Sam is gonna help me," Derek cried. "Aren't you, Sam? Papa said so."

"Yeah, 'cause you're so stupid," Nathan taunted.

"You shut up." Derek pushed him.

His brother pushed him back. "No, you shut up."

Sam looked down at the boys. "All right, all right, hold it." He pulled them apart. "No more of that kind of talk. You two are brothers and you're lucky to have each other."

Derek looked up at him with wide, hopeful eyes. "You mean we're gonna go fishing?"

Sam sighed heavily. "Yeah. I guess we're going fishing."

He cast Anna a sour look and followed the cheering boys around the house.

Satisfied, Anna took Molly and Elizabeth into the kitchen.

The baby gradually calmed, but burst into tears again each time Anna tried to set her down. Molly was hungry and claimed she would only eat cookies.

"Okay," Anna said. "We'll have cookies."

The process was slow and messy with Molly doing most of the work herself. But Anna's patience held through spilled flour, the dropped butter, the egg shells in the batter, holding Elizabeth on her hip the entire time. Despite the problems, Anna enjoyed it.

Shadow's barking sounded in the backyard as Anna was taking the last batch from the oven. Feathers, who had been napping under the cookstove, took off at the sound. The boys burst through the door.

"Look! I gotted two!" Derek held up the fish he'd caught.

Nathan pushed him aside. "I got three and mine are bigger."

"Uh-uh. Mine are." Derek thrust the fish at Anna. "Aren't they."

"We'll, let's see." Anna studied all the fish. She shifted Elizabeth to the other hip. "They're all big. Where's Sam?"

Derek's eyes widened. "We saw'd a big, big wasp nest."

"The biggest I ever saw in my whole entire life," Nathan added.

Concern creased her brow. "So, where's Sam?"

Shadow barked again and the back door opened. Sam walked inside. Molly took one look at him and ran behind Anna.

"And all these wasps came flying out at Derek," Nathan explained.

"And Sam grabbed me like this." Derek pulled up on back of his collar. "And it hurted my chin."

"Oh, dear. Let me see." Anna knelt down and examined the boy's chin.

"I ran away as fast as I could, but I fell down. See?" Nathan held out his hand to show her a tiny scratch on his palm.

"We must fix that right away," Anna told him and stood.

"I hurted my knee." Derek pulled up his trouser leg.

"I've got medicine for that too." Anna transferred Elizabeth to her other hip and opened the cupboard. "We'll get you boys taken care of right away."

Sam stepped forward frowning. "What have I got to do to get some attention around here? Puke up a lung?"

They all turned and looked at him.

"Sam got stungded," Derek announced.

"Oh dear. Let me see. Where?"

Irritably, he leaned down and showed her the back of his neck where the wasp had stung him.

Anna examined it closely. "Sit down. I'll put something on it."

The boys crowded around Sam as he sat at the table.

"Does it hurt a whole, whole lot?" Derek asked, sympathy pains showing in his young face.

Sam sat up straighter. "No. Not at all."

"Gosh. . . ."

Awestruck, both boys watched as Anna tended to Sam.

"Next time, watch where you're going. We could have all got stung, stupid," Nathan said to his brother.

Derek's chin went up. "You're not supposed to say that no more, remember? Sam said so. 'Cause we're brothers."

"Sam says we're special 'cause we're brothers," Nathan explained to Anna. "He never had no brother."

"Yeah, and we're supposed to be nice to each other and look out for each other," Derek added.

Anna's hands froze in their work. "Did Sam say that?"

"Uh-huh." Derek nodded earnestly.

Nathan's head bobbed in unison with his brother's.

She coated the bee sting with baking soda, working gently. She couldn't see Sam's face, but he sat still and looked at no one. He rose abruptly when she was finished and headed for the back door.

"Come on, boys, let's clean those fish. I'm hungry."

Anna's heart ached a little as she watched him leave.

She prepared their noon meal, Molly clinging to her skirt and Elizabeth in one arm. Sam broke up a water battle the boys got into when he sent them out back to wash, and set the table. Derek didn't like the peas, Nathan wanted to bring Shadow into the kitchen, Molly turned over her cup and spilled milk in Sam's lap.

The afternoon progressed no better. Elizabeth refused to sleep, Nathan fell and ripped his trousers, and Shadow dug under the chicken coop. Molly turned over the sack of flour in the pantry and was so frightened by Sam when he attempted to sweep it up that she knocked over the cornmeal. Feathers hid under the stove and showed no signs of coming out.

"Come along, Molly, I need your help." Anna held out her hand and shifted Elizabeth higher on her shoulder. "Derek, Nathan, you two come along too."

Sam placed the broom and dust pan back in the pantry and looked at Anna with the same questioning eye as the boys.

"I've got to get Elizabeth to sleep a bit, and I need your help." Anna took Molly's hand. "Come along."

Derek followed but Nathan hung back. He looked up at Sam. "Do I got to go too?"

Sam wished he'd been called on to help get the baby to sleep. He didn't remember the last time he'd worked this hard.

"I need Nathan outside with me for a while," he said to Anna. "He'll be in soon."

Anna nodded and took the other three down the hall and into her bedroom. "We have to help Elizabeth with her nap today. Slip off your shoes and lie down."

The children did as she asked, their tiny shoes dropping to the floor as they climbed onto the bed. She laid the baby between them. "Close your eyes now so Elizabeth will do the same."

Molly sat up. "You too."

"No, I—" Anna stopped. The bed looked awfully inviting, and it was important the children got their rest. "Well, all right. For a few minutes."

Anna kicked off her slippers and stretched out on her side next to Molly. The little girl snuggled close, pressing her back against Anna's chest.

It felt good, having the warm, soft little body next to her. She stroked Molly's hair and reached farther to pat the baby's back. Derek gave her a sleepy smile then buried his head in the pillow and closed his eyes.

It felt good, Anna thought again. It felt right. Children were the most wonderous gift of all. She closed her eyes thinking of all the children in the world who had no one to hold them, no one to cuddle them. Anna tightened her arm around Molly. She'd cuddle everyone she could, once she got her orphanage.

In the barn, Sam and Nathan were busy feeding the horses.

"Have you got chores at home?" Sam asked as he held open the lid to the grain barrel.

On tiptoes, Nathan leaned down and scooped the grain into the measuring can. "Yeah. Some. Papa does most of them."

"With a big fellow like you there to help?"

A proud smile crossed Nathan's face as he climbed the stall and dumped the grain into the trough, spilling only a little in the process.

Sam looked around the barn. "Well, I guess that's about it for now."

He frowned. "Do I got to go take a nap now?"

"Let's have a seat in the shade for a spell and rest a bit," Sam told him.

He led the way to the bench by the wall of the barn, bathed in the afternoon shade. Sam took off his hat and sat down. Nathan scooted onto the bench beside him.

The boy pointed to the scar on Sam's temple. "What happened?"

"Horse threw me." He wasn't about to tell anybody, not even a child, that he'd fallen off.

"Gosh."

Sam rolled back his sleeve and pointed to a scar on his forearm. "See that? That's where I got into a knife fight."

Nathan's eyes widened. Tentatively he reached out and touched the scar with the tip of his finger. "Gosh. A real fight?"

Sam nodded. "Yep."

"My papa says you're not supposed to fight. He says the Bible says so."

"Your papa is right." Sam rolled down his sleeve. "But sometimes, a man has got to fight. He's got to stand up for himself."

Nathan frowned. "Yeah? Like when?"

Sam rubbed his chin. "Well, like when somebody is trying to hurt you."

"Papa says you're supposed to turn the other cheek. It's in the Bible like that."

"It's in the Bible all right," Sam agreed. He shrugged. "Sometimes, though, a man's got to make his own decisions."

"Like if somebody is trying to push you down?"

Sam thought for a moment. "Yeah."

"Or take away your lunch pail?"

Sam looked down at the boy. He seemed so small and frail, carrying a load of troubles on his slim shoulders.

"Somebody been bothering you?"

Nathan looked away and nodded. "Eddie. At school. He's always hitting me and calling me names, and one time he took away my pail and I didn't have nothing to eat all day."

"Did you tell the teacher?" Sam asked.

He looked up at Sam, anger in his expression. "Yeah, but Eddie called me a baby and he hit me again anyway. 'Cause he knows my papa says I can't hit him back. How come God wants me to get hit all the time?"

"God doesn't want that."

"Then how come my pa says to turn the other cheek? My pa will be real mad at me if I don't."

Sam ran his fingers through his hair and blew out a heavy breath. "I don't know all there is to know about God or the Bible, Nathan. And I can't say your pa is wrong, because he isn't. But sometimes you've got to make up your own mind about things. Sometimes you've got to listen to your own heart."

They were quiet for a long moment, and Sam realized he'd stumbled upon the cause of Nathan's hostility toward Derek.

"Hitting Derek won't make up for Eddie picking on you,"

Sam said softly. "Derek is just a little fellow. He looks up to you because you're his big brother."

Nathan nodded. "Ma says Derek has to go to school next year."

"He'll be glad to have you there to look out for him."

"'Cause we're brothers?"

Sam smiled. "Yes. Because you're brothers."

Nathan studied the tips of his boots, then looked up at Sam. "Too bad you didn't never have no brothers."

The loss of something he'd never had bore heavily on Sam. He patted Nathan's knee. "Let's go up to the house. Maybe we can sneak a couple of cookies before the others wake up."

Nathan slid off the bench and walked with Sam across the field.

The afternoon wore on into early evening, with the children needing constant attention. By the time their parents arrived, Sam and Anna were exhausted.

"Oh, no, they were no trouble at all," Anna said as she handed Elizabeth up to Sarah seated in the wagon beside Jamie.

Sam lifted the boys onto the wagon. "You two come over anytime and we'll do some more fishing."

Derek leaned between his mother and father sitting together on the wagon seat. "We founded a special place, Pa, way up in the hills."

"There's an old swing there, and Sam says next time we come he's going to fix it for us," Nathan added.

Jamie offered his hand to Sam. "Thanks for looking after my young 'uns."

Sam shook his hand. "You've got a good family here. You ought to be proud."

Anna and Sam waved good-bye as the Calhoun family drove away. Wearily they trudged to the house and collapsed on the front steps. Anna's arms ached from holding the baby all day. Sam's neck hurt each time he moved his head.

They sat in silence for a long moment. Finally Sam pulled his white handkerchief from his pocket. He waved it weakly. "Truce?"

Anna nodded wearily. "Truce."

She was tired. Tired from the children, tired of fighting with Sam, tired of that damnable money that was still wreaking havoc with her life.

"There must be some other way to settle this."

After spending a week's time and energy, neither was any closer to finding the money than when they'd started.

Sam leaned back on the step behind him. He liked looking at Anna from this angle. "You were real good with the children today. I can see why you want to open an orphanage."

She turned on the step and looked back at him. "Does this mean you're giving up on the money?"

Sam shook his head. "No. But if I know you, you'll find a way to get that orphanage, regardless."

Tired as she was, a little smile crept over her lips. "I am a bit headstrong. My mother warned me about it."

"I wish somebody would have warned me."

Anna laughed. "What was that special place Derek was telling his pa about?"

Sam lifted his shoulders. "I figured you knew about it. A place back in the hills with a tree swing and a little stream running by. Right pretty little spot, nearly hidden behind a stand of white pines. You've never seen it?"

"No." Anna shook her head. "It must have been the folks' who rented the farm when we weren't here."

"Maybe so." A long silence passed before he spoke again. A soft, cooling breeze wafted by. "We haven't solved our problem with the money."

"You could just leave," she suggested lightly.

He sat forward and braced his forearms against his knees. "Can't do that."

Anna twirled a stray lock of hair around her index finger. "Maybe if you hadn't been so wasteful with your money all these years you could have bought yourself a farm by now."

His brows went up. "How much do you think a ranch hand earns?"

"I'm talking about the money from all the banks and trains your father robbed."

Sam frowned. "He didn't give that money to me. He didn't even keep any of it for himself."

She sat up straighter. "You mean that what they said about Jimmy Rowe was really true? He gave the money away?"

"Damn right. His gang kept a share for their families, and he settled some on the folks that took me in. But the rest he handed out to people in need, people the government had stolen from. Like they stole from him."

"But it wasn't his money to give away. Surely you don't think what he did was right."

Sam shook his head. "He was a soldier, fighting for what he believed in. After the war was over, he had nothing to go home to, so he kept on fighting the Yankees. Robbing their trains, hitting their banks, doing what he could to keep them out of the South. After a while, he was in too deep. He couldn't quit."

A pain of sympathy and regret squeezed Anna's heart. "Did you see your pa much?"

"Some." He rubbed his forehead and looked down at Anna. "But I wouldn't have taken any of that money from him, even if he'd offered."

"Yet you'll take the money that's hidden here."

His expression hardened. "My pa was killed because of that money. He was left laying in the dirt to bleed to death like an animal."

Anna shuddered. "I'd heard that. It's . . . awful." But it had never seemed awful to her before. She'd thought Jimmy Rowe got what he deserved. Yet now, knowing he was Sam's papa, it seemed callous and cold.

"The government owes me now." Sam tapped his finger against his chest. "Me."

They both had too much at stake to work out a compromise, but Anna tried.

"How about if we turn in the money and I split the reward with you?"

"Half of five hundred instead of fifty thousand? Never." Sam stroked his chin. "What do you say if you take me to the money and I give you five hundred, same as the reward."

"But I have to turn in the money. It's the only way to clear my family's name."

It was useless. They both knew it and were too tired to argue about it.

Anna rose. "I'm going to take a bath."

Sam followed her up the steps. "I'll help you with the water."

It was too personal a task, and she should have told him no. But he was so strong. Anna watched as he went down the hallway ahead of her. His shoulders were wide and his arms heavily muscled. He could accomplish the job with such ease, and she would have to struggle if she faced it alone. For a fleeting second, the thought of having him with her forever was a comforting one, for his strength was not in his muscles alone.

Sam heated the water and filled the wooden tub inside the pantry for Anna. He still bathed in the creek, for a number of reasons.

"Thank you." Anna stood by the door, her wrapper and night rail draped over her arm.

Sam placed the bucket by the cookstove. The house seemed quieter now, the room smaller—and Anna prettier. "Take all the time you need. I've got chores to see to."

He went outside and breathed deeply. The sun was going down and the air was cool. The hills behind the house drew his attention and he gazed at them as he had so many times, wondering where among them the money was hidden.

It was his future. Everything he'd dreamed of since he was a boy. A home he belonged in, a family of his own, a life he could be proud of.

It was all out there.

Sam heard water splash in the tub.

Wasn't it?

CHAPTER 11

Whatever had caused her to be so agreeable all of a sudden, Sam didn't know. But he didn't question it; he just took advantage of it.

Sitting beside him on the wagon seat, Anna gazed off toward the mountains. The woman was always contemplating something, he thought as he stole a glance at her. He wondered if she suspected the real reason he'd wanted to go into town this morning.

Sam pulled the team to a stop in front of Palmer's General Store and helped Anna down. His hands lingered at her waist a moment longer than was necessary.

"I need to talk to the blacksmith about getting the horses shod," Sam explained. "Do you want to do some shopping on your own for a while?"

Anna nodded and headed off down the street. Sam watched her bustle bobbing through the crowd of Saturday shoppers. She was quiet today—too quiet—it made him jumpy.

But he'd gotten the time alone he needed, so he headed in the opposite direction.

Jonas Fry jumped when Sam entered the express office.

"Morning, Jonas."

He busied himself at his desk behind the counter, stacking and shuffling the papers there. "Morning," he mumbled without looking up.

"I've been expecting a telegram. Has anything come in?" He should have heard from Otis DuBerry in Raleigh a couple of days ago. Sam was getting anxious.

"Well, let's have a look-see." Jonas peered up at the pigeon holes above his desk. "Just this one. But it's for your wife."

"Who?"

Jonas looked over the tops of his spectacles. "Anna. She's your wife, isn't she?"

Sam cleared his throat. "Well, yes . . . but—"

"Came in last night. I was going to send it out to your place this afternoon." Jonas passed the envelope across the counter.

Sam tapped it against his palm. "That's it? Nothing for me?"

Jonas averted his eyes. "If anything comes in, I'll send it out to you."

Sam nodded and left the express office. On the boardwalk he looked down at the telegram addressed to Anna Fletcher. It was bad enough that he hadn't heard from Otis DuBerry, but a telegram for Anna could only mean more trouble. He glanced around, then ripped the envelope open.

Sam cursed softly. It was worse than he'd imagined. Anna's uncle was on his way to the farm. He'd arrive any day.

Anna wrung her hands and bounced on her toes, unsure of what to do. It had seemed so clear a few days ago, but now she wasn't sure.

She stilled her runaway thoughts—nothing was different, she told herself. Nothing. Certainly Sam had seemed like a different person the day the Calhoun children were at the farm—caring, tender-hearted, kind. But that had changed as soon as they were gone. He was never going to let her get to that money. Anna knew she had to take matters into her own hands.

She looked up at the door to the sheriff's office. She had to talk to Brett.

Cautiously, she went inside. It was a small, dim room with a cluttered desk and racks of guns on the wall. She glimpsed the jail cells down the hall. She shivered and her stomach pitched; it made her think of her father.

Sheriff Pond set aside his coffee cup and rose from behind his desk. He was a slender, clean-shaven man who looked more like a clerk than a sheriff. "Can I help you, ma'am?"

Anna clutched her reticule to keep her hands from shaking. "I'm looking for Brett—Deputy Morgan."

The sheriff squinted at her. "Aren't you that Fletcher girl?"

Anna's cheeks colored. She'd never escape that stigma. It reinforced her notion that she was doing the right thing.

"Yes," she replied. "Is he here?"

"Nope. Don't expect him back before nightfall." He eyed her curiously. "What you need him for?"

"Nothing," she said quickly and backed toward the door.

"I'll tell him you came by."

Anna hurried outside without answering. It had been pure luck that Sam had wanted to come into town this morning, allowing her this opportunity to seek out Brett. It might be weeks before she got the chance again.

She threaded her way down the crowded boardwalk. Somehow, she'd have to figure a way to see him.

Sam was already in Palmer's General Store when she arrived, talking with several men around the pickle barrel. She eased between the aisle of yard goods and cooking utensils to catch her breath after the brisk walk.

Ben Atkins was standing with Sam, she noted as she peered between a blue-speckled coffee pot and a copper kettle. She hadn't expected to see him until church tomorrow. Anna smoothed down the skirt of her blue print dress. Maybe she couldn't talk to Brett today, but Ben was right here, and he was an important part of her plan as well.

"Sam, honey. There you are." She smiled sweetly as she glided across the store.

The men tipped their hats and murmured a greeting, with the single exception of Sam. A guarded look crossed his face as she joined them.

"Have you ordered the supplies, sugar?" She touched him gently on the arm.

His brows drew together. "No, I was waiting for you."

She smothered a giggle behind her hand. "You're such a dear. But you know I don't know a thing about what to get. You go on and order." She turned her smile on Ben. "I'll just have a nice, neighborly chat with Ben. Let's step outside into the sun. I'm getting a little chill in here."

Without waiting, Anna slid her arm through Ben's and pulled him outside, leaving Sam behind. They stood in the morning sunshine beside the wagon.

"How are things going for you, Ben? My mother used to say what a good farmer you were."

Ben rubbed his hand over his whiskered chin to hide the faint blush. "Elsa said that, did she?"

"Oh, yes, all the time. I remember quite well how you used to come over and tend to things that needed fixing. Mamma thought it was grand," Anna told him. "Papa wasn't much of a farmer. You remember."

"Yeah, I remember." His expression grew somber. "I remember what a pretty young girl Elsa was, sweet and kind as the day was long. Nobody could figure why she up and married him. Why, it was done before I had a chance to—"

Ben stopped and drew in a deep breath. "Your pa was a good man. Always neighborly, as best he could be. Had me over for supper so I wouldn't have to be alone so much. I appreciated everything he done for me. Guess I should have told him at the time. Who'd have thought. . . ."

"I'm sure Papa knew how you felt," Anna offered.

Ben shook his head. "Naw. I should have told him. Maybe I'll send him a letter up there to the prison. I'm not much with writing, but I can get by. I guess the man ought to know what I'm saying, even if I should have said it years ago."

"No!" Anna pressed her lips together. No one knew her pa had died, thanks to Brett caring enough to keep the news to himself and save her from being the object of more gossip; surely word of his death would only stir up the town again. And though she felt close to Ben and carried fond memories of him, she wouldn't be the one to make that fact known.

She smiled. "What I mean is, no need to worry about how the letter will turn out. Papa would like to hear from you, just the same."

Ben nodded. "I guess you're right."

Anna glanced over her shoulder at the general store. Sam would be out any minute and she had to speak to Ben in private. The older man seemed to be lost in the past again, but she was running out of time. She came right to the point.

"Ben, since you're such a good farmer, I was wondering if you'd thought about expanding your farm. I'm planning to sell out and you seem like the perfect buyer since our properties adjoin."

"Huh?" He squinted at her. "But Sam said you all had moved back here permanent."

Sam again. It irritated her no end that he was going around talking on her behalf, ruining her plans. Not wanting her feelings to show, Anna forced a smile. "He's changed his mind. So what about it? Are you interested?"

Ben chuckled. "Naw, honey. Actually I was thinking about asking Sam if he wanted to buy my place. My sister's husband passed on a few months ago down in Savannah, and she's been after me to move down with her. I've about decided to do just that."

"And leave your farm?" Anna was stunned.

"I'm getting too old now to work it alone. Besides, I got no young 'uns to leave it to, so what's the point?" He shrugged indifferently. "Do you think Sam might be interested in buying my place?"

"I might be."

Sam appeared between them, a sack of flour balanced on his shoulder. Anna's hopes sank.

"Come on over to the house and we'll talk about it," Ben said to him.

"Sounds good."

Ben winked. "I got me a jug we can bust open."

Sam laughed. "Count on me."

It was as if she didn't exist anymore. The farm was hers—hers alone—and they were acting as if she should have no say in the matter. But they were men. In their eyes she had no business being involved. It made Anna's blood boil.

She sat on the wagon seat while the supplies were loaded, refusing to look at—let alone speak to—anyone. Finally Sam climbed aboard and headed the team out of town.

"All right, let's have it," he said. "What's wrong?"

Her back stiffened and her nose went a little higher in the air.

"Come on, spit it out. You're going to pop if you don't."
Sam looked down and nudged her with his elbow. "You
know, you're kind of cute when you're mad."

She jerked away from him. "Don't touch me, you worm."

He rolled his eyes skyward. "Just like a dam breaking.
Here it comes."

"You are the lowest, sneakiest polecat I've ever known!"

He shook his head and muttered to himself. "Well, I asked
for it."

"Is there no end to the tricks you'll pull? Would you just
tell me? Is there anything you won't stoop to?"

He looked down at her. Her eyes were blazing, her cheeks
flushed. She really was cute when she was mad, he decided,
though he didn't know why it had taken him so long to realize
it, given the number of times she'd been angry with him.

"What are you talking about now?" he asked calmly.

"Oh!" She flung out both hands. "I can't believe you have
the gall to sit there and pretend you don't know. What gall!
What gall!"

He lifted one shoulder. "Well, are you going to sit there
sputtering all day, or are you going to tell me what's eating
you?"

"As if you don't know." Anna planted her hands on her
hips. "Since you seem to be suffering from another bout of
amnesia, I'll tell you—"

"I knew you would."

"Oh! Stop patronizing me!"

A sly grin curled the corner of his lips. "You know, Mrs.
Rowan, if you could get all of that emotion of yours
harnessed in the right direction, you could satisfy a man's
needs till his dying day."

Anna's mouth clamped shut. Her eyes bulged. Anger roiled
inside her. "How dare you say such a coarse and disgusting
thing to me."

His eyebrows bobbed. "I meant it as a compliment."

Her chin went up a notch. "I do not find that complimentary in the least."

"Well, you ought to. A respectable woman with that kind of
charm is not easy to come by."

"You are crude and vulgar, Sam Rowan, and I forbid you to speak to me that way again."

Their gazes locked in mortal combat. Her eyes were narrow with determination; his, dancing with defiance.

A slow, devilish smile spread over his face. "You've got nice bosoms, too."

Anna gasped in outrage. "You pig. You vile, disgusting pig! Stop this wagon. Stop it right now!"

He sighed heavily. "I'm sorry. I shouldn't have said that." He knew he'd gone too far, but the woman had egged him on. He couldn't abide being told what to do.

"I said stop this wagon. I'm not riding with you another foot!"

"I said I was sorry."

Anna jumped to her feet. "Stop this instant!"

He grabbed her arm. "Sit down before you fall."

"I'll jump if I have to!" She pulled against him to free her arm.

Hampered by the reins in one hand, he tightened his grip on her. Things had suddenly gotten serious. She might really fall and hurt herself.

"Sit down, I told you."

"No!"

"Damn stubborn woman." With a flick of his wrist he whirled her around and pulled her onto his lap. He locked both arms around her.

Anna squirmed and kicked her feet. "Let go of me!"

She worked one arm free and her breasts pressed against his hard chest. His mouth was inches away. She could feel his breath, warm against her skin. And instead of striking him, she curled her hand around his neck and pressed her lips against his.

His mouth was assaulted by the sudden sweetness of her kiss. The sway of the wagon tantalized his chest with the motion of her breasts undulating against him. Soft fingers curled through the hair at his nape. He was mesmerized— tantalized—and thoroughly captivated.

Her unpracticed lips plied his, bringing on a firestorm like none he'd felt before. Slowly her lips parted, and he touched his tongue to the soft warmth of her mouth. She tasted sweet. He held her tight and pressed further. Anna leaned her head back and gave him entrance. He caressed the warm depth of her mouth, slowly, deliberately, making a place for himself where so obviously no man had been before. Then he withdrew, suddenly afraid that his boldness would frighten her. Instead, she followed him, doing as he had done.

Her tongue slid across his teeth, and pressed further, acquainting herself with the hot, masculine taste of his mouth. She lingered, darting in and out, over and over again, while a new burning urge consumed all rational thought.

Panting, their lips parted. They looked at each other, stunned. Anna slid her hand down his chest. She could feel his heart pounding against her palm. She could feel her own heart beating with his.

The wagon hit a pothole, jarring them. Her weight shifted, and she felt his hardness pressing against the back of her leg. Her eyes widened. He looked at her with no apology in his expression.

Anna blushed and tried to push herself off him. He grabbed for her arm to help her up, but she moved quickly and his hand closed around her breast instead.

Anna fell back on his lap to escape his touch, and his maleness again made itself known through the layers of her dress and petticoats, this time pressing against her soft bottom. It grew harder at the touch.

He groaned and covered her mouth again with his. A soft sigh slipped from her lips as his tongue caressed hers and his big hand gently kneaded her breast. Waves of yearning pulsed through her. She splayed her hand across his chest and touched his tiny nipple. He groaned again and plunged his tongue deeper inside her. Her hips moved rhythmically against his maleness, sending fingers of heat through both of them.

Suddenly Sam broke off their kiss again. He had to stop now, or he wouldn't be able to stop at all. They looked at each other, both breathing heavily, lips wet from their kisses and their desires.

Anna blushed. "I'm—I'm sorry. . . ."

"No, don't. Don't say anything." Sam sat her on the seat beside him. She straightened her dress. He adjusted his trousers.

An awkward silence stretched between them. Birds chattered in the trees and the breeze blew gently. Sam and Anna gazed off in the distance, looking everywhere but at each other. Finally, he picked up the reins and urged the team forward. Anna stared at her hands folded in her lap.

She didn't know how she would ever look him in the eye again. She'd behaved like a harlot. What must he think of her!

Anna agonized over her unseemly conduct all the way home. But once they arrived, they busied themselves unloading and putting away the supplies, then preparing their supper. Sam was more quiet than usual as they ate and washed dishes. He then went outside saying he needed to check the livestock.

Anna watched from the window as he crossed the yard and stopped under the oaks. He didn't go up to the barn, but just stood there in the dusk staring at the hills in the distance. For once, she was certain he wasn't thinking about the money that was hidden there. He was remembering her wanton behavior in the wagon this afternoon. Anna cringed. Surely, he now thought her no better than the soiled doves who worked the saloons in town. Tears welled in her eyes.

And she didn't know why it bothered her that he now thought so little of her. How could he think otherwise? Certainly he'd seen how much she'd enjoyed it.

Anna turned away from the window. It was good she'd decided never to marry. What would a man think having such a strumpet for a wife?

Anna paid her proper respects to Reverend Langford as they left church the next morning with Sam at her side. The congregation had spilled out onto the churchyard, chatting in small groups. Sam joined the men by the church steps, and Anna wound her way through the crowd until she found Sarah.

After lying awake most of the night, unsure of how to face Sam, Anna decided to discuss the subject with Sarah. She was the only woman she dared mention it to. But seeing her now, in the cold light of day, Anna didn't dare broach the subject. Instead, she asked her for her peach pie recipe.

Anna glanced across the churchyard at Sam as Sarah rattled off the ingredients. He was tall and handsome and stood out among the other men. A sudden pain constricted her heart.

Any woman would want him. Was her conduct yesterday in the wagon really that bad?

Before she could come to a decision, Brett Morgan appeared beside her, smiling broadly.

"Morning, pretty lady." He swept his hat from his head. "And good morning to you, Mrs. Calhoun. And surely it's too fine a day for such a sad face. What's troubling you, Anna?"

She cast a quick glance in Sam's direction. Yesterday's incident in the wagon was further proof that she had to get Sam Rowan out of her life.

With no intention of telling Brett what she'd been thinking, she latched on to the notion that this might be the only chance she would get to see Brett for quite some time. She needed to talk to him. If he couldn't help her, no one could.

Sarah's baby started fussing and Anna took the opportunity to slip away. Brett followed her.

"You said I could come to you if I had a problem," Anna began.

His expression grew somber as he edged closer. "You know you can count on me, Anna."

She hardly knew where to begin.

"Go ahead, Anna," he encouraged. "You can tell me anything."

She took a deep breath and closed her eyes. Yes, she told herself, telling Brett was the right thing to do.

Across the churchyard Sam was talking with Jamie as Nathan and Derek ran between them. The boys laughed and darted through the crowd, racing each other to the church steps.

Sam smiled. "Those are two fine boys you have there, Jamie."

He nodded proudly. "And getting along much better now, thank the Lord."

"Has Nathan quit hitting Derek?"

"I think I took care of it, once and for all."

Sam was relieved. Nathan and the schoolyard bully had been on his mind since the boy had confided in him. But Sam didn't know anything about giving advice to a child. It was good his pa had handled it.

Jamie nodded. "I had a long talk with Nathan and explained how God wants us to live our lives. It must have stuck with him because he's getting on just fine with Derek now."

"That's good." But Sam couldn't help worrying about what would happen when Nathan went to school in the morning. He wondered if Jamie had really handled the problem.

Sam was searching the crowd for the boy when he spotted Brett Morgan approaching Anna. Sam's belly coiled into a knot. Morgan was wearing that moon-sick smile like he was courting her. For all anybody knew, he and Anna were man and wife. Yet Morgan acted as if she was there for the picking. It riled him, but good.

Sam pulled his hat low on his forehead and strode across the churchyard.

"It's time to go home."

Brett's eyes met his in a silent challenge, but Sam stared him down. He took Anna's arm and led her away.

He was in no mood for her sharp tongue and didn't want to have words right here in front of the whole congregation. He expected her to protest, but she said nothing. In fact, Anna almost looked guilty. That made his belly knot tighter.

At the wagon Sam lifted Anna onto the seat and was ready to climb up himself when Charles Hampton walked up. Sam had the feeling he'd been waiting for him, and he was in even less of a mind to deal with the retired clerk from Richmond. Sam gave him a curt nod.

"Morning." Hampton tipped his hat in Anna's direction, then turned to Sam.

But he gave the man no opportunity to speak. "Ben Atkins says he's looking to sell his farm. You ought to talk to him. That is, if you're honestly looking to buy a place."

Sam's tone and glare threw down a challenge. Hampton glanced at Anna then back at Sam. "Much obliged for the information." He lingered for a moment then walked away.

Doubly annoyed now, Sam climbed onto the wagon and left the church.

Once at the farm, Sam changed from his Sunday clothes and went out to the barn. His days had been filled with hard, back-breaking chores before he had come here, and now he needed the work to burn off the anger that had built up inside him, even though it was Sunday. He cleaned the stalls, fed the horses and cow, then took the hammer and banged out his feelings repairing the barn roof.

The day grew hotter. Sweat trickled down his face and soaked his shirt as he pounded nails into the boards and refitted the sheets of tin that he'd recovered from the corral and fields.

Sam sat back and wiped his brow with his shirtsleeve. From his position on the roof he could see out into the field behind the house, past the creek, and to the hills. The sky overhead was a rich blue, and bright sunlight bathed the greens of the meadows and trees in intense light. It was beautiful here, he decided, as beautiful as Kentucky.

The tension that had held him tight since church this morning left as a cooling breeze blew in. Anna came into his thoughts. His gaze settled on the house. What was she doing in there? Reading her Bible? Maybe she'd started preparing their meal.

Sam leaned back on one elbow and pushed his hat up. It wasn't Anna's fault that Morgan bastard kept coming around. She was a pretty woman. Men were going to look at her. She'd done nothing to encourage him. He shouldn't take his anger out on her.

From his trouser pocket he pulled the crumpled telegram he'd gotten in town the day before. Sam opened it and read the message again. He hadn't told Anna her uncle was on his way, and now seemed like a good time to give her the news. The man was the only family she had and seeing him would make her happy, even if it delayed his own plans for a few days.

Sam picked up the hammer. He'd fix the front step too, he decided. Anna's ankles were so tiny she'd break them for sure if she fell on that step.

He slid the telegram back into his pocket and climbed down the ladder.

"Brett? What are you doing here?"

Anna slipped out onto the front porch and closed the door behind her.

"You were about to tell me something at church this morning before Rowan showed up. I came out here to find out what it was." His brows were furrowed, his mouth drawn in a hard line.

She glanced around quickly. "You shouldn't have come like this."

"I always told you, Anna, to come to me if anything was wrong." His face softened. "Now, tell me what's bothering you."

"It's not that—it's just—" She couldn't take a chance that Sam might overhear her conversation. Anna sighed. "I can't go into it now, Brett."

"We go back a long way, Anna, you and me. We're alg like family."

Anna twisted her fingers in her apron. "I can't talk Not now."

He nodded slowly. "All right."

They walked together to the edge of the yan had tethered his horse.

"I still want to know what's on your mind hat on. "Promise me you'll tell me soon

Anna gazed up at him. He was say wanted to hear. He'd done so many t about her. But Brett's eyes smolder she stepped too close, she'd get h

"I don't know, Brett."

"Promise me." He put his f her face. A smile parted his l I'll haul you off to jail fo flowers."

A little laugh bubbled up. "Brett, what am I going to do with you?"

He chuckled and gave her chin a squeeze. "I'll be back," he promised.

Maybe he'd get the sickle out and cut these weeds, Sam thought as he rounded the corner of the house. The flowers were trying to come up and Anna surely would like the place spruced up a bit. Especially since her uncle was coming. The picket fence needed repairs but that wouldn't take much time either, he decided. Just some whitewash and a few—

Sam froze in his tracks. Across the yard, Anna and Brett were laughing into each other's eyes.

A hot flash of pain shot up his spine and stabbed his chest. He stood there watching while Brett caressed Anna's face and spoke softly to her and they laughed together. He watched as Brett climbed onto his horse and Anna stood by the road, waving as he rode away.

Sam's chest constricted. His limbs shook.

Anna called farewell to Brett. Her voice carried like a melody on the gentle breeze.

Sam's belly coiled into a knot. He looked down at the telegram in his fingers. His hand curled into a fist.

He shoved the paper into his pocket and walked away.

"Uncle Lloyd? Uncle Lloyd? Oh my word! Uncle Lloyd!"
Anna bolted off the porch steps and raced across the yard the horse that had stopped by the picket fence. She threw rms around her uncle as he climbed to the ground.
an't believe you're here! It's so wonderful to see you."
d Caldwell was a stout man, whose waistline told of chant for good cooking. His hair and mustache were ith age, and his eyes, weakened by hours of reading, d by small spectacles that frequently slid to the end e.
ped Anna in his full embrace. "Don't act so oney. I saw you waiting for me."
st sitting here thinking. A visitor left a few nd—" Anna stopped herself, not wanting to go

into Brett's visit. "Anyway all that matters is that you're here. Why didn't you tell me you were coming?"

He lifted his carpet bag and satchel from the saddle horn. "You didn't get my telegram?"

"Telegram? No."

He shrugged. "No wonder. Bad storm north of here. Lines are probably down. Now, let's get inside. I want to hear everything you've been up to these past three months, and more important, whatever possessed you to come back to this place."

Anna slid her arm around him as they walked toward the house. She was so glad to see him. She hadn't realized how much she'd missed him.

Lloyd eyed the house. "Looks like the place could use considerable fixing up. I don't think it's safe, you living out here alone."

"But I'm not—" Sam!

Anna stopped still in her tracks. Sam! How was she going to explain him living here? Living here with her!

She dashed up the steps and into the house in front of her uncle. She had to get to Sam. She had to tell him her uncle was here and be certain they had their facts straight on their supposed marriage.

Anna turned in a nervous circle and laced her fingers together as her uncle followed her into the foyer. "Just make yourself comfortable, Uncle Lloyd. I'm going to run down to the spring house and get a jug of cider."

Lloyd's right brow crept upward. "What's wrong?"

"Nothing. Nothing at all." Anna backed down the hall away from him. "I've got a—a surprise for you. Yes that's it. A surprise. Just wait here. I'll be right back."

Anna bolted down the hall before her uncle could voice the confusion that reflected in his face. She raced through the kitchen, gathered her skirt, and leaped down the back steps. Curls bouncing, she ran across the yard and flung open the barn door.

"Sam! Sam!" She stepped inside and turned in a circle, her footsteps silent on the dirt floor. It was cool in the barn's dim interior. It smelled of horses, leather, and hay.

"Sam!" Where was he? She gnawed her bottom lip, her heart pounding. The stallion in the stall beside her snorted. "Sam! I need you!"

"I'm right here."

She whirled and saw him step through the door that led from the corral. His wide shoulders blocked the light. His face was hidden in the shadow of his dark hat. He lingered in the doorway.

"Oh, Sam, thank goodness." She splayed her hand across her chest, nearly out of breath. "You're not going to believe this. My uncle is here. Here! We've got to get our story straight. He's bound to ask about our wedding."

Slowly he pulled off one leather glove. "Is that so?"

"Yes. Now listen. Tell him we met in Salem right after he left for Boston."

Sam slowly pulled off his other glove. "Okay."

"And that we fell madly in love."

He nodded. "Got it."

Anna paced fitfully then stopped suddenly. "He might be hurt that we didn't hold off on the wedding until he got back. Tell him—tell him we were so much in love we couldn't wait that long."

"Couldn't wait," he repeated.

She whirled around and snapped her fingers. "And you must tell him that we're here to sell the farm because that's what I told him in my letter."

Sam tossed his gloves aside. "Anything else?"

She bit down on her lip. "No, I don't think so."

"Okay. Whatever you say."

Anna hurried over and took Sam's arm. She heaved a sigh of relief. "I'd just die if Uncle Lloyd thought even for a second that we weren't really married. Now don't be nervous about meeting him. He'll think you're a fine husband. I know he will."

Sam allowed her to grasp his forearm. "I can be a great husband."

She pulled him toward the door. "I'm sure you can. Come on now, Sam, we have to hurry."

He didn't budge. "I can be the best damn husband money can buy."

Anna froze. She looked at Sam. His eyes were cold. Colder than she'd seen them. Ever. A chill swept over her. She released his arm.

"You are going to tell my uncle we're married, aren't you?"

A smirk twisted his lips slightly. "Oh yes, ma'am. I'll tell him we're married. I'll keep your reputation lily-white." The line of his mouth hardened, and his eyes turned a steely blue. "And all it will cost you is fifty thousand dollars."

CHAPTER 12

"What?" The word slipped through Anna's lips in a whisper. She pushed a strand of hair behind her ear.

Sam stood straighter and hung his thumbs over his belt. "You heard me right."

Dumbly, she shook her head. "You don't mean. . . ."

"I want it all. Every cent of it."

Anna blanched. "You can't be serious."

The line of his mouth hardened. He didn't flinch a muscle.

A silly, inane laugh escaped her lips. "Is this some kind of joke?"

His jaw tightened. Determination was chiseled in every line and curve of his face.

"After all I did for you?" Her brows drew together in disbelief. "After I took you in and nursed you back to health? After all I gave to you unselfishly?"

His cold stare held steady.

"And now you're treating me like—like this?"

He didn't move a muscle.

Anna's temper flared. "You're a bastard. A rotten, sniveling, cold-hearted bastard!"

He shrugged indifferently. "Maybe. But I'll be a rich bastard."

Her hands curled into fists. "I won't let you get away with this. I'll go tell Uncle Lloyd the truth. He'll get the sheriff out here and have your filthy hide hauled off to jail!"

Anna spun around and headed for the door, her heart racing.

"And have the whole town know we've been living out here together all this time?"

She turned, her cheeks flushed. "We haven't been living together! Not like you mean."

He stepped closer. "And who's going to believe that?"

"Uncle Lloyd will believe me. And I don't care what the town thinks, anyway." She flung the words at him, knowing there was no way he could stop her now.

"Do you think your uncle is going to believe you're a pure innocent when I tell him exactly how many pairs of pantalettes you own and which ones have lace and which ones have bows?"

Anna gasped.

"And when I go into your room and show him exactly where that little pink dress is hanging, do you think he'll believe you then?" Sam advanced on her. "How about when I describe the mole on your butt?"

Anna's cheeks flamed. "How do you know about that?"

"And when I tell him exactly how big it is and which cheek it's on, is he still going to believe you?"

Shocked, the color drained from Anna's face. Sam came closer, taunting her unmercifully until he was only inches away. He leaned down.

"What's he going to say when I tell him how your breast feels cradled in the palm of my hand?"

"Oh!" Anna swung at him. He grabbed her wrist. Their gazes took over the battle, cold, hard blue against angry, determined brown. She pulled her arm away.

She hated him. Plain and simple. Raw emotion burned into every fiber of her body. It seeped in with every breath she took. It scorched her soul.

She glared at him as the realization came clear to her. Because of Sam Rowan the blight on her family name would never be removed. The dream she'd kept secret since the day she and her mother had left Kemper in disgrace would never be realized. Her act of kindness to this stranger had been her undoing.

She'd find a way, Anna swore silently. Somehow, someway, she would get even with Sam Rowan.

She let out the heavy breath she'd been holding. Her gaze riveted him. "You've left me no choice. You win. It's all yours." The words were bitter on her tongue.

He relaxed his stance but only marginally. "You take me to the money, and I'll play your little game for your uncle."

Anna wanted to slap the words from his lips but didn't. At least she'd have her reputation intact.

She sealed their agreement with a curt nod. "Agreed."

The look of grim relief shadowed his face. He took her arm. "Come on. Let's go get it."

She pulled away. "What kind of fool do you take me for? I'm certainly not going to take you to the money this minute."

"And why the hell not?"

"What's my uncle going to think when my supposed husband suddenly abandons me and the farm? I'm not taking you anywhere until my uncle is gone."

He didn't like it. She saw it in the set of his jaw and the tenseness in his shoulders. Yet he had no choice. It was a small victory, but she savored it.

"All right." He pointed a finger at her. "But if you don't tell me where that money is buried as soon as he's gone, I'll track him down and spill everything."

She met his harsh gaze. "And if you don't keep your end of the bargain, so help me God, I'll take out a full-page ad in every newspaper in the state and announce the money is hidden here. This farm will be so thick with treasure hunters you won't have room to swing a shovel."

They sealed their pact with a final harsh stare.

"Come on. Let's get this over with." Sam headed for the door.

Anna stopped him with a hand on his arm. "I expect a fifty thousand-dollar husband."

His brows furrowed. "Don't you worry your pretty little head. You'll get your money's worth."

Sam gestured grandly toward the door. "After you, Mrs. Rowan."

Anna's stomach was in a knot by the time they got into the house. Above all, she had to convince her uncle she was

married to Sam. Somehow, she had to see this charade
through.

He was in the parlor, pacing among the shrouded furniture.
Anna forced herself to smile.

"Uncle Lloyd, this is—" She cleared her throat. "This is
Sam Rowan, my hu—hu—"

He stepped from beside her and offered his hand. "I'm Sam
Rowan. Anna's husband. Pleased to meet you, sir."

He peered at Sam over the top of his spectacles, then
accepted his hand. Lloyd turned to Anna, his brows drawn
together in a deep frown.

"Do you want to tell me what this is all about, child?"

Anna twisted her fingers together and forced a bigger
smile. "It's true. Sam is my hu—hu—"

"Husband." Sam finished the word for her, then turned to
Lloyd. "I owe you an apology for not talking to you first and
asking for her hand proper. I hope you won't hold it against
me."

Lloyd eyed him skeptically but didn't say anything.

"I fell in love with this niece of yours the minute I laid eyes
on her. I thought she was the prettiest little thing I'd ever
seen. I knew my life would never be complete if I didn't have
her at my side." Sam circled her shoulder and drew her closer.

The old doctor studied Sam, not speaking.

"You don't know me, Dr. Caldwell, so all I can do is ask
you to take me at my word and have some faith in your
niece's judgment." Sam squeezed her again. "I love Anna.
She's the best thing that ever happened to me. I'll take care of
her and treat her right. She'll never want for anything. I
swear."

Lloyd considered his words for a long moment, then asked
Anna. "Do you love this man?"

Her stomach rolled over. Anna glanced up at Sam, then at
her uncle. "Well . . . I . . ."

Sam's grip tightened on her shoulder and he gave her a
little shake.

"Yes!" Anna blurted out her answer. "Oh, yes. Yes, I do,
Uncle Lloyd."

He nodded slowly. "How did you two meet?"

This is what she feared most from her uncle, a barrage of questions about a past that didn't exist. She cleared her throat. "Well, Sam and I met when . . . well, it was when—"

"It was the luckiest day of my life," Sam broke in. "Of course, it didn't start out that way. I was stupid enough to fall off my horse and bust my head open. Anna did a fine job of patching me up."

Anna smiled up at him, relieved that he hadn't told her uncle they'd met over a bullet wound—one she'd threatened to inflict herself.

"So you two met in Salem," Lloyd concluded.

Anna's head bobbed. "That's right."

He eyed Sam. "I don't recall knowing any Rowans in Salem."

"I'm from Virginia, originally. More lately from Kentucky," Sam said. "My family's all passed on now, and I came to Salem looking to start over."

"And you two got married there?"

Anna nodded. "It wasn't too long after you left for Boston, Uncle Lloyd."

His frown deepened. "Then why didn't you write to me and tell me what you were doing?"

Her eyes widened. Why wouldn't she have written her uncle and told him she'd gotten married? Her mind spun. She needed a brilliant excuse—fast.

Anna looked up at Sam, desperation in her eyes. He gave her a squeeze and smiled broadly. "Go on, honey. Tell him."

Her long lashes fluttered rapidly. "Well, Uncle Lloyd, actually, I . . . ah . . . I—"

"Never mind, sugar, I'll tell him." Sam took over the conversation again. "It was my fault, anyway. You see, Dr. Caldwell, Anna wanted to wait until you got back from your trip up north and have a proper engagement and a proper wedding. In fact, she insisted. She didn't want to make a move without you there at her side. But I'm not a patient man and I didn't want to wait. I was afraid some other man would come along and snatch her away from me. It took a lot of talking but I finally convinced her. So don't hold it against Anna. It was all my doing. I hope you won't hold it against me either, Dr. Caldwell." Sam looked down at Anna snuggled beneath his arm. "I just love her so much I couldn't stand the thought of losing her."

The rich timbre of his voice and the warmth in his eyes held Anna spellbound. She gazed up at him basking in the glow of his loving words, secure in the feel of his strong arm around her.

Her uncle's intrusive voice-clearing brought her back to reality. "You're not angry with me—I mean—us, are you Uncle Lloyd?"

He looked Sam up and down one final time. "No. No, I don't see how I could be when Sam here is so honest and open. Besides, what's done is done. Welcome to the family, son."

The men shook hands and pounded each other on the back. Anna heaved a silent sigh of relief. It was over and done with. Sam had convinced her uncle they were husband and wife and had even taken the blame on himself for all the wrongdoing in the matter. And he had sounded so convincing at confessing his love for her. For a moment, she'd almost believed him herself.

But why shouldn't his performance be believable, Anna realized. She was paying him fifty thousand dollars for it.

"Honey, why don't you take Dr. Caldwell out to the—"

"Call me Lloyd."

"Thank you, Lloyd, I will. Honey, take Lloyd out to the kitchen for some coffee while I get his horse bedded down." Sam muzzled his lips against Anna's ear and whispered, "Keep him out there while I clear my things out of the spare room."

He ended the message with a warm kiss against her ear that tingled all the way down to her toes. Flustered, Anna took her uncle's arm and led the way to the kitchen.

"This won't take a minute," she said as she stoked the fire in the cookstove.

Lloyd seated himself at the table. "This comes as quite a shock, Anna. Are you happy?"

"Oh, yes. Yes. Very." She kept her back to him, afraid he would read the lie in her face. She changed the subject. "How does it feel being back in Kemper again? Back in the house? It must bring up a lot of old memories from growing up here."

"That it does." Lloyd sat back in his chair. "I've got some catching up to do with the folks around here. Haven't seen them since the trial."

Anna cringed. It seemed everything in her life revolved around the robbery in some way.

"It helped Mamma so much when you came down from Salem and stood by her during that time. I remember her telling me that she could always count on you." Anna placed the coffeepot on the stove and turned to face her uncle. "I was grateful, too, that you took us in after Papa was sent up to Raleigh. You did so much for me, Uncle Lloyd. You got me away from this place, gave me a chance at a new life. There's no one else who would have done that for me. So it's important you understand about this business with Sam. I wouldn't hurt you for all the money in the world. Truly, I wouldn't."

He held out his arms, and Anna sank to her knees in front of him. He took her hands. "It's a funny thing about love, child. You don't get to pick when it's going to hit you. I'm just glad you found happiness."

Anna closed her eyes and felt the kiss he brushed against her forehead. Right now she had the most expensive happiness in the world—fifty thousand dollars' worth.

Uncle Lloyd told her about his trip to Boston while she poured coffee and sat across the table from him. Feathers curled up in her lap while Anna stroked its soft fur. Things were happening quickly in the medical field these days, and Anna listened attentively; it was an interest they had shared since Anna and her mother had moved in with him.

"You should make a point of seeing Dr. Sawyer while you're here," she suggested.

Lloyd nodded. "I'll do that."

Sam came through the back door. "Your horse is all bedded down for the night."

"Much obliged, Sam." He peered over the top of his spectacles as Sam got a cup from the cupboard and poured coffee for himself. Lloyd's brows drew together as he glanced at Anna idly stroking the cat on her lap.

"Would you like to look around the place?" Sam asked as he sat down beside Anna. "I've got some plans you might be interested in hearing about."

The doctor set his coffee cup aside. "Anna's letter said you were going to sell out."

"We are." The edge on Anna's voice was sharp.

Sam smiled indulgently. "I've decided to keep the place."

"Good. Glad to hear it." Lloyd rose. "Let's clear out of here so Anna can get supper on the table."

Sam's face lit up as it dawned on him what that meant. "Yes, let's do that."

He threw Anna a smug smile as he strode out the back door.

Anna stuck out her tongue as he walked away.

The men returned just as Anna was taking a pan of biscuits from the oven. They were deep in conversation about improvements to the farm. They milled around so that Anna had to squeeze between them, washed their hands at the sink, dripped water on the floor, and left the dish towel in a wad on the sideboard. Sam smiled knowingly at Anna's glare.

"Supper looks great, honey." Sam slid his arm around her waist as she threaded her way past him with the fried chicken, and bent to drop a kiss on her forehead.

Anna pulled away and placed the platter on the table. She hadn't had to cook a whole meal by herself for some time now, and she especially wanted this one to be nice for her uncle. Sam was just gloating because he'd gotten out of helping her, and it annoyed her that he was taking advantage of the situation.

Lloyd caught their exchange. Sam shrugged helplessly as they sat down.

"Anna has been busy helping the ladies at church with their stitchery for the Founders' Day booth," Sam said as he passed the bowl of peas to Lloyd.

His bushy brows rose. "Is that so?"

"Anna's been helping on the sewing and helping out the

neighbors. She spent a whole day cooking for the Huntberrys' barn-raising, and another day looking after the Calhouns' children." Sam smiled proudly. "She's really taken root here."

Anna felt her uncle's gaze on her, and she looked up from her plate. While it was true she had been doing all those things, it was not for the reason Sam implied. Still, she wanted her uncle to believe she was happy here.

Anna smiled. "I've been really busy with all sorts of projects."

Lloyd nodded. "Glad to hear it, but knowing how you feel about coming back to Kemper, I guess I owe it to Sam for getting you involved in things so quickly. Looks like you've got yourself a good husband here." He looked across the table at Sam. "Thank you, son."

Anna nearly choked on her peas. Sam had pawned her off on every old busybody in town, had nailed her shut in her bedroom, and even now, was blackmailing her out of her life's dream—and her uncle thought he was a good husband!

The men went on with their conversation oblivious to Anna's outrage. Finally they wiped their mouths and pushed their plates aside.

"Good supper, sugar." Sam gave her a little hug. "You're usually a lot quicker getting the meal on the table, almost like two people are in the kitchen. But it's okay, honey."

She bristled and continued pushing her food around her plate.

Lloyd sat back and patted his round belly. "Fine supper, fine indeed." He looked across at Sam. "Let's go have a cigar and get out of Anna's way."

"Sure thing, Lloyd." He headed out the door behind the older man.

"You needn't look so smug, Sam Rowan," Anna hissed.

He turned back, unable to wipe the grin from his face. "Did you say something, honey pie?"

"For your information, I'm glad to have you out of my kitchen." She jerked her chin and began gathering the dirty dishes. "You're nothing but a bother, anyway, big as a grizzly bear and always underfoot. I can manage perfectly well without you."

"It breaks my heart to leave my little bride in here, all alone, with so many dirty dishes." Sarcasm dripped from his words. "And it was my turn to wash, too."

Anna drew back a chicken bone ready to fling it at him.

"No, no, darling." He wagged his finger at her. "We don't want Uncle Lloyd to think there's a problem in our love nest."

"Shut your stinking mouth, Sam Rowan, and wipe that goofy grin off your face." Anna planted her hands on her hips. "Just get out of my kitchen and stay out."

"Yes ma'am. Whatever makes you happy."

Anna seethed with anger as the door closed and she heard Sam chuckling.

Her foul mood wore off quickly as she washed and dried the dishes, scrubbed and put away the pots and pans, wiped down the sideboard, swept the floor, and banked the fire in the cookstove. She hung her apron beside the door and appraised her work. It had been easier with Sam's help, she admitted to herself. Easier and quicker.

She stepped out onto the back porch. It was almost dark. Fireflies blinked in the meadow beyond the house and crickets chirped in the distance. From the hills she heard the call of a whippoorwill. The evening breeze was cool, a welcome relief from the heat of the kitchen.

Sam and her uncle were standing at the plot of land that was once the vegetable garden. She wondered how they found so much to talk about. They'd never even met until a few hours ago. Anna crossed the yard toward them. That was Sam, though, surely the friendliest person she'd ever known.

The men stopped talking when Anna approached and Sam drew her to his side. "What took you so long with the dishes, darling? You're usually done in half the time."

She couldn't voice the words that clamored to be said, so Anna clamped her mouth shut and looked away.

Sam gave her a squeeze. "I just missed you, sugar, that's all."

Anna pressed her lips together tightly to hold her anger.

"I've got to go check on the stock." Sam planted a kiss on her forehead and left her alone with her uncle.

Anna shuddered involuntarily. She shook her head to throw

off the bad mood Sam had caused. At last she was alone with her dear uncle, and she had wanted to have him to herself all evening. But he spoke before she had the chance.

"Since your mamma passed on before you were married, Anna, she didn't have the opportunity to talk about certain things that marriage entails." Uncle Lloyd cleared his throat uncomfortably.

A nervous giggle bubbled up as Anna realized what he was about to say. "I'm not a silly young schoolgirl, Uncle Lloyd. I know about . . . that."

He stepped closer and pulled on his mustache. "I'm sure your mamma told you all about the birds and the bees some time ago. But what she couldn't tell you about were the other things."

"Other things?" Alarm spread through Anna. What other things? She didn't know about any other things.

Lloyd slid his arm through hers, and they slowly walked toward the house. "I'm talking about making a home. You didn't get a chance to see it with your folks, you were so young when your pa was sent away. But it's up to you, Anna, to make a home for your husband."

Anna wanted to retch. Every fiber of her being cried out to pull away from her uncle and tell him what a conniving, black-hearted bastard her supposed husband was. Instead all she could do was grit her teeth and listen.

"Sam's a good man," he went on. "I can see he's already done a lot around the place to fix it up. But as I see it, Anna, you haven't done your part. Now, take the house, for example. A man needs a comfortable parlor to come to at the end of a hard day, and you haven't done a thing to fix it up."

"I haven't had time." Anna blurted out the words in her own defense.

"I know that. I understand completely." He patted her arm. "But you're going to have to stop all this church work and neighborly assistance. Sam's a permissive husband—maybe too permissive. A woman's primary responsibility is to her husband and her home."

Anna did a slow burn. Sam had been the one who had involved her in all those activities to occupy her time so he could bilk her out of a fortune. Now she ended up looking like a terrible person.

"And one more thing, Anna, honey."

They had reached the back steps, the evening shadows making it almost impossible to see her uncle's face. But his tone told Anna she was going to like this part of their conversation even less.

"Like I said, you didn't have your ma and pa around to take notice, but it's natural for a husband to be affectionate towards his wife. You act like you can hardly tolerate his touch."

She didn't want that snail-trail of a man to put his hands on her, but she could hardly tell that to her uncle. "I don't think he should be so . . . demonstrative in front of you."

Uncle Lloyd chuckled deep in his belly. "That's my little Anna—always the perfect lady." He took her in his arms. "Don't you feel uncomfortable about a little hug or peck when I'm around. I like to see it, to know you two are in love. I'll make a point of telling Sam the same, just to be sure there's no misunderstanding on his part."

He gave Anna a kiss on the forehead and walked off toward the lamplight that shone in the barn. Glumly, she sank down on the porch steps.

Anna propped her elbows on her knees and planted her chin on the palm of her hands. She gave up her dream of clearing her family name, gave up a fortune in cash, perpetrated a hoax on her only family left in the world, and made a pact with the devil, all to keep her reputation intact and to salvage what honor was left in the Fletcher name. And still—still—it wasn't enough.

Now, on top of it all, she had to be a proper wife.

Anna lowered her head to her knees. Not only did she have to be a proper wife, but a proper wife to Sam Rowan.

"I hope you'll be comfortable in here, Uncle Lloyd."

Anna smoothed out the blanket on the bed in the extra room and plumped up the pillow. This was where Sam usually slept. She wondered how he got his big frame into a bed so small. Did he sleep curled up? On his stomach?

Heat flashed through Anna at the mental image of Sam in the bed and jumped back as if she were bitten.

"I'm sure I'll be fine." Uncle Lloyd ambled into the room behind her, carrying his satchel and carpetbag. He chuckled. "I guess it won't be long until you'll be opening the upstairs rooms. With a man like Sam for a husband, you'll be turning out sons every year."

Anna blushed from head to toe.

"Now, now, don't go looking so shocked by such talk. You're a married woman now." He chuckled again and patted her hand affectionately.

"Is there anything else you need?" It was a stark, little room, furnished with only a bed and bureau. Hardly a fitting place for her uncle to sleep. And for a fraction of a second, Anna almost felt bad that Sam had to sleep in here.

"Can I put your things in the bureau for you?" She had checked the drawers earlier, and as Sam had promised, all his things were removed. The room still smelled vaguely of him, Anna realized. She hoped her uncle wouldn't notice.

"I can take care of my things. You run along. Your husband is waiting for you." Uncle Lloyd kissed her on the cheek and shooed her out the door.

For the first time that day Anna allowed herself to believe things might turn out all right. Uncle Lloyd seemed convinced she was actually married; his approval meant everything to her. She twisted the wedding band on her finger, Sam's mother's wedding band. Now she was grateful she hadn't taken it off.

Anna slipped down the hall into her own room and closed the door behind her. Her emotional state today and the responsibility of doing all the cooking and cleaning had taken its toll. Anna pulled off her slippers and stockings and lit the lantern at her bedside.

A hinge squeaked louder than thunder in a summer sky. She whirled around. Sam strode into the room.

She gasped. "What are you—"

"Shhh." He eased the door shut and waved his hands for silence. "Calm down. I can't very well be knocking on my own bedroom door, now can I?"

"This is not your bedroom."

"Do you want your uncle to think we don't sleep together in the same room?"

His words brought a deep blush to her cheeks. "No—no, of course not."

"Well, then. . . ."

She rubbed the tight muscles of her neck and walked to the bureau. Anna heaved a heavy sigh. "Run on, Sam. I'm awfully tired."

His eyebrows popped upward. "Run on?"

"Yes, run on." Anna pulled open the bureau drawer. "I want to—"

A squeal of horror slipped from her lips as she jerked her hand back from the bureau drawer.

Sam bolted to her side. "What? What's wrong?"

"Your long johns are in my drawer."

He sighed heavily. "Christ, Anna, I thought you'd seen a snake or something coiled up in there."

"I'd rather see a snake than your underwear. What is it doing in there?" she demanded.

"I had to put my things somewhere when I cleaned out my room. What did you want me to do? Pile them up in the hallway?"

Anna crossed the room and threw open the door of her armoire. There hung Sam's shirts and trousers alongside her skirts, dresses, and blouses.

"Take them out. All of them. Get them out of my room this minute."

Sam folded his arms across his chest. "You're being silly, Anna."

Her back stiffened. "No, I'm not."

"You are and you know it. My things are staying in here until your uncle is gone and that's final. I'm not taking any chances on him doubting we're married. I've got too much riding on this. And so have you."

She hated it when he was right. "All right. Now, please just leave so I can go to bed."

He straightened. "Leave? And go where?"

"I don't care. You can sleep wherever you want as long as it's not in here. Try the barn."

"The barn!"

"Shhh!"

"The barn?" He whispered the words through clenched teeth.

"You're being paid very well for a night or two of discomfort," she said tartly.

Sam muttered an oath and reached for the doorknob.

"No, not that way. Uncle Lloyd might see you leaving." She gestured toward the window. "Go out this way."

He raked his fingers through his hair, sighed resolutely, and pulled the window open. Sam threw one long leg over the sill and climbed out. He stuck his head back in through the chest-high opening. "Goodnight, Mrs. Rowan."

"Goodnight."

Then he was gone and only blackness lay outside the window. The pit of her stomach felt suddenly empty.

Fatigue swamped Anna. She pulled her night rail from the drawer and poured water into the basin on her bureau to wash with. Her every thought was focused on falling into bed, when she heard a sound at the window. Anna turned. Sam's face filled the opening.

She rolled her eyes. "Is there nothing you won't sink to?"

"Huh?"

She walked to the window, hands on hips. "Skulking around in the dark, peering through windows—that's how you found about my mole, isn't it?"

"No!"

"Then how? Peeping through the keyhole waiting for me to undress?"

Sam glanced over his shoulder. "Let me in."

"We've already settled this." Anna's chin went up. "You can sleep in the barn with the other animals. I'm only sorry we don't have a pigsty so you'll feel perfectly at home."

He ignored her tirade. "Move aside. Your uncle is on the back porch. I saw him when I was heading for the barn."

"Oh no." Anna stepped aside. "He didn't see you, did he?"

Sam pushed himself up on his arms and climbed into the room. "No. I was in the shadows."

"Thank goodness. That would have been hard to explain. What's he doing out there?"

"Having a smoke."

"Oh, yes. I'd forgotten Uncle Lloyd likes to have a cigar before bed. Well, you'll just have to stay here until he goes back inside."

Sam nodded. "That's how I see it."

They looked at each other in the faint light. A gentle breeze blew in through the open window. The room suddenly felt small.

"I suppose we may as well try to make the best of it." Anna crossed her arms in front of her.

There was a long moment of awkward silence before Sam finally sat down in the chair beside the bed. "Don't let me interrupt what you're doing."

"You've already interrupted my entire life." Anna plopped down on the end of the bed and curled her bare legs under her skirt.

"You haven't exactly played into my plans either," Sam said sourly and stretched his long legs out in front of him.

Anna gestured grandly. "Oh, yes. Your plan to make yourself wealthy using stolen money."

"Keep your voice down," he cautioned. "You don't want your uncle to think we're arguing."

"Ah yes. Something else I'll be blamed for."

Sam looked up at her. "What are you talking about?"

"I think you know," she told him, "after the way you've been carrying on today."

"Carrying on?"

"Don't act as if you don't know what I'm talking about."

Sam rubbed his forehead. "Anna, why do you always make me guess at what you're trying to say?"

Her gaze riveted him. "I'm talking about your gloating."

"Oh." He shifted uncomfortably. "But I was bragging on you too."

"Well, don't. Just don't say anything."

"And how is that going to look?"

She glared harder at him. "And I'll thank you to keep your affection to yourself."

A little grin tugged at his lips. "My what?"

Anna pursed her lips. "You know exactly what I mean."

He sighed. "Okay, I'll admit I said a few things today that maybe I shouldn't have. But the rest of it was how I figured a man ought to act toward his wife."

She looked up at him. "You mean you've thought about it?"

"Sure I have. I told you I was getting married. And I'm having a house full of kids."

"Yes, you did tell me that." Anna uncoiled her legs from beneath her. "And I suppose you've worked it all out in your mind."

Her bare feet and legs dangling down the side of the bed caught his attention. He'd never seen them before. Her toes were tiny and her ankles small, fine-boned, and delicate; like the rest of her had looked the time he'd seen her naked in the bathtub. Sam's mouth grew dry and he shifted in the chair.

Achingly conscious of her bare legs and Sam's gaze upon them, Anna curled them under her again and tugged down her skirt. It was an odd feeling have attracted such rapt attention because of her feet, of all things.

"My uncle is probably finished with his cigar now."

"Huh?" Sam looked up at her. "Oh, yeah, your uncle. Well, I'd better get going."

He rose and went to the window. "Well, good night again."

"Good night."

She sat on the bed as Sam climbed out the window and disappeared. The room seemed oddly empty now and cool, as if he had taken all the warmth with him.

Anna pulled the curtain closed. She unpinned her hair and washed at the basin, then put on her night rail. Settled in bed, she brushed her hair with slow strokes.

This was the first time in weeks Sam hadn't slept under the same roof with her, she realized. Despite how unwanted his presence had been in her life, he at least made her feel safe.

Anna laid the brush aside and slid beneath the quilt. Uncle Lloyd was with her now. He meant everything to her. He'd done so much for her and her mother. Anna desperately wanted to please him. The only problem was that it meant being a good wife to Sam. And she didn't exactly know how to go about accomplishing that.

Anna blew out the lantern and stared at the darkened room. It seemed that Sam had put a lot of thought into how to be a good husband, even if she didn't agree with all of it, he at least had a plan—and she didn't. Anna had never intended to marry. She didn't have the slightest idea of what to do.

She rolled over and pulled the quilt up around her. She'd have to come up with some sort of plan, and soon. Because tomorrow morning she'd have to be the perfect wife—to Sam Rowan.

CHAPTER 13

"Where is Sam?"

Where was Sam? A proper wife would know where her husband was. Wouldn't she? Anna glanced over her shoulder at her uncle entering the kitchen pulling up his suspenders.

"He's up and out already. Sam always likes to get an early start." It was all she could think of to cover for Sam's absence from the house. She poured a cup of coffee and passed it to her uncle.

He nodded, satisfied. "He seemed like that kind of man to me."

Anna smoothed down the apron that covered her pale-blue dress. She took a deep breath. She'd lain awake half the night formulating a plan. It was time to put it into action.

"I hope you're hungry," she said brightly. "I like to be sure Sam's day starts off with a big breakfast."

"A man needs a good breakfast," he agreed and sat down at the table.

Anna poured flour into the mixing bowl and glanced out the window. The sun was peeping over the mountains and everything was covered with morning dew. The grass sparkled in the sunlight.

She spotted Sam walking toward the house. He was wearing the same shirt and trousers he'd had on the night before. Anna hoped her uncle wouldn't notice.

"Good morning, dear," Anna crooned when Sam stepped inside the kitchen. He looked tired, his face shadowed with whiskers. Obviously his night in the barn hadn't been a good one. She handed him a cup of steaming coffee and smiled brightly.

Sam cast her a grim, wary look as he accepted the cup. His eyes were red from lack of sleep.

"I told Uncle Lloyd you were out working already, and in the barn, I see." Anna plucked a straw from his dark hair. She gestured toward the table. "Come sit down, honey. I'll have your breakfast ready in just a few minutes."

Anna ducked inside the pantry, mentally rehearsing all the words and actions she'd planned the night before. Juggling the blue-speckled dishes, she left the pantry, then froze in her tracks, stunned.

Sam was standing at the sink, naked to the waist. The taught muscles of his back rippled as he pumped water into the basin.

The dishes clattered to the floor.

Sam whirled around. Dark, curly hair covered his chest and arrowed down the center of his tight belly and disappeared into his trousers that rode low on his hips.

She'd not seen him like this since the afternoon at the pond, the afternoon he'd paraded himself in front of her totally naked.

Suddenly conscious of both men staring, Anna dropped to her knees and gathered the dishes. Sam knelt beside her, their heads together.

"What's gotten into you?" he whispered as he picked up the plates.

"What are you doing in here dressed like—like—that?" she hissed. "You're supposed to wash outside."

"That would look pretty funny, wouldn't it?" He looked down at himself as he picked up the remaining cups. "Besides, what's wrong with having no shirt on?"

Anna kept her head down. "What would you think, Sam Rowan, if you walked out of the pantry and saw me dressed that way?"

The dishes now tumbled from Sam's hands and again clattered to the floor. Their gazes locked and raw, unchecked emotion flashed between them.

Anna's cheeks burned. Sam swallowed hard. Suddenly

aware of their closeness, they gathered the dishes, both picking up the same plate. They tugged it back and forth between then until Anna finally let go, nearly sending Sam backwards across the room. He rose and dumped the dishes on the sideboard and went out the back door. Anna placed the cups aside and attacked her biscuit dough. Seated at the table, Lloyd took in the exchange over the top of his spectacles.

By the time Anna put breakfast on the table, Sam had washed and shaved at the pump out back and changed clothes in Anna's room. She smiled and uttered endearments, served his food first and gave him the last biscuit even though she wanted it for herself. Sam regarded her with wary suspicion throughout the meal, unaccustomed to this different side of her.

It was a show she was putting on for her uncle's benefit, and Lloyd gave her a nod of satisfaction as she cleared away the dishes and poured Sam a final cup of coffee. It seemed to be working, Anna thought. She wanted to be a good wife in her uncle's eyes.

"You two run on," Anna said as they rose from the table, and shooed them toward the back door.

"Sam and I are going to ride over the property this morning," Lloyd told her as he pulled on his hat.

"I'll have dinner ready when you get back. Be careful now, honey." Anna stretched up and placed a kiss on Sam's cheek.

Her lips froze there for a moment. His face was soft and slick and smelled of his shaving soap. Her breast tingled where it brushed lightly against his arm. Her fingers burned where she touched his muscular arm to steady herself.

Reluctantly she moved away. "Keep an eye out for hunters," she cautioned.

Sam frowned, confused as much by her remark as her actions all morning. She waved good-bye as the two men left the house.

Anna sighed with relief that they were gone. Now she'd have a respite from pretending.

Without Sam standing in the way or dripping water on the floor or working at a snail's pace, Anna got the kitchen chores finished quickly. She fetched the basket of dirty clothes from the corner of her bedroom and hauled them out back. It was Monday—wash day.

Anna gazed out at the hills as she fetched water for the wash tubs. In the distance she saw two riders among the trees. It was Sam and Uncle Lloyd looking over the property. She was sure Sam was looking for something more, despite the bargain she'd struck with him.

Anna blew out a heavy breath as she dumped a pail of water into the tub. Perfect wife or not, wash day was a far sight easier with Sam around.

An uneasiness had plagued Sam all morning and he wasn't sure what to attribute it to, though he thought it was most likely the man who now rode next to him.

Sam glanced at Lloyd Caldwell as they ascended the hills behind the farmhouse. The old doctor hadn't spoken a word since they'd left the barn; lost, it seemed in memories of his boyhood days spent here on the farm. Sam hadn't intruded, using the time to ponder Anna's odd behavior this morning. She'd smiled and nodded and agreed with every word he'd spoken at the breakfast table, and called him every sweet name he'd ever heard. She'd been kind and considerate, and fawning over him. He should have loved it. But all he could do was wonder what the hell was wrong with the woman.

"Brings back memories."

Sam looked over at Lloyd, the past apparently having relinquished its hold on him. "Must have been hard to leave this place. It's a fine piece of land."

Lloyd nodded. "I'd been called for something else. My pa knew it and didn't ask me to stay. Besides, Elsa was about to marry Cyrus around that same time, and we all thought he'd work the land. My pa passed on without knowing how things turned out."

"It's a shame to just let the place go to seed," Sam agreed.

"That's why I'm glad to see you and Anna back here." Lloyd looked across at Sam as they rode side by side. "To tell you the truth, I figured Anna would never marry. She gave the boot to every young buck in Salem who chanced a smile at her. She's got a lot of spirit—too much to make a good wife."

Sam's back stiffened. He knew it was true, but he didn't like Lloyd Caldwell saying it.

"You seemed to have tamed her, though, and more power to you."

Sam nearly laughed aloud. Obviously, the man knew very little about his niece.

"It was rough on Anna when her pa was sent to prison. She and her ma spent a lot of time reliving what had happened, trying to change things that had already been done." Lloyd shifted in the saddle. "I'm glad she married. Damn glad."

Sam's head was beginning to ache, partially from lack of sleep, but mostly because of the conversation. He changed the subject.

"Let's ride east. There's something over there you might shed some light on."

They turned the horses and followed the creek back into the hills.

The sun was directly overhead when Anna pinned the last shirt to the clothesline. Time to cook again. Uncle Lloyd and Sam would return soon and they'd be hungry. She looked out at the hills and realized she'd been watching for them all morning, hoping to catch sight of Sam.

Anna stopped short, the thought startling her. She hurriedly wiped her hands on her apron and grabbed the empty laundry basket. No, she told herself, it wasn't Sam she was watching for. It was her uncle. It had to be. Anna flew into the house without another glance at the hills.

The men strode into the kitchen just as Anna slid the biscuits into the oven. Their deep male voices boomed as they talked and took up what little floor space was available as they washed at the sink. Anna weaved her way between them as she placed the food on the table.

"Sam's got some good ideas for getting the farm producing again," Lloyd said after they were all seated.

Anna cast a quick glance beside her at Sam. Evidently he was playing his role to the hilt. Well, so could she. Anna smiled sweetly. "Sam knows everything there is to know about farming," she bragged.

"Seems so. Just what this place needs." Lloyd helped himself to the bowl of beans Anna offered. "I've got no idea about that spot you showed me in the hills, Sam. Must be something set up by those folks who rented the place."

"What's this?" Anna asked.

"That place I stumbled on when I took the Calhoun boys fishing," Sam explained. "The place by the stream with the broken-down swing."

Anna nodded. She'd forgotten about the find that had excited Nathan and Derek so.

"The family who had the farm had some children, didn't they, Uncle Lloyd?"

He shrugged. "I expect they did."

"I saw tracks in the hills again." Sam helped himself to another piece of chicken.

Anna felt him tense beside her. "Probably just someone hunting for game again."

Lloyd looked over the top of his spectacles at Sam. "You'll want to put a stop to that."

"I'll see to it."

Their meal concluded, Sam rose from the table. "I've got chores to take care of."

"I'll give you a hand." Lloyd wiped his mouth and stood up.

"Good meal." Sam bent down and kissed Anna on the forehead.

Startled, Anna felt the color rise in her cheeks. She looked away, hoping her uncle hadn't noticed. "Thank you . . . sweetie." She busied herself with the dishes until the men left.

She made quick work of cleaning the kitchen, now that she'd gotten her routine set, and ventured down the hallway. Anna stood at the parlor door. As much as she hated the thought, she was going to have to clean this room, since, according to her uncle, that would please her supposed husband. Anna sighed and walked inside the room.

The first thing she did was to pull down the curtains. She stood on a chair, dirt and dust billowing around her, and fiddled with the hardware. The thought skittered across her mind that if Sam were here he could accomplish this task much more easily than she.

Anna sneezed as she pulled the curtains down. They would have to be washed, so she carried them to her bedroom and dropped them in the empty basket in the corner. As she turned to leave, she caught sight of a shirt lying on the floor beside the bed. Anna picked it up and saw Sam's trousers and socks lying there as well. They were the ones he'd worn the day before and slept in last night in the barn.

Annoyed, Anna tossed them into the clothes basket. She could have washed them this morning. Now, they'd have to wait until next Monday when she washed again. Why couldn't Sam have put them in the basket? He'd thrown them on the floor. Couldn't he as easily have thrown them in the basket?

With her uncle judging her every move, Anna knew she didn't dare mention it to Sam. She went back to the parlor and slowly turning in a circle, tried to summon the courage to begin cleaning. The room was hopeless. She sighed heavily and walked out again. She'd rearrange the pantry instead, she decided.

It was a mindless task but made the morning pass quickly. She had to stop before she was finished, though; it was time to cook again.

Anna hummed to herself as she moved about the kitchen. Feathers wandered in and sat down beside the stove, curling her long, white tail around her feet.

"How do oatmeal cookies sound?"

The cat tilted his head and stared blankly at Anna.

"Don't you think a good wife would fix oatmeal cookies for her husband?" She brought the ingredients from the pantry and assembled them on the sideboard. "Hopefully my uncle will think so; and besides, cookies sound good to me too. What do you think, Feathers?"

Anna looked down. The cat was gone. She turned around, but there was no sign of Feathers. Anna sighed heavily. She was alone. Again.

The kitchen grew hotter with the cookstove on, but she baked the cookies and arranged a dozen on a plate. Juggling it along with two cups, she made her way to the spring house, got a jug of cold cider, and walked out to the barn.

"Hello! Anybody home?"

Anna stepped into the barn. Shafts of sunlight streamed in between the boarded walls, highlighting the dust motes that floated in the stagnant air. Uncle Lloyd was by the door pitching hay into the corral. Sam was standing in the loft, shirtless, the sleeves of his long johns tied low on his hips, pitching the hay to the floor. They both stopped their work when Anna walked in.

She felt as though she'd intruded upon a male sanctuary. Uncle Lloyd peered over his spectacles at her. High in the loft, Sam leaned against the pitchfork and gazed at her from beneath the brim of his dark hat.

"I thought you might like a snack." It sounded incredibly silly, so she quickly added, "And something cold to drink."

Lloyd leaned his pitchfork against the wall. "That ought to hit the spot. Come on down, Sam. Let's see what this little wife of yours has got for us."

He jabbed the pitchfork into the hay and climbed down the ladder. His face was beaded with sweat; his chest was slick with it.

Anna set the plate of cookies on the bench beside the toolroom and poured cider into the cups. "I thought some cider would taste good."

Lloyd smiled broadly and accepted the cup. "I'll say."

Sam approached slowly and pulled off his gloves. He eyed Anna, then accepted the cup. Cautiously, he peered inside. He gave Anna a wary glance before taking a sip.

"I baked cookies."

Sam choked on the cider. He coughed and wheezed. "You . . . you did what?"

Anna plastered on a smile. "I baked cookies. Oatmeal. They're your favorite. Aren't they, Sam?"

Uncle Lloyd took a cookie from the plate she offered. "Fresh baked—none better."

Sam coughed a final time and then took a cookie. But his eyes were on Anna—every second.

He tasted it. He chewed slowly, cautiously. "Good," he finally said.

"It sure feels good to work on the farm again," Uncle Lloyd declared. He gestured to the barn around him. "I'd forgotten what it felt like to do an honest day's work."

"Sam knows all about hard work." Anna praised as she poured more cider into her uncle's cup. "He's always busy out here, tending to one thing or another."

Uncle Lloyd nodded. "I guess I can tell you now, Anna, how pleased I am you're not selling the farm. I'd like it to stay in the family. I'm glad Sam changed your mind about selling it."

"Well, he's the man of the house. It's really his decision." Anna nearly gagged, but she got the words out.

Sam's brows drew together and his hand froze as he reached for another cookie. "Did you bump your head on something this morning?"

Anna forced herself to smile sweetly. "No, of course not . . . darling." She looked at her uncle. "He's always so concerned about me. What a dear he is."

Sam's frown deepened. He took another cookie and popped it into his mouth.

Anna had endured all she could. "I've got things to do in the house. Supper will be ready when you get there."

She turned to leave, but remembered that wives were supposed to kiss their husbands. She stretched up and pressed her lips against his cheek.

"Is there anything special you want for supper, sweetie?"

Looking thoroughly confused, he replied, "No."

Anna smiled and waved as she left the barn. Her stomach was in a knot. She said a quick prayer that her uncle's visit would end soon—before she exploded.

Anna fed the chickens, took down the wash and put it away, then fixed supper. The men came in and discussed their day's work while they ate. By the time she'd cleaned the kitchen, it was dark and Anna was exhausted. She told her uncle goodnight and went to her bedroom. She'd been there only a moment when the door opened and Sam strode in.

He pushed the door shut and faced her, his feet braced wide apart, his jaw set. "What the hell is the matter with you?"

Anna looked up from the bureau drawer, startled. "What do you mean?"

"You know damn well what I mean." He took a step closer. "All this sweet-talking and—and cookie-baking."

She felt like he'd plunged a knife in her heart. "You—you didn't like my cookies?"

"I'm not talking about cookies," he snapped.

"But you just said—"

"Why you're carrying on so peculiar is what I want to know."

"Peculiar?" She'd knocked herself out trying to be a good wife, and he thought she was acting peculiar? It was more than she could take—arguing with Sam these past weeks, giving up the money, cooking and cleaning, pleasing her uncle, trying to figure what a good wife should be. She just couldn't take any more. Anna sniffed twice. Tears welled in her eyes and spilled down her cheeks.

Sam was dumbfounded. "Hold on, now. I didn't mean—"

"It's not your fault. It's me. Just me." Anna sobbed harder. "I—I'm not a good wife."

"Huh?"

"I'm not." She walked across the room, tears pouring down her face. It was a cleansing experience, a relief to say it aloud. "I thought I could do it, just while Uncle Lloyd was here, but I can't. You're right. You're absolutely right."

He followed along behind her. "What's your uncle got to do with this?"

Anna sank into the chair beside the bed. "He—he said I was spending too much time doing charity work and I wasn't keeping the house clean enough and I wasn't being a—a good wife . . . to you." She wiped her cheeks with the backs of her hands. "So I tried being nice to you and—and I spent this whole day cleaning and cooking. And you didn't even like my . . . cookies."

Tears gushed and she covered her eyes, sobbing hysterically.

Sam stared at her. She was crying. He didn't know what to

do with a crying woman. He waved his arms around helplessly then sat on the edge of the bed across from her.

"Don't cry, Anna." He took her hand. "Please don't cry."

She pulled her hand away. "See? I can't even cry to suit you."

"It's not that—it's just—"

Anna rose, fresh tears wetting her face. "I never planned on being anybody's wife in the first place."

Sam shook his head, more confused than every. "But—"

She turned away. "Just leave, Sam. Just go."

He looked up at her, overwhelmed by the need to take her in his arms. He couldn't leave her. Not when she was upset.

"I'm not going anywhere until we get this straightened out." He stood and walked around in front of her. "So, is that what all this has been about? You're trying to please your uncle by being a certain kind of wife?"

Anna stared at the floor and nodded. She sniffed loudly.

"Well, to tell you the truth, I like you better the other way."

Anna's head came up quickly. "You do?"

"Yes, I do." He rubbed his forehead. "I don't understand it, but I don't think I'd want a wife who agrees with everything I said just because I was her husband. A woman like that would be—. Well, she'd be just plain boring, as I see it."

She sniffed again. "Do you mean that?"

"I mean it." Sam pulled a handkerchief from his pocket and wiped her tears. "Don't worry about your uncle. I'll take care of him. You just be yourself and that will be good enough for me. Your uncle will see we're happy like this and he'll be pleased."

Anna took the handkerchief from him and blew her nose. "Thank goodness. I don't know how much longer I could have gone on like this."

Sam chuckled. "And your cookies were perfect."

She smiled up at him. "You really are a sweet man—at times."

He laughed again. That was more of a compliment than he'd ever expected to hear from Anna Fletcher.

"I know I fussed about you being underfoot in the kitchen, but I miss you when I cook," Anna told him. "It's lonely."

"I never thought I'd admit it, but I kind of miss it too." It was true, he realized. He missed seeing her bustle about the kitchen, licking batter from her dainty little fingers while she cooked, standing beside her, smelling how sweet she was, watching her bend over to use the oven. Sam grinned. "I miss it a lot."

Anna worked the handkerchief between her fingers. "I guess things were going better between us before my uncle came along."

"I guess so."

She grinned up at him. "Does that mean you're ready to start washing dishes again?"

"Hell no."

They laughed together.

Sam touched her shoulder. "We'll get along as best we can until your uncle leaves, then——"

Then it would all be over. Anna's heart constricted. Once her uncle was gone she'd be honor-bound to show Sam where the money was and he'd be gone and she'd return to Salem penniless, with little hope of opening her orphanage.

Anna backed away from his touch. "I think you'd better go."

Sam nodded. The empty feeling in the pit of his belly grew wider each second he looked at her. He mumbled a goodnight and climbed out the window.

There was little else they could do but continue their charade, and that meant convincing Uncle Lloyd they were both happily married and anxious to get the farm going.

Anna filled the next day performing the endless list of chores: cooking, cleaning, gathering eggs, mopping, and sweeping. She saw Sam and Uncle Lloyd only at mealtime and when she visited them at the barn with the last of the oatmeal cookies. Sam was working as hard as she, fixing and repairing everything in sight. It was a relief that she didn't have to force herself to be nice to him. They talked to each other much as they had done before her uncle had come along, but without the threats and the name-calling.

Sam and Lloyd were returning from the barn at day's end

as Anna was going out to gather wood for the stove. The sun was setting. Shadows stretched across the yard. A gentle breeze stirred.

"Don't be lifting that heavy wood." Sam stopped beside her as Lloyd headed on to the house."

"I can carry it," she told him.

He took the wood from her hand and tossed it back on the pile. "So can I."

Anna brushed her hands down the front of her apron. "What have you and Uncle Lloyd been doing all day?"

"Working on the fences." He dragged his shirtsleeve across his brow. "I was thinking we ought to start on the vegetable garden."

"I was thinking that very thing today." Putting in the garden was the next logical step. Besides, it would keep her from having to clean the parlor.

"Thinking the same things now, huh?" Sam chuckled. "I guess we're acting almost like a real married couple."

She glanced up at him. "Almost."

Sam pointed past her. "Did you see the sunset?"

Anna turned. The sky was ablaze with streaks of orange and red fanning out from the deep-blue horizon. She sighed longingly. "Isn't it the prettiest thing you've seen in a long time?"

"No."

His arms closed around her waist, pressing her back against his chest. His breath was warm, caressing her cheek with its closeness.

Startled, Anna tried to pull away. He tightened his grip.

"Don't move. Your uncle is watching." He whispered into her ear, his lips brushing softly against her skin. She tried to turn her head. "And don't look. You don't want him to think we're doing this for his benefit."

"Aren't we?" Anna's flesh tingled. His arms were strong around her. She sensed the power he possessed, countered by his gentleness when he held her.

Sam shrugged. "Partly because of him. But mostly because the sunset is so pretty."

He held her for a moment, arms locked around her, his

cheek resting on hers as they gazed at the distant horizon. Anna relaxed against him. She felt warm and contented; she hoped her uncle watched until sundown.

Sam released her. He picked up the wood and headed for the house. Anna looked around. There was no sign of her uncle anywhere.

By the end of the week a great deal had been done to get the farm back in order. Sam had gotten the barn and corral to his liking and had done extensive work to the chicken coop, spring house, and woodshed. He'd repaired things at the house, too: the roof patched, the broken step replaced, the front-porch swing fixed and rehung. He'd cut the weeds back in the yard and straightened the sagging picket fence. He and Lloyd had made plans to get the crops in the ground next week.

Anna spent time outdoors too. She worked alongside Sam as they readied the vegetable garden for planting. They hoed and raked and decided together what should and shouldn't go into their garden. This necessitated a trip to the root cellar to get the seeds left behind from last summer's crop. Luckily, the folks who had rented the farm had left plenty. Anna hated the dark, damp room under the house and rushed through as quickly as possible. They planted the vegetables in long, narrow rows and surrounded the garden with zinnias, marigolds, and sunflowers to keep the bugs away. Sam promised to help her construct a scarecrow soon.

In the evening, they sat on the front porch, since Anna was dragging out the work in the garden to avoid cleaning the parlor. It was comfortable there, watching the fireflies and sipping cool cider from the spring house. They talked mostly about plans for the future of the farm.

"Ben Atkins says he's been thinking of selling out." Sam spoke the words into the dusky evening from the swing where he sat with Anna. With one foot planted on the wide boards of the porch, he kept the swing gliding gently.

Lloyd was seated across from them in the only serviceable chair left in the parlor. Sam had hauled it outside, and Anna had beaten the dust from it.

"It would be a good addition to the farm," Lloyd said. "Ben's got a good piece of land."

"He's been a good neighbor, too," Anna said. "I'd hate to see him leave."

"No reason not to profit from it." Lloyd took a final puff from his cigar and tossed it into the yard. "Well, I guess it's time to call it a day."

"Goodnight, Uncle Lloyd."

He rose from the chair. "You two staying out here for a while longer?"

It had become their custom to sit on the porch together, then simply outwait the older man. Finally, when he'd gone to bed, Anna would go inside and Sam would slip off to the barn.

"We'll sit here a little while," Sam said. "Goodnight."

Lloyd disappeared into the house leaving Sam and Anna alone on the porch together.

As a boy Sam had dreamed of finding himself alone on a dark night, seated by a pretty girl on a porch swing. He'd imagined feigning a yawn, then stretching his arm behind her for a hug, stealing a kiss. A kiss was as far as his imagination had taken him then. But none of that had been possible when he was young. The family he lived with seldom socialized, and by the time he'd figured what girls were all about, he was on his own, working on farms, living in bunk houses, seldom welcome in the homes of nice girls. He'd gone from nothing to whores.

Now he looked at Anna seated beside him on the swing, the dim light playing favorably on her soft expression, the sounds of the night creatures singing their familiar chorus around them. He gave an exaggerated yawn, stretched his arms high over his head and settled one arm on the back of the swing.

"Nice night."

Anna felt the pressure of his arm behind her. The old yawn-and-stretch routine. No one had tried that since she was fourteen. And the last one who did had paid dearly for it. Anna shifted her shoulders. "Yes, very nice night."

Sam wound his finger around a stray lock of hair at her

nape. His knuckles brushed gently against her neck. She sure was soft.

Anna's senses came to life, tingling from his touch. It felt delicious, and she suddenly wanted to melt against him. That fourteen-year-old boy who had last sat on the porch swing with her hadn't made her feel these things. Anna glanced at Sam beside her. He wasn't fourteen. But he made her feel as though she were.

Sam closed his fingers around her shoulder, stroking her arm gently. He edged closer. "I never sat on a porch swing with anybody before."

Her heart began to beat faster and her stomach coiled into a knot. Captive in his embrace, Anna tilted her face up to his. His lips were inches away. "I have."

A little grin tugged at his lips. "I had no idea I was dealing with an experienced woman."

Anna lowered her eyes and batted her lashes. She blushed. "It was only once. And the boy didn't fare very well."

Sam closed his other arm around her. "What happened?"

"He kissed me."

The idea sounded so appealing, emotion swelled inside Sam. Gently he brushed his lips across her forehead. God, she tasted sweet.

"You didn't like being kissed on a porch swing by a boy?" Sam asked.

"No."

He tightened his grip. "How about being kissed by a grown man?"

"A grown man never tried," she whispered.

Need flowed through Sam unchecked. He bent his head and touched his lips to hers. Soft and compliant, her mouth moved against his, drawing him in. Sam moaned contentedly.

It felt good. It felt right. Anna hoped he would go on kissing her, here, on the porch swing, forever. But he didn't.

Sam ended their kiss. Not because he wanted to, he had to. He loosened his grip on her and sat back against the swing, gulping in breaths of the cool, night air.

With the warmth of Sam's body gone from her, a chill

swept over Anna. She folded her arms over her middle, composing herself.

"Maybe you'd better go in now, Anna," he said softly.

It was a warning, spoken gently, but a warning just the same. Anna looked up at Sam and saw the yearning etched on his face. And for an instant she was tempted not to heed his request.

She rose and walked across the porch, pausing at the front door. "Yours was better."

Sam's heart flipped over. "My what?"

"Your kiss." Anna smiled. "Good night, Sam."

"Good night."

Sam sat on the swing for a long moment, thinking and wondering.

Wondering if maybe he'd be wise to take the swing down.

By Saturday morning, they were all ready for a respite and a change of scenery. It was Founders' Day, the day of the big celebration in town.

Anna hurried out to the wagon, where Sam and her uncle waited, and placed a box tied with string in the back.

"What did you fix?" Uncle Lloyd asked.

She'd gotten up extra early this morning and prepared a box lunch to enter in the raffle today. Anna smiled at her uncle. "I'm not telling. You'll have to bid for it if you want to find out."

Uncle Lloyd nodded toward Sam. "I'll leave that to your husband. Wouldn't be proper, otherwise."

"You'll have to find you some widow woman's lunch to vie for," Sam suggested.

He winked. "Maybe I'll do just that."

Sam helped Anna onto the wagon seat, and he and Lloyd squeezed in on each side of her. Their thighs rubbed together as the team drew the wagon toward town.

Most of the days activities would be held at church. There, the booths were set up selling rag dolls, doilies, stitchery, jams and jellies, shawls and scarfs, baked goods, pastries, and candies. Pie-eating contests were scheduled, and sack races were planned. There were lots of games for children, rope-jumping contests for girls and marble-shooting for boys. The box-lunch raffle would be held on the church steps. A horse race was set for afternoon. People came from miles around to join the fun and excitement of Kemper's Founders' Day celebration.

The churchyard was already crowded with wagons, buggies, and horses when Sam pulled the team to a stop under the oak trees. Children were running about, playing games, and laughing. Men and women were gathered together talking, looking over the merchandise for sale, signing up for the days contests.

And on the church steps, with a commanding view of the whole area stood Brett Morgan. Waiting.

CHAPTER 14

Lloyd joined a group of men standing under the trees. He knew them from his boyhood in Kemper and hadn't seen them in years. They had a lot of catching up to do.

Sam took the boxed lunch from the back of the wagon and walked Anna over to enter it in the raffle. Emma Langford, wearing a hat decorated with huge purple daisies, registered Anna's entry and stacked it with the others on the table beside the church steps.

"Looks like quite a turnout," Anna commented.

Emma pressed her lips together and nodded. "You'd better hold tight to your purse today. We get a lot of riffraff in along with our good Christian townfolk. Now, you see those men over by the wall? That's the Johnson family and everybody knows they're—"

"We'll see you later, Emma," Anna interrupted. "I want to show Sam around."

Emma smiled and adjusted her hat. "Have a good time today—but be careful."

Anna slid her arm through Sam's and hurried away.

"Do you really want to look around?" Anna asked as they stopped beside the pickle booth. She had fond memories of Founders' Day but didn't know how Sam would feel.

He grinned. "Shoot, yes. I haven't been to anything like this since I was a boy."

They toured the booths and looked over the items offered for sale. Sam sampled the fare of everything edible. They saw many of their friends and stopped to talk.

Anna was especially glad to run into Sarah and Jamie.

They were standing under a shade tree while the children played around them.

"You look so pretty today," Sarah told her as Sam and Jamie talked.

Anna smoothed down the skirt of her pink dress. It was the one she'd refused to wear, simply because Sam had requested it. But she wanted to wear something special today and aggravating Sam didn't seem as important as it once did.

"Thank you," Anna replied. "Are you feeling all right? You look a little drawn today."

Jamie slid his arm around his wife. "I think she just overdid things yesterday. She's been cooking and cleaning like there's no tomorrow."

"I want things to be ready when the baby gets here." Sarah rested her hand on her full belly.

"But you've got lots of time yet. The baby isn't due for another month, is it?" Anna asked.

Sarah glanced at Jamie. "That's what the doctor says, but. . . ."

"Dr. Sawyer knows what he's talking about, honey." Jamie chuckled and looked at Sam. "These women, they think they know more than a doctor. Let's head on over to the horseshoe-pitching contest, Sam. I see Hugh Palmer over there. He's won the tournament last two years."

Sam hung back as Jamie walked away. "Keep an eye on Sarah until we get back," he whispered to Anna. "She doesn't look so good to me."

"I will." Anna turned to Sarah. "Let's go over by the steps and sit for a while."

Sarah rubbed her lower back and grimaced. "Let's do."

The boys had run off after Sam and Jamie, so Anna herded Molly and Elizabeth along with them and settled on the church steps. Sarah gingerly lowered herself to sit beside Anna. They were there only a moment before Molly grew restless.

"Cookie, Mamma. Cookie." She pointed a chubby finger toward the booth across the churchyard.

Sarah shifted uncomfortably. "Wait, honey, until Papa gets back."

"Cookie, Mamma. Cookie."

"But honey—"

"I'll take her." Anna rose and lifted Elizabeth into her arms.

"Thank you." Sarah's smile was genuine.

"Come on, Molly." Anna crossed the churchyard with Elizabeth in one arm and Molly skipping along beside her.

"Cookie! Cookie!" the child exclaimed as they reached the booth. She stretched up trying to see over the ledge.

Anna shifted Elizabeth to her other hip and dug through her reticule. "Four sugar cookies, please."

A hand from beside her dropped two pennies on the counter. "We'll let the taxpayers cover this."

Startled, Anna looked up to find Brett standing beside her.

"Morning, Anna." He grinned. "I remember how partial you are to sweets. I knew if I waited here long enough you'd show."

Anna glanced at Pervis Dooley, who was manning the booth, and felt herself blush at the disapproving look the deacon tossed back and forth between her and Brett.

"Brett, I can't let you buy me—. I mean, it wouldn't be—"

He chuckled and gestured to the coins on the counter. "Too late, it's already done."

Brett shot Pervis a scowl. "The lady asked for some cookies." His tone was icy.

Anna took the cookies from Pervis and passed one to Molly. Before she could say anything, Brett picked up the child and walked toward the trees at the edge of the churchyard, away from the crowd. Anna was forced to follow.

They stopped at the corner of the yard, near the woods, well away from the Founders' Day activities. Anna glanced back over her shoulder, annoyed with Brett and uncomfortable with the situation he'd created. She was sure someone had seen them leave together; someone always saw everything that happened in Kemper.

"Don't fret. If Rowan can't hold on to you, he doesn't deserve to have you."

Stunned, Anna looked up at Brett. He smiled and set Molly on the ground.

"Besides," he said, "I've been worried about you, Anna. I

knew something was wrong last time we talked, and I want to find out what it is."

It had been only a week since Brett had come by the house, but it seemed longer. So much had happened. And everything was changed.

There was no longer a reason to take Brett into her confidence, hoping he might help her get rid of Sam. She'd made a deal. She'd given her word. And despite how cooperative Sam had been this week, he'd confess the whole sordid scheme to her uncle if she didn't lead him to the money. He'd do it. In a heart beat.

Still, she had to tell Brett something. After all, she had scoured the town for him and had been brazen enough to barge into the jailhouse and ask for him. She'd hinted something terrible was wrong when he'd come by the house. She had to say something. He was concerned and worried—a true friend. One of the few she had in town.

Anna smiled. "This may seem silly to you, but it means the world to me, Brett. I wanted to thank you for not telling anyone in town about my pa dying in prison. It would have brought up the whole robbery story again, and people are talking about the Fletchers already, with me back in town."

Brett frowned, then nodded. "I wanted to protect you, Anna. I'd never do anything to hurt you by telling anyone about your pa. He'd been sick for a while. I guess it was bound to happen."

"Yes. He started going downhill after Mamma died last fall." Anna shuddered at the memory. "Just by looking at him, anyone could see he wouldn't last long."

Brett nodded wisely. "I'm surprised he held on as long as he did."

Confused, Anna looked up at him. "How did you know he'd been ill? How did you know it wasn't an accident or something?"

"Oh, well—" Brett shuffled his feet. "I told you my cousin was a guard up there at the prison. Remember?"

She had forgotten that. Still, it struck her as odd that Brett and his cousin would be discussing her father.

Brett seemed to read her thoughts. "I settled back in

Kemper not long after your ma passed on, and I went up to visit my cousin at the prison. He remembered that you and I had practically grown up together, so he mentioned your pa to me while we were catching up on the years I'd been away."

His story made sense. Still, she didn't like knowing that people were talking about her and her family.

Anna took Molly's hand. "I've got to get back."

Brett blocked her path. "I told you, Anna, I'm here to help you. You just say the word."

A chill slithered up Anna's spine. For a moment she thought she'd read something frightening in Brett's eyes.

"Thank you." Anna skirted around him and hurried back to the church.

It seemed every eye was on her as she sat down on the steps beside Sarah again.

"Feeling better? " She settled Elizabeth on her lap.

Sarah shifted uncomfortably and rubbed her back. "Not really."

"Maybe I should have Jamie take you home." Anna scanned the churchyard looking for him.

"No." Sarah touched her arm. "No, please don't do that. He'll just start in again about me thinking I know more than Dr. Sawyer."

"But you're the one who has already given birth four times." Anna's eyes flashed. "You should know if you're not feeling right. Dr. Sawyer has never had a baby."

"No, no, it's fine. I'm sure the doctor is right. He is the doctor, after all. Maybe if I walk for a bit, I'll feel better."

Anna helped Sarah to her feet, then gathered the baby into her arms and took Molly's hand. They strolled through the booths and wound up at the horseshoe-pitching tournament. A crowd of men and a few women were gathered there. Sam and Jamie and the boys were among them, Sam's tall frame towering over the others.

Maggie Fry was there chatting with the men, winding her way between them in a dress cut scandalously low for a function held on the church grounds. Anna had seen Maggie several times today; she always seemed to be wherever the men were clustered. Anna was sure Emma Langford was about to pop a stay over Maggie's behavior, but like everyone else in town, never said a word out of respect for Deacon Fry.

The crowd shifted as people watched the match for a while, then moved on. Anna found herself standing beside Charles Hampton. He tipped his hat.

"Good day, Mrs. Rowan."

She smiled. "Nice to see you, Mr. Hampton."

"I wouldn't have missed the Founders' Day celebration for the world." He gazed across the crowd at Sam, who was engrossed in conversation with several other men and watching the tournament. "Looks as though your husband is enjoying himself."

"Sam fits in here better than I. Why, I don't believe the man ever met a stranger."

Charles gazed at him for a long moment. "Sam seems to have found a home for himself here. I'm glad to see that."

The familiarity of the comment startled Anna.

"I believe that's Mrs. Calhoun's child, isn't it?" He looked at the baby in Anna's arms.

Anna angled the baby so Hampton could get a better look at her. Her cheeks and chin were covered with crumbs from the sugar cookie she was still working on.

"Her name is Elizabeth and she's truly an angel."

Mr. Hampton smiled warmly. "Spoken like a woman who truly loves children."

Anna smiled. "Oh, yes. I wish I could gather every child in the world around me and hug them and never turn them loose."

He nodded wisely. "It is hard to let go of your children." He smiled proudly. "I have grandchildren, you know."

"You must miss them terribly."

"I do indeed." He ran his finger softly across the baby's cheek. "I can hardly wait to see them again."

"Will the rest of your family be moving down from Richmond to join you?" Anna asked.

Mr. Hampton withdrew his hand. "No." He tipped his hat. "Good day, Mrs. Rowan."

How odd, Anna thought. He seemed so genuinely concerned about his family and yet had simply moved away and

left them all behind. But maybe there was more to the story
than Mr. Hampton wanted to discuss. Maybe something had
happened between him and his family. Anna understood how
circumstance could change a family and felt bad for Charles
Hampton. He was a hard man to read, with eyes that seemed
to take in everything around him and a mind that was always
clicking. Anna liked him, though, regardless of what Sam
said about him.

Anna wiped the crumbs from Elizabeth's face and walked
over to stand beside Sarah and Jamie.

Nathan sidled up next to Sam. "You gonna pitch horse-
shoes?"

"No, not today."

"How come?"

"I haven't—"

"Hey, baby pants!" A taunting voice interrupted them. Sam
turned and saw another boy about Nathan's age a short
distance away. He sneered and wagged his tongue, then
disappeared into the crowd.

Sam looked down at Nathan. His small body was rigid.
"Eddie?"

"Yeah." Nathan looked at his father standing nearby, then
at Sam. He bolted into the crowd, away from Eddie.

Sam's belly churned. He couldn't stand it anymore. He
approached Jamie. "Let's go talk for a minute."

Jamie followed him to a quiet spot under the trees away
from the crowd. "What's wrong, Sam?"

"First of all, I know this is none of my business. They're
your boys and you can do with them whatever you think
best." Sam took a deep breath. "But something's eating at
Nathan and you ought to know about it."

A deep frown creased Jamie's brow. "Nathan? What's
wrong with him?"

"Some kid at school named Eddie keeps hitting him and
taking away his lunch pail. But Nathan won't hit him back
because you told him fighting is wrong."

"Nathan told you about this?" Jamie shook his head slowly.
"I wonder why he never told me?"

"Because he's trying to please you. He wants to make his

pa happy." Sam vividly recalled the many times he'd tried to win the approval of the man who'd taken him in as a child. Tried, and never succeeded.

"I probably stuck my nose in where it didn't belong," Sam went on. "I told Nathan that fighting was wrong, like the Bible says, but that sometimes a man's got to make his own decisions."

Jamie nodded thoughtfully. "Thanks, Sam." He walked away.

At noon, everyone gathered at the church steps for the box-lunch raffle. It was a favorite event, where lunches were awarded to the highest bidder, with proceeds going to the church. The women were flattered by the attention their lunches received and considered the bidding the ultimate compliment of their cooking skills. To men it was a territorial issue, a way to publicly stake a claim on the woman they sought. Many a romance had begun at the Founders' Day box-lunch raffle.

Clara Abbot's lunch with her much-sought-after apple pie went for forty cents, while Emma Langford's, whose culinary skills were even less impressive than her millinery talents, brought twenty cents. Huge Palmer's bid of thirty cents for Mildred's lunch brought no challenges, since it was unheard of that any man would bid for the lunch another man's wife had prepared. Hugh's oldest son, Boyce, bid fifty cents for Adalie Reynold's lunch, and the young girl blushed a rosy red as Boyce escorted her away from the gathering, box lunch securely in hand.

Anna almost wished she hadn't entered the raffle. This morning when she'd packed it, she indulged in the same daydream she'd had as a girl, the same daydream every girl had. Her lunch sought after by every handsome young man in the county, the bids growing higher and higher until one champion, one true love, beat out all challengers, declaring his feeling for her in front of the entire town with a final bid that shocked everyone.

Now, Sam was obligated to buy the lunch she prepared and she was certain he'd do just that; Sam had shown himself to be as territorial as any man she'd known. But it was all so fake, so false, a mockery of a relationship the gesture should have been a tribute to.

Anna took a deep breath as Emma placed her lunch on the table, and Reverend Langford called out her name.

"Now, who will start the bidding for our little Anna's lunch," the reverend called out. He smiled and looked pointedly at Sam. "There's only one person who really knows what kind of cook she turned out to be. Do I hear an opening bid?"

"Fifty cents," Sam offered.

A murmur went through the crowd. His was the highest bid of the day, so far. Emma squealed with delight and smiled at Anna.

The reverend looked pleased. "Fifty cents. My, but she must have become quite a cook!"

The townspeople chuckled. Standing beside Sam, Anna felt her cheeks flush.

"Fifty cents it is," the reverend said. "Going once, going—"

"Seventy-five cents."

A collective gasp broke the silence as Brett Morgan stepped from the crowd. "I bid seventy-five cents," he repeated.

Anna's stomach flipped over. She saw every eye in the crowd turn to her.

Reverend Langford's brows drew together as he glanced from Sam to Brett as they stood at opposite ends of the auction table. He cleared his throat. "I—I have a bid of seventy-five cents."

All eyes turned to Sam now.

"One dollar."

The crowd turned back to Brett.

"One twenty-five."

Anna wished the ground would open up and swallow her. The bidding war she'd dreamed of as a child had become a nightmare.

"One-fifty," Sam called.

"One-sixty," Brett countered.

Lloyd Caldwell came through the crowd and stood beside Sam. Jamie moved over next to him.

Sam's cold, icy gaze impaled Brett. "Two dollars."

The onlookers gasped again. Such a high bid was unprecedented in the history of Founders' Day.

Brett locked gazes with Sam. People gathered at that end of the table fell back, leaving the deputy to himself.

"Two-fifty."

Reverend Langford looked on in horror as the dueling bidders drove the price up to three dollars. This had never happened before. Never!

Brett took a step forward, his gaze resting for a moment on Anna before returning to Sam. "Three-fifty."

Sam stood ramrod straight, his feet braced wide apart, squarely facing his opponent. It was high noon and the sun was clear and bright overhead. His eyes were cold beneath the brim of his dark hat.

"Ten dollars."

Emma Langford's mouth fell open. A ripple went through the crowd as Reverend Langford announced, "Sold to Sam Rowan for ten dollars!"

Anna heaved a sigh of relief, as did the rest of the crowd.

"Wait!" Sam's voice broke through the noise. He hadn't moved a muscle. "I believe he has the right to answer the bid."

The crowd fell silent again and drew in a collective breath. Reverend Langford's forehead popped out with beads of sweat. Anna's heart rose in her throat. Every eye turned to Brett. Clearly, Sam wasn't done.

Brett drew in a deep breath as he once again locked gazes with Sam. They held steady for a long moment, then looked away.

"No bid."

Chatter broke out in the crowd as the reverend declared the lunch sold for ten dollars, and Emma looked as though she might swoon. Lloyd and Jamie patted Sam on the back. Anna wished she could dissolve in a puff of smoke.

For once, Emma was struck speechless as she accepted Sam's money. He took the boxed lunch and escorted Anna away from the auction table. The crowd parted, giving them a wide berth.

"You didn't have to do that," Anna said quietly when they reached the wagon.

"Like hell I didn't." Sam pulled the blanket from the back of the wagon. "Did you think I'd stand there and let somebody insult my wife like that?"

Anna's heart swelled. Sam was looking at her with an intensity she'd never seen before. "But I'm not your wife," she said softly. "Not really."

"Yes, you are." His expression grew fierce. "I don't want that bastard around you anymore. I don't want to see him at my house ever again. And I don't want you talking to him again—ever. Do you understand that?"

She should have protested. She should have told him to keep out of it. She should have told him to mind his own business. But the pit of her stomach was glowing and her heart was pumping wildly. Sam was a strong man. He was a capable man. She'd always known that about him. Now she knew he was a possessive man and that he wanted to possess her. And oddly enough, that didn't bother Anna.

She looked up into his determined face. "I understand."

The tension left him slowly. "Good. Now let's go eat this lunch."

They walked toward the church again when Sam noticed Nathan standing alone by the hitching post.

"You go ahead. I'll catch up," he said to Anna. She took the blanket and left.

Nathan saw him coming and hurried over. The boy's chin went up defiantly. "I done it."

Sam bit on his lower lip to keep from smiling. "What did you do?"

"I hit him. Right in the belly. Just like this." Nathan demonstrated his swing, punching his fist into the air.

"You got him good, huh?"

"Yep. And I told him he better not never hit me or call me no more names again."

Sam couldn't hold back the smile anymore. "Feel better now?"

"Yep." Nathan nodded emphatically. "And if he bothers me again, he's gonna get it again."

Jamie stepped from behind one of the oaks. "What's this?"

Nathan shrank back. Fear showed in his features. He looked up at Sam.

"I heard about that boy who was picking on you," Jamie said gently. "You should have told me, son. I don't want other kids hitting you."

"But you said—"

"I know what I said." Jamie knelt down in front of him. "But I guess I'd better change my thinking on that. If someone hits you first, it's okay to take up for yourself. How's that?"

"Whew." Nathan wiped his brow with the back of his hand. "Thanks, Pa."

Jamie laughed and wrapped his son in a big bear hug. Nathan hugged his neck.

"How about we go have some of your ma's fried chicken?" Jamie suggested.

"Yeah! Let's go!" Nathan wiggled free and took Jamie's hand. "Come on."

Jamie looked back at Sam with gratitude as he followed his son through the crowd.

Nathan released his father's hand and ran back to Sam. He buried his face against Sam's belly and threw his small arms around him, then raced over to his father's side.

Sam watched as Nathan pulled his father toward the spot under the oak where Sarah and Anna had spread their blankets. For all the happiness he felt at seeing father and son happy together, an emptiness filled him for all the same reasons.

Sam followed them to the picnic spot. Uncle Lloyd was the highest bidder for Irene Sanders' lunch and they ate with them also. Several men stopped by to shake Sam's hand and offer support for the bidding war he'd won.

There seemed to be new respect for Sam in the community, Anna thought as Hugh Palmer walked away. She wasn't sure that respect extended to her as the one who had seemingly instigated the whole affair.

After they'd eaten, Jamie said, "The horse race will be starting in town pretty soon. Let's head on over."

"You run on," Sarah told him. "I don't feel much like watching the race this year."

He looked at Sam. "How about it?"

Sam didn't want to leave Anna alone, and he was sure she wouldn't go off and leave Sarah behind, especially when the woman looked so miserable.

"You head on over," Sam told him. "I'll catch up with you later."

Jamie nodded. "Okay. Come on, boys."

Nathan and Derek hurried off after their father.

Irene Sanders gathered up the remains of the lunch she'd shared with Lloyd. "It's my turn to handle the church booth. I've got to run along."

Lloyd got to his feet. "That was a fine meal you fixed, Irene."

"Well, you didn't have to mortgage your property to pay for it, but I suppose it was palatable," she replied.

Lloyd chuckled and helped her to her feet. "Allow me to walk you to the booth, would you?"

"Very well." Irene pressed her lips together primly as they walked away.

Sam, Anna, and Sarah were still seated on the blanket, with little Elizabeth sleeping soundly beside them. Molly was busy finishing off the last of the sugar cookies Anna had bought.

"I'd better get her cleaned up," Sarah said as Molly finished her cookie.

"I'll do it," Anna offered.

"No, Anna, you've looked after the girls all day." Sarah's protest was weak.

"I don't mind," Anna told her.

Sam rose and helped Anna to her feet. Sarah lifted her hand.

"I'm not near as light as your wife, but I certainly could use your help."

Sam smiled and assisted Sarah to her feet.

"We'll be right back," Anna called as she and Molly headed for the pump behind the church.

Sam and Sarah watched them go.

"Anna's so good with children," Sarah said. "She ought to have a dozen of her own."

Sam nodded as he gazed at Anna crossing the churchyard holding Molly's tiny hand. "That's for certain. She'll make a fine mamma."

A pang of guilt stabbed his conscience about that; now, thanks to him, Anna wouldn't be able to open her orphanage. And bullheaded as she was, Sam was sure she'd never marry. Her uncle was most likely right when he'd said Anna was too strong-willed to be a good wife.

Of course, the elements that make up a good wife are relative, Sam decided as he watched Anna swing Molly into her arms. Some men may be content with a docile, soft-spoken woman, who carried out her responsibilities dutifully and produced a baby every year or so and kept a clean house and put a hot meal on the table three times a day. That was a wife's place, Sam told himself. He tried to imagine himself married to someone like that, a woman who never questioned his word, who did as she was told, who allowed him his husbandly rights when it suited him. That was what a wife was supposed to be. And that certainly wasn't what Anna Fletcher was like. Anna was none of those things. She was—Fingers suddenly clamped around Sam's arm and dug into his flesh with such strength that he winced. Sam turned to find Sarah clinging to him, her other hand on her belly, her face contorted with pain.

"What the . . ."

Her fingers dug deeper into his arm and her knees bent. "Sam . . . it's the. . . ."

His eyes widened and his heart lurched. "Oh my God. . . ."

"The . . . the baby." Sarah gasped through clenched teeth.

"Oh my God." Sam grabbed her arms to keep her from falling. "It's—it's not time."

"It's time."

"No, it's not." He looked around for help. No one was in sight.

Sarah managed a small smile as the contraction eased. "Sam, it's time. Believe me, it's time."

"Well to hell with that damn doctor!" Sam swore. Then he remembered himself. "Excuse my language, Sarah."

"I agree with you completely. To hell with him." Sarah straightened and rubbed her back. "I have to get home, Sam."

"Right, right." His heart was pounding. Sarah clung to him totally helpless. And suddenly he felt helpless too. He'd never been around anyone giving birth before. He'd spent his life in bunkhouses and barns. Frantically, he searched the church-yard and, thankful, there was Anna.

Sarah's grip on his arm suddenly intensified and her face contorted once more.

"Anna!" Sam bellowed across the yard. Sarah gasped and her knee gave out. Sam lifted her into his arms. He saw Anna suddenly break into a run, pulling Molly along beside her.

"What's wrong? What happened?" Anna asked as she reached them.

"It's time," Sam told her.

"But the doctor said—"

"It's time!"

The urgency, the near panic in Sam's voice spurred Anna into action. She jerked the blankets from the ground, save the one Elizabeth was sleeping on.

"I'll make a bed for her in the back of the wagon and go find the doctor."

Anna rushed to their own wagon and quickly spread out the blankets, then hurried off to get her uncle. As expected she found him at the doily booth with Irene Sanders.

"But where is Dr. Sawyer?" Lloyd asked when she'd told him the situation.

"I don't know." She grabbed his arm. "Come on, Uncle Lloyd, we can't have the baby born in a wagon."

"I'll go find Dr. Sawyer and send him to the Calhouns' house," Irene offered.

"And find Jamie, too," Anna instructed. "He's over at the horse race in town."

By the time they'd gathered the sleeping Elizabeth and gotten to the wagon, Sam had already placed Sarah on the blanket in the back. Molly was sitting on the tailgate swinging her feet.

Lloyd climbed into the back and spoke softly to Sarah.

"Let's get her home," Lloyd called to Sam as he climbed onto the seat beside Anna. "Nice and gentle."

Sam wanted to whip the two old horses and get to the Calhoun place at a dead run, but came to his senses and coaxed the team home as gently as possible.

Sam carried Sarah into her bedroom and rushed out so quickly he nearly collided with Anna in the hallway holding Elizabeth. Molly scurried past him into her own room. They both looked at each other, frightened and excited.

Lloyd appeared in the bedroom doorway, coatless, rolling up his sleeves.

"Sam, put on some water to boil," he ordered. "I haven't got my medical bag with me so find some twine and scissors."

Sam's stomach rolled. "Twine and scissors?"

"Anna, get in here. I need your help." He disappeared into the bedroom again.

She held Elizabeth out for Sam. He backed up. "I don't know anything about holding babies."

"Look, Sam, you can either hold this one or go inside and deliver the other one."

"Give me that kid." Sam pulled Elizabeth from Anna's arms. "Get in there and help your uncle."

He found a crib in Molly's bedroom and placed Elizabeth inside; thankfully the baby kept sleeping. He wasn't sure how much water was needed to deliver a baby, so he filled four pans and set them on the stove to boil. After an extensive search, he found scissors and twine and passed them to Anna through the bedroom door, trying to block out the sounds of Sarah's mournful moans.

Within the hour, Jamie arrived home with the boys, accompanied by Irene Sanders. She took over the water-boiling while Sam and Jamie paced the front porch together.

"What the hell is taking so long?" Sam asked.

Jamie stopped his pacing. "Could take hours. Days, sometimes."

Sam cringed. "Days. . . ."

"It's worth it." Jamie gave him a consoling pat on the back and the men began pacing once more.

Justin James Calhoun was born shortly before sundown. He came into the world screaming and kicking, with Anna assisting at the birth. Tears of joy trickled down her face as she wrapped the baby in a blanket and placed him in his mother's arms.

"He's beautiful." Sarah's eyes were wet also. She looked up at Anna. "Go get Jamie, please."

Anna stood in the corner of the room while the two proud parents fawned over their new son. Exhausted, Sarah fell asleep.

Jamie took Lloyd's hand and thanked him for delivering the baby, then turned to Anna. "Would you like to show this little fellow off?"

A big smile spread over Anna's face. "I'd love to."

Anna gathered the baby in her arms and carried him into the hallway. Irene was waiting there and the two women cooed and fussed over him together.

"Go show him to Sam," Irene told her. "He's been pacing the porch with Jamie like it was his baby coming into the world."

Anna went outside and found Sam. He looked haggard and worn, as if he'd given birth to the child himself. He backed up when Anna approached.

"He's a beautiful baby, Sam. Don't you want to see him?"

He didn't move.

Anna drew the blanket from the baby's face and angled the child in Sam's direction. "See? Isn't he precious?"

"Jesus. . . ." Sam stared at the child, awestruck. Slowly he ventured closer.

"Isn't he tiny?" Anna pulled the blanket away exposing the delicate body swathed in a white gown.

Sam wiped his brow. "That thing—that big thing—came out of her?"

Anna smiled. His face was colorless and his expression

was one of cold terror. "Haven't you ever seen a newborn baby before?"

Numbly, Sam shook his head. "Horses. Just horses."

"No cousins or brothers or sisters?"

He lifted his shoulders helplessly. "I didn't have any."

She'd forgotten he'd grown up alone, in a house where he'd been only tolerated. Her heart suddenly ached.

Anna inched closer. "It's God's way, Sam. Babies are the most precious gift of all."

Cautiously, he reached out and rubbed his finger against the baby's cheek. Sam smiled and looked up at Anna. "It's soft."

Jamie walked out onto the porch. "You'll be seeing your share of babies, Sam. Just give it a little time."

Sam's grin widened. "Yes, I guess I will. I'm going to have me a lot of these."

With some Kentucky woman, Anna thought bitterly. She gathered the blanket around little Justin and went back into the house. Sam would have lots of babies. He'd have a home of his own. He'd have a family. Bought and paid for with her money.

Anger, deep and rancid, coiled in Anna's stomach and spread its hot tentacles through her. Her own future flashed before her, a life without a husband or child. A lonely spinster destined to live out her years in her uncle's home, with nothing to call her own. No one to comfort her. No one for her to nurture. A bleak, desolate existence, devoid of love.

Anna held the baby tight in her arms as she looked out the door at Sam standing on the porch talking with Jamie. He'd taken it from her; all of it, and he intended to go on his way and leave her behind, cast aside like so much garbage while he built a rich, fulfilling life for himself.

Tears threatened, but Anna held them back. She would find a way to get even with Sam Rowan, she swore. She'd make him give her back the life he'd taken from her.

Her belly coiled into a knot. She'd get even. No matter what it took.

CHAPTER 15

Was it happiness? Or was it envy?

Anna admitted to herself that she didn't know which she felt. Maybe it was a little of both.

Quickly, she took the chicken from the pan and piled it on the platter. She glanced out the kitchen window. The sun had risen above the mountains now, its shafts of light illuminating the barn and the corral. Sam was driving the team toward the house. She'd have to hurry or they'd be late for church this morning.

She wrapped a fresh linen towel around the platter of chicken she intended to drop off at the Calhouns' after services and tossed her apron aside. Thoughts of Sarah and little Justin came to mind once more. It was all she'd thought of since leaving the Calhoun home last night.

Yes, Anna thought as she hurried to her bedroom, she was happy for her friend. It was wonderful that Sarah had a good husband and beautiful children. As for herself, Anna had decided years ago that she wanted no part of marriage.

She studied her reflection in the mirror as she pinned her hat in place. She'd always thought she'd have her orphanage, though, with lots of children to care for and love. Now, it was unlikely she'd realize that dream. With Sam keeping all the robbery money for himself and her uncle's admission that he wanted the farm to stay in the family and never be sold, it was very doubtful she'd ever get the funds together to open her orphanage.

So that meant she was envious, Anna decided with a heavy

sigh. Envious of her friend for the loving family she had, the full life Anna would never know.

Envy. Anna thought it must be a sin; another to add to her recent list. She looked glumly at her Bible resting on the bureau. Maybe she'd discuss it with Reverend Langford this morning. Her outlook brightened a little. Maybe the reverend's sermon would give her hope.

Her spirits slightly buoyed, Anna took her reticule and Bible and left.

Once in church, seated between Sam and her uncle, Anna's hopes were dashed as Reverend Langford announced the scripture lesson for the day. Deuteronomy, Chapter 19. God's Law.

Reverend Langford's voice boomed as he pounded the pulpit with his fist, warning of God's punishment for sinners.

"An eye for an eye! A tooth for a tooth!" The reverend's gaze raked the congregation. He lowered his voice. "A soul for a soul."

Silence hung heavy in the church. Gazes cast toward the pulpit riveted on the reverend, waiting, while others less comfortable with the sermon eyed their own laps.

"Sinners among you, repent." Reverend Langford paused. "God's law is a just law. But God is merciful, and He's a loving God. His law is applied when absolutely necessary to carry out justice and executed on those who fully deserve the punishment." The reverend waved a finger over the congregation. "Those among you deserving of punishment know who you are. God knows also. Repent now, my children."

Anna chanced a glance around the gathering, her gaze settling on Maggie Fry, the deacon's wife. Certainly that woman should be squirming in her pew. Anna looked up at Sam as he listened intently to the sermon. Surely there was no bigger sinner in the church than Sam Rowan, she thought. And if God's law prevailed, what punishment would fit his sins? Anna could think of nothing horrid enough to equal what he'd done in stealing her life from her.

Reverend Langford cleared his throat. "Now let's all turn to page twenty-four in the blue hymn book."

Miss Marshall pounded the organ, hat bobbing, bringing

the congregation to its feet for the closing hymn, "Onward Christian Soldiers."

Outside in the churchyard, Anna chatted with Emma and Mildred Palmer about the Calhouns' new baby. As was Anna's plan, most everyone else intended to drop off a dish for Jamie and the children today after church.

From the corner of her eye, Anna saw Deacon Fry and Deacon Dooley with their heads together whispering and glancing her way. She had the uncomfortable feeling they were talking about the incident with Brett at yesterday's box-lunch raffle. Anna cringed.

The last thing she wanted was to be the topic of gossip once more. So when she saw Brett heading toward her from across the churchyard, and with the reverend's eye-for-an-eye sermon fresh in her mind, Anna turned the other way. She grabbed the first person she knew. It was Ben Atkins.

"Morning, Miss Anna." He pulled off his battered hat.

"Ben, it's good to see you." She chanced a glance over her shoulder. Brett was still weaving through the crowd in her direction.

Anna slid her arm through Ben's. "Why don't you come have supper with us this afternoon?"

"Well, I don't know." He worked his hat in his hands. "I don't want to be a bother."

"It's no bother. Sam would love to have you over. Let's go tell him." She pulled Ben along beside her. "Sam! Sam!"

He stepped away from the group of men he was talking with.

"I invited Ben over for supper," Anna announced.

Sam's brows drew together at the sight of Anna, slightly breathless, dragging Ben toward him. He nodded slowly. "Glad to have you join us, Ben."

Anna settled next to Sam, in the company of all his friends, while the men talked about farming, crops, and the weather. She prayed Brett wouldn't approach her, not with Sam at her side. She didn't want to start another confrontation between the two of them. She figured Brett would simply go away.

Yet when she peeked around Sam, she saw Brett across the

churchyard, his hat pulled down low on his forehead, watching her.

Having Ben over for supper reminded her of years gone by. He'd been a frequent guest and having him seated at her kitchen table now brought back lots of memories.

Anna pulled the corn bread from the oven and placed it on the sideboard. The memories were all pleasant ones, she suddenly realized, then was more surprised to realize that many of her recollections lately had been happy ones—from before the robbery. Christmas and birthdays, spring mornings, helping her mother tend the flower garden, anxiously waiting by the back steps for her papa to come home at night.

Anna placed the corn bread on the table where Ben, Sam, and her uncle were already seated. For years, like her mother, she'd dwelled on the robbery, the trial, the townspeople. Why, she wondered, hadn't she thought of those happy times before?

She sat down at the table. And why had the house come to feel like a home again? Anna's gaze met Sam's as she passed him the beans. He smiled, a warm, familiar smile. Anna turned away quickly.

"I've given some thought to making you an offer on your farm," Sam said to Ben.

The older man spooned gravy over his potatoes. "I'd be right proud to see you have it."

Sam shook his head. "But, to be honest with you, Ben, it would be a year or so down the road before I'd be in a position to buy you out."

"You've got your hands full getting this place up and running," Ben agreed.

"And doing a fine job of it," Lloyd agreed.

Sam sighed. "So, if you need to take Hampton up on his offer, I understand."

Ben squinted at him from across the table. "Hampton?"

"Is that Charles Hampton?" Lloyd asked.

Sam nodded. "He was asking around about buying this place, so I told him you were looking to sell. You mean he hasn't talked to you about it?"

Ben shrugged. "Nope. Not a peep. And I saw him just yesterday in town. He never mentioned a word about looking for a place to buy."

The men all exchanged a puzzled look.

"Well, it doesn't surprise me."

As one, they all turned to Anna. She gulped down the bite of potatoes she'd just taken.

"I talked to Mr. Hampton at the horseshoe-pitching tournament," she explained hurriedly. "I don't think he'd ever settle here permanently."

Sam's brows drew together. His jaw tightened. "Why not?" Strained patience was in his tone.

Anna shifted uncomfortably, unsure of what she'd said that had upset him so.

"Grandchildren."

Sam rubbed his forehead. "What?"

"Grandchildren." Anna repeated the word thinking that it explained everything.

Sam's frown deepened.

"Mr. Hampton has grandchildren in Richmond. His whole family is there. He misses them terribly. I can't imagine why he moved here in the first place."

Lloyd nodded. "Makes sense."

"Well," Ben said, "I don't cotton to the notion of selling out to some stranger. If I decided to hold on to the place for another year, you and me will talk about it then, Sam. Fair enough?"

Sam nodded. "Fair enough."

After supper the men headed for the front porch for a smoke. Sam hung back in the kitchen.

"I'll be out in a minute," he called.

"Sure thing," Lloyd said as he and Ben disappeared down the hallway.

When their voices faded, Sam whirled around to Anna. "Why didn't you tell me about Hampton?"

Anna looked up from the dishes she was gathering. "Tell you what?"

His gaze was dark with accusation. "About his family in Richmond."

"I didn't think anything of it. It hardly seemed important."
She carried the plates to the sink.

He picked up the cups and followed along behind her.
"We're partners in this. I expect you to tell me everything."

Her eyes bulged as if he'd taken leave of his senses. "I'm
not your partner. I'm a victim of your blackmail."

Sam tensed. He studied her for a long moment, then
dropped the cups in the sink. He blew out a heavy breath.
"Yes, I suppose you would look at it that way."

She turned back to the table and gathered the serving
dishes.

Absently, Sam pumped water into a pan and put it on the
stove to warm. "Too bad you and I couldn't have teamed up
under some other circumstances. I think we'd have made
good partners."

Anna grinned as she returned to the sideboard. "Do you?"

He looked down at her and grinned slowly. "Yes, I do. You
seem to know more about keeping house than I'd given you
credit for."

Anna pumped water into the sink. "Are you suggesting we
should open a maid service together?" she asked with a grin.

Sam moved to stand beside her. His gaze captured hers.
Gently he touched her chin with the tip of his finger and
traced the line of her jaw. A hot trail blazed her neck to the
collar of her blouse.

"No, no maid service." Sam stepped closer.

Anna's heart began to pound. Her senses flamed. "You
don't mean you want to run an orphanage with me, do you?"

Sam splayed his hand across her neck and dug his fingers
into the hair at her nape. He edged closer. "I'd thought of
children. But not orphans."

Anna touched her tongue to her dry lips. His hand gently
kneaded her neck sending waves of pleasure pulsing through
her.

"I hope you're not asking me to team up and rob the mint
again."

A chuckle rumbled deep in Sam's chest. His gaze searched
her face. "I can picture you and me pulling off a holdup,

arguing over who was going to hold the gun and who was going to grab the money."

Anna laughed with him. She touched his arm. Through his shirt she could feel his corded muscles drawn tight. Her knees felt weak.

"I can't imagine anything else you and I could be partners in." She whispered the words.

"How about this."

Sam's lips touched hers, softly, gently. The sensation overwhelmed her, and Anna fell against him, wrapping her arms around his waist. Her breasts tingled as they pressed against his powerful chest.

He groaned and deepened the kiss, pressing more intimately. Lost in the masculine taste of him, Anna let him pull her closer in his embrace, locking her in his arms.

She was helpless against the spell he cast over her, mesmerized by the whirling sensations that pulsed through her.

Then he broke off the kiss, but his gaze held hers—firmly, deliberately.

"Anna . . ."

He breathed her name hoarsely. The deep resonate sound seeped inside her, washed over her like a wave.

"Anna . . . I . . ."

He stopped. His brows drew together in an unreadable scowl. She thought it was anger, or indecision, she saw on his face. Anna's heart lurched. He opened his mouth to speak again, but hesitated, then stepped away.

Sam turned abruptly and walked out of the room and down the hallway toward the front of the house.

She tingled all over, her body still throbbing from Sam's touch. Was he angry with her, she wondered. Was he displeased with her kiss?

Anna stared at nothing for a long moment. No, she realized, it wasn't anger she'd seen in Sam Rowan's face tonight.

It was fear.

Sam cursed softly as he felt in the darkness for the lantern. The acid scent of sulfur burned his nose as he struck a match against the wooden stall door and touched it to the wick.

Light filled the corner of the barn that had become his bedroom since Lloyd Caldwell's arrival.

And tonight, this drafty, smelly barn was the last place he wanted to be.

Sam cursed again as he sat down on the small bunk he'd built into the stall by the tack room and kept covered with harnesses during the day. He'd nearly made a complete fool of himself tonight. He'd nearly given away everything he'd worked toward these last weeks.

The wait tonight for Ben to leave and Lloyd to have his smoke had been unbearable, especially since Anna had never appeared on the porch to join them after supper. He could only imagine what she must be thinking.

"Jesus. . . ." Sam stood quickly and paced the narrow stall. His footsteps were silent against the soft earth.

Children. He'd brought up children to her. What the hell had he been thinking? She didn't want children. She'd said so a thousand times.

And he'd mentioned a partnership. Where had that idea come from? Anna didn't want a partnership of any sort. She'd made her position on that subject very clear. Numerous times.

Sam kicked at the bottom rail of the stall. Farther down the barn, Fortune whinnied and tossed his head.

It was useless. Hopeless. Pointless. It was the most frustrating situation he'd ever been up against.

Sam plopped down on his bunk and braced his elbows against his knees. It was no good thinking about it or mooning over it or wasting a good night's sleep over it, he told himself. Even if she did believe him, she'd never want any part of it. Yet Sam knew he had to tell her. He was going to bust if he didn't.

Somehow, he was going to have to tell Anna he'd fallen in love with her.

Anna lifted the clothes basket onto the bed and began sorting through the laundry. She was tired this morning, having rested little last night. Sam's strange behavior and abrupt departure had kept her tossing and turning, speculating on what he'd been trying to work up courage enough to tell her.

Everything had flashed through her mind, from absurd to sobering, but she'd not settled on any real possibilities. She'd dreamed of him all night, images of the two of them riding the country together, holding up orphanages, taking children to their secret hideout to raise.

Ridiculous dreams, Anna thought as she slid her fingers inside the pockets of one of Sam's shirts. She pulled out two nails and tossed them on the table beside the bed.

Sam looked like he'd slept no better than she when he'd come in for breakfast this morning. He still had the peculiar look in his eye that he'd had last night. She wasn't sure what it meant, but before he left for the field, he'd hauled the water and filled the washtubs for her. There was extra laundry to do today, with Uncle Lloyd still staying with them. He'd promised, too, to set aside some time this afternoon and help her make the scarecrow to put in the garden.

Anna sank down onto the bed amid the mound of dirty clothes. She picked up another of Sam's shirts and mindlessly ran her hands through the pockets.

He'd been different with Uncle Lloyd there. Attentive, complimentary, kind. He was a hard worker, too. Already he'd accomplished a great deal around the farm. And it pleased her, she realized, that the place was starting to take shape. It reminded her of the "before" times, and all those memories were good ones.

Anna picked up a pair of Sam's trousers. What had he been trying to tell her last night?

She slid her hand into the back pocket. Talk of partnerships. What did it mean?

Her fingers closed over a piece of paper. And children? Why had he brought up children?

Anna withdrew the paper from Sam's trouser pocket. She'd already come across a variety of nails, his pocket knife he was no doubt searching for, and several coins, and she nearly tossed the paper aside with the rest of the collection when something written there caught her eye. It was a name. Her name.

Slowly Anna unfolded the telegram. Her eyes scanned the message quickly. Her stomach coiled into a knot.

It was from her uncle. He was coming to visit her. Anna

re-read the telegram. She studied each word carefully so there was no mistaking the meaning. Her heart began to pound.

Reluctantly, without really wanting to, her gaze searched the crumpled paper. Anna's blood ran cold. There, in Deacon Fry's careful script, was the date of the telegram. Over a week ago. Before Uncle Lloyd had appeared so unexpectedly. Before she'd run to the barn and pleaded with Sam to save her reputation. Before she'd had to bargain away her future. Sam had known.

Anna came to her feet, spilling the dirty clothes to the floor.

Sam had known. He'd gotten the telegram intended for her and kept it a secret.

Anger flamed in the pit of her stomach. He'd known her uncle was coming. He'd plotted to use that knowledge against her and get the money all for himself. And that's exactly what he'd done.

Fury ripped through Anna as she closed her fist around the telegram. He was a bastard. A conniving bastard. And she'd been a fool to think otherwise. She should have never softened her feelings or let down her guard. He'd used her. Again.

Anna stuffed the telegram back into the pocket of Sam's trousers and hurled them across the room. Her limbs shook. Her breath came in short, rapid puffs.

There wasn't much time left. She'd have to move quickly. Her uncle would be gone any day, and soon after, Sam would follow. And she couldn't let him get away until. . . .

Anna's hands curled into fists. She couldn't let him get away until she'd gotten her revenge.

Anna ran to the barn. Hard, cold determination was etched in her face as she scoured the tool room for hammer and nails and slipped them into the pockets of her apron. Then she climbed the ladder to the loft and kicked hay down to the floor.

She hauled it all to the back porch and stuffed the hay into Sam's trousers and one of his shirts. Anna worked feverishly, mindless of the dry straw that pricked the soft skin of her hands.

When she'd finished, she dragged it to the garden and nailed the scarecrow to the post that Sam had already planted there. Anna stood back and brushed the straw from her skirt. She nodded her head slowly, satisfied with her work.

The scarecrow wore Sam's trousers and inside the pocket was the telegram. Planted there in the middle of the garden, it would be a constant reminder of what Sam had done. A flag. A beacon. An ever-present symbol of the bastard he was. Never again, she vowed, never again would she fall victim to his tricks.

Anna turned her anger to the laundry, scrubbing and wringing the garments with a vengeance. Sam was uppermost in her mind. The despicable deed he'd done, the unforgivable trick he'd pulled, and her desire for revenge.

By the time she'd washed, rinsed, and hung the laundry, most of Anna's anger had dissipated, along with her energy. She looked out over the farm, the barn, the corral, the garden, and the scarecrow. Anna didn't know why, but her friend Sarah came to mind. Lucky Sarah, with a husband and a new baby. A life. A real life.

Glumly she turned toward the house, feet dragging slowly across the yard. Reverend Langford could preach a whole sermon on her own life, Anna decided. Revenge, vindictiveness, envy, coveting other people's babies. But if the message in his last sermon was to be lived out, she was justified in her thoughts, she decided. Sam deserved to be punished—an eye for an eye—that was what the Bible said.

Anna stopped. Her stomach began to tingle. Sam had taken away the life she'd planned for herself. So, according to Reverend Langford's sermon, his punishment should fit his crime. Sam would give her another life.

A slow smile spread across Anna's face as an idea took root. It spread quickly and grew fully.

Yes, she'd have the ultimate revenge. Sam would give her another life to make up for the one he'd taken. Anna's heart soared.

Sam would give her a baby.

CHAPTER 16

"I would like to purchase your services for the night. Just take it out of the fifty thousand dollars I've already given you."

Anna spoke the words aloud to the mirror above her bureau. It sounded all right, she supposed. A simple business proposition. Maybe, on those terms, Sam would go along with it.

Anna patted the back of her hair and laid her brush aside. There was only one way to find out.

Sam came in through the back door just as she reached the kitchen. She glanced out the window beside the cookstove.

"Where's Uncle Lloyd?"

Sam took the linen towel from the sideboard and dried his face and hands; he still washed up at the pump out back.

He nodded toward the backyard. "He stopped to pull a few weeds from the vegetable patch."

Anna tied her apron on. Her stomach tingled. Now was as good a time as any to propose her business arrangement.

"Speaking of the vegetable patch—" Sam tossed the towel aside and cast her a harsh look. "I see you made your scarecrow today."

Anna froze as she poured flour into the mixing bowl. Yes, the scarecrow. Her banner. Her flag.

The anger she'd felt in finding her uncle's telegram in Sam's pocket coiled deep in her stomach. An outright confrontation, complete with accusations, name-calling, and shouting was what she preferred. Instead, she'd chosen to keep silent and finally, at long last, get even with Sam. She had to hold tight to her resolve.

Anna glanced back over her shoulder. "Yes. I finished it this afternoon. I know you said we'd work on it together, but I decided not to wait. It turned out rather nicely, don't you think?"

"I think it's the best-dressed scarecrow I've ever seen." His jaw tightened. "That's probably because it's wearing my trousers and shirt."

Anna turned to face him. His gaze bore into her. She batted her eyelashes. "I needed to dress it in something."

"For chrissake, Anna." Sam touched his forehead then planted both fists on his hips. "It's not like I've got drawers of clothes to wear."

She pursed her lips. "A temporary problem, I'm sure you'll agree. As soon as my uncle leaves, you'll be able to buy yourself most anything in the state."

Anna whipped around and plunged her hands into the biscuit dough. "Unlike me, who'll never be able to purchase decent yard goods for a dress, let alone anything so extravagant as a new hat."

Sam exhaled heavily and pulled at the tight muscles of his neck. He could hardly disagree with her.

"What's for supper?" he asked and poured himself a cup of coffee from the pot on the stove.

Anna glanced at him as she rolled the biscuits. "Chicken."

"Again?" He leaned a hip against the sideboard, watching her. "There's half a cow in the smoke house. Can't we have a steak or roast sometimes?"

"Beef is expensive," she explained. "I was being cautious with it."

He shrugged. "Well, like you just said, I guess I can afford it."

She could have cried. He hadn't said it in a mean way, but the finality of their arrangement still tore at her. Anna toughened her feelings. It was time to get on with her revenge.

"So, tell me, Sam, what do you plan to do with all that money?"

He took a sip of coffee. "I already told you. I'm buying me a farm. I'm going to raise horses."

Anna pressed the biscuit cutter into the soft dough. "You can make a living doing that?"

"Sure. Between selling off the yearlings and putting the stallions out to stud, I figure I'll do all right." Sam took another drink from his cup.

Anna frowned. "Putting them out to stud. What's that?"

He gulped down a mouthful of coffee. This was hardly an appropriate topic to be discussing with a proper, decent woman like Anna.

"I'd get paid for my stallions mating with mares." Sam took another sip, satisfied he'd been delicate enough.

"Like a whore?"

Sam choked on the coffee. He coughed and sputtered. "What? Where'd you hear that word?"

"Isn't that right?" Anna looked up at him, her big, brown eyes wide.

"Yes—no! No, it's not like that. Who told you about—that?"

Anna wiped her hands on her apron. "Then what's the difference?"

Sam plopped his cup down on the sideboard. "There's a big difference."

"Then what is it," she challenged.

"I'll tell you what the difference is." Sam searched feverishly for some shred of logic. He shifted uncomfortably. "The difference is that with stallions it's business, and with . . . women . . . it's—it's . . . different."

Anna nodded slowly. "So what you're saying is that as long as it's the man that's being paid, it's all right."

At the moment, Sam wasn't sure what point he was trying to make. He'd agree with anything, though, to end this conversation.

"Yes, that's it."

"But if it's the woman that's being paid then it's not all right."

"Exactly."

"But men pay women all the time, don't they?"

She was looking at him funny, as if she were sizing him up, determining something. He didn't like it. Not one bit.

"I'm going to help your uncle pull weeds."

Sam bolted for the door.

Well, so much for the business proposal, Anna thought as she watched Sam striding across the backyard. Now what was she going to do? She'd have to think of some way to get him into her bed. The only problem was, she didn't have the slightest idea of how to go about it. She wished now she'd paid more attention to the gossip about Maggie Fry.

Anna went about getting supper ready, toying with all sorts of ideas from making a clandestine call on the soiled doves who lived on the other side of town to joining Sam at the creek for his nightly bath. Maybe something drastic would do the trick, Anna thought, as she put a pot of water on to boil. Maybe if she—

"Yooooo-hooo!"

Anna turned to find Emma Langford walking through her back door.

"Your uncle said for me to come on in. He and Sam are out front walking with Pa. We're just out calling on folks this evening." Emma smiled brightly, her freckled cheeks beaming.

"It's nice of you to stop by." Anna wiped her hands on the towel. "I'll have supper on soon. Will you join us?"

"Oh, no. Pa promised we'll have supper at the hotel tonight." Emma's smile stayed firmly in place but her gaze swept the entire room. "Really, Anna, I don't remember the last time I was here, but I didn't realize the place was so small. You've surely got your work cut out for you."

"It's coming along." Anna turned back to the stove, not wanting Emma to see that her words had hit a nerve. Certainly not Emma, of all people. She carried gossip from person to person, spreading it faster than the plague.

"We were just out to see the Fosters." Emma wandered to the hutch and eyed the dishes stacked there. "Vera is just beside herself, of course, and Jack is fit to be tied. I think they really needed Pa's help."

Anna stirred the potatoes. The Foster family lived on the

other side of Ben Atkins's farm. "What's wrong with Vera and Jack?"

Emma gasped. "Well, hadn't you heard?"

"Heard what?"

Emma pursed her lips and crossed the room to stand close to Anna. "It's just the scandal of the county," she whispered.

Gossip. She should have known. Anna wished she hadn't asked.

"Vera and Jack's daughter Ardeth is—" Emma glanced around the empty kitchen. She edged closer to Anna and whispered, "—is in the family way."

"Ardeth?" Anna's eyes popped open. "But she's only fourteen. And she's not even married."

Emma nodded wisely.

"Oh, my." Anna shook her head. "No wonder her mother is so upset. But what happened? Ardeth seems like such a nice young girl."

Emma pressed her lips primly. "It was that Perkins boy."

"Danny Perkins? Little Danny?" She was acquainted with the Foster family and the Perkins clan from seeing them at Sunday services. "He seems like a nice boy, hardly the type to—"

"It was liquor." Emma nodded solemnly. "It's the devil's brew—Pa always says so."

"Danny was drunk when it happened?"

"Oh, yes," Emma said. "Liquor makes men lose all control. Why, you get a man drunk and who knows what he's liable to do."

Anna paused as she rolled chicken pieces in flour. She turned to Emma. "Drinking really affects men that way?"

"Certainly. I suppose that's one of the reasons Vera feels so bad. She never warned Ardeth about men and drinking. Anyway, it looks like they'll be getting married any day."

"I hope they'll be happy," Anna mumbled, her thought on a different subject.

"I suppose they will. You just wouldn't think this could happen to a nice girl like Ardeth." Idly, Emma strolled around the kitchen. "But that Maggie Fry. Now there's a different story."

Anna turned back to her chicken. Emma made no bones about it, she simply did not like Deacon Fry's young wife. In truth Anna didn't care much for her either, thinking her too familiar when it came to Sam.

"I don't know why Maggie has never gotten . . . caught," Emma said. "That woman is a disgrace, the way she's always fawning over men, touching them, giving them the eye. She thinks no one sees, but everybody knows. Why, Deacon Fry must be so sorry he ever married her."

"Do you think she does that on purpose?" Anna asked. She thought back over Maggie's behavior while in the company of other men—including Sam—and was willing now to be objective if only because Emma was so judgmental. "Maybe she's just friendly."

"Humph!" Emma blinked her short lashes rapidly. "She knows how to lure a man."

"Lure?" Anna's attention was piqued.

Emma laughed. "Really, Anna, don't be silly. After all, you attracted that husband of yours."

She'd never attracted a man in her life. But she did have extensive experience in driving away every one she could, every prospective suitor who'd looked her way in Salem. She didn't know the first thing about getting a man's attention.

Emma laughed again. "Goodness, Anna. Think about when you and Sam were courting. You complimented him, told him what a strong, capable man he was, fixed him special meals, catered to him, went out of your way to please him." Emma's expression turned hard. "And that's exactly what Maggie Fry does—only to everyone else's husband instead of her own."

Anna didn't respond. She clung to each of Emma's words, committing them to memory. Complimentary . . . special meal . . . pleasing. . . .

"I saw Brett Morgan today."

She felt Emma's gaze upon her, waiting for a reaction. Determined not to be the grist for her rumor mill, Anna kept her expression steady.

"Oh? That's nice."

"He asked about you."

Darn his hide, Anna thought angrily. Why didn't Brett

leave her alone? She hadn't seen or spoken to him in days. But she had the sinking feeling that she'd never see the end of Brett Morgan.

"Have you seen the Calhouns' new baby?" Anna asked.

"Yes, yes. Little Justin. Such a dear." Emma said. "Well, I suppose I'd better go."

Emma appeared to have grown bored with their conversation. Anna wiped her hands on her apron. "I'll walk out with you."

The two women went out the back door and around the house to where the men stood beside Reverend Langford's buggy. Emma climbed in beside her father.

"Glad you stopped by," Sam said as he shook the reverend's hand. "Come on back soon. Have supper with us."

The reverend picked up the reins. "I'll do just that." He turned to Lloyd. "These two are a welcome addition to our community. You ought to be proud."

Lloyd smiled broadly. "I am, Hiram. I am."

The reverend flicked the reins, and the horse pulled the buggy toward the road.

"Oh Anna!" Emma turned on the small leather seat. "I forgot to tell you. Your hat is ready."

"What?"

"The hat you said you liked so much when you were in the shop is ready. Come by and pick it up." Emma waved good-bye as the buggy pulled away.

Anna shuddered. She'd forgotten about the hideous hat Emma was working on that day. "Thanks," she called and waved.

"What was that all about?" Sam asked.

"Nothing," Anna said. "Just a hat Emma showed me in her shop."

Lloyd stroked his chin. "She's got quite a flare for headwear." Today's monstrosity was fashioned like a boat with a fisherman seated in the crown and fish dangling from lines over the sides.

Sam touched Anna's arm. "Do you want the hat?" he asked gently.

Good heavens, no! Anna wanted to scream at him. But her

uncle was watching and this seemed like a prime opportunity to make a good-wife remark. She smiled. "You're a dear for asking, Sam, but no. We need our money to get the farm going. You two get washed. Supper will be ready soon."

Confused, Sam watched her trim form swaying across the yard. They'd just had a similar conversation with her saying how she'd never afford a bonnet or decent yard goods and he'd have the cash to buy anything he desired.

Sam stroked his chin and watched Emma and her dangling fish disappear down the dusty road.

As soon as Anna closed the back door behind her she hiked up her skirt and dashed down the hall and into her bedroom. Emma Langford, of all people, had given her tips on getting Sam into bed with her.

She opened the armoire and pulled out Sam's saddlebags. She'd left them there the first night he'd come to the farm and she'd forgotten all about them until Emma's gossip had given her a sure-fire solution to her problem.

Feeling inside the leather pouch, Anna located the small whiskey bottle and pulled it out. The liquor was a deep amber as she held it in the sunlight. The devil's brew, Emma had called it. Anna tossed the saddlebag back into the armoire. She hoped she'd brew up the kind of trouble she wanted.

Her knowledge of drinking was even less than her experience with men, so Anna could only guess how much liquor was enough to make Sam lose control, as Emma had put it.

Should she dribble some into his food? She stared at the pots and pans on the stove. It might have a distinctive taste, she thought.

Anna pulled out the cork and took a tiny sip. The hot liquid burned her mouth and throat and spread fingers of fire through her belly. Anna coughed. Her head reeled. Anna grabbed the sideboard for support.

"What's wrong?"

It was Sam!

Coughing and wheezing, Anna grabbed for the bottle of whiskey. She had to hide it! Instead it tipped over and spilled onto the sideboard.

"Are you all right?"

She deliberately presented her back and tossed the linen towel over the spill. But it was no good. Sam reached over her shoulder and picked up the whiskey bottle.

"Where did you find this?"

"I don't know." She coughed again.

His brows drew together. "Were you drinking this?"

"No!" She batted her watery eyes at him and cleared her throat. "Pepper—I just swallowed a little pepper."

He didn't look as though he believed her but corked the bottle and turned away.

"Don't you want some?" Anna asked hopefully, following him to the pantry.

"I'm not much of a drinker." He placed the bottle on the top shelf. "I take a nip sometimes when I feel the croup coming on."

Now she was confused. "But I thought men like to drink."

"Where did you get an idea like that?" Sam chuckled and headed out the back door. "Holler when supper is ready."

Undaunted by one seemingly bad piece of Emma's advice, Anna pressed on. She conjured up the memory of every moment she'd seen the seductive Maggie Fry in action and tried it out for herself when Sam and her uncle came in to eat. By the time she'd served supper and their meal concluded, Anna had managed to "accidentally" bump nearly every part of her body against Sam. She brushed her bottom across his as she took the biscuits from the oven and slid her breasts along his back when she turned to get the platter of chicken. Seated at the table she rubbed her leg against his—twice— and each time he ignored her, as if she hadn't touched him at all.

Refusing to be discouraged, she hurried through the dishes and headed out to the porch where they always spent their evenings. She would sit next to him on the swing, she decided as she hurried down the hallway. But when she reached the porch her hopes fell. "Where's Sam?"

The swing creaked as her uncle puffed his cigar and gazed idly into the distance. "Said he needed a bath."

"A bath?" Anna plopped down on the swing. Sam bathed

every night at the creek, she knew, but never this early in the evening.

She waited on the porch until the sun had dipped below the mountains and her uncle had finally retired, and still no sign of Sam. She went off to bed alone.

Sam splashed another handful of water in his face, sending icy rivulets trickling down his back and chest. He shifted on the rocks. It wasn't helping, he thought miserably. Even seated as he was, waist deep in the middle of the creek, his body was still on fire.

He'd felt like a moose at a tea party tonight in the kitchen, big and clumsy. Every way he'd turned he bumped into something of Anna's—something soft and yielding, something he wanted to grab hold of with both hands. He'd wanted to take her right there in the kitchen, right when she'd bent over to take the biscuits from the oven.

Desire surged through him at the thought. He was stiff and swollen and achy—and he hated himself for it.

Anna was completely innocent. She'd had no experience with men. She probably thought him a brute for bumping into her all evening.

He'd control himself from now on, Sam vowed as the freezing water swirled around him. Even if it meant sitting in the creek until he got pneumonia.

The next morning Sam rushed through breakfast and headed out the door without a look and scarcely a word for Anna. He awakened this morning to find himself in the same condition as when he'd gone to bed last night, and he couldn't chance spending too much time with her. If she dropped something, God help him when she tried to pick it up.

Inwardly, Anna sighed when she saw Sam leave. It would have been easy to become discouraged, since he seemed to be so uninterested in her. But she had a new plan. One which required her uncle's help. He was one man she could count on.

"Uncle Lloyd?"

"Yes, Anna?" Lloyd reached for his hat by the door.

She waited a minute until she saw that Sam was well across the yard. "Today is the anniversary of my first meeting with Sam and I wanted to do something special for him."

"Oh?"

"I planned to make him a special supper tonight." She dipped her gaze hoping to look like a blushing bride and not a lying skunk.

Lloyd nodded and gave her a wink. "I'll just go into town later on and give you two some time together."

Anna smiled shyly. "Thank you, Uncle Lloyd." She wondered if people went to hell for telling lies.

She left a light meal for them at noon, and just as they'd planned, Uncle Lloyd came back to the house by midafternoon. He changed his clothes, kissed Anna's cheek, and headed back to the barn.

With the men gone, she'd spent the whole morning preparing. She'd bathed and washed her hair with rainwater and taken extra care in styling it with rows of curls in the back. Now, dressed in a black skirt and pale-pink blouse with ruffles all down the front, she was ready as she supposed she'd ever be.

Sam came through the back door. "Your uncle said you wanted me."

"Supper's ready." She cast him a slow smile from the sideboard where she stood slicing cornbread.

He didn't move from the doorway. "This early?"

"I fixed what you asked for last night," she explained. "It got done a little quicker than I thought it would."

Her hair was different. He wasn't sure how, exactly, but it was different. It made him want to plunge his hands into the curls.

"Sam?"

"Huh?" He snapped out of his own thought.

"You are hungry, aren't you?"

He was starved. But the meal she'd prepared had little bearing on his problem.

"I made roast, like you asked. With onions and carrots and potatoes. It's ready now."

Well, he could hardly say no. "I'll go wash up."

"No, wait!" She gestured to a bowl by the sink. "You can wash here. I've got a pan of hot water for you."

His eyes narrowed. "Where's your uncle?"

Anna shrugged. "He wanted to go into town for the evening."

Something was wrong. A tiny voice somewhere deep in his mind was sounding an alarm. It went unheeded, however, as the rest of him took notice of the ruffles that covered her blouse, moulding the rise and swell of her ample breasts.

He rolled back his sleeves and scrubbed his hands, arms, and face with the bar soap she'd laid out for him, then dried with the fresh linen towel.

"How does this look?"

Sam turned to see her bending over, pulling the roast from the oven. His knees nearly buckled.

"Are you ready to sink into it?" she asked.

"Oh, God, yes."

Anna brushed past him and placed the roast and vegetables on the table. "Sit down."

He had to. Before he fell. Before she saw.

Anna took the chair across from him, pleased that the meal had turned out so well. The roast was perfectly cooked, the vegetables tender. And Sam was eating it, though he seemed distracted.

She tried joking with him, talking, complimenting him, asking about the work he was doing at the barn, but he managed only mumbled responses. Finally she couldn't stand it anymore.

"Is something wrong?"

The edge of her voice brought him out of his ruffle-stupor. "No, uh-uh."

She drummed her fingers on the table. "You've hardly said a word."

Had he? "Oh, well, I pulled a muscle or something in my shoulder a while ago. It's just hurting a little, that's all." It wasn't a lie, except that he hadn't felt anything from the waist up since she'd taken the roast from the oven.

"Why didn't you tell me?" She got out of her chair.

Sam swallowed hard. He knew where she was headed. "No, Anna, it's okay."

"This will fix you right up." She took a bottle of liniment from the cupboard where she kept her medical supplies. "Take off your shirt."

Sam bolted to his feet. If she touched him—just once—

"I've got to go." He skirted around her and went out the door.

"But where are you going?"

"Into town!" he called as he hurried toward the barn.

Her hopes fell. Anna sank into the chair. Not only had she not gotten him into her bed, but she'd managed to run him off the farm completely.

He was going to find him a woman. Come hell or high water, he was going to be between somebody's legs before the night was over.

The thought burned through Sam as he touched his heel to Fortune's sides and galloped away from the house. He rode the stallion hard all the way into Kemper, slowing him to a walk only when he reached Main Street. The run seemed to release much of the horse's pent up energy; it did nothing to relieve Sam.

He cut down the alley, so as not to be so noticeable on the busy street, and rode to the big white house with the red shutters on the opposite end of town. It was still early—the sun wasn't even down yet—which suited Sam perfectly. It shouldn't be busy yet, and he wasn't in a mood to wait.

Sam tied Fortune to the hitching post out front and crossed the porch. A woman with rouged lips and cheeks and huge bosoms spilling out of her red silk wrapper answered his knock.

Her gaze ran the length of him, eyeing him seductively. "Come on in, sugar."

Sam stepped inside the parlor. It was decorated with heavy red drapes, dark, ornately carved furniture, and gold-framed paintings of naked women frolicking in meadows and streams. His stomach coiled.

"I'm Mable," the woman said. "You're new. Just passing through?"

Mable seemed to be looking straight through him. She was probably in her forties, he guessed, and this was probably her house. She'd been around.

"Want a drink?" she offered.

Sam's palms began to sweat. He shook his head.

"Just want to get right to it?"

"Yeah."

"Do you have a preference? Blonde, brunette, thin, short?"

"I don't care."

Mable grinned, a slow, knowing grin. "Been a while, huh?"

Sam threaded his hand through his hair. "Yeah."

"Ruby! Come on out here, honey. I've got a gentleman for you to meet."

From behind the curtain across the room stepped a dark-haired beauty. She wore a floral drape, open to the waist and tied loosely with a gold sash. She held out her hand. "Let's go up to my room."

Sam's mouth suddenly went dry. Her hair. It was the same shade as Anna's. Maybe not as shiny, but so close in color that he couldn't look at Ruby without seeing Anna.

"Have you got one that doesn't have brown hair?" he asked Mable.

Ruby looked disappointed, but left.

Mable gave him a wink. "I've got just what you need. Pearl!"

She was a tall, buxom woman with thick blond hair swirling around her shoulders. When she stepped through the curtains she eyed Sam hungrily.

Sam cringed. Her eyes! They were deep brown—just like Anna's.

"Well?" Mable asked.

"Blue eyes. I need one with blue eyes."

Slightly miffed, Mable sent Pearl away. "Sapphire, honey!"

The redhead walked in wearing a wrap that was split up to her hip and opened to her waist. Her bosoms were round and full, peeking at him through the thin fabric.

Anna's breasts had looked just like that when he'd caught her rising naked from the bathtub. And it was hers he itched to touch, not this woman's.

"What now?" Mable asked sourly.

"Smaller bosoms," Sam requested.

She sent Sapphire away with a nod of her head and called, "Garnet!"

Sam sighed with relief when he saw her, blonde, blue-eyed, with small mounds of breasts barely visible through the opaque wrap she wore. This one was perfect. Except—

She was the same age as Anna. He knew it without a moment's hesitation.

Sam turned to Mable. "Have you got anyone older?"

Mable rolled her eyes. "Well, there's my grandma, but she's dead and buried out behind the privy!"

Sam shrugged helplessly.

"Come on, sugar." Mable took his arm and led him back to the door. "You're just going to have to find a way to bed down with whoever it is that's got your privates in a pinch, honey, because I don't think anybody but her is going to do you any good."

Sam dug coins from his pocket. "Thanks anyway."

"You keep it, sugar." Mable folded his hand over the money. She smiled. "Something tells me you're going to have to marry her to get her between the sheets with you, and you're going to need that money more than me. Goodnight, sugar."

Dejected, Sam climbed on Fortune and headed back through town. Anna. He just couldn't get her off his mind. He couldn't even go to a whorehouse, for chrissake, without thinking of her. Sam cursed his body and its needs. Needs that could only be satisfied by Anna, it seemed. He pictured her as she had been when he'd left the farm, in her rows of ruffles, looking confused and hurt when he'd run from the kitchen. And after she'd gone to the trouble of making a special supper for him. Sam sighed. He felt like a louse. Maybe he could think of a way to make it up to her—without getting too close to her, of course.

"Yooo-hooo! Saaaaam!"

Emma Langford. Good God.

Sam pulled his horse to a stop in front of the millinery shop just as Emma was crossing the boardwalk.

"Evening, Miss Langford."

"I knew you'd be here, I just knew it." She giggled and adjusted her hat, fashioned like a stage coach with purple and green horses galloping around the brim. "I told Mildred Palmer, I said, 'That Sam Rowan will be in my shop before the end of the week.' I said it."

What the hell was she talking about? He forced a smile. "Well, here I am."

"So you are." Emma dug through her reticule and came up with the key to the shop. "Come on in. I was just closing, but you just come right on inside."

Sam groaned inwardly, wondering what the devil he'd gotten himself into. He climbed down off Fortune and followed Emma into the store.

"Don't feel uncomfortable in here, it's not as scarey as it looks." Emma lit the lanterns and turned them up. "I know men don't like it in women's places, but this won't take a second."

Women's places. Did that include whorehouses, Sam wondered.

Emma lifted a hat from the display in the front window. "This is it! Isn't it gorgeous."

It was a fruit bowl. A big green fruit bowl-shaped hat, with an orange, an apple, and a banana exploding out of the top and a bunch of grapes dangling down the side.

"Anna will just look so pretty in this."

Sam gasped.

"And it's so sweet of you to make a special trip into town and get it for her." Emma beamed happily. "I knew you would, after you heard us talking about it at your place the other night."

Sam remembered Anna had mentioned a hat, but he couldn't imagine her wearing something like this. He glanced around the store at the smaller, more fashionable bonnets. They looked like they belonged on Anna's head.

"Are you sure this is the one she wanted?"

"Of course," Emma said. "I made it myself."

"Well . . ."

There was just no way to disguise a hatbox, Sam realized, much to his embarrassment, as he was riding out of town. For one thing, it was about six times bigger than the hat. And it was decorated in pink and lilac with ruffles around the bottom, a bow on the top, and a string of lace where a handle ought to be. People were watching him as they finished their evening shopping and closed their stores, heading home for the night. The women all looked at him with endearing smiles, as if he'd recited a poem correctly at a grade-school play, and the men all appeared sympathetic, as if he too now belonged to the great fraternity of husbands forced to buy gifts to get back in the good graces of their wives.

Sam was glad when he arrived home. And glad too, in a way, that Anna was already closed up in her room and Lloyd wasn't anywhere to be seen; at least he didn't have to explain to her uncle why he'd been absent from the farm in the first place. Sam shoved the hatbox on the top shelf of the pantry and went out to the barn.

He lay wide-eyed on his bunk in the darkness and listened when the old doctor arrived some time later and bedded his horse down for the night at the far end of the barn. Something would have to change. Sam knew it in his heart. He couldn't go on feeling this way about Anna and doing nothing about it. Maybe Lloyd Caldwell would leave soon, he thought. At least then, things could go forward.

She slammed the bowl of oatmeal down on the table in front of him. "If you want more, it's on the stove. I've got work to do."

Anna stalked out of the kitchen.

"Oh, no, honey, it's fine," Sam called to the empty doorway.

He glanced at Lloyd eyeing him over the top of his spectacles from across the table. It was a sympathetic look.

"Guess it didn't go well last night."

Sam picked up his spoon. "What?"

"The special dinner she planned for your anniversary."

"Anniversary?" Sam frowned.

Lloyd shook his head in dismay. "Now you've done it."

"Christ . . ."

Sam left the table and took refuge in the barn. Presently Lloyd joined him but neither spoke as they went about their chores. Finally, Sam gave up.

"I'm going back up to the house for a while."

Lloyd gave him a nod of encouragement. "Good luck, son."

The parlor was filthy and she was sick of looking at it. She'd have it spotless by sundown, Anna swore, one way or the other.

The morning had grown warm so Anna had thrown open both parlor windows, letting in the small breeze. She was hot from the work she'd already done in the room, uncovering the furniture, knocking the cobwebs from the corners, sweeping up the dirt, and cleaning out the fireplace.

Beads of perspiration dotted her nose. She'd opened her blouse all the way to the top of her chemise and removed her petticoats, stockings, and slippers. Her hair was wrapped in a scarf to protect it from the dust.

Anna picked up the hem of her skirt and fanned her face as she gazed up at the window she'd just washed, checking for streaks. The breeze felt good on her face and swirling past her bare ankles, calves, and feet.

She heard a board creak in the foyer and caught sight of Sam from the corner of her eye. She didn't bother to drop her skirt. Apparently she could run through the house naked and not make an impression on him.

"Anna?" He stepped into the parlor fumbling with his hat.

She kept fanning herself. "It's not feeding time yet. Go back to the barn."

"I didn't come to eat, Anna."

"And all this time I thought the only miracles were in the Bible." Anna rolled her eyes and climbed up into the chair she'd placed under the window.

Her trim little figure was outlined by the sunlight pouring in around her. Sam swallowed hard.

"Anna, you ought not be up there. You might fall."

She plunged the scrub brush into the bucket of water balanced on the window sill. "Oh my word, then you'd have to wash your own clothes. I can see why you're worried."

Sam sailed his hat across the room, landing on the settee. He could see her legs outlined through her skirt. The tops of her breasts swelled out of her blouse when she scrubbed. His mouth went dry.

"I came to tell you I was sorry for taking off like that last night."

She paused in her scrubbing. Water ran down her bare arm and dripped onto her breast, seeping into the fabric. She looked down at him. "Oh?"

He ventured closer. "Please get down."

She started scrubbing again. Her bottom swayed softly in rhythm with the scrub brush. His smoldering desire flamed.

"I shouldn't have done it." His throat constricted. He coughed. "I bought you something in town."

She stopped. The hard edges of her face softened. "You did?"

He bobbed his head eagerly. "Sort of an official apology. Want to see it?"

She shrugged. "Maybe."

She seemed to be weakening. Sam forced a smile. "It's real pretty."

She shouldn't give in so easily, Anna told herself. But Sam had said he was sorry. She'd made her point.

"I got it just for you."

Anna sighed. "Where is it?"

"In the kitchen."

She stepped down from the chair, eyeing him suspiciously. "You didn't get me a new pot or pan, did you?"

"Oh, no," he assured her, and said a silent prayer of thanks that Emma Langford didn't work in a dry goods store.

"Close your eyes," he told her when they reached the kitchen.

"They're closed. Hurry up."

"I see you peeking."

"Oh, all right." Anna squeezed her eyes shut. She heard him fumbling with something.

"Okay. Open."

He stood before her, his big suntanned hands holding the dainty lace handle of a hat box. "Oh, Sam."

He grinned when he saw a smile break out over her face. "I got it from Emma."

Anna hurriedly wiped her hands on her apron and pried the top from the box.

"Emma showed me the one you said you wanted."

Thrill and excitement hardened into a cold lump in the pit of Anna's stomach. Please, no, she prayed, don't let it be one of Emma's creations. Slowly she lifted the lid.

"But I told her no, I didn't think it was right for you."

She moved aside the delicate paper and saw a tiny blue hat.

"It's lovely." She smiled up at him.

He stepped closer. "Is it all right?"

"And to think that last night I believed you couldn't stand to be around me and all the while you were buying me this hat."

"Don't think that, Anna. Sometimes I just look at you and—"

He couldn't stand it any longer. Sam crushed her to him and covered her mouth hungrily. He groaned deep in his throat.

Then just as quickly he set her away and hurried out of the door. Stunned, Anna watched him go. Her body tingled with the feel of his chest, his hands, his lips.

She had tried to seduce him last night with a fine meal and her best blouse, and had driven him off the farm. And today, dressed like a scrub woman he'd kissed her with such passion, it was almost frightening.

Anna rubbed her finger over her lips. Deep in her heart she knew that come sunrise tomorrow, Sam Rowan would be in her bed.

CHAPTER 17

Anna stood by her bedroom door, alone in the darkness, listening to the male voices on the front porch. It seemed an eternity passed before she heard Uncle Lloyd wish Sam goodnight and enter the house.

Anna held her breath and eased her door open a crack. Uncle Lloyd walked past her room and into his own. The door closed firmly behind him.

A moment later, Anna heard footsteps on the front porch. Her heart began to beat faster. She hurried to her window and crouched on the floor, peeping over the sill. In the moonlight she saw Sam crossing the meadow toward the barn.

Anna sprang to her feet. She didn't let herself think about what she was planning to do, afraid that she might back out. She undressed and washed at the basin on her bureau, then pulled a night rail from the drawer. It was a simple white gown with long sleeves, a high collar and a tiny pink bow at the throat. Would it be enough to entice Sam back to the house, she wondered? Back into her bed?

It was all she had—it would have to do. Anna slipped into the gown and pulled the pins from her hair. Dark thick tresses fell to her waist. She grabbed the brush from her bureau and whisked it through her hair.

Anna knelt at the hearth and stacked logs in the grate. Her fingers trembled as she struck the match and held it to the kindling. The tiny chips of wood caught and orange and yellow flames spread slowly up the logs.

She stepped into her slippers and threw a shawl around her shoulders. Cautiously she crept to the door and eased it open.

She held her breath and listened. From the room next door, she heard Uncle Lloyd's soft snoring.

Relieved, Anna turned back to her room. The fire from the hearth cast flickering light across the floor. Her gaze fell to rest on the bed.

Anna's stomach clenched. Sam would be here tonight, with her in that bed. He'd give her a new life. He'd give her a baby. No matter what she had to do, no matter how awful it might be, she would go through with it.

Anna dashed to the bed and folded back the covers, then grabbed an extra blanket from the bottom drawer of her bureau. Quickly she slipped out into the hall.

She tiptoed across the foyer and eased the front door open. The hinges creaked. She held her breath, as if that might soften the sound. She listened. There was no disturbance from her uncle's room, nothing more than his soft snoring. She sighed and hurried outside.

The grass, damp with dew, rustled as Anna made her way around the house and across the meadow. She clutched the shawl around her shoulders to ward off the chill of the evening. The barn loomed before her, dark and ominous. Anna said a silent vow that she wouldn't lose her nerve when she came face to face with Sam.

Butterflies took flight in the pit of her stomach as she stepped into the barn. It smelled of leather and hay and horses, earthy smells that soothed her nerves. Her slippers were silent on the dirt floor as she walked past the stalls. There, at the far end of the barn, she could see a lantern burning. Anna's heart skipped a beat. That's where Sam would be.

Anna held tight to her shawl and clutched the extra blanket under her arm as she advanced on the stall. Her mind raced. She'd thought that once she was here, once she confronted Sam, somehow she'd know what to say or do. Now, her mind was totally blank.

She glanced back across the barn at the door. It wasn't too late. He hadn't seen her yet. She could get away unnoticed.

Anna drew in a deep breath. No. No, she wouldn't run. She'd been running for the last ten years.

With that thought held firmly in mind, Anna stepped into the stall. Her hopes fell. Sam wasn't there.

She turned, taking in every corner of the stall. Bathed in a pool of lamplight, there wasn't much to see. A small bunk against the back wall, a crate where the lantern sat—and no Sam.

Anna's shoulder sagged. It had taken all her nerve to come here. It had never occurred to her that Sam wouldn't be here.

Maybe he was only at the outhouse. Maybe he was still bathing—his baths seemed endless these days, and she didn't think he was that dirty in the first place. Or maybe he'd taken Fortune out for a late-night run. Whichever it was, Anna knew she couldn't wait around for him to return. Her nerves were already strung tight. The wait might kill her.

Anna whirled around to leave, then froze. Sam stepped into the stall.

He wore only his trousers, opened at the waist, as if he'd pulled them on in a hurry, and his boots. His chest was bare; it sparkled in the lamplight. His hair was wet. A deep frown creased his forehead.

"What are you doing out here?"

Anna fell back a step. "I—I thought you weren't here."

He gestured with the clothing bundled in his hand. "I was at the creek."

Anna felt her cheeks color. "Oh."

"What are you doing out here?" he asked again.

She swallowed hard. Opportunity stood before her. This was what she wanted. But she hadn't expected him to be half naked already. Seeing his bare chest always unnerved her.

"Well?"

Anna drew in a quick breath. "Oh, well, you see, I thought it might get cold tonight, so I brought you an extra blanket." The notion seemed ludicrous since Sam appeared to be smoldering from some internal fire.

Sam's eyes narrowed. He shifted, but didn't relax his stance. "All right."

The butterflies in Anna's stomach suddenly hardened into a knot. A wave of calm washed over her. "I'll fix it for you."

He tossed the bundle of clothing aside. "No. Leave it. Get back to the house."

"I don't mind." She smiled. "It's the least I can do."

Anna opened the blanket and spread it across the bunk. She bent over, tucking in the corners. She stretched farther, smoothing the blanket, and the fabric of her night rail draped her bottom and rose to expose the silky white skin of her calves.

Sam's loins reacted swiftly, pulsating with desire. A fire flamed low in his belly and threatened to consume him. He fought against it with all his strength.

"No—stop—that's fine," he stuttered.

Anna rested one knee on the bunk, her bottom bobbing as she tucked in the opposite corners.

Sam's mouth went dry. Instinct as old as mankind, clutched him, robbing him of words.

Anna straightened and turned to face him. Her shawl slipped off her shoulder and hung there. "That should keep you warm tonight."

He could only stare at her. She was beautiful. She was alluring. He wanted her like he'd never wanted any other woman in his life. But he wouldn't take advantage of her. He loved her too much. Sam curled his hands into fists as if that might help him win the battle that raged inside him.

Anna turned her head slowly, looking at the meager surroundings. "It must be lonely sleeping out here every night." Her long hair fell forward, cascading down her shoulders. "Are you lonely, Sam?"

"No." He forced himself to say the word, though it was far from the truth. The sight of her was tantalizing. His loins ached with need.

Anna slid her tongue along her bottom lip. She sighed heavily. Beneath the flimsy gown she wore he could see her full, ripe breasts rise and fall. She couldn't know how tantalizing she looked. She couldn't know what she was doing, he told himself. She was far too innocent.

And the thought of her innocence sent a new wave of desire through him, strong, urgent, bordering on lust.

"All right," Anna said softly. "I'll go, if you're sure that's what you want."

What he wanted wasn't fit to speak of. Not to Miss Anna Fletcher. Especially since he was sure it would send her running back to the house and the safety of her uncle if she had the slightest inkling of what his body was demanding of him.

Anna looked up at him. Her eyes—those big doe eyes—regarded him expectantly. His knees threatened to buckle.

"Go," he croaked. "Go now, before. . . ."

"Before what?"

Anna stepped to the side directly in front of the lantern. Light filtered through her gown.

All rational thought left Sam's head. Outlined before him were her shapely calves, her thighs, the curves of her hips. Need—primal need—coursed through him. He loved her. His head and his heart loved her. Now, the rest of him demanded that he show her his love . . . all night long.

She'd never seen such wanting before. It was etched in each line and curve of his face. It shone in his eyes, deep, dark, and searing. Anna knew she was tempting him, knew where it would lead. But she didn't feel afraid. The pit of her stomach glowed, and fingers of hot fire stretched downward, stirring something she'd never felt before. Something she'd never wanted before, until now.

Slowly she walked toward him and allowed her shawl to inch down her arms. Her gaze held steady with his as she stopped before him and dropped the shawl at her feet.

"Do you want me to go?"

She was only inches away. Her sweet fragrance wafted around him. Sam ached for her. Every fiber of his body cried out for her. He strained for self-control.

"You'd better go." His words were a warning. "You'd better go now before I—"

She slid her tongue along her lower lip. "Before you kiss me?"

His heart thundered in his chest. "Before I do a lot more than kiss you."

Heat radiated from him. His every muscle was drawn tight.

He exuded an aura that penetrated deep inside her, pulling her toward him—uncontrollably. But nothing about him frightened her—the tightly contained power, the lustful gleam in his eye, the huge bulge in his trousers—none of it. She wanted to experience it. With him.

Anna leaned her head back and angled her mouth toward his. "Maybe I want a lot more than a kiss."

Her breath was hot, sweet. His resolve began to crumble. "Anna, honey, you don't know what you're saying."

She splayed her hand across his chest. His muscles jumped. "Yes I do."

"Anna, don't . . ." Sam squeezed his eyes shut.

She wasn't tall enough to reach his mouth so Anna placed her lips against his chest. His flesh was hot.

"Oh, God . . ." Sam opened his eyes; they smoldered with naked desire.

"I want this." Anna whispered the words. His gaze locked with hers, searching. "I want you."

Anna rose on her tiptoes, her mouth open, seeking his.

Sam's lips covered hers hungrily. He groaned deep in his chest as his tongue slid across her lips. She gave him entrance and he plunged deep inside her mouth. Anna's breath caught in her throat.

He wrapped both arms around her, crushing her against him. The feel of her soft breasts pressed to him, even through her gown, unleashed the torrent of desire he'd held in check. Passion overcame him. He thrust his tongue into the deep recesses of her mouth over and over, driven by a need too strong to control.

Sam pressed her back onto the bunk and positioned himself above her, one knee between her thighs. He levered himself up, fumbling with his trousers and pulling her night rail upward. He loved her with all his heart. Now he was going to show her how much.

Beneath him Anna squirmed and turned her head away. Sam's heart squeezed almost to a stop. He wasn't showing her his love, he realized. He was frightening her.

"No . . ."

Sam rose from the bunk. His breath was heavy. She looked up at him, confused and unsure of what was happening.

"No," he said again. "Not like this. Not in a barn." Not like an animal, he nearly said.

Sam lifted her into his arms and carried her out of the barn. He crossed the meadow with long, striding steps. Anna curled her arm around his neck and buried her head against his shoulder.

He climbed the front steps and entered the house quietly. Inside the bedroom, he pushed the door shut silently and laid Anna on the bed.

He stood over her for a long moment watching her curled up on one elbow, her night rail tugged primly down to her ankles. The light from the fireplace cast a soft glow over her. Sam's heart surged. God, how he loved her.

Slowly, he sat down on the edge of the bed beside her. He threaded his fingers through her hair pushing the thick tresses off her shoulder.

"Are you sure?" If she said no, he didn't know where he'd find the strength to leave.

She sat up, facing him, their bodies inches apart. "Yes." She touched her lips to his, delicately.

Sam groaned and closed his mouth over hers. She sighed and fell back onto the bed, kicking off her slippers. He followed her down.

Their tongues dueled intimately, renewing their acquaintance and rekindling the fire that had sparked between them in the barn stall. Sam stroked her hair, feeling the silkiness. He kissed a hot trail across her cheek and buried his face against the curve of her neck. She smelled so sweet. He groaned with pleasure.

Tentatively Anna slid her hands up his arms, responding to some unseen force that demanded she answer his kisses. His muscles bulged. They were hard as stone. She'd wanted to touch him since she'd seen him at the pond, she realized. She'd wanted to know how his strong, rippled muscles felt beneath her hands. Now, she could explore him. All of him.

Her fingers sought out and found his broad shoulders, the column of his neck. She plunged her hands into the thickness of his hair. It felt soft and full. Like the rest of him. Solid. Strong.

Sam broke off their kiss suddenly and pulled off his boots and socks in a swift motion. He stood and hung his thumbs in his waistband, anxious to shed the confining trousers. She was watching him. Her eyes were wide, her lips wet and full with his kisses. She looked beautiful . . . innocent.

Sam stopped. She'd glimpsed him naked once and seen him in his long johns when he was ill, but, surely, she wasn't prepared to see now what he'd kept hidden in his trousers so many times over the last few weeks.

He circled the bed and wiggled out of his trousers as he sat down, then pulled the quilt up to his waist and turned to face her. He propped himself up on one elbow and covered her mouth with his.

Slowly, he ran his fingers across her cheek, down her delicate throat to the buttons of her night rail. He opened them carefully, one after the other and slid his finger inside the gown. Her skin was warm. Soft. The softest thing he'd ever felt.

Beside him, Anna tensed, and he stopped, wanting to go slow, wanting not to frighten her, but wanting to make her his. Completely.

Sam deepened their kiss and Anna responded. The feel of his tongue against her, his lips pressing intimately, touched a wellspring of desire she'd never known existed. She couldn't deny it. She couldn't deny him. Or herself.

Sam slid his hand further inside her gown until his fingers closed over her breast. Hot tentacles of fire shot through him. He caressed the soft mound, squeezing gently, filling his palm. It was the most exquisite thing he'd ever felt. His thumb circled the crest and the tiny bud of her breast came to life. Anna moaned and writhed. His loins, already swollen and anxious, demanded fulfillment. He couldn't wait any longer.

He slid his hand past her flat stomach, over the curve of her hip, and down her thigh until he found the hem of her gown. Passionately he smothered her face with hot kisses as he pulled the gown up over her head. He flung it across the room.

In the golden fire light she lay before him, her dark hair splayed across the white pillow, her naked body soft and delicate as the first flower of spring. Sam's heart rose in his throat. She was beautiful. He loved her. And now he would show her how much.

Briefly, it crossed Anna's mind that she was naked, but only because the thought brought with it the realization that being naked for Sam seemed natural. She didn't question it. There was no time. Sam's kisses, the heat of his strong body, the tenderness of his caresses sent all logical thought from her head, leaving her to rely solely on these newly discovered feelings.

Sam rose above her and slid his knees between her thighs. He kissed her softly as his loins sought and found the heart of her femininity. She stiffened, and he cursed himself silently, hating that he had to hurt her. For an instant, he wanted to withdraw. She was so tiny. And he had never felt so swollen in his life. But instead, he kissed her; tender, coaxing kisses along her cheek, her eyes, her forehead until she relaxed.

Cautiously he began to move, slowly, carefully, and she responded. Sam curled his fists into the pillow beneath her head, struggling for control. He wanted to drive himself into her and release the ache in his loins, but he listened to his heart instead.

The rhythm of his movements was mesmerizing, leaving her no choice but to respond in kind. Deep inside her grew an urge too great to resist. She wrapped her arms around his neck and grabbed a handful of his hair. The desire became stronger, rising to a higher level. Sam moved faster, pushing it farther. It overwhelmed her. It burst inside her. She called his name as great waves of pleasure broke inside her over and over again.

Sam bit down on his lip, struggling for control as her hips thrust violently against his. And when he could no longer wait, when he was certain she was ready, he moaned her name and drove himself deep inside her, time and time again, pouring out his love for her in an ancient primal release.

*   *   *

What had she done?

Muted sunlight from the overcast morning filtered through the window as Anna came awake. She knew without looking that she was still naked; she clutched the quilt closer.

Curled on her side, facing the cold gray ashes of the fireplace, she could feel the warmth of Sam's body behind her. She heard his even breathing. A wave of humiliation washed over her. He was undoubtedly still naked too.

Instinct told her to run. But she was afraid he'd wake and see her striding stark naked across the room. Anna cringed. What had she done? What had come over her?

She chewed her bottom lip. Visions of the night came back like scenes from a play—only she was the one at center stage, acting like a harlot. Anna's stomach knotted. She couldn't think of a word bad enough to call herself. Good grief, she fretted, what would Sam think of her.

"I thought you were an angel."

Anna tensed as his voice washed over her. She hadn't known he was awake. The bed shifted and she felt his chest brush lightly against her back.

He picked up a strand of her hair and wrapped the silky curl around his finger. He wanted to pull her into his arms and smother her with kisses, but thought better. He was going on instinct alone now, having never had a newly deflowered woman in his bed before. He had to get it right. Everything was riding on it.

"When I was sick," he said, "I had only your voice to listen to. I thought you were an angel."

His tone was gentle. It soothed some of her internal quaking. She felt his hand toying with her hair. It was comforting.

Sam chuckled. "Of course, then I woke up and found what you were really like."

A tiny giggle escaped her lips. "That must have been quite a shock."

"There's nothing about you that's ordinary, honey, that's for certain."

His words uncoiled the knot in her stomach by a small degree.

"Kind of awkward, isn't it," Sam said, "waking up like this."

Anna rolled onto her back, clutching the quilt above her breasts. He was propped up on one elbow watching her. He looked as if he'd been awake for some time, a lot longer than she.

Anna frowned. "But haven't you—I mean, this wasn't the first time you. . . . Was it?"

"It's the first time I ever woke up with someone." He gazed at her earnestly. "That makes it extra special to me."

Anna relaxed her death grip on the quilt.

"You don't mind, do you, that last night wasn't the first time I'd done this."

"No," Anna said thoughtfully. "I suppose one of us should have known what to do."

Sam chuckled low in his chest. A practical woman. It was one of the things that made her dangerous. And one of the reasons he loved her.

"I thought it would be different."

Her words sent a chill over him. How he'd wanted to give her pleasure. He'd tried to ensure her enjoyment. And he'd thought he'd done it. He'd lain awake half the night reliving it again and again.

Anna frowned and gazed up at the ceiling. "I thought it would be. . . ."

Sam swallowed a cold lump of emotion. "What?"

She turned her head and gazed at him. "I thought it would be bad."

He began to breath again. "Who told you that?"

"Everybody. They say it's a woman's duty and that only men like it. But I liked it." Crimson crept over her cheek. "I shouldn't have said that."

Sam smiled broadly. "There's nothing wrong with liking it."

"But doesn't that make me just like those, you know, those soiled doves?"

"Oh, no, honey. You're nothing like them."

Anna smiled. "I'll have to take your word for it. You are the expert here."

Sam's chest puffed out. "I wanted you to like it."

Anna's brows drew together. "It was like doing the dishes."

Over the years he'd enjoyed a lot of comments on his love-making, but he'd never been compared to a household chore before.

Sam shifted in bed. "Could you explain that please?"

"Like when we wash dishes." Anna rolled over and faced him. "This time you did a lot more than your half."

His heart thundered in his chest. Leaning toward her, he placed a kiss on her forehead. "You could drive a man to do all sorts of things, honey."

A knock sounded at the bedroom door.

Anna gasped. "Oh, no. It's Uncle Lloyd!"

Sam mumbled under his breath, cursing the man, cursing his bad luck. He threw back the covers.

"My goodness," Anna whispered. "What will he think!"

"He'll think a man and his wife are in bed together."

Sam rolled out of bed. Anna gasped again and pulled the quilt over her face.

Grumbling, Sam strode across the room and opened the door. He didn't bother pulling on his trousers. Better to let the old doctor know what he was interrupting, and get rid of him.

"It was getting late and I—" Lloyd looked Sam up and down, then took in the mound of covers in the bed that Anna was hidden under. "Oh. I'll go into town for a spell. Be back this afternoon sometime."

Sam nodded. "Take your time."

The doctor disappeared down the hall, and Sam closed the door firmly. At least he'd had the good grace to leave them alone for a while.

Sam caught a glimpse of Anna peeping from under the quilt as he approached the bed again. Quickly she pulled the cover over her completely.

"It's all right," he said. "I don't mind if you look."

"I was not looking at you," came the indignant, muffled reply.

He stood by the bed. "Did those same people who said you

weren't supposed to like it also tell you it wasn't proper to look?"

Beneath the quilt Anna frowned. She'd been given a great deal of bad information. She didn't know who to trust.

Sam bent down and lifted the cover back until he saw one wide, brown eye looking up at him. He straightened.

Anna pushed the quilt from her face. He stood naked before her, with no inhibition, no shame, and let her look at him. She remembered the feel of his furry chest against her breasts during the night and his strong arms locked around her; his thighs rubbing intimately with hers; and his maleness probing her best kept secret.

As she watched, he responded, as if he was remembering the same things as she.

Sam eased himself into the bed and locked his lips with hers in a strong kiss. He sighed contentedly.

"All you have to do is look at me and it drives me crazy," Sam whispered.

"I think I know what you mean."

He kissed her again and gently stroked her supple cheek. Anna pulled away.

"But what about Uncle Lloyd?"

"He's gone to town for the day."

She shook her head, embarrassed. "But what will he think?"

Sam chuckled. "He's not thinking anything, Anna. He knows."

He covered her protest with a deep kiss, driving thoughts of her uncle from her head. Their embrace, their kisses demanded more; driven by the fresh memories of their union the night before, Sam joined them together, making them one. Quickly their passion grew and exploded between them like thunder clouds in a turbulent summer sky. Then, sated, they lay in each other's arms and slept.

He woke and found her head resting on his shoulder, her dark hair tousled. Her arm was stretched across his chest and her legs were entwined with his.

Sam buried his face in the sweet fragrance of her hair and

breathed deeply. He tightened his hold on her, careful, though, not to wake her.

She was a hell of a woman. Passionate, willing. Both giving and demanding. The kind of woman a man would work himself into the grave for. Give up his life for. Sam frowned. Give up a fortune for?

He'd really messed things up, he decided with a silent curse. He looked at Anna curled contentedly in his arms. He should have told her he loved her before taking her to bed. He should have told her how he felt. At the very least, he should have told her he'd deceived her about her uncle coming to visit.

But the money—that damned money—was always between them. How could they ever be together with fifty thousand dollars separating them?

Sam shook his head. They would have to work it out somehow. There was still time. As long as Lloyd Caldwell was at the farm, nothing would change. But once the man left Anna would lead him to the money and he'd have to take it and go. Unless—

It scared Sam to think of it, he wanted it so badly.

Unless he could convince Anna he loved her—her alone, and not the money—and come to terms on what to do with the cash once it was recovered.

Sam snuggled closer to her. Finding the key to her heart would be far more difficult than finding the money.

Anna woke feeling safe and secure wrapped in Sam's arms. She stretched up and planted a kiss on his lips.

He grinned. "You're mighty bold."

She tilted her head coyly. "I think I've got this whole thing figured out."

Intrigued, his body responded quickly. "Do you?"

A mischievous smile spread slowly over her face. "Let me show you."

Anna pushed away the quilt and rose above him kissing her way down his body, seeking out the most intimate places. Her fingers, then tongue found and caressed the coppery discs hidden in the swirling hair of his chest. Sam moaned helplessly. She continued downward, touching, sampling, teasing, returning over and over again to bring him pleasure. And finally, when Sam could no longer endure the ecstasy, she rolled off him and urged him above her. He entered her swiftly, bringing her with him to the height of pleasure. Together they shuddered in agonizing delight and collapsed into each other's arms.

"Are you hungry?"

"Starved."

"Me too."

Reluctantly Sam untangled himself from Anna and sat up on the edge of the bed. He gazed out the window, cursing the number of hours that had passed. Her uncle would likely be home soon.

"I'll heat up some water." He looked longingly at Anna curled against the pillow. "I thought you'd like a hot bath."

She blushed. "Thank you."

Sam located his trousers across the room and shoved into them as he headed toward the kitchen.

Anna sat up and pushed her tangled hair off her shoulders. Without Sam there, the room felt cold and empty.

Just as her life would be when Uncle Lloyd left and she gave Sam the money and he rode away to buy his farm in Kentucky. It was a dismal outlook. Even the thought that she might now be pregnant brought her no pleasure. Without Sam there to share it, would it mean as much?

Anna slid out of bed, the chilly air tingling against her skin. She went to the armoire for her wrapper, but, instead, her hand fell on Sam's white Sunday shirt. She sniffed the sleeve. It smelled of him, a rich, masculine scent. She pulled it from the hanger and slipped it on, wrapping her arms around her middle to hold the oversized garment closed.

For an instant she wanted to cry. Why wouldn't he just let her turn that money in? Why was he so stubborn? If it wasn't for that money maybe they could—

Anna stopped herself. He'd promised her nothing. He'd not even been the one who'd initiated their love-making last night. It had all been her doing, and she couldn't expect something from Sam that he'd had no inkling of giving.

This was her revenge, Anna reminded herself. She rubbed her hand across her belly. But if it was supposed to be revenge, why did it feel like—love?

"The water is almost rea—"

She turned to find Sam frozen in the doorway gazing at her with unmasked wanting.

He swallowed hard. "Oh, God . . ."

Dark tussled hair hung around her shoulders like a silken drape, and his Sunday shirt had never looked so fine. The sleeves hung over her hands, and the hem barely covered her most desirable features.

"Oh, God . . ." Sam shucked off his trousers.

Anna curled her arms around his neck as he lifted her onto the bed. "Is this supposed to keep happening?" she asked as she parted her thighs for him.

"Oh, God . . ."

Lloyd Caldwell came through the back door relieved to find Sam and Anna standing at the stove cooking; he'd guessed correctly at staying in town for so long.

"Afternoon," he called as he hung his hat by the door.

"Hello, Uncle Lloyd." Anna glanced around Sam, and a rose blush covered her cheeks. Sam moved closer sheltering her protectively.

"How's things in town?" Sam asked, though his tone displayed little interest.

"The usual." Lloyd hitched up his trousers. "But I do have some news. I'm leaving today."

They both froze. Anna's eyes widened. Sam's brows furrowed in a deep crease.

"Within the hour, actually." Lloyd pulled his watch from his vest pocket.

"Now?"

"Today?"

"Yep. Train leaves soon." He snapped the timepiece closed and tucked it away.

"But—"

"How—"

"I checked the schedule when I was in town just now."

Anna wrung the skirt of her apron. "But Uncle Lloyd, this is so sudden." She looked desperately at Sam.

"Yeah, what's the big rush? Stay on for a while."

Lloyd shook his head. "No, it's time for me to get back home."

"But you can't leave now," Anna pleaded. "Not now, not until—"

She felt Sam's gaze on her. What was she about to blurt out? That her uncle couldn't leave until things were settled between her and Sam? Things that were never going to be settled, Anna realized.

"At least stay until tomorrow," Sam said. That would give him another night, a few more hours to work out something with Anna and that money. Damn! How he hated that money.

"No, no. It's time for me to go. I've got patients waiting in Salem." Lloyd bustled out of the kitchen.

Sam and Anna gazed helplessly at the doorway, as if they might get him to stay longer by sheer force of will. Then slowly, they turned to each other, both looking lost, feeling lost.

Anna's heart constricted. Her uncle was leaving, and in the next moment Sam would demand the money. He'd ride out of her life with no idea that he was leaving behind her broken heart. And how could she tell him now? He'd think it was a ploy to keep from giving him the money.

Sam felt sick. He couldn't let it end, not like this. They had to settle the matter of the money and get on with their lives—together.

He took her hand. "Anna, we've got to talk about that money. Your uncle is about to leave and—"

His words ripped through Anna like a firestorm. She jerked her hand away. "You could at least wait until he's out of the house."

Anna fled the kitchen, choking back tears, leaving Sam open-mouthed. She helped her uncle pack, dragging out the chore as long as possible in a vain attempt to delay the inevitable.

When they finally walked out onto the front porch, Sam was already there waiting beside Lloyd's horse. The sky was a dull gray. It did nothing to lift Anna's spirits.

"Take good care of this girl of mine." Lloyd shook Sam's hand.

"I'll do that."

He gave Anna a hug and kissed her cheek. "Try to get up to Salem and see me sometimes."

Anna fought back tears. "I'll be there before you know it."

"So long." Lloyd tied his bag and satchel on the saddle and rode away.

Anna stood for a long moment, watching him draw away. She could feel Sam beside her. Funny, she thought, how she'd grown so accustomed to his presence. But then she stopped herself and willed her emotions to subside. He'd promised her nothing, suggested nothing. It had been she who had given of herself, as now she must give him the money and send him on his way. Somehow.

Anna cleared her throat. "I suppose now you want to know where the money is."

"No, not really. Not this very minute."

"That was our agreement." Anger tinged her voice. "So you can leave this place and get back to where you belong."

"Then tell me!" His emotions were running high. They slipped easily into anger. Had he been a fool to think she'd want him? "Where is it?"

Anna was taken aback by his outburst. Had she really expected him to say he didn't want to leave?

He stepped closer. "You're so damned anxious to get this over with, take me to it—now!"

"Well . . ." Anna backed up a step. He towered ominously over her. "I can't, exactly."

His eyes narrowed. "What do you mean you can't?"

Anna twisted her fingers together. "You see—" She licked her dry lips. "You see, I don't know where the money is."

CHAPTER 18

"You what!"

Anna cringed beneath his glower. "I don't know where the money is, exactly."

She'd tricked him. She'd lied to him. She'd used him to save face with her uncle. It was like a mule kick in the gut.

Sam pointed a finger at her. His voice was low, threatening. "I told you what I was going to do if you didn't tell me where that money was hidden."

"But I can't tell you where it is!"

He shoved past her, striding down the road after her uncle.

"No!"

Anna raced after him and grabbed his arm. He pulled her along with him.

"No, Sam! Don't tell my uncle. You promised!"

"You lied to me!"

Anna held his arm with both hands and dug her heels into the dirt road. "I can't tell you where the money is because my father didn't tell me."

Sam stopped. His gaze impaled her.

"He tried to tell me," Anna explained desperately, "but I couldn't understand. He kept talking about Christmas, and—and—"

"What?" Sam wondered if she'd taken leave of her senses. He pulled his arm from her grasp. "Slow down."

Anna took a deep breath. "He was giving me clues, I think. But they were all jumbled."

"Clues? What kind of clues?"

Anna waved her hands fitfully. "It was his final moments.

He must have turned to religion because he kept talking about God."

Sam nodded slowly. "So that's why you've had your nose buried in the Bible every spare minute."

"I thought I might understand what he was trying to tell me," she admitted.

Sam just stared at her. All this time and she never knew where the money was hidden. He strode up the road, scooped a loose stone from the weeds and hurled it into the trees sending a measure of his anger with it.

He looked back at Anna and sighed heavily. "Let's get back to the house."

Sam waited until Anna caught up with him, shortened his strides to match hers. They returned to the kitchen and Sam poured them each a cup of coffee; their half-cooked meal was long forgotten.

"Okay, what did Cyrus tell you, exactly." He sat down across the table from her.

Anna sipped the coffee he'd placed before her. "Like I said, he talked about Christmas and—"

"What about Christmas?"

She drummed her fingers on the table. "The Christmas tree. The angel we always put on the top."

Sam stroked his chin. "What else?"

"Adam and Eve."

Their gazes collided across the table. Sam shifted in his chair. Anna looked away.

"What about Adam and Eve?"

"The Garden of Eden."

Sam thought for a moment. "A Christmas angel and the Garden of Eden. What else did he tell you?"

She shrugged. "Nothing."

"Nothing?" Sam's eyes widened. "He was giving you directions to a buried treasure and that's all he said!"

"He was dying!" Tears welled in her eyes. "He was lying in that stinking, miserable excuse for a hospital talking about that robbery. Of all things! He said he wanted me to have the money—as if I'd actually take one filthy dime of it!"

Sam took her hand across the table and folded it between his. "All right, honey, it's all right."

His voice was comforting. Anna calmed herself and withdrew her hand from his. She sniffed. "Anyway, that's about all I can remember."

Sam sat back. "What about the night of the robbery?"

She'd struggled for ten years to put the whole thing out of her mind. Now he was asking her to recall it in detail.

"I remember Papa going to work that afternoon. Mamma gave him a dinner bucket and he kissed me good-bye, like always." Sadness gripped Anna's heart. "I never saw him again, except in jail. The sheriff came to the house the next day and told us Papa had been arrested."

"So after your pa got to work, the train left the mint at Charlotte with him in the baggage car along with two strongboxes containing fifty thousand dollars each." Sam rose and paced the floor. "There was another railroad guard in the car with him along with the federal marshals."

"The train was stopped just east of here," Anna said, "between the farm and Charlotte. That's where your papa's gang robbed it."

Sam shoved one hand in his pocket and stroked his chin as he walked back and forth in front of the table. "There was a shoot-out. My pa and some of the marshals were killed. The four gang members took the two strongboxes and left. Your pa went along with them."

"He was taken hostage," Anna corrected. "The gang split up, each pair taking one of the strong boxes. My pa was with the Kyle brothers."

"The posse found them in the hills that night. Arlow was dead and Buck had been shot. There was no sign of your pa or the money." Sam paused and gazed out the window. "And he buried it out there somewhere."

"I suppose so." Anna pressed her lips together. "But Papa never said it."

Sam's head came up quickly. "He never actually told you he'd buried it in the hills."

"No." Anna shook her head. "He never said it. Not in so many words."

Sam snapped his fingers. "What if he hid it here in the house?"

"I guess he could have."

Sam flipped the chair around and straddled it. "What do you remember about the night of the robbery? Are you sure your pa didn't come home? Did your ma ever mention seeing him that night?"

She shook her head, thinking. "No, never."

"Did you wake during the night? Did you hear any hammering or digging?"

"No."

Sam rose. "Show me where you put your Christmas tree."

Anna led the way into the parlor and stood in the space between the window and the fireplace. "Right about here." She made a circle with her arms.

Sam studied the floor boards beneath her feet. He stepped on each, testing its strength, listening for squeaks.

"Do you think he might have pried the boards up and buried it underneath?" Anna asked.

Sam shook his head. "Come to think of it there's nothing under this end of the house, except—"

"The root cellar."

He nodded slowly. "You could be right."

"I guess there's only one way to find out."

Sam fetched a shovel and pick from the barn and descended into the dark room under the house with Anna following reluctantly. The cellar smelled of years of stored foods, the timbers of the house, and the dirt floor. The ceiling was low, causing Sam to stoop as he walked.

He eyed the far corner of the room, judging the placement of the Fletcher family Christmas tree in the parlor overhead. He drove the pick into the soft earth.

Anna shivered as she stood by watching him. The root cellar always made her skin crawl. She rubbed her arms to keep away the chill.

Sam dug into the ground opening a hole several feet wide and just as deep. Shovelful after shovelful of dirt he tossed aside until sweat broke out on his brow.

"Do you think Papa really buried it here?" Anna asked.

"Seems logical," Sam grunted as he drove the shovel into the dirt once more.

Anna frowned. "Then why didn't he just tell me it was in the root cellar? Why did he talk about the angel on the tree?"

Another scoop of dirt went flying. "I don't know, Anna. You were with him, not me."

Anna paced the room, thinking, remembering, trying to decipher the clues her father had given her. Sam kept digging.

"And why would he have mentioned the Garden of Eden?"

Sam wiped the sweat from his brow with his shirtsleeve. "Maybe because this is where seeds are stored for the next year's garden."

Anna sat down on a crate. "Maybe he meant vegetable garden or the flower garden. Mamma had lots of flowers. Is there a flower or vegetable called angel? Or one that looks like an angel? Could he have meant something special from the garden that we ate only at Christmas? Around the tree?"

Sam kept digging.

Anna's mind whirled. The possibilities were endless.

Sam shoveled until the entire corner of the root celler had been dug down nearly three feet. He jabbed the shovel into the mound of loose dirt. "It's not here."

"It was worth trying."

Sam stepped out of the hole. "I need some air."

They left the root cellar and Anna worked the pump while Sam splashed cold spring water over his face and neck and washed his hands. He stood there dripping, catching his breath.

"That puts us back where we started," he said.

"At least we've ruled out the root cellar," Anna offered, though it seemed a feeble accomplishment in light of Sam's hard work.

It was growing dark. The overcast sky had shortened the day. Sam shook the water from his hands. "I'm hungry."

Anna smiled. There was something extraordinarily handsome about Sam when he worked, she thought; the strength of his muscles, maybe, or the sweat on his face. The exhibition of his abilities, perhaps. She wasn't sure why he was so attractive to her or why she found it endearing that he was hungry afterwards or why it brought her pleasure to feed him. It touched something inside her that she couldn't name.

"I'll cook us some supper." She headed toward the house.

He fell in step beside her. "I'll help you."

They cooked their meal together in the kitchen, neither talking much, then sat down to eat. Sam seemed far away, Anna thought, and she was sure his mind was still searching for the money, though his body was seated across the table from her.

Inwardly she sighed. That money meant so much to him, it seemed. Watching him toy with his potatoes and gazing blankly at his plate, she wished she could understand why.

"You must have missed your pa a lot when you were growing up."

Jolted from his thoughts, Sam frowned and shook his head. "No. I never knew him much. I was just a kid when he went off to war. I don't remember much about him."

He grew silent again and gazed off at nothing. Anna figured he was thinking of the money again.

"He used to take me fishing," Sam said suddenly. He looked at Anna. "I'd forgotten that. But there was a pond not far from our house and we'd go fishing together. He called it our secret fishing hole. Sometimes he'd take me into town with him and buy me hard candy from Cooper's Dry Goods. And at night after supper he'd sit me on his lap and—"

Sam stopped and looked down at his plate. He shoved a forkful of potatoes in his mouth.

Anna's heart ached seeing the pain that flashed across his face.

"What about the people who took you in?" She hoped another pleasant recollection would make him feel better. "Were they nice to you?"

"Sometimes."

She wished she hadn't asked.

Sam laid his fork down and rubbed his forehead. "I left when I was twelve or so and found a job as a barn boy on a farm over in the next county. A widow owned it. She never asked much about me, but a few weeks later when the sheriff came around she told him she'd never seen me."

"You didn't want to go back?"

He shook his head and started eating again. "The widow took a liking to me, and she'd have me come up to the house nearly every night. She taught me reading and writing and ciphering. I never had much schooling before that."

Anna smiled. "She was good to you?"

Sam chuckled. "Looking back I think she had designs on me, but at the time I was too young to know it."

"Did you stay there long?"

"No. She sold the farm the next spring, and I moved on to work for somebody else." Sam looked across the table at her. "But my pa always kept up with me, somehow. No matter where I'd go, he'd show up one day out of the blue and we'd visit for a while. He couldn't stay long, of course . . ."

"How about some apple pie?" Anna popped out of her chair. She couldn't bear to hear another word. It made her feel guilty for having a mother and a home and an uncle who cared about her.

"Pie sounds good." Sam carried the dishes to the sideboard.

She took his hand as he stood next to her. "I didn't mean to upset you."

The feel of her hand, soft and tender upon his, drained the tension from him. Damn, he liked the way she felt. And the way she looked. The scent of her had driven him to distraction more times than he could count. Sam savored the feel of her flesh against his. He liked this house, too, he decided. It felt warm and comforting. As Anna felt to him. His belly glowed with a pleasing ache.

They sat at the table and ate their pie together. Sam scraped his plate clean and rose. "I'll be back in a while."

"Where are you going?" Her eyes widened.

"I've got chores to attend to."

Her gaze pointedly swept the kitchen, taking in the dirty dishes, the pots, and pans.

"Uh-uh. No." Sam pulled on his neck. "You don't think I'm going to start doing half the housework again, do you?"

Anna took the dishes to the sink. "That was our agreement."

He planted his fists on his lean hips. "But that was before

we got the chickens and the cow and planted the garden and everything. I've got a lot of work to do."

A tiny smile tugged at her lips, though she tried hard to hold it in. "I guess we'll have to do those things together, too."

Oh well, maybe this halves thing wouldn't be so bad after all.

"Pump some water for me, please, Sam. I'll wash."

They stood side by side, washing and drying, talking. They were comfortable with each other. The tension brought on by her uncle's presence in the house was gone now, and they were left alone with no false pretenses between them.

Anna slipped her shawl around her shoulders and helped Sam feed the chickens and stood by while he chopped some wood. They walked around the garden together, looking for the first vegetable shoots to appear.

The barn was quiet when they entered, the stalls empty. Sam poured grain into the feeding troughs.

Anna turned around, looking up at the vast, dark corners of the loft. "Maybe it's here."

"What's here?"

"The money." Anna waved her arms to encompass the entire barn. "Maybe it's hidden in here."

Sam banged the feeding can against the wooden boards of the stall and Fortune nickered in the corral. The stallion tossed his head and trotted into the stall.

"Could be." Sam stroked the horse's head as he ate. "But this place doesn't look like a Garden of Eden to me."

Bob and Bill plodded in from the corral and settled into the next two stalls. They chewed the grain with far less enthusiasm than the stallion.

Anna walked over to the stall and stood by Sam. "It could be anywhere."

He nodded. "It could take days to find."

"Days." She stroked the stallions neck. "Probably."

"Weeks, maybe."

They looked at each other in the fading light. Unabashed wanting bound them together.

In that moment Anna knew she couldn't stay here with

Sam for that long. As it was, her feelings were strong for him. She couldn't spend that much more time with him, then watch him ride away when the money was recovered.

It would never work. Sam realized in that instant there could be nothing between them until the issue of the money was resolved. Regardless of what he said to her now, she wouldn't believe him as long as the strongbox was out there somewhere. It had to be found. Immediately.

"I'm going back to the house," Anna said softly.

He turned back to the stallion. "That would probably be a good idea."

Sam milled around at the barn making half-attempts at doing needless chores. By the time he went back to the house, Anna's bedroom door was closed.

His shoulders sagged as he stood in the hallway staring at the brass doorknob. He hadn't really thought she'd wait up for him, but still, he'd hoped.

Sam locked the front and back doors then retired to his tiny bedroom off the kitchen and the hellish bed Lloyd Caldwell had occupied these last days. He stripped off his shirt and trousers, thinking of Anna in the next room. Was she wearing that white night rail? The one he'd taken off her last night and flung across the room? Was her hair down? Dark thick tresses curling around her shoulders, fanned out across the pillow.

"Damnit . . ." Sam strode out of the tiny bedroom dressed in his long johns. He was finding that damn money. And he was getting on with his life.

Old Cyrus's clues had to be deciphered. He had to figure them out or he might well wind up digging into every square foot of the two hundred-acre farm.

Sam only knew one place to start—Anna's Bible.

After he'd searched the kitchen and parlor and came up empty, he knew there was only one other place it might be.

Sam stood before Anna's bedroom door. His heart began to beat faster. Should he knock? Last night he'd been inside rolling around in the bed with her. But tonight the closed door looked mighty formidable.

Maybe he'd just sneak in, he thought. She could be

sleeping already, and if he tiptoed, perhaps he could slip in and out without her knowing.

Sam's body coiled tight. Who was he trying to kid? There wasn't a shred of a chance that he could walk into Anna's room and not crawl into bed with her.

Sam mumbled a curse and walked back to his room. He jerked his clothes on and stormed out of the room again. He was going to find that money, and he was going to start by tearing the house apart, board by board, if necessary.

"Get up! Get up now!"

Anna roused from a restless sleep at the sound of Sam's gruff voice and his fist pounding on her door. She dragged the quilt with her as she opened the door.

"What's wrong?" Her eyes barely crept open.

He turned away and headed down the hall, not chancing a look at her. "I'm going to find that goddamn money today and I need your help to figure out those half-witted clues your pa gave you. Get dressed. Breakfast is ready."

Anger drove the veil of sleep from her thoughts. "Maybe I don't want to look for the money today!"

He spun around. His brows were creased, his jaw set. "You can either put some clothes on and have your breakfast or I'll take you like you are. Either way you're coming with me."

Anna wagged her tongue at his back as he disappeared into the kitchen. So, that was the way he wanted it. Fine! She'd be just as happy as he to locate that money. Anna slammed her door shut.

She washed quickly and pulled on the trousers she'd hidden in the bottom of her bureau along with her tan work shirt. She tied the bow into her long single braid as she stepped into the kitchen. Sam was seated at the table eating a plateful of eggs.

"And good morning to you, too." She spat the sarcastic words across the room at him.

Sam looked up, his mouthful of biscuit. His loins clinched. God help him, she was wearing those trousers again.

He swallowed hard. "What the hell are you doing?"

Anna tossed her head and walked to the stove. "I'm just

doing as you instructed, oh great lord of the manor." She picked up the breakfast plate he'd left warming on the stove.

Sam gulped down his coffee to clear the food that hung in his chest. He was already so randy he couldn't see straight, and here she was flouncing around in those trousers. He didn't have time to argue with her; they could be here the whole day trying to get her to change clothes.

"Just hurry up," he barked. "We've got to get going."

She pointed toward the window with her fork. "It's still dark outside."

"Just eat and come out to the barn." He took his hat from beside the door and started out.

"Hold on. Just where do you think you're going?"

He waved his arm over the stack of dirty dishes. "Leave them."

"It will draw bugs," she protested.

"I don't care if the bugs carry off the whole damn house. Pack some biscuits and cold meat for us to eat today. And hurry up." Sam yanked his hat down and strode out the door.

"Ooooohhh!"

Anna would have flung her plate after him but she didn't want any more mess to clean. He'd left her enough already.

A short while later, Sam rode into the yard on Fortune. She caught sight of him through the kitchen window.

"Anna! What's taking you so long!"

She ignored him and scrubbed the dishes faster.

"Anna!"

She could see his deep frown under the brim of his hat.

"Anna! Are you washing those damn dishes?"

Droplets of water splashed on the floor as she set the last cup on the sideboard to dry. She grabbed the sack of food she'd prepared and hurried out the door.

He glared down at her. "You were washing dishes, weren't you."

"Of course."

Sam pressed his lips together and slapped his hand against his thigh. "I told you to leave them."

She shrugged. "Whatever made you think I'd start listening to you now?"

His ego deflated a fraction. What had he been thinking?

Anna handed the sack of food up to Sam. "Where's Bill?"

He hooked the sack around the saddlehorn. "At the barn."

She crossed her arms under her breasts. "Do you think I'm going to walk?"

"No. You're riding with me." He pulled his left foot from the stirrup. "Come on up."

Her brows drew together. "I'm not riding with you. Go get Bill, or Bob."

"Oh, no. No, no." He shook his head slowly. "I'm not spending the whole day hunting you down because you're too pigheaded to ride where I tell you."

"Well, my, but aren't you the charmer this morning."

"Just get up here."

Sam reached down to help her as she slid her foot into the stirrup. Anna pulled away.

"Don't touch me."

"Christ . . ." Sam held up both hands in surrender. "Pardon me all to hell, Mrs. Rowan. Climb up here the best way you can."

She shot him a scathing glare and reached for the saddle horn. Sam grabbed the waistband of her trousers and pulled her up.

Anna squealed as she threw her leg over the back of the horse. She dug her fingers into Sam's ribs in the ticklish spot she'd discovered quite by accident the night before last. He yelped and twisted to the side. Fortune shifted suddenly. Anna grabbed Sam's shoulders to keep from falling.

"Settle down back there," he told her crossly as he got the horse under control.

"If you can't keep this horse in hand, maybe I should ride up front." It was the most hateful thing she could think to say, given her precarious position.

"You're riding where I tell you to ride," he snapped and headed the horse across the meadow toward the hills and the rising sun.

They had only gone a few yards when Sam realized that having her ride behind him may not have been the wisest decision. He could feel her thighs against the backs of his legs and occasionally when the horse shifted in just the right way, her breasts brushed over his back. He pictured her soft round bottom swaying with each step the stallion took. The pressure behind his fly increased.

"What are we doing out here?"

Anna's words tickled his ear, she was so close. He shifted uncomfortably in the saddle.

"We're looking."

"For what?"

"The Garden of Eden."

They rode through the woods, across streams, over fallen trees, up and down hills. Spring had brought the hills to life, with wild flowers, saplings, budding trees and bushes. Sam had spent most of the night searching the house. He'd checked for loose stones in the fireplace, planks in the floor that didn't fit perfectly, and tapped on the walls hoping for a hollow sound that would indicate a hidden room. He'd even tested the barrier that blocked off the second story. And he'd been thinking the whole time. Cyrus Fletcher loved his wife, it seemed, and it was doubtful he would involve her in the robbery by bringing the strongbox to the farm. Finally Sam had come to the conclusion that the money was hidden in the hills. All he had to do was find paradise.

After many hours they stopped at the creek to let the horse drink. Wide and shallow, the water drifted lazily past them. Anna slid off the stallion.

"If the Garden of Eden is in these hills, I haven't seen it." She walked stiffly down the bank.

"Me either." Sam climbed down and stretched.

Anna knelt at the water's edge and cupped her hands into cool liquid. Something in the soft earth caught her eye. "Are we close to Ben's place?"

Sam led the horse up stream and stopped beside her.

"No. Why?"

Anna stepped back and pointed to the ground. "Hoof prints."

Sam knelt and studied the tracks that ran along the creek bank then disappeared into the shallow water. "Two riders."

Anna bit her bottom lip. "Hunters?"

"Maybe." He stood and pushed his hat back, turning around to take in the thick wooded mountains that surrounded them.

An eerie feeling swept over Anna reminding her of how vulnerable she'd felt at the pond the day she'd come across Sam. These hills were isolated. No one knew where she and Sam had gone and no one expected them to return. She edged closer to Sam.

"How fresh are the tracks?"

"Last night. Maybe this morning."

A chill ran up Anna's spine. "They're just hunters, don't you think?"

Sam pulled his hat down. "Let's keep riding."

Anna hurried after him and didn't protest when he helped her onto the stallion's back.

Hours dragged by until every tree looked like the last tree Anna had seen, and absolutely nothing resembled her mental image of the Garden of Eden. She'd directed Sam to the spot where her father had usually selected their Christmas trees and answered his endless questions concerning gardens of any type that her family used to tend. And no, she'd told him, there had been no angels spotted on the farm that she could recall. She was getting tired. Sam had had little to say that didn't relate to their search and had even asked her to be quiet twice as he strained to hear something she couldn't; she wondered if he thought the voices of her father and the Kyle brothers might be actually calling to him, directing him. Sam seemed as irritable as she felt.

"Aren't you hungry yet?" She prayed he'd say yes so she could get off of the horse for a while.

"Getting that way." He looked up at the sun. It was midafternoon. "We'll stop soon."

"I want to stop now."

He nodded. "I know a special place. We'll eat there."

It piqued her interest enough that she waited patiently while Sam took them eastward into the hills. They followed the stream to a stand of white pines.

"This is it." Sam stopped the horse.

The spot looked no different than the other scenery they'd

taken in all day. The little stream had cut a deep bed over the years several feet deep and just as wide in front of the row of pines. Behind them a mountain, thick with trees and brush, rose sharply.

"We're not too far from the house." Sam pointed to the northwest. "It's just on the other side of that ridge."

Anna turned in that direction. She considered making a break for it.

Sam threw his leg over the stallion's neck and dropped to the ground. "Don't you like it here?" he asked as he lifted her down.

She rubbed her bottom and gave the trees a cursory glance. "It's nice."

"This is the spot I told you about." Sam tied Fortune to the lower branch of a tree, giving him enough lead to graze on the sweet grass and drink from the stream.

She seemed vastly disinterested in what he'd brought her to see, so Sam unpacked the food and canteen and blanket and jumped across the stream.

He turned back and held out his hand. "Come on."

She didn't move. His stride was long enough to leap the stream bed easily. But she would have to make her way down one side, jump the stream, and climb up the other. And that was the last thing her sore butt and legs wanted to do.

She rubbed her backside again. "Can't we eat on this side?"

His heart melted and he hated himself for it. He'd been gruff with her all day and bounced her delicate little bottom around for hours, and she hadn't complained half as much as he'd expected or nearly as much as he deserved. Sam put the blanket and food on the ground and jumped back over the stream.

Anna eyed him suspiciously. "What are you doing?"

He swept her into his arms and crossed the stream again before she could protest.

But he didn't put her down. Her face was inches from his and her breasts were snuggled against his chest. She felt good in his arms. He wanted to hold her forever.

Instinctively she'd circled his neck when he'd lifted her and now she couldn't let go. For an instant his mouth hovered above hers and she thought—hoped—he'd kiss her. Instead he set her on her feet and picked up the supplies.

"Come on. It's right through here." He strode away without waiting.

Anna followed him between two of the pines. Their soft needled branches had grown together to form a wall of sorts. There she found a large open area backed by the curving mountain on three sides and fronted by the stand of pines. It was shady and cool there. A carpet of soft grass covered the area. The only sound was the water from the rushing stream beyond the pines. In the center stood an oak tree with a broken swing dangling from one of its limbs.

Her spirits lifted slightly. "This is the place you found with the Calhoun boys, isn't it?"

Sam spread out the blanket. "It was a lucky find. If the boys hadn't chased their dog through the pines, I'd have never known it was here."

Anna nodded. "It's nice."

It was secluded. Isolated. Sam sat down on the blanket. It was dangerous.

"What did you bring us to eat?" He dug through the sack, trying to keep his thoughts—and imagination—from getting him into a situation he'd decided to avoid, for now.

Anna sat beside him on the blanket and nibbled at the cold chicken, cheese wedges, and homemade bread she'd packed for them. Sam ate hungrily, concentrating on the food.

"At least we won't have any dishes to do," Anna said.

A laugh rumbled deep in his chest. "Yeah. And it was my turn to wash."

Anna stretched her legs out on the blanket and braced her elbows behind her. "Uncle Lloyd must be back in Salem by now."

He studied her for a moment as she gazed up at the blue sky. "You're anxious to get back there too, huh?"

She looked at him. "As much as you're anxious to get home to Kentucky, I'll bet."

At that moment he didn't care if he ever saw Kentucky again. Sam drew his knees up and draped his arms over them. He took a deep breath.

"To tell you the truth, I've gotten pretty attached to this place." There—he said it. He made the first effort. Sam held his breath waiting for her response.

Was that a sign? she wondered. Did it mean he cared? Or was she just grasping at straws?

"Actually," she said slowly. "I don't mind it here as much as I did when we first got here."

"No?" Sam asked hopefully.

She shook her head. "No. But it helped that you were with me. I don't think I would have spoken to one person in town if it hadn't been for you."

A proud grin parted his lips. He stretched out alongside her, propped up on one elbow. "I thought at one time you hated me for that."

"I could never hate you, Sam."

Her words were spoken with such sincerity that his heart squeezed nearly to a stop. She had good reason to hate him. And she still might, once she learned the dastardly secret he'd kept from her.

Sam sat up again. He raked his fingers through the hair at his temple. "Look, Anna, I've got something to tell you. At the time it seemed like it was all right, but now—well, now I wish I could take it back."

Her stomach fluttered. She sat up. "What is it?"

He took a deep breath. "I knew your uncle was coming before he got here, and I didn't tell you so I could make you give me all the money." He sighed heavily, relieved that his confession was off his chest. Still, though, he couldn't look at her. He braced himself for a verbal assault.

"I know about the telegram," she said softly. "I've known for some time now."

Stunned, he looked up at her. "You knew? And you didn't say anything?"

"I did something horrible, too." She twisted her fingers together. "Something absolutely horrible."

He couldn't think of one bad thing she'd ever done. "What?"

"I lured you into my bed just so I could have my way with you."

Sam threw back his head and laughed, a deep masculine sound that echoed off the hills surrounding them.

Annoyed, Anna punched his arm. "It isn't funny."

He splayed his hand across his belly trying to control himself. "Anna, honey, there was nothing horrible about that."

"Yes it was," she insisted. She waited until his laughter had settled down. "I did it for revenge. You'd taken away my chance to have an orphanage, so I decided you should give me another life by giving me a baby." Ashamed, Anna dropped her gaze to her lap.

"So you were just using me?"

"Well, yes." She looked up again. "But I didn't know it would be so much fun or that I'd like it so much. I didn't know it would make me feel differently about you."

His heart slammed against his chest. "Different how?"

"I guess I'd felt that way all along and didn't realize it until we—" Her cheeks turned pink. "—you know."

Sam nodded slowly. "I guess that makes us both pretty rotten people."

"But we confessed. Doesn't that make it all right?"

Sam captured an errant strand of her hair and smoothed it behind her ear. "You just used me to get a baby?"

She nodded miserably. "You don't hate me, do you?"

He pressed her back onto the blanket and took her in his arms. "Mrs. Rowan, you can use me like that any time."

They both laughed and Sam kissed her gently on the lips.

"You must think me a devil instead of an angel." Anna coiled her fingers through his hair.

His lips covered hers again, stronger, deeper this time. She tasted exquisite. "You're an angel." He muzzled her neck. "I know because right now I'm in heaven."

She wiggled closer to him. Her body tingled even through the thickness of their clothes. She stroked his cheek.

"Heaven?" She giggled. "I think we would both be cast out of heaven. Just like Adam and—"

Anna froze.

Sam didn't notice as he kissed her lips again.

"Oh."

He drew back.

"Oh!"

"Anna, what the hell—"

"Oh!" Anna pushed him away and sprang to her feet.

"Christ—"

"I know!" She danced in a circle waving her arms.

Sam clambered to his feet. "What's the matter with you?"

She touched her hands to her chest. "I know where it is, Sam. I know where the money is!"

CHAPTER 19

"Calm down before you bust something." He took both her hands.

She pulled away. The solution to the riddle had come to her suddenly. The clues had simply fallen into place. And if she didn't say it out loud, she might well bust something.

"My papa called Mamma 'Angel'—that was his pet name for her." Her eyes were wide with excitement. "He told me the money was under the angel. He had to have meant my mother."

Sam frowned. "He put the money under your mamma?"

"In paradise." Anna wrung her hands. "In paradise, Sam. He said he put the money under his angel in paradise. I was thinking of the Garden of Eden, but he actually used the word paradise."

A jolt like a bolt of lightning ran up Sam's spine. His heart pumped wildly.

As one, they turned and gazed at the dilapidated swing hanging from the limb of the oak.

Emotions swelled inside Sam. "This is paradise. We're standing square in the middle of it."

They returned to the farm and Anna gathered more food and a bottle of cider from the kitchen while Sam hitched up the wagon. He loaded it with picks and shovels, a hammer and chisel and all the lanterns in the barn. He drove the team up to the house.

"I'm almost ready," Anna said as he walked into the kitchen. Her stomach tingled with excitement.

"Better bring your cloak. It will get cool tonight."

Sam gathered the spare lanterns from the pantry and took down his rifle. He offered no explanation to Anna's questioning stare as he strode out of the house again.

It was dark by the time the team pulled the wagon out to the edge of the woods. Sam and Anna carried the supplies in on foot. It was slow going on treacherous ground with only the lanterns to light their way.

Sam placed the lanterns on the ground, their flames casting tiny circles of light in the pitch-black forest. He tore down what remained of the swing and tossed it into the woods. Anna handed him the pick. He raised it high over his head and plunged it into the earth.

For hours he dug, tossing aside great shovelfuls of dirt until the moon rose over the mountains. Anna took over the shoveling while he caught his breath.

"So it was your folks who used to sneak off out here for a few minutes alone," Sam speculated as he sat against the trunk of the oak.

Anna looked up from her feeble attempt at shoveling and made a face. "Yuck. Don't talk about my parents and things like that."

"Your pa must have been the romantic type." He took another drink from the canteen. "Women like that, or so I'm told."

"Why don't you try it sometimes and find out?" She grinned playfully at him.

He rose and took the shovel from her hand. "Give me this thing before you hit me with it."

"Not a bad idea," she muttered and stepped aside. "But to tell you the truth, I'd rather have a man who knows how to use a hammer and nail and can plow a field. Can you plow a field, Sam?"

"I can plow a hell of a field," he told her and thrust the shovel into the ground again.

The night wore on. Anna huddled against the tree, wrapped in her cloak and dozed. Sam kept digging.

She roused from a light sleep to the steady sound of Sam's

heavy breathing and the thud of metal against the earth. He was knee deep in a cavernous hole.

Anna rubbed her eyes and got to her feet. "Are you hungry?"

He didn't answer, just shook his head and kept working.

She took a hunk of bread from the food sack and knelt beside the hole. The ground was cold where he'd opened it. "Want a bite?"

Sam didn't respond, unwilling to use breath or energy on anything but the digging.

He was a man possessed, Anna thought as she watched him. But she might have been the same, she decided, if one single cent of the money buried there was going to be hers.

"You won't be able to spend your money if your heart gives out before you get it out of the ground."

He spared her a look this time. "I'm fine."

"I'm just concerned about your health."

"I've got to find this money. It's too important to stop." He thrust the shovel deeper into the ground.

The sound of metal against metal rang through the night like the crack of a gunshot.

Sam froze. Anna dropped to her knees in the dirt at the edge of the hole.

"Move the light closer."

Sam dug fitfully while Anna repositioned the lanterns. Through the loose dirt a rectangular-shaped object appeared. Sam dug down the sides then threw the shovel away and dragged it out onto the floor of the deep, wide hole.

It was the strongbox. On the front was a heavy lock with the words "Property of the U.S. Government" engraved in the metal.

Sam fell to his knees. Anna crept into the large hole and knelt on the opposite side of the box, facing Sam. Her thoughts and her heart were racing.

Solemnly Sam ran his hands over the top of the box brushing away the dirt, caressing it. Here was his farm, his home, his future. In his mind he saw the faces of his children seated at his supper table, loved and secure and happy. He saw himself rooted in a place that belonged to him—that he belonged in—that no one could take away.

Sam sat back on his heels. He took a deep breath. "It's yours, Anna. All of it."

She gasped. "What are you saying?"

He waved the box away with his big hands. "Take it. Go clear your family name and open an orphanage if that's what you want."

"Did you suffer a heat stroke while you were shoveling so hard?"

He shook his head. "All I've been able to think of since last night is finding this money and giving it to you."

Anna sat back, stunned. "You deserve this money, Sam. You lost your pa, your mamma, your home—everything. Don't you want your farm and your family?"

All the years he'd thought of nothing else, the image he'd thought was perfect, could never be complete now unless Anna was part of it.

"I'm not taking it," he told her.

He meant it. He was giving her the money—all of it. Anna's thoughts reeled. The blight on the Fletcher name would be lifted at long last. She'd be free of the heavy burden she'd borne for so long.

But in exchange for what?

Anna looked across at Sam. The robbery, the trial, the gossip, even her parents were all in the past. The present was the important thing. That's what Sam had always shown her. And the future—living with her uncle, raising unwanted children alone—suddenly seemed bleak.

Tears welled in her eyes. "I don't want it."

Sam tossed his hat side and rubbed his forehead. "Anna, honey, think about what you're saying."

"I want you to have it."

"I don't want it!"

"Neither do I!"

The unmistakable sound of the lever action of a rifle exploded in the silence.

"Now aren't you two lovebirds just something else."

Sam leapt to his feet and whirled around, his gaze

sweeping the darkness. Anna rose. He grabbed her and pulled her behind him.

A menacing chuckle emanated from the row of pines and Brett Morgan pushed his way between the trees. Light from the lantern reflected off the badge on his chest and the rifle in his hands.

Sam made a move for his own gun propped against the trunk of the oak.

"Don't try it." Brett raised his rifle. Sam froze. "I don't want to have to shoot you. Yet. Get your hands up."

"Brett, what are you doing?" Anna stepped from behind Sam, stunned.

A sardonic smile twisted his face as he advanced on the hole where Sam and Anna stood.

"Sweet Miss Anna Fletcher. I wanted to take you and the money. And it might have worked. You might have come along with me if it hadn't been for Rowan here." He waved the rifle at Sam and the smile disappeared from his face. "I should have made sure you were dead."

The horrifying truth came to her. "Oh, Brett, no. It was you?"

Sam's eyes narrowed. "What are you talking about?"

Brett laughed. "It was me that shot you."

"Shot me?" His gaze impaled Anna.

She blinked up at him. "The cut over your ear was a gunshot wound. I thought you knew."

"Christ . . ." Sam rolled his eyes. "The next time you know I've been shot would you please say so?"

Anna licked her lips and glanced nervously at Brett. "I think that might be real soon, Sam."

"I swear, you two carry on as if you really were married." Brett motioned with the rifle. "Drag that box out of the hole."

Sam tensed, looking for an opportunity to get the jump on him. Brett swung the rifle and pointed it at Anna.

"Nice and slow, Rowan."

With the barrel boring down on Anna, Sam couldn't chance it. He dragged the strongbox out of the hole, then stepped back in alongside Anna.

"Brett, I don't understand," Anna said. "Why are you doing this?"

"A lot of reasons." Brett circled the hole and rested his foot on the strongbox. "Fifty thousand reasons."

"But you have a job, a good job."

Brett uttered a short laugh. "Chicken feed."

"I've known you nearly all my life, Brett. I can't believe you're doing this." Anna felt betrayed, and stupid too, that she'd trusted him, that for a while she'd thought she cared for him. Now, she hated the sight of him. "Just go, Brett. Just take the money and leave us alone."

He shook his head. "Sorry, Anna, I can't do that."

"He's going to kill us." Sam spoke to Anna, but never took his eyes off Brett and the rifle.

Anna gasped. "But why?"

"Witnesses," Sam explained.

"And I appreciate you going to the trouble of digging this big hole, Rowan." Brett laughed. "You and the little missus should be real happy in there together."

Anna's stomach rolled. He sounded like a crazy man— crazy enough to do as he threatened.

"At least tell me why you're doing this, Brett."

He hesitated, eying both Sam and Anna, then shrugged. "You remember I told you my uncle was a guard up at the prison? He knew all about your pa, of course. He wrote me when your ma died last fall and your pa took a bad turn. Things were heating up in Galveston, and it was time I moved on, anyway. I got my own pa to get me a job as deputy right here in Kemper. And I just sat back and waited."

Revulsion curdled Anna's stomach. "You waited for my father to die in prison."

"Yep. There was a lot happening up there once you left carrying that secret inside of you. Otis DuBerry got word to your supposed husband here right away." Brett gave Sam a smug grin. "Too bad about your telegram, Rowan. Seems it never made it out of the express office. But don't blame the good Deacon Fry. It was a small price to pay for having that young wife in his bed every night. Well, most every night."

Sam's spine stiffened. He'd figured Morgan was up to no

good. But what of his other suspicions? Would they prove correct, too, before the night was over?

"And I thought you'd told no one about my papa's death to protect me from the gossip," Anna realized. "But it was only to keep others from speculating and maybe guessing the truth of why I'd returned to the farm."

Brett nodded. "I figured once I'd gotten Rowan out of the way, you'd be easy pickings. I'd just sweet talk the location of the money right out from under you. I'd even thought once about taking you along with me."

Anger flashed in Anna's eyes. "I'd have never gone off with you and that stolen money."

"Yep, I figured that too." Brett scowled. "The worst whipping I ever got was when we stole that hard candy from Palmer's General store when we were kids. You couldn't stand it until you confessed, and I paid the price for your honesty. That was always your problem, Anna, you thought that justice should prevail, that the scales should balance out. Well, darling, they don't. And that's why you have to die alongside this worthless, coward's son."

Brett stepped back from the hole and raised the rifle to his shoulder.

"Brett, no!"

Sam stepped in front of Anna, his muscles taut, ready to dive for his rifle resting against the tree.

"Everybody freeze! United States Marshal."

The pine limbs rustled and Charles Hampton stepped into the clearing, sighting a rifle at the three of them. Brett pivoted. Caught in the crossfire, Sam pushed Anna to the ground and covered her body with his. A shot rang out. Then another, followed by a heavy thud.

Sam lay still for another moment, listening. He felt Anna's body trembling beneath him.

"Stay down," Sam whispered.

Terror constricted her heart. "No, Sam, don't."

Sam sat up cautiously peering over the mound of dirt that surrounded the hole. In the darkness beyond the lantern light lay Brett Morgan. He looked back over his shoulder at Charles Hampton and the gun he held.

"Federal Marshal," he repeated. "Climb on out of there, son."

Sam uttered an oath as he slowly got to his feet. "I knew I didn't like you for some reason."

"Mr. Hampton?" Anna climbed to her feet, her eyes wide with bewilderment. She turned. "Brett?"

"Don't look," Sam turned her back to face Hampton. "Morgan's dead."

Anna only looked at him, too shocked to speak.

"Mr. Hampton here is a federal marshal," Sam told her. "On the trail of the money, all along."

Anna stepped away from Sam. "Did everybody in the whole world follow me to this farm to get the money!"

Sam pulled at his neck. "Hampton is the only one who matters." He sighed resolutely. "And we're going to jail for it."

"Jail . . ." The word slipped from Anna's lips in a stunned gasp. She looked at Hampton. "But why?"

"I've been on the trail of that money since the night of the robbery. You see, I was one of the marshals on the train the night the Rowe gang hit it."

"You were there?" Anna's heart pounded. "Then you saw that my papa was taken hostage."

Sam's eyes narrowed. "You saw my pa die."

"I saw the whole thing," Hampton lowered the gun. "I had my suspicions about Morgan since I got into town. He didn't cover his trail in Galveston like he thought he had. I've kept my eye on him."

"Those were his tracks and yours I kept seeing in the hills," Sam said.

Hampton inclined his head toward the lifeless body lying in the dark. "Good thing I followed him tonight."

"Lucky, all right," Sam muttered. "Now we get to spend the rest of our lives in jail instead of dying."

"I don't know about that." Hampton studied them as if confirming in his own mind a decision he had already made. "Seems to me a lot of lives have already been wasted because of this money. I don't see any use in adding two more to the list."

Stunned, they only stared at him.

"As far as I'm concerned," Hampton said, "Morgan recovered the money, and I shot him trying to escape with it. That will be the official version. But there is a reward for the return of the money and seeing as how it was found on your farm, I guess the five hundred dollars should go to you."

"But we don't deserve that money," Anna said.

Hampton grinned. "I'm sure you two young people will put it to some good purpose."

He was giving them their freedom, exonerating them from the whole matter, but Anna couldn't leave.

She climbed out of the hole. "Mr. Hampton, I have to know. The night of the robbery my father was taken hostage, wasn't he? He didn't go willingly, like everyone said. I know he didn't. You were there, Mr. Hampton. What happened?"

He studied her for a moment. "The Kyle brothers took him at gunpoint," he said softly.

Tears welled in Anna's eyes as the weight of ten years lifted from her shoulders. "I knew it. Thank you, Mr. Hampton, thank you."

He looked past her at Sam. "And I guess you heard the stories of how your pa died."

Sam gave him a curt nod. "I heard."

"Lies," Hampton said. "It was a single gunshot wound to the head. Jimmy Rowe was dead before he hit the ground."

Sam turned away, fighting back the lump of emotion that rose in his throat.

An odd look in Hampton's face caught Anna's eye. "That was true, wasn't it?" she asked him quietly.

He glanced at Sam, then back at Anna. "I've known Sam since long before he knew me, in Kentucky, tracking his father when he'd come to visit. Sam came a long way trailing fifty thousand dollars. No need in him going home empty-handed."

Reality struck Anna like a slap in the face. Yes, Sam would be going home. To Kentucky. And she would return to her uncle's home in Salem as if none of this had ever happened. She wouldn't clear her family name, nor open her orphanage, and Sam wouldn't have his farm or raise his horses. Sadness overwhelmed her.

Anna darted through the soft pine branches and across the tiny stream. Tears slid down her cheeks as she hurried through the woods, aided on her way by the first rays of the morning sun spilling over the mountains. She wound her way out of the trees and past Bob and Bill still hitched to the wagon at the edge of the meadow.

Far below she could see the farm house and the clothesline Sam had repaired, the chicken coop he'd constructed, the corral and barn he'd fixed, the garden they'd planted together. A sob tore from her throat, and she hurried toward it.

Halfway across the field she stopped suddenly. Was it the breeze? She strained to hear. Someone was calling her name. Anna turned. It was Sam.

"Anna! Wait!" He stopped when he saw her turn. "Come here!"

Anna sniffed and drew in a deep breath, unsure what this meant. She walked back toward him, halfway, and stopped. Her chin went up a notch.

Sam chuckled. He walked up to meet her.

She sniffed again. "What do you want?"

Golden rays of sunlight splashed over them as the sunrise brought a new day.

"I was thinking . . ." Sam ran his fingers through his hair and glanced at the ground, the woods, and sky before settling on her again. "I was thinking that, well, this farm isn't a bad farm. Maybe it's not so big, but Ben might be willing to sell out in a year or so. And this house is a good size if we opened up the second floor."

She swallowed her rising emotions. "What are you talking about, Sam?"

He pulled at his neck. "I wanted a farm to raise horses on, and here we've got one. And the house is plenty big for your orphans . . . unless you'd rather fill it up with kids of our own."

Her heart soared. "I—I don't understand,"

Sam looked deep into her eyes. "What I'm trying to say, Mrs. Rowan, is will you marry me?"

"Oh, Sam . . ."

"Will you?"

Anna choked back her tears. "Do you love me?"

"Oh, God, yes." Sam enclosed her in his arms and pulled her tight against him. "I love you with all my heart." His lips covered hers in a deep, generous kiss.

"So how about it?" he asked. "Will you marry me?"

Tears of joy welled in her eyes. "I love you, Sam. Of course I'll marry you."

Sam swept her into his arms and whirled her in a circle, kissing her passionately.

Anna pulled away. "But Sam, we can't have the ceremony here. Everyone thinks we're already married."

"We'll talk about the wedding later." He headed across the meadow toward the house. "Right after the honeymoon."

EPILOGUE

Anna awoke with a start. She sat up and pushed her hair off her shoulder. The room was dark, lighted only by the embers glowing in the fireplace. The bed was cold. Sam was gone—again.

She tossed back the quilt and left the room, confident of where she'd find him. This had happened so many times in the past few months, it no longer surprised her.

In the doorway of the small bedroom beside hers, Anna paused. Sam was there, dressed in long johns and socks, trousers pulled hurriedly on. He was seated in the rocker, the light from the lantern on the dresser cast soft shadows. Cradled in his arms was six-month-old Carrie.

A smile spread across Anna's face as she walked toward him. "Was she fussing?"

Sam looked up at her. "Yes . . . sort of."

"I didn't hear her."

"Well . . . she was going to wake up . . . soon. Probably."

She'd chided Sam a few times about picking up the baby when she was sleeping, but it had done no good. He'd forged a deep bond with the tiny, dark-haired baby from the moment he'd laid eyes on her. Born to one of the girls at Mable's place on the far end of town, no one had wanted the baby when her mother had died in childbirth. Destined to be whispered about the rest of her life, it had seemed right that Sam and Anna should take her in, and when Reverend Langford had suggested it, they had readily agreed. Since then, Sam had hardly been able to put her down.

"You need some sleep tonight too, Sam," Anna said gently. "I'll be in after a while."

Anna held out her arms. Sam reluctantly gave the baby a kiss and handed her over. She snuggled little Carrie into her crib and covered her with a soft blanket.

She took Sam's hand. "Come on."

"No, not yet." Sam pulled Anna onto his lap. She came willingly, drawing her knees up and curling against his shoulder. He held her close. "There. That's better."

Slowly he ran his fingers through her thick hair, down her arm, and settled his hand on the curve of her hip. Anna shifted his palm to her belly. "Girls," she said.

He kissed her forehead. "What?"

"Girls. I want girls next time," Anna said. "Carrie and I are outnumbered now."

Sam chuckled and looked over at the two cradles situated next to Carrie's crib. Inside, three-month-old Jimmie and his twin brother Cy were sleeping peacefully. "I'll try my best, Mrs. Rowan."

Anna rested her head against Sam's shoulder. "I've been thinking."

He rocked them gently. "About what?"

"About the other fifty thousand dollars that was taken in the robbery."

"Five hundred dollars wasn't enough for you?"

It had taken over a year to actually get the reward from the government that Charles Hampton had promised, and now it was tucked away safely in the bank in Kemper. They didn't need the money. Sam's reputation as a horse breeder had begun to spread, and in the last year he'd made a modest profit. They'd decided to put the reward money away for a rainy day.

Anna sat up. "How do we know what really happened to the other strongbox taken in the robbery? Maybe the other two gang members didn't have it. Maybe it's hidden right here on the farm too."

Sam snorted. "That's doubtful."

"You don't care that there may be another fifty thousand dollars buried right here on our farm?"

"No."

"Why not?"

Sam pulled her head down onto his shoulder again and kissed her forehead. "Because I've got all the riches I need," he told her. "Right here in this room."

FREE

Romance

(a $4.50 value)

Send in the Coupon Below

To get your FREE historical romance and start saving, fill out the coupon below and mail it today. As soon as we receive it we'll send you your FREE Book along with your first month's selections.

Mail To: **True Value Home Subscription Services, Inc. P.O. Box 5235**
120 Brighton Road, Clifton, New Jersey 07015-5235

YES! I want to start previewing the very best historical romances being published today. Send me my FREE book along with the first month's selections. I understand that I may look them over FREE for 10 days. If I'm not absolutely delighted I may return them and owe nothing. Otherwise I will pay the low price of just $4.00 each: a total $16.00 (at *least* an $18.00 value) and save at least $2.00. Then each month I will receive four brand new novels to preview as soon as they are published for the same low price. I can always return a shipment and I may cancel this subscription at any time with no obligation to buy even a single book. In any event the FREE book is mine to keep regardless.

Name _____

Street Address _____ Apt. No. _____

City _____ State _____ Zip Code _____

Telephone _____

Signature _____
(if under 18 parent or guardian must sign)

Terms and prices subject to change. Orders subject
to acceptance by True Value Home Subscription
Services, Inc.

0069-7